THE LADY AND THE ASSASSIN

A FANTASY ROMANCE

The Lady and the Assassin

For sheltered Lady Ruvona, visiting Devenmere Manor to investigate her father's disappearance is a chance to escape her dull life. In Netherbury, the nearest town, the malevolent Lord Emil is taxing and starving the people, and a mysterious dark force is draining the land. Determined to help the townsfolk and save her father, with her magic and the skills her guardian taught her, Lady Ruvona disguises herself as the lad, Robbin.

Assassin Warric masquerades as the new Sheriff of Netherbury and is tasked to thwart Emil. What he did not expect to encounter was beautiful Lady Ruvona bathing in a moonlit river. Nor did he expect an ally in the outlaw Robbin. Aiding the lad is in line with Warric's task, but it doesn't take him long to realize who Robbin is.

Together, with magic and swords, they try to save her father, take on Emil, his ancient amulet, and the plot to destroy all they stand for. While trying not to fall in love.

This is a work of fiction. The characters, incidents and dialogues in this book are of the author's imagination and are not to be construed as real. Any resemblance to actual events or persons, living or dead, is completely coincidental.

Published by Sevannah Storm.

~~~

First Edition 2023

Copyright © 2023 - 2090 Sevannah Storm All rights reserved.

Cover Art by Sevannah Storm

This eBook is licensed for your personal enjoyment only. This eBook may not be re-sold or given away to other people. If you would like to share this book with another person, please purchase an additional copy for each recipient. If you're reading this book and did not purchase it, or it was not purchased for your enjoyment only, then please return to your favorite retailer and purchase your own copy. Thank you for respecting the hard work of this author.

https://sevannahstorm.com/

Version_1
~~~

Also by Sevannah Storm

The Blood of Legends Series

The Huntress

The Healer

The Gifting Series

Soul Forged

Fate Forged

Sun Forged

War Forged

Star Forged

Shadow Forged

Earth Forged

Lust Forged

Standalones

Xiaxan Fox

Ire of Silver

The Shikari

Sol Survivor

Plump Playwright Series

Plump Jane

Seducing Amelia

Loving FinleyKeeping Tessa

Kissing Navy

COMING SOON

Inkoded

Fire Forged

The Crucible of the Eternal

Contents

PROLOGUE

Warric closed his knee-length coat against the chilled wind sweeping across the campsite as it stirred up smoke, reignited embers, and lifted the lingering stench of gunpowder. The sun set on another day with the skirmish unresolved. Soldiers, in dark-blue and gold uniforms, gathered around small fires. Great cannons, mounted on formidable wagons, glowed red as they cooled from the day's barrage. Metallic gyros bobbed, tiny white lights flickering on each ball—no doubt soldiers communicating with loved ones.

How the gyros worked wasn't something Warric could wrap his mind around. Slowly, weird contraptions powered by magic had begun to form part of his life. He grimaced and fingered the pouch of iron balls hanging off his belt alongside a pistol. A dagger or an arrow was silent and the best way to assassinate. No matter his skill, he couldn't beat the speed of a pistol.

General Jacut Devenmere of Bennedor strode out of the tent, then paused to run his hazel gaze over the campsite while donning calfskin gloves. His dark-blue coat piped in gold flickered in the wind. He glanced at Warric, tossed his blond hair off his temple, and grinned. "He is in a foul mood this night, Assassin."

"Perhaps I will soon find out why." Warric smirked.

"Aye, he seems...troubled. I head northwest to tackle the Briv-ela." Jacut grimaced.

Warric offered a nod in condolence. "A tiresome tribe and quite barbaric in their practices."

"Or so I have heard." Jacut stomped his foot, shaking a fleck of mud off the polished leather. "Imagine claiming a woman as wife by stealing her?" He scoffed. "There have been a few I wished I could silence but none worthy of a good kidnapping."

Warric chuckled. The idea of stealing a woman to wed was ludicrous when most gave out their *favors* for a kind word. "Are they not all too much effort?"

"Spoken like a man who has never known love." Jacut gazed at the unscalable stone wall as it snaked west for miles. "My sister is quite special. Mother and Father sacrificed much for her, and the little minx knows nothing of it." He squared his shoulders. "We pray she never learns the truth." He forced a smile after delivering that cryptic bit of information. After dusting his wide-brimmed hat in matching beige calfskin across his thigh, he marched off.

"Assassin." The voice, thick, educated, and filled with author-ity, belonged to Warric's lord, Baron Gregory of Kenningthain.

Only those in the baron's confidence knew Warric's true name. In private, the baron used it, but anywhere else, Warric was known as 'Assassin.' He flipped the tent flap back but halted. Awareness rippled across his skin, raising the hairs. Someone lurked, watched, their intentions ill.

A quick scan of those hovering nearby showed no one glancing in his direction. He ducked inside the massive tent, then let the flap fall, waiting a moment to ensure the guards didn't encroach. With a side glance, he located the baron and crossed the burgundy and periwinkle blue Eryssian rug to stand beside the war table. A detailed map sprawled across it, littered with iron figurines representing the wildemen from the north or the baron's soldiers.

While sucking air through his teeth, the baron ran a finger along the rim of a gold goblet. Warric remained still, expectant, patient for his lord to elaborate on why he'd been summoned. The wind shook the tent, yanking on its supports. From outside, the incessant murmur of camp life, along with sharp clashes of metal, penetrated the crackle of the fire pit inside the tent keeping the chill at bay. The magical flames fed on nothing. A standalone clock in gilded bronze ticked as each second passed. All this was noted in a cursory glance. Once he'd settled, he didn't shift, didn't focus anywhere but on Gregory's rugged face, half-hidden by a sculpted beard.

Yet, Warric's senses prickled.

The tent trembled with what he might have attributed to the gusts whipping across the campsite. Rolling his hand, gesturing to Gregory to talk, Warric cast out his magic—air and darkness. He searched for the void among the noise and dusky light.

Stiffening, Gregory nodded and droned on about his favorite horse as a boy growing up in Kenningthain.

Instincts snapped Warric's gaze to the side of the tent, mere feet from where the baron sat on a bench. No movement, sound, or shadow warned of an impending strike. In an instant, the shape of a man flickered to life, glowing like a lantern at the center of Warric's senses, despite not being visible through the tent cloth. He grabbed Gregory by the forearm and yanked him off the bench. At the same time, he unsheathed his dagger then plunged it downward, sinking it into the attacker.

Had he been wrong, the worst was a hole in the cloth.

"Hell's teeth," Gregory spat and bolted out of the tent.

Warric scowled, pulled the bloodied dagger from the man, leaving crimson stains on the tear. Cursing under his breath, he followed the baron. Sprawled in the gap between tents writhed a 'servant' clutching his chest. Blood saturated his cream garments.

"Who sent you?" Gregory roared, grabbing the man's tunic and bringing him off the ground to within an inch of his face.

The man smirked. Blood dribbled over a bottom lip. He slumped, his head falling to the side.

"Shit, Assassin, you could have stabbed him somewhere less lethal. I need answers." Gregory hooked a finger at a nearby guard, then pointed at the dead servant. With a glance at Warric, the baron stomped into the tent.

He withdrew a bottle from a wooden chest. "Wine?" He uncorked it with his teeth, poured a healthy amount, then held out the goblet.

Warric had just saved the baron's life, again. Something he'd done many a time. Yet the baron didn't bark out commands? No, he seemed...resigned. "So, the dead servant is not up for discussion?"

Gregory met his gaze and wiggled the goblet. "This is the last in a line of attempts on my life. This you know."

"I was here for a few of those, milord." Warric wrapped his fingers around the warm metal, drew the goblet under his nose for a deep inhale, then twitched. Sickly sweet almonds infused the fruity and not-yet-matured wine.

"As I expected." The baron ran a hand through his pale-blond hair. A military man in every aspect of his life from discipline to routine, it showed in his physique, as honed as if he was decades younger. Unlike his brother, whom the baron had often lamented being forbidden to kill.

"The wine is from your brother, Emil, milord?" Warric couldn't bring himself to call that child-man a lord.

Only Emil was cowardly enough to use poison. Then again, if it was said he'd killed the baron, the Conclave would deny him the right to rule. Should Gregory die on the battlefield—a hero's death—then the Kenningthain holdings and all its fiefdoms would become Emil's duty. Warric smothered a snort. Duty? The man knew not the meaning.

At Gregory's nod, Warric lifted the bottle off the table then angled it into the light. Dregs of some sort of powder lay at the bottom.

"I hoped to have his name from the dead servant." The baron took the bottle and poured the contents into the piss pot. "My little ass of a brother is stirring up mischief. I was tolerant when he wasted gold to find some lost amulet. That futile search kept him out of my hair. Now, he's taken over the Netherbury seat, and the rumors...well, you know." Gregory closed his eyes and inhaled, then slowly exhaled. He opened his brown eyes to meet Warric's gaze. "That is where you come into this, Warric. This is a personal matter, and for that, I apologize. We are at war, and yet, I must deal with—" He grimaced. "You are the only one I can trust. I need you to replace the new Sheriff of

Netherbury en route to his post. Become Emil's right-hand man by all means necessary. Thwart every vile act without revealing yourself and send me regular updates."

He yanked open a drawer and placed two gold discs on the table—intricate patterns were carved into them. In the center of each was a needle. "State of the art, or so I am told. Will allow two-way messaging." Gregory pursed his lips while staring at the discs. With a squaring of his shoulders, he pressed a thumb over the needles. On each, a drop of blood sank into the grooves. White light burst outward. "Newfangled gadgetry powered by wind and air magic? The pistols and cannons, those I can grasp, but these?"

Warric followed suit, pricked his thumbs, and watched as his blood merged with Gregory's. Still glowing white, he palmed one metallic disc then slipped it inside his coat. "I agree, but adapt we must, milord." He gestured to the baron's plated armor—riveted, curved metal sheets, strong enough to stop a pistol, never mind an arrow.

"If these blasted Northerners would quit attacking my lands..." Gregory wiggled his fingers at the tent flaps. "The sheriff leaves Lorden in two days."

With a bow to the baron, Warric strode out of the tent to his horse tethered nearby.

He grabbed the bridle and rested his temple on Serenity's forelock. "We have been tasked, my dear boy."

Serenity snickered and stomped a foot, as if to say he was prepared for anything. Two pistols slapped Warric's thighs when he mounted. He threw a hand back to check the placement of his shotgun on the right. To the left was his freshly oiled crossbow nestled in its holster. Pulling his hood up, he nudged Serenity, spurring him into a trot.

They veered around small tents, campfires, and wagons carrying anything from boom cannons to cannon balls to rations. It would take a day to reach Netherbury. He might camp along the Olion river or perhaps find a tavern close to the Conclave Way and await the sheriff's passing.

Out of all the assignments, this one irritated Warric. He clenched his jaw, rolled his shoulders, and urged Serenity into a gallop as soon as they breached the camp's perimeter. Infiltrate a northerner's tribes? Happy to do it. Kill a deserter or betrayer? What a pleasure. Seduce a fair maiden to reach her father? Whatever Baron Gregory needs, but this? Bow to lazy-as-shit Lord Emil? Warric grimaced. He'd rather lick sweat off a bull's balls.

Chuckling at his thoughts, he hunched his shoulders and faced ahead. If Gregory hadn't chosen Warric's scrawny ass decades ago, where would he be? Stuck in a brothel? Babysitting a sop of a lord? Days wasted guarding a treasured library? He shuddered. No, as a sentinel, he served the baron. If he could ease one of those frown lines etched into Gregory's brow, then Warric had served well.

ONE

THE AIR SHIFTED BESIDE Vona's ear, giving way to the precise swing of a sword. She ducked while raising her weapon. Blades struck. The force reverberated up her arms, but she gritted her teeth and parried. Darkness filled her vision, her breathing loud and labored in the courtyard. Only her senses could guide her, and of course, her magic. In water, she was unparalleled. In air, her weakest, she was a sitting duck.

Still, Yrsa of Chalimar insisted on testing this as if magic could be improved with practice. Vona huffed. Many a Conclave noviciate had tried. Each child, known as the untested, was born with the five elements—fire, earth, air, water, and darkness. Though magic could be replenished from its element, the size of the 'jar' deep within each individual couldn't be increased. So, when Vona stated air was her weakest, it truly was, and no amount of blindfolding could help improve its power.

A blade bounced off her knuckles. She cried out, leaping back while swinging her sword wild.

"Channel the pain," Yrsa commanded from Vona's left.

"You say that every cursed time, Yrsa. Injuring me only drains my magic." Vona focused on her hand, the tickling of blood as it trickled down her fingers, making the grip she had on the sword slippery. A warmth swept along her arm, honeyed sweetness that brought instant relief. High in earth and water, she could heal and replenish.

"Wasted magic," a man said, his deep voice bouncing off the stone walls—Uldane Tellalouise of Harvet, Head of the Conclave's military division known as the Sundowners, and dear friend to Mother and Father. Before the blindfold, Vona had admired the forest-green of his jerkin catching the sunlight streaming from the massive windows set high in the vaulted arches.

She tilted her head in his direction.

At the same time, Yrsa nudged her.

Having not expected it, Vona tumbled to the side. She halted her sprawl across the stone-carved floor. Glaring in the direction of Yrsa's voice, she held up the sword just in case.

"Talking to me is not helping, Uldane," she sang.

"No battle is without distractions, sweet one," he chuckled and snapped a scroll closed.

Yrsa remained silent. When she spoke to Vona, steel hardened her voice. "Focus. Recite the levels of magic and their purposes."

A blade cut through the air, forcing Vona to leap aside or lose a limb.

Uldane's steps led to the door to the inner house.

Yrsa muttered a curse.

Vona frowned. "What is it about Uldane that angers you so?"

"I am aware he is a friend to the Devenmeres, to your mother, but he is still Lord Sundowner and as such, has power over me."

"You are stronger than he, Yrsa."

Yrsa laughed. 'Tis good you think so." She tapped Vona on the shoulder with the blade. "Recite."

"Again?" Vona whined, thrusting more earth magic into her limbs. They'd been at this for hours. What she wouldn't do for a goblet of brandy.

"Again." Yrsa was a harsh taskmaster but one of the best Sundowners the Conclave had ever seen.

Striking with her shaved head, she towered over all in the Conclave's hallowed halls. Her muscles rippled with each movement revealed by the furs and armor she wore, that of her heritage from the east of Sagua, in the Osiree Mountains of Chalimar. On her right upper arm, inked into the skin by the magic of darkness, was the Sundowner mark. A griffin and a lion guarded a pentagonal shield. All recognized the symbol and feared the bearers.

"Fine. First are the untested, as of age seven. Their magic and natural power are assessed." Vona lunged, thrusting her sword forward then cursing when she met nothing.

"Second level are the guided, their primary magic identified." Swish, slash, and still, she hit air.

"Third are the noviciates, having mastered elementary spells." She ducked, grateful she'd done so when the air stirred above her head. Sure, she could heal minor wounds but a beheading? There was no coming back from that.

"Fourth are the surpassors, learning to focus their magic on noble pursuits in music, weaponry, or exploration." A tap of blade along blade had Vona spinning toward it. She grimaced, having not heard the woman move.

"Fifth level are the proficient, skilled in their chosen fields. Most do not venture past this level." *Like myself.* Gasping for breath, she willed the sweat droplets dripping off her chin to sink into her skin. Coolness swept over her, a trail of goosebumps in its wake.

"Level six?" Yrsa's voice hardened.

Vona instinctively leaped back and again, avoiding the swish-swish of another strike. "They're the sentinels, masters in their craft. They may choose to educate the lesser levels or make their mark across Sagua."

"Good." Yrsa grunted. High praise, indeed. Vona knew better than to let it go to her head. "What am I?"

"You, my dear tall one, are an envoy—a level seven assigned to guard a Conclave member. In this case, my mother." Vona lowered her sword, assuming they were done for the day. But the slap of the blade across her upper arm had her crying out. She lifted the sword again.

"Level eight? Why do you forget?"

"An empyrean is legend, Yrsa." Vona gritted her teeth while glaring through her blindfold. "There has not been someone at that magic level for centuries."

The older woman snorted. "Because 'tis legend does not mean 'tis forgotten."

The blindfold unraveled and flew across to Yrsa, who caught and slid it into a pocket. Vona blinked at her and pouted. She hadn't worked up a sweat while Vona wasted magic re-absorbing hers. As an envoy, Yrsa's inner well was massive, her magic extraordinary.

"Come, we have...more guests." Yrsa tilted her head, then scowled. "Bringing bad news."

Vona gave her a token smile. "Not every guest is—"

"I am a level seven in air, Vona. Piers natters like a simpleton, sharing news with each breath he spills." Yrsa stomped toward the foyer, crossing through marbled arches three-men high, her boots thudding along the stone floor. Vona hurried to keep up, tripling after the giant of a woman.

The great doors opened. Vona trailed Yrsa down the circular steps to the pebbled road. Clinking like the tinkerman he was, old Thack slid off his horse.

A skinny runt of a man with a swath of golden hair, Piers of Ruarden bobbed on his donkey. When it brayed and bucked, he clambered off, jangling the qitary in his hand. He juggled the musical instrument to rub his ass in purple, velvet, brocaded breeches. Even his boots had bells.

While waving parchment, Thack wheezed past Vona, offering her a dusty kiss on the cheek before disappearing into the estate's library—her mother's domain.

"I swear, either that donkey is losing weight or I am," Piers grumbled. Raising his deep blue gaze to Vona, he beamed. "Lovelier than the sunset across the Somerto Sea." He sniffed then sobbed into a red silk kerchief. "You've grown so much since we last saw you, my pet."

"Missed you too, Piers." She hugged him, then stepped back to hitch a thumb in the library's direction while he blew his nose.

"Do not glower at me, Yrsa the Great. 'Tis been a while since I last saw Ruvona. She is as breathtaking as the moon and stars, as the sky after a storm..."

Yrsa muttered when his face crumpled, "Do not start—"

He threw his arms around her and wailed. His qitary clanged across her back with each jarring breath he took. Instead of shoving him aside, she patted his shoulder and let him have this moment.

Vona danced around Yrsa to peek at Piers. "Is it bad news?"

"Aye," he sniffed.

Vona chewed on her lip while frowning. "My father—?"

"Best to ask your mother," Yrsa said, then with a gentle hip thrust, nudged Piers off her. "Come, to the library we go." She strode ahead, but a side glance didn't put Vona at ease. If Yrsa was worried, then so should she be.

Piers dabbed his eyes with a delicate touch, straightened his purple and gold jerkin then holstered his qitary to his back. He offered Vona his elbow. She accepted and allowed him to escort her to her mother, like a gentle maiden. Giving into his gallantry was far easier than arguing with him while dodging his hand. He was as stubborn as his donkey, Kit.

The library always took her breath away. Books lined the walls as high as the arches. Artifacts served as bookends. Stacks of rolled manuscripts filled shelves behind the great wooden desk dominating a handwoven circular rug from Isamölk. The rich gold, azure, and forest-green threads complimented the dark wood of the desk and shelves. Sconces with flickering flames lit the vast room. Not an inch of sunlight was allowed entry. The windows, visible from the outside, were covered with more bookshelves. Mother took her sentinelship seriously, spending weeks hunting a specific artifact or the lure of a magical fountain purported to expand inner wells.

The main topic at this year's Conclave moot was the search for the fabled manuscript, *Whispers of the Lost Ones*. Mother had obsessed over this adventure for the last ten years. She'd narrowed the possible locations to two, or so Vona had overheard.

A thump snapped Vona's gaze to Thack who was waving his arms as he paced, danced, and jumped up and down. His mouth opened and closed as he ranted, but no sound escaped him. He stamped his muddy boots, spraying dirt onto the rug and polished wooden floor, then paced in front of Mother. She didn't glance up from her work, her focus clear in her furrowed brow.

"Ailith, listen to the poor man." Uldane laughed. Under his arm, he'd tucked a few scrolls and balanced an open book on his palm.

With a sigh, Mother placed the quill into its inkpot and flicked her wrist at Thack.

"—in danger, and all you can do is shut me up. He is missing, I tell you. One night, we bid each other 'sweet dreams,' and in the morning, he was gone, taken from his bed. Not a peep I heard."

"Not a peep," Piers sang in a croaking voice. He was a self-appointed bard who couldn't sing, but none of them had the heart to tell him.

Thack's great barrel chest shuddered on an exhale. "I found Hayworth's study ransacked and this letter tucked in his favorite boot."

"How uncivilized to take him without shoes." Piers patted Vona's hand. "We came as fast as we could."

Mother snatched the letter, rising to run her gaze along the scrawled words. She pursed her lips as she studied the document she'd been working on. Uldane dropped the book and the scrolls onto the desk to read the letter over Mother's shoulder. He stiffened.

"What did Father say?" Vona tried to step away from Piers, but he drew her back.

"Some darkness has taken over Netherbury." Mother met her gaze, glanced between Yrsa, Piers, then settled on Thack. "I cannot leave, not now. Uldane and I are so close to— The Conclave is about to meet for the annual moot. Can you return to Devenmere, Thack?"

He nodded.

"Good." Mother handed the scroll to Uldane, veered around the desk and grasped Vona's hands, breaking Piers's hold on her. "You, my dear, must go in my stead. Head to the northern border and locate your brother." Her grip tightened. "We cannot wait for his weekly call. He will speak to Baron Gregory to ask for a leave of absence."

Her brother? Vona jerked back. "But—?"

"Uldane is with me, so Yrsa will guard you." Mother shook her head. "A girl alone is always an easy target."

Vona winced. *Girl?* Like she hadn't spent every morning in the last four years mastering her weaponry.

"Of course, Piers must accompany you." Mother flashed him a smile. "Without his gallantry, the trip would not be a success."

Grinning at Mother's blatant flattery, he dipped in a flourished bow, waving his hand wide and almost smacking Yrsa in the chest. Mother opened a drawer in a tallboy nearby and dug out two discs and a bag of gold. She dumped them on the desk, careful not to touch her documents.

After bleeding into the discs, she shoved them at Yrsa, who stepped forward to press her thumb to the needles. Vona froze, blinked, then gritted her teeth when her mother didn't ask her to bleed. This said it all. She was to journey to find her brother, but under the supervision and command of Yrsa. How her mother saw Vona was the same as her opinion of Piers—pointless.

"We leave within the hour." Yrsa shoved the disc in the back pocket of her breeches and grabbed the gold.

Without a word, Vona turned on a heel and marched to her chambers. She wasn't about to plead with her mother about this lack of trust or how sadness squeezed her heart. Perhaps on this journey she could prove herself?

"Oh, so now you return?" A voice came from her leather satchel. She ignored it. "Or do you plan to punish me some more? Huh?"

She undid the buckle. As soon as the satchel gaped, a gyro slipped out, rolled across the wooden floor then shot into the air. It twirled into a stop in front of her to shine a light into her eyes.

"Quit it, Orv. You are a distraction during training, and you know it. Not that Yrsa has ever harmed you, but you shy away from her and act as if every swing of her sword will kill me." Vona flopped onto her bed and threw an arm across her face. "Hell's teeth," she cried out, slapping the bed. Tears stung behind her eyes. She missed her father. Her mother was a ball of ice that only melted when Father was home. That had been months ago.

Vona was a disappointment. Her well wasn't more than a five at best. She would never be a sentinel like her brother, Jacut, who'd chosen to serve Baron Gregory of Kenningthain. Which meant she couldn't bring honor to the Devenmere name except through marriage. What family wanted a worthless level five? No, she would go on this quest and earn her honor, her place in this world.

"You seem upset? Did Fearless Yrsa best you again?"

Vona ground her teeth. Even her personal gyro revered Yrsa. How could Vona compete when the odds were against her? "Listen here, you worthless ball..." What could she say? He was an it, an inanimate object made lifelike through her frequent blood donations. A gift from her father when she was six, Orv was supposed to be her biggest champion and protector.

"Milady, we must pack." Mags hurried in, heading for the double doors of Vona's wardrobe.

"Why?" After casting a glare at her now-silent gyro, Vona fell back onto the bed. "I will go as is."

"Do not be silly, milady." Mags removed breeches, tunics, leather jerkins, a coat, a hat, pistols and their holsters. She draped a blue silk gown over the pile.

Vona kicked, dislodging the objects covering her shins. "Mags, we will not be traveling by wagon."

The serving girl pursed her lips. "The silk will crease in your saddle bags. Perhaps the linen gown instead?"

Vona shrugged then folded her arms behind her head to stare at the ceiling. "Whatever my horse can carry."

While Mags darted around the room, muttering and cursing, Vona ventured onto the balcony to watch the grooms saddle the horses and tend to Kit and Thack's warhorse, Baston.

Orv trailed her, and in privacy, it whispered, "So, what happened?"

"The usual." She didn't need to go into detail. The poor gyro had endured many a rant at the injustice of it all. Still, as she shared her attention between the grooms and Mags, she had to admit, her life was preferable to a level four or lower.

"Will you change before you depart, milady?" Mags held up a cream-colored tunic.

Vona frowned.

Mags tugged on the fabric of the tunic Vona was wearing. "Your sleeve is bloody."

Slumping, Vona tossed a glance at the horses then entered her chambers to whip off the tunic she wore. First, she slipped on her chest holster, tucking in the tiny pistol between her breasts. While she dressed, Mags tried to brush her hair. "Braid it, Mags," Vona snapped, then grimaced. "Sorry, it...has not been a good day."

Once again, she had failed to best Yrsa at weapons training and under Uldane's watch. No doubt, something her mother was more than aware of. Vona curled her lip. Perhaps it was time. At the age of twenty-two, she was old enough to no longer need her mother's approval. Still, it hurt. Each failure dug into her heart like the piercing of a dagger, twisted when her mother revealed her disappointment or said nothing. Releasing a long breath, Vona tapped her foot while she waited for Mags to finish braiding.

"Piers is at the door," Orv whispered a second before the knock.

"Come in, Piers," Vona called.

The door creaked open, then he popped his head around it. Seeing her standing there, he pushed the door wide to saunter in, his boots jingling. "You all right, my pet?" He cupped Vona's cheeks and held her still for a long perusal.

"I am, why do you ask?"

He smiled. "You know me, your personal empath."

Vona smothered a snort at that little bullshit. "I am well, Piers." She forced a smile. "Excited for our little adventure. When last did we travel anywhere together?"

He hummed. Releasing her to lean back, he folded his arms across his chest and gripped his chin. His thin mustache quivered like a golden caterpillar wiggling to escape. "I do believe it was on a trip to Devenmere when you were ten."

She pinched her lips, having not realized she hadn't left her home for twelve years. Her days had been filled with tutors and training. Father had been there for most of it. She'd spent afternoons in his company. His office, to the rear of Bennedor, their Lisbay estate, was filled with artifacts, weapons, and trinkets. If he needed a manuscript or book, he would visit the library.

"I hope Father is well, wherever he is, Piers." She blinked back tears, not wanting to appear weak.

Without saying a word, Piers yanked her into a crushing hug, then engulfed her in some sort of scent—a mixture of mint and sugar. She sniffed, pressed her temple to his shoulder, and let him hold her.

"You are packed, milady. Will there be anything more?" Mags wrung her hands.

Vona pulled away to glance at the satchels at the foot of the bed. Her dagger and pistols sat on top of the pile. "Thank you, Mags."

"I shall send a groom to collect your things." She dipped into a curtsey and darted out, leaving the door gaping.

Piers bent to catch Vona's gaze. "Meet you downstairs?"

He left before she could respond. Alone, she added bags of gold to the satchels, preferring to be prepared for the worst scenario. After a deep pull, in went her favorite flask holding Brederburg brandy, the finest this side of the northern wall. The smoky flavor coated her tongue then set her throat and innards on fire.

"Orv," she called.

The gyro shot up from behind a velvet arm chair in the corner of the room. "Aye, milady?"

"Ready for an adventure?" She chuckled when it bobbed. "Come on, then." Marching through the door, she skipped and danced down the stairs. Even though she would be under Yrsa's thumb, she was away from her mother's vigilance and disapproving stare.

The horses and donkey were waiting, fed, brushed down, and re-saddled.

"Should we not let them rest?" she asked while stroking Kit's beard.

"Sir Thack stated 'twas not necessary. Said they spent the night in Lisbay."

She flicked a glance at Bent, Mag's brother. "Here I thought Thack and Piers had slept on rocky ground and suffered all manner of hardships."

Bent chuckled. "Perhaps on lumpy beds? Those can do a person's back some harm."

"With plump partners, no doubt." She grinned.

"A lady does not banter," Mother bit out, sashaying down the circular steps, her arm looped through Uldane's. Resplendent in a ruby-red gown, her hair pinned up, she had never looked more beautiful.

Vona dipped her head but not before smirking at Bent. He wisely sidled away.

Mother snagged Vona's hands and steered her around. "Now, take care, my girl. Do as Yrsa instructs."

Uldane broke Mother's hold on Vona. "You are acting as if Vona is unskilled and unguarded, Ailith. Trust that you have raised her well." He glanced over his shoulder at Yrsa marching toward them. "If you have further instructions, now is the time." When Mother hurried away, he grabbed Vona's shoulders, holding her in place. "Enjoy this adventure, my dear. Find your voice and inner strength." His green eyes narrowed. "I pray you find what *completes* your soul." He brushed a curl off her temple, then gripped and released her chin.

What an odd thing to say. It had an old-world feel so she smiled her thanks and let him draw her into a stiff hug. "You keep Mother safe, Uldane," she commanded, her voice smothered by the fabric of his jerkin.

"For as long as I am able." He helped her mount her horse, Honey.

Thack clanked as he hoisted himself on his warhorse. Piers, however, needed two stable hands to climb onto Kit, his qitary strapped to his back, his boots jingling when he forced his toes into the stirrups. He was huffing by the time he held the reins.

Yrsa's glower couldn't dampen Vona's spirits when they finally set off.

Two

Rain poured down in sheets, obscuring the road ahead. The Conclave Way lead from village to town to Lisbay with wagons, fellow horsemen, and an occasional goat. Warric's coat kept the water off him, but rain pooled at the juncture of his thighs, saturating his breeches and chilling him. Now if he had any competency with fire magic, the droplets would sizzle as they hit him. Alas, air and darkness were his gifts to Sagua and more than utilized in the service of Baron Gregory.

The next town was Borfort. He would settle at the Black Dog tavern and watch the road. Anyone riding past would be within sight. Having never met the Sheriff of Netherbury, Warric didn't know his appearance. He would rely on instinct, the image the man presented in his posture and attire, and if the Lord was willing, arrogance would drive the sheriff to announce his new position while downing an ale.

Warric dismounted, landing in a puddle, splashing his breeches and boots with mud. He pressed his temple to Serenity's neck. "Sorry, old friend. I cannot control the weather."

When he whinnied in response, Warric gathered the reins and urged Serenity into the stables.

"The best for my horse," he said, leveling a glare on the hapless stable master. "Touch my things and die." He patted the saddle, the butt of his shotgun sticking out.

The man gaped then curtsied. Tossing him a gold coin, Warric strode across the busy road to the tavern. A warm glow from the windows and door spilled across the dismal ground. As soon as he stepped inside, an elderly woman screamed for him to wait.

"Let me dry you, kind sir." She waved a hand, and in an instant, he was dry and clean.

He grunted at the immediate warmth bathing his body. Fire and earth magic were a wonderful combination. He gave her a silver in thanks and let her usher him to a table near a roaring fire.

"Ale and a bowl from your pot." He sat and rested his elbows on the table.

She hurried off to do as asked. Wall-mounted sconces added light, their bases old and tarnished. Still, about a hand's width above, a ball of flame spun and flickered. Fire magic indeed. He could fade into shadow, kill without thought or emotion, and manipulate sounds. None of those granted him any comfort.

A warm ale and a bowl of...he sniffed...goat stew was set before him. He pushed a coin across the scoured wooden table to the serving wench, who snatched it up and darted to the kitchen. Mm, skittish. Scanning the crowd, he tried to assess the level of danger in the room.

A tall man, wide in shoulders and girth might pose a problem. The wily man beside him, scrawny and hunched, more so. Taking a long drink from his ale, Warric set the tankard down and dug into the stew. It tasted like the ass-end of the goat, but it was hot, heating him from the inside.

The conversations resumed, most about the shitty weather, some about farming and livestock, and one about the blacksmith's daughter. None of them were Warric's business. He kept his head down but his focus on the road he glimpsed through the grimy windows. Wagons passed. Horsemen headed to Lisbay, so the wrong direction, and those riding north had the look of farmers or soldiers. By his third ale, he'd taken an interest in the blacksmith's daughter. Their comments weren't savory other than mentioning her beauty and innocence. He clenched his jaw against having to kill more than planned. The sheriff, sure, as per Gregory's instructions, but these men... Warric had no doubt they'd done these vile deeds before. What other innocents had suffered?

He had a mission. If he dallied in an alley, giving each man a crimson necklace, he might miss the sheriff's passing. Time dragged, with his attention split between the road and the two men. When they stood, the sun had begun to set. Warric rose on instinct, trailing the men while they staggered out of the tavern. He paused and raised his face to the clearing sky. At least, the rain had stopped. The men had taken up vigilance opposite the blacksmith. Smoke still bellowed out of its chimney, the store open to the elements. A young woman stoked the furnace, sweat glistening off her heaving bosom still perky in her youth. The smithy was older than Warric would have liked.

Had the men continued past, Warric might have warned the smithy and left it at that. Palming his dagger, he strode along the muddy road, dodging puddles and horse shit. His boots were beyond salvation without magic, but cleaning shit off was a no. He shuddered.

Dipping to the left, he 'bumped' into the scrawny man, sending him flying into the heftier one. As expected, they grunted and spun on him. Warric held up a hand, pretended to sway then 'stumbled' into the alley while jangling his pouch of coins.

With a flick of a wrist, he faded, allowing the shadows to swathe him in darkness. Warmth flowed through him as his magic fed off and replenished itself. A shimmer circled his vision, outlining everything in purple. The men called out, spinning and peering into the shadows. Warric moved, targeting the most troublesome of the two. By the time they realized they were in danger, the heftier one gurgled, fell to his knees, bounced off his face, and sprawled in eternal silence.

"Hey—" Scrawny's eyes widened. His hands flew to his throat. Blood trickled through his fingers. With a last gasp, he hit the ground, spraying mud onto Warric's left boot.

He grimaced and wiped his dagger across the dead man's jerkin. Keeping his gaze on the road, he dragged the bodies deeper into the shadows. The pounding of hooves and the rickety creaks of wagon wheels added to the laughter and cries from the tavern. No alarm sounded. He tilted his head to listen, honing air magic to be certain.

Voices, scratching, coughing, hammering, hoofbeats, the crack of a whip, the sizzle of a fire reverberated in his ears. Air magic was a gift and a curse.

Into this cacophony came the plaintive cry of a kitten. He jerked back, scanned the alley, then smiled at the muddy bundle of fur shivering in what moonlight spilled into the darkness.

"Look at you," he whispered and scooped the kitten into his arms, taking a moment to check the sodden creature's sex—a male. "Where's your mother, mm?" He listened for a mother cat's cries, but there was nothing. "You're stuck with me, Mud."

Slipping out of the alley, he hurried to the tavern and waited at the door, expecting the old woman from earlier to wave her hand and clean him *and* Mud. A service he was more than happy to pay for. As he waited, a man shoved him aside.

Warric ground his teeth, fighting for patience. "I beg your pardon," he snapped.

"You should." The man swept off his wide-brimmed hat and slapped it across his chapped thigh. "I need a hot meal and an ale. See to it."

Warric narrowed his eyes and assessed the man. He started with the polished boots, high-quality breeches, and fine-leather chaps. Two exquisite gold-filigree pistols looked like they'd never been fired. His bulging gut stretched a crisp white tunic. A thick moustache squatted like a weasel on his top lip. Ruddy cheeks and a semi-smooth jaw worsened Warric's opinion of him.

"Unless you want it poisoned, I suggest you find a tavern maid and ask her..." Warric leaned in, bringing his darkness with him. "Nicely."

The man stepped back, arched a brow, then snorted, giving Warric a cold shoulder.

The skittish maid from earlier offered a tentative smile to Warric. "Oh, you have returned, sir. Would you like your old table?"

"I was here first," ground out the other man.

"Thank you, the same table would be wonderful." Warric gestured to his coat and blood-splattered breeches. "Would you mind asking your mistress—"

"See here," the pompous man spluttered.

Losing his patience, Warric leveled his gaze on him. The man choked, clutched at his throat, then coughed as he fought for breath. Before releasing the stranglehold Warric's darkness had on the man's throat, he gave it one last squeeze.

"I said...nicely." He tossed a silver to the maid. "Another ale, please."

"Of course." She bowed her head then scurried to the barkeep.

"Sentinel Warric of Auriville, I serve Baron Gregory of Kenningthain." Sharing his real name wouldn't matter. Not when the man would die knowing it. "You are?" He put enough disdain into his voice to make any man shrivel.

"Thomas of Hasden, Sheriff of Netherbury," the man spat. "I serve Lord Emil of Kenningthain."

Warric stilled and blessed him with a broad smile. "A pleasure to make your acquaintance, sirrah. Care to join me?" He swept out a hand, gesturing to the table by the fire.

Taken aback, Thomas gaped, straightened his spine so his gut bounced, then flounced to the table. The poor chair squeaked in protest when the man sat.

"Ale?" Warric waved a hand at the maid to bring another tankard. "The stew is hot. That's all that recommends it."

Thomas chuckled. "Hot is just what I need. The weather has been abysmal."

"Indeed." Warric stroked the kitten's head as he studied the man he would kill. The maid placing brimming tankards on the table broke Warric's focus. "Pray, ask your mistress for her service. My garments are in a state." He slid two silvers across to her. "Any scraps for my cat."

"Aye, sire." She hurried off, granting them privacy.

"I assume you are headed for Netherbury?" Warric took a long pull from the insipid ale, his gaze fixed on Thomas.

"Aye, and yourself, to the north?"

Warric nodded. "I will be riding through Netherbury if you care for company." It wasn't meant as a question. Whether the man agreed or not, Warric would remain close to him—in the shadows behind him or by his side, he cared not which one.

"A man of your caliber would be an asset, to be sure." Thomas tapped his pudgy fingers on the table.

The elderly woman from earlier stopped by the table, placed a plate of chicken innards before Warric, and waved her hand, cleaning him and Mud. She faced Thomas, did the same, dipped into a short curtsey and was off.

"A lovely magic to have." Warric downed his ale.

A lad whipped out a qitary and filled the common room with jaunty music, his voice pleasing. For a time, as Thomas spilled his life's story, Warric could pretend he was among friends, with no obligations weighing on his shoulders. Mud gobbled his meal then curled onto Warric's lap, contentment in his steady purring.

His last pet had been a baby bird that hadn't survived its broken wing. Perhaps, when he was but a child, if he'd had someone to care for, then he wouldn't have this need for companionship that asked nothing from him but his time. Perhaps he ached to be something more than a killer, someone who could be gentle, could show mercy. Hell's teeth, could love.

He shoved the tankard aside. Having another would be foolish if these maudlin thoughts continued.

"Staying the night, or are we pressing through?" He stroked Mud's neck, wincing when the kitten's claws dug into his unprotected inner thigh.

"The weather has improved." After drinking from his tankard, Thomas licked his lips. "I might take advantage of it while it lasts. Mayhap we reach Netherbury in good time."

"If need be, we could camp alongside the Olion."

"True, but I prefer a softer bed than the forest floor." Thomas rubbed the back of his neck. "These old bones..."

"Do you have lodgings in Netherbury or must you still acquire them when you arrive?" Warric gathered Mud and slid him into his inside pocket. It was the largest and warmest spot for the cat.

"All part of the contract." Thomas beamed.

"That was most generous of Emil."

Thomas frowned. "*Lord* Emil."

"My apologies. I have spent so much time with Baron Gregory that I have picked up his mannerisms." Warric grinned. "Pray I do not meet *Lord* Emil." He smothered a wince at showing the man any sort of respect. "How goes his search for the amulet?"

"I do not know," Thomas replied as he pushed himself to his feet.

Warric followed suit and trailed the man out of the tavern. "I am most curious. 'Tis said to have belonged to the Last Empyrean."

"What could such an artifact do?" Thomas mused while they strode to the stables. "It might lead one to a hidden treasure? Offer wisdom?"

Warric shrugged. "'Tis for us mere servants to ponder."

Serenity's coat, now dry, glistened under the lantern's light. A glance confirmed the satchels untouched. Mounting, Warric accepted the reins the stablemaster held up to him, and with a nudge of his heel, lurched into a canter.

Night had truly fallen. Although darkness for one such as he offered refuge and opportunities. He feared it not. Adjusting his vision allowed the road and the surrounding forests to appear as if bathed in purple light. Sunlight and firelight was the antithesis of darkness and of no use to him. If he had his way, he would sleep all day and work at night. Alas, Baron Gregory expected Warric to do as commanded, no matter the hour.

The Conclave Way was abandoned the longer the moon crossed the sky. At least, Thomas had ceased his chatter, allowing the night creatures to serenade Warric. He could give his magic free reign, to warn him of approaching trouble, to whisper of passing predators or fellow travelers. It also allowed him to track the Olion river running along the road.

As anticipated, when they had yet to reach Netherbury by midnight, Warric gestured to a secluded corpse of trees. "Shall we?"

Thomas grunted, steered off the road, then dismounted with a whimper before tethering his horse to a nearby tree. Warric did the same, sans the whimper. Within minutes, he had a fire going and his bedroll set out. He took the time to brush Serenity down, then draped a blanket across his back, to ward off a chill. Lying on his bedroll, he watched Thomas struggle, groaning when he kneeled and rolled onto his back.

Warric said nothing. What more was there to discuss? He planned to wait two more hours. No sympathy rose to sway him. Besides, his instructions were clear. Kill the man and assume his position as sheriff. Letting Thomas live would complicate things.

Warric must be getting soft to be contemplating other scenarios. Mud mewled. He withdrew the kitten, rolled onto his side, and let Mud scramble around and over him. Time ticked by and still, he waited...for Thomas's snoring.

A man that unhealthy surely had to snore.

THREE

"The bonny lass was naught but sass,
With curls of fire and eyes of green,
Her coffers were full, her tongue crass,
For a silver, her sweet treasure—"

"Piers," Yrsa snapped, spinning in her saddle to glare at him.

He paused mid-wail, his fingers still strumming the qitary. At least he could play the instrument. So much better than his caterwauling. As he beamed at Yrsa, Vona smothered a chuckle. While Yrsa was distracted, she snuck her flask out of the satchel for a sip. They'd been on the Conclave Way for hours. Already the sun had set, and the moon glowing bright in the cloudless sky.

Thanks to Yrsa's fire magic, the rain had made no impact on them or their mounts. It had been odd to ride through a downpour and not feel it. Vona had longed to soak the droplets into her skin, savor the sweet wealth of energy filling her well. Alas, she wasn't allowed such an opportunity.

This adventure so far had turned out to be as dull as ditch water. She sighed at her reflection in a moonlit puddle. Brown hair and eyes stared back with boredom etched into her brow. Tugging her hat down, she hid her face. She resembled her father. Jacut had their mother's pale blonde hair and hazel eyes.

Vona slumped. She even had Father's snub nose—sitting like a ripe cauliflower on her face. Piers claimed it was adorable.

Pushing her disappointment aside, she cleared her throat and broke into song, *"Her kisses are honey sweet. Her arms heaven divine."*

"Vona," Yrsa cried out. "A lady—"

"Could die of boredom, and since you shut Piers up at the best part..." Vona grinned when Orv whispered from her satchel, "I know how you feel." She'd tried to break it of its shyness, but to no avail.

"Your voice is that of an angel," Piers sniffed, balanced his qitary on his lap, and dabbed at his eyes with his kerchief. Lagging behind, he bobbed on his donkey, its steps shorter than that of their horses. Piers had a fear of anything taller and faster. Nor did he care that he was a sight to behold in his bright purple garments.

"I suggest we camp for the night." Thack's gravel voice sliced through the tension growing under Yrsa's glower.

"Alongside the river, please." Vona pinched her lips. She hadn't meant to reveal how desperately she yearned for a source of water. The scent and lure of it had trailed them since they started along the Conclave Way. To have magic's warmth rushing through her, the influx of energy so exquisite, it was almost addictive. "A bath would be wonderful," she said, ruffling Honey's mane.

"A bath?" Piers shivered. "It's sure to be freezing."

"You will not be taking liberties with your person, Ruvona." Yrsa adjusted herself in her saddle. "'Tis dangerous and—"

"With an envoy in our party? Who would dare?" Vona gave her a wide smile.

"Let the lass," Thack said. "Besides, you'll guard her as usual."

Yrsa harumphed and said no more.

He tossed a wink at Vona. She thanked him by sliding her flask between their mounts, making sure to hide her actions from her ever-vigilant nursemaid.

"How much longer?" Vona tried to strip the whine in her voice, but her ass was numb, and her left foot itched inside the boot. She'd drained her earth magic hours ago, and until she could sink her bare feet into soil, healing her ass and thighs wasn't going to happen.

Yrsa growled, "If you ask me one more time—"

"Devenmere is a half-a-day's ride." Thack hiccupped then pocketed her flask as if it were his own.

Under Yrsa's watchful eye, Vona was grateful he hadn't thought to return it to her. 'Ladies do not drink brandy,' her mother had stated with her top lip curling in disgust.

"We could push through, but I would prefer to arrive when 'tis daylight." Thack studied the moon's position. "I did not like how your father was taken, Vona. The darkness does offer cover for those with nefarious intentions."

Yrsa faced forward, her shoulders stiff.

Vona tried not to dwell on what this trip would have been like without Piers and Thack. More like her training sessions where she'd be told to suck it up, to have a backbone, to imagine herself as stronger and not this weakling her mother had birthed. What awaited her in

Devenmere and north, Vona couldn't say, but at least her life was disrupted. Hopefully, it would be a while before she needed to attend daily training sessions or suffer through old-as-dust tutors.

She longed to be out from under their thumbs, learning to survive on her own, to meet new people and discover what their lives were like. Wiggling in her saddle, she rolled from ass cheek to cheek, hoping to ease the burn. If she was in agony, how did Honey feel?

"Are we there yet?" Orv muttered.

"Do not ask," Vona hissed. "I did and got snapped at."

"Over the rise and to the west is a small camp site. 'Tis close to a secluded pool," Thack whispered while slipping her flask into her satchel. Despite his size and girth, he sat a horse like a true equestrian. When she was younger, Thack had tucked her into bed while regaling her of his travels and service to a baron drunk on adventure. She missed those carefree days.

Thack snatched a whimpering Orv out of her satchel and began to tinker with it, a strange tool in his right hand. With each poke or nudge, lights would flicker and Orv would gurgle in delight.

Trusting that no harm would befall it, she asked what had been on her mind since they'd departed Bennedor. "What do you think happened to Father?"

"Lord Emil," Thack snarled. "That man is slimier and more slippery than an eel. He has the morals of one too. Pity the baron has not done the deed."

"Rumors state he promised his mother he would not," Piers called out while thrumming his qitary. He dug into his pocket and popped a gumdrop into his mouth. No wealth dangled from his belt, but his garments, satchels, and any available space held confectionary.

When Vona was younger, she had tried to out-eat Piers and paid the price. Thankfully, one severe stomach ache put an end to her liking for sweets. Sneaking sips from Father and Thack's goblets had introduced her to wines and brandies. Of course, Mother hadn't...*didn't* approve, but Father had brushed her complaints aside.

Thack guided the party across a narrow wooden bridge to the other side where he dismounted under an ancient oak tree. Yrsa and Vona followed suit, tethering their horses alongside Thack's warhorse, Baston. Within minutes, Thack had a fire blazing. Piers bobbed in, clambered and jangled off his donkey, then with a grimace, adjusted his tight breeches at his crotch.

He scowled. "Mayhap I should bathe as well."

Thack chuckled. "Just do not cook the fish."

Piers grinned. "A lesson learned." He rubbed his stomach. "Although, dinner was delicious."

Vona didn't hesitate to set out her bedroll while they chattered. She knew the story. Piers could use his earth magic to clean himself, but this one time, he'd opted for a proper bath. Except the water had been too cold for his liking. He'd set his fire magic to heat the river and had gone to extremes. Thack had needed healing when Piers had scorched his ass and legs. They joked about it now, but Thack had been livid, threatening to castrate poor Piers, who'd squealed like a girl and burst into tears.

While they bantered now, she grabbed Orv, shoved it in her satchel, and bolted for the river.

"Vona." Yrsa's call halted her.

Vona slumped and faced her nursemaid. "Listen, do you hear anything to worry about?" She tilted her head. "No? Then I am sure nothing will befall me mere feet from you."

Yrsa frowned. "Your mother—"

"Leave me alone for once." Stomping off, Vona headed for the river glistening in the moonlight. A circle of rocks had formed a pool, calmer and more inviting. She tossed the satchel down and sat on the grass. Orv rolled out, teetered as if assessing its surroundings then rose to eye level.

"What has you so grumpy? My circuits are zinging and strangely itchy."

Vona ignored it to yank off her boots and stockings. She shoved her feet into the damp sand. A green glow swirled around her toes and rushed up her legs before fading into her skin.

On a muted groan, she closed her eyes and tilted her face to the moon. Her backside and thighs quit throbbing and cramping. What exhaustion had plagued her, vanished. Giggling, she peeled off her knee-length coat, unbuttoned her tunic, then unbuckled and slithered off her breeches. Standing naked, she shivered when a cool breeze swept across her skin, inspiring a surge of goosebumps.

Once more wriggling her toes in the sand, she studied the pool, then waded in, making sure she touched the river bed. A shiver raced across her skin, her nipples pebbled into tight buds, but she didn't care about the cold. Green and blue light bathed her, saturating her with warmth and sweet ecstasy. Her well filled, tension eased from her body, and she sank deeper. She dipped her head under the surface, spending a few moments submerged despite being unable to see much in the green-blue glow.

Desperate for air, she pushed off from the bottom to burst out, sucking in great gulps.

"I was about to call for aid," Orv said where it bobbed above her.

"I am good. Better than that, I am well." She beamed, swirling the water with her hands as she crossed to her satchel for a bar of soap. Unraveling the cloth, she sniffed, inhaling the sweet fragrance of Jasmine. Mags knew her well. She smiled and sank into the water to soap and rinse.

Humming a haunting tune about lost love and wasted death, she took her time washing her hair. In that moment, life was perfect.

THE FIRST WHISPER REACHED Warric's ears where he lay waiting. Thomas had yet to settle deep into slumber. A sleeping man was easier to kill. Warric wasn't in the mood to expend energy more than he had to. Mud clambered along the banks, chewing on grass, lapping water, shitting in the sand and burying it. Entertaining to watch while time passed.

The dulcet tones of a woman stirred Warric's interest. She bathed nearby and at this time of the night. When Thomas didn't stir, Warric settled, content to listen to the ancient song she hummed, one he hadn't heard in years. If he recalled, the story was of two lovers doomed to be apart and destined to die alone.

He grimaced when Thomas launched from his bedroll to face the river.

"What was that?" he rasped, his hand on his pistol, orange swirls rippling down his arm.

"A woman bathing," Warric said, keeping his tone bored. He wasn't, not in the least. Her presence intrigued him.

"Oh?" Thomas cackled and inched toward the rushes shielding them from view.

Sighing, Warric slipped the dagger from his boot and enshrouded himself in purple-tainted darkness. With a flick of a wrist, Thomas slumped to the ground, guided there with Warric's gentle touch.

"Are you done yet, Ruvona?" a woman snapped.

Warric parted a few rushes with his bloody blade, blinking at the mountain of a woman standing on the opposite bank.

"Did you hear that?" She stilled and tilted her head, white magic circling her.

He grimaced. An envoy, here, and with air magic?

Thomas gurgled. Without glancing at him, Warric pressed a hand over the man's mouth, silencing him while sending out a sound dampener. He could thwart the eager hearing of a sentinel but an envoy? While the man died, Warric let his focus shift to the woman in the river.

His breath caught. His eyes narrowed. Into this, his heartbeat thundered in his ears.

She was beautiful. A nymph bathing, her pale skin illuminated by the moonlight. Her dark hair clung to her back, partially obscuring her form. Blue glowed where she touched the water, screaming her magic-gift. She twirled, peering into the shadows, stirring the water, and blessing him with a full view of her body. Feminine softness was there in her youthful breasts, but her stomach had definition, her arms and shoulders appearing strong...capable.

Hell's teeth. He gritted his, while savoring the burn of lust setting his body ablaze. It had been a while since a woman had inspired something as potent as desire within him. His focus was always on the task, the next step, the situation, or saving his ass.

"What do you hear?" she fake-whispered, then waded across to swing her hand as if it were a sword, whacking at the rushes. She was close enough to touch. "See. Nothing."

Mud meowed, tumbled through the rushes and into the river with a *plonk*. Warric jerked forward and froze. Thomas was gasping his final breaths. Warric couldn't move without alerting the envoy. Air magic could silence but not blind. She'd see him for sure if he plunged into the water to save his pet.

"Oh." Ruvona leaped across and scooped Mud out of the water. "A kitten attacked me, Yrsa." She cuddled Mud to her chest, hiding her dark nipples from Warric's gaze. "We are in such dire straits."

"We are not keeping it," the envoy growled.

This close, Warric feasted his eyes on Ruvona in all her bare beauty. They were inches apart. If she peered through the rushes, she would see him. Dark brown eyes glanced in his direction. Her adorable nose softened the harshness of a square jaw, and her mouth tugged downward in a perpetual frown, made bewitching by the plumpness of her lips. Her magic was weaker though. He threw out his senses to confirm her level as proficient. Why would an envoy be watching over this young woman? He hadn't heard of a sentinel on the Conclave dying.

Nor would the Conclave assign an envoy to anyone with magic this insignificant.

With a sweep of a hand, Ruvona encircled the kitten in blue light, drying him. He mewled and received a cuddle in return. "Listen for its mother, Yrsa. She cannot be far."

Warric whipped his gaze to the envoy. He stilled, held his breath, and waited for her to pick him out of the shadows.

"We're not keeping it," she repeated. "Now, out you get. Piers wants fish for dinner."

"Truly?" The younger woman laughed, then swallowed it at Yrsa's glower.

Sighing, Ruvona waded across the river and stepped out, passing Mud to the reticent Yrsa. With a grunt, the massive woman placed the kitten on her shoulder, giving it a quick stroke. Ruvona glowed blue briefly before she donned a cream tunic, breeches in dark gray, knee-high boots, and a coat, each item hiding her from his admiration. A hat, pinned on one side and adorned with grouse feathers and a large gold brooch, she slapped against her thigh.

When she stamped her boots, she faced the river again. "Orv?"

"Coming," a gyro called, peeking from behind a rock to shoot across the bank and dive into a satchel.

As their voices faded, Warric sat frozen. A glance at Thomas's lifeless eyes confirmed one task was done. Creeping close to the river, Warric washed his hands and dagger while staring across the bank. Anger warred with fascination. For even though he'd been blessed to see Ruvona in all her fine glory, the woman had stolen his cat.

FOUR

After searching Thomas for any parchment confirming his position as sheriff, along with valuables and gold, Warric hid his body under a pile of rocks and debris. He did all this by rote, his focus on how to get his cat back. With the letter of appointment in his pocket, he packed his bedroll and satchels, doused the fire, then unsaddled Thomas's horse to set it free. He mounted Serenity and headed south, planning on approaching Ruvona's party from Lisbay's side, as if he was merely a traveler en route to Netherbury. Simple enough.

That was as far as his plan went. What worried him was deceiving an envoy. They were notoriously skeptical, and as a fellow air-gifted, he prayed his smile worked. Charming one's prey was an acquired skill. In his case, it had been ages since the baron had used that side of him.

He cantered toward their encampment, one he knew well yet didn't often use since it was on the west side of the river. "Greetings, fellow travelers," he called as he intruded into their clearing.

As expected, Yrsa was on guard, her pistols unholstered. Ice chilled the blood in his veins at the sight of a Sundowner mark on her upper arm. Shit. Why hadn't he noticed it? He willed himself not to snort at his stupidity. He'd been ogling a fine pair of breasts like an untried youth.

He bowed his head at Yrsa, dismounted, and lifted his hands in a show of surrender. "I mean you no harm. I wish to share your fire this night." It took all his strength not to search out Ruvona among the faces. "I am the new Sheriff of Netherbury."

Ruvona's cry whipped Yrsa's attention to her. It granted him the opportunity to do the same, to admire the firelight playing off Ruvona's skin and the way her breeches pulled tight over her legs. Mud scrambled out of her arms, bolted across the clearing, and climbed Warric like a tree.

"Whoa," he chuckled. "What is this?" He cuddled the kitten, taking the time to stroke his little head.

Yrsa lowered her pistols. "Do you have proof?" she demanded.

"Yrsa," the older man scoffed. "My apologies, young man, she is naturally distrustful."

"Something I understand." Warric withdrew the parchment and handed it to the envoy. She snatched it out of his hand for a quick perusal then passed it back to him.

"Welcome." She gestured to an empty spot between two bedrolls. On the right sat the older man, sturdy in physique and dark in skin tone, his head bald. Beside him was Ruvona's bedroll. Guarding her was a petite man in bright purple. His qitary on his lap said it all. A few fish roasted above the fire.

"My thanks," Warric beamed, meeting the gaze of everyone around the camp. He dared not linger on Ruvona's large brown eyes. "Name's Thomas."

"Help yourself to our bounty," the purple man sang, croaking the words like stone on stone.

Warric smothered a wince. He tethered Serenity beside a donkey, of all things, and set out his bedroll again while cradling Mud to his chest. Passing the kitten to Ruvona granted him a chance to admire her upturned face, the darkness of her braided hair, and her deep soulful brown eyes. She blessed him with a smile so mesmerizing, it took him a moment to break the daze. Striding away from her, he tried to gather his thoughts, to build a resistance to her wiles. He'd met beautiful women. While summoning memories of said women, he brushed down his horse then lengthened the tether so the sweet grass and river were accessible.

When Warric settled onto his bedroll, Mud was making grumbling noises while eating pieces of fish out of Ruvona's palm. The traitor, but Warric couldn't blame him. Warric dragged his gaze away and stared into the flames burning without wood. Someone here had fire magic. Common enough.

Yrsa joined them, her focus remaining on him. Not an expression crossed her features nor did she reveal anything but wariness in her posture. A tap on his upper arm drew his gaze to the older man, who offered him a flask.

"The name's Thackeray or Thack." His grin was full of teeth and bright against his dark cheeks. "This is Ruvona. That's Piers, and the termagant glowering at us is Yrsa."

Warric sipped from the flask without sniffing it first. Trust mattered, especially when he wanted to reclaim his cat licking his paws and cleaning his face close to the fire. The sweet smokiness of Brederburg brandy coated his tongue. He jerked back and studied the flask. R.D. was engraved in the metal. Flowers and weapons decorated the top half. The bottom sat snug in a leather casing. R for Ruvona? This was *her* brandy? How wealthy was this woman?

"My thanks," he said, handing the flask to Thack. "I will not pry. We just met so sharing your business is irresponsible." He smiled to soften his words. "Shall we discuss the weather?"

"Miserable earlier," Piers muttered, pulled a brown ball out of his pocket, and popped it into his mouth. The familiar crunch of crystalized sugar identified it.

Beside Ruvona, a gyro peeked out from her satchel. Its flickering lights meant it was active, yet no one spoke to it. Not making a call, perhaps it recorded the scene? Warric doubted that, not after it had answered Ruvona when she'd called it. This party was an odd assortment of characters. He'd said he wouldn't ask, but he was desperate for answers.

Into the silence, he said, "I stopped at Borfort where a woman warmed me. Truly worth every coin."

Ruvona gaped at him while Thack snickered. Piers giggled like a girl.

Realizing what he'd said, Warric chuckled. "My apologies. I meant the old woman working in the Black Dog tavern would not let me in until she waved her magic over me." He fiddled with his duster coat's collar. "I was wet to the bone and splattered with mud." *And blood.*

His kitten meowed and scampered over to him to climb onto his lap. He stroked his head, relishing his sweet purr.

"Disappointing," Piers said. "I would have loved a salacious tidbit to pass the time."

"Within Ruvona's ears?" Yrsa said.

Ruvona shrugged. "I have heard worse."

Yrsa harumphed but said no more.

Warric smothered a chuckle. Seemed to him, Ruvona had three nursemaids. Interesting. "I promised not to pry, but are you heading through Netherbury per chance?"

"Aye," Thack grunted. "We might stay a day or two at Deven-mere."

Ruvona's eyes widened. She dipped her chin, hiding a smile. Warric tried not to stare. With three strong personalities, figuring out hers was harder, as if she kept it hidden. She smarted at her protection, resenting it. At least he'd gathered that from the little he'd seen. Two pistols rested beside her satchel, so she was skilled with weapons. Then again, how hard was it to point and click? The ornate buckles and holsters around her thighs implied daggers, but none were in sight.

Closing his eyes as if exhausted, he used his senses to ascertain their magic.

Yrsa's came across loud and clear—fire and air, smelling of coal and crispness. Ruvona's was water and earth. The first he'd witnessed when she'd rescued Mud and absorbed water droplets into her skin. Thack was air and water with the latter the strongest. That left Piers who was fire and earth, like the old woman at the tavern, explaining his tidy appearance. Not a smidge of dirt marked his body or garments. 'Twas a pity cleaning was taught only to fire-earth-gifteds. But there was something else to Piers, something volatile simmering under the surface.

Thack clambered to his feet amid clangs and clinks, snapping Warric's eyes open. An odd-shaped gadget fell out of the old man's pocket. He scooped it up and vanished behind the trees, no doubt taking a piss.

"I will patrol," Yrsa said to no one, grabbed her pistols, then faded into the shadows.

"That means she's keeping an eye on you," Ruvona whispered.

"I heard that," Yrsa called but didn't reappear.

"Of course you did," Ruvona muttered. "Got a gumdrop for me, Piers?" She held out a hand, and the man grudgingly dropped a brown hardboiled sweet on her palm. Popping it into her mouth, she shimmied into her bedroll and lay on her side, resting her head on her folded arm. Her gaze settled on Warric. He tried not to fidget. As an assassin, he had trained to control his reactions, expressions, instinctive tells that revealed his thoughts or intentions. Under her innocent attention, he struggled not to react.

Tucking a dozing Mud into the inner coat pocket, he crossed his legs and spread out on his back, praying she didn't notice his...*interest* in her.

"Ruvona is well, milady." Yrsa's distant voice grabbed Warric's attention, but he didn't glance away from Ruvona whose eyelids had drifted shut. Yrsa spoke to someone, reported in, to be specific. "A half-day away." She paused. "Nothing eventful, and in Lisbay?" She hummed. "Aye, good night, milady."

Ruvona's mother, perhaps? Warric smiled. So, her mother was a sentinel, which explained Yrsa's presence and Ruvona's quiet personality. The woman was sheltered, no doubt having been tutored and trained in the privacy of her home. Yet, by her words, she'd been exposed to experiences beyond her innocence and Yrsa's protection.

Mud stretched and sank his claws into Warric's tunic. Well, at least he had his cat back. He could part ways with this strange party and be done with them. A pang of sadness sliced through that notion. Something about this niggled, like a torn fingernail snagging on garments. The oddity of this party? What their motives were for heading north if they hailed from Lisbay? Ruvona had been delighted to stay a few days in Devenmere, which meant they intended on traveling onward.

Devenmere? Warric stilled while he feasted on her sleeping beauty. She was Ruvona Devenmere, daughter to Lady Ailith, a Conclave sentinel, and the renowned adventurer Lord Walter. Sister and minx to General Jacut. Mystery solved. He grinned. No doubt she hoped to spend time with her father at their Devenmere estate just east of Netherbury.

Under Warric's jurisdiction. Hell's teeth, he hoped she stayed for longer than a day or two. Why, he couldn't say. Didn't want to prod his thoughts or emotions regarding her. Beautiful women were common, yet something about this one...

As hardened as he was, as tainted and black his soul, perhaps her innocence called to him. She was pure, untouched, he was sure. Her lips parted. He narrowed his focus, allowing his magic to reach out and absorb her breath. Mint saturated his nose. For a moment, he savored the connection to her.

Perhaps she shouldn't stay long in Devenmere if this was how he reacted. He didn't need a weakness nor a distraction. Not with this task at stake. Emil was up to something, and Lord willing, Warric would find out sooner rather than later.

Thack slunk to his bedroll, clanking as he did so. The noise he made didn't stir Ruvona who'd buried her fingers in the soil beside her. Green tendrils spiraled over her skin. She moaned, her eyelashes fluttering.

"Dream well," Thack said after tossing orange magic into the silent fire. It swelled, cast out more heat, before settling into a steady burn. What was missing was the hiss and crackle while it consumed wood or coal.

"You too," Warric said, admiring the starlit sky. In the morning, he prayed his fascination with Ruvona would have dwindled. With one last glance, he threw his arm over his eyes and allowed the calls of the night's creatures to lull him to sleep.

FIVE

HELL'S TEETH, THE STRANGER was handsome. Something about him drew Vona's gaze, like the lure of a beautiful sunset or a master's artwork. Tall, broad-shouldered, big hands, and with black hair falling in waves to his shoulders, he would turn many a head. The type of man she rarely met. His voice rasped when he spoke, as if from disuse, and his eyes were a cerulean blue—like the seas south of Sagua she'd seen paintings of.

River, the kitten, had taken to him. He'd cradled the tiny thing in his large yet gentle hand. It said much, the way a man treated a smaller-than-him creature. She flicked her eyes open to study Thomas's profile while he slept. His nose was slightly hooked at the tip, yet she couldn't imagine him with it straight. At some point, it had been broken and healed crooked, which implied he hadn't been able to find a healer in time. She liked what it did to his face, changing it from heavenly to mesmerizing. His wide forehead, thick eyebrows, high cheekbones, and angular jaw into a square chin added to the attraction. When he'd intruded, her breath had caught. She hadn't reacted to any of the popinjays mother had brought round to meet her.

Even his hands were weathered, callused.

Thomas? His name felt...wrong. She expected him to have a bold, strong name, not something so common. Nor that he was from Hasden? A farming town south of Lisbay? She couldn't imagine him tending to his crops, although, his touch would be gentle when he tested the ripeness of plums, greeted a lamb, or stroked the forelock of a breeding mare.

She sniffed, trying to sense his magic. Air was easy, smelling similar to Yrsa's but not as potent. As expected, otherwise he wouldn't be a sheriff but an envoy at the Conclave's service. His other magic was a mixture of rain hitting soil, of sunlight baking rock. It wasn't like hot coals, tilled dirt, or damp foliage. Her heart leaped. Darkness? She hadn't met anyone with such a magic. Then again, how many people did she meet? Not many. As a sheriff, perhaps darkness was needed? In her studies, she was taught that such a magic was used for war, spying, or murder.

Despite the pale color of his eyes, an intensity and a soul-deep exhaustion shone out, like he'd seen and done much. Aye, he could be an assassin in that long duster coat. What had surprised her was that Yrsa let him stay. She'd half expected her nursemaid to shoot the man and his horse. Perhaps River bolting across the camp to Thomas had spared his life. An animal wary of a man was cause for alarm. A kitten taking to him was sweet and endearing. Even now, River was tucked in his pocket, one extended paw lying across his chest.

His lips twitched when claws dug in, but he didn't shove the kitten aside or harm it in any way, not even in his sleep. There was just something fascinating about him. She wanted to know more, bask in his gaze, listen to his voice and easy laughter. A weird reaction to be sure.

If she had her way, they'd spend more time in Devenmere. Why couldn't she solve her father's disappearance? Why did Jacut have to be involved when he had his hands full? Lack of trust, that's why, and her mother's low opinion of Vona's capabilities. True, she hadn't given her mother any reason to believe she could do this, but then again, no opportunities had arisen.

She was simply expected to attend her lessons and training and keep out of Mother's hair. Easy to do but oh-so-boring. Vona wanted to see the Ravelhern Mountains, past the battlegrounds to the northern most reaches of Sagua. It was said they were white, coated in snow yards thick beneath her feet. A chance to visit Yrsa's homeland would be wonderful, and even more, to sail across the crystal blue waters of the Somerto Sea.

She wanted to dance in the moonlight in her lover's arms, savoring the sweetness of his kisses, and the love for her shining in his eyes. Life had to offer more than this mundane existence.

Sleep eluded her. Piers snored, occasionally breaking into a mumbled song that grated along her nerves. Thack jangled whenever he rolled over, snorting and snuffling as he did so.

Yrsa had returned an hour ago, sliding into her bedroll and falling asleep in an instant, marked by her faint huffs. Desperate to relieve herself, Vona waited, not wanting to disturb Yrsa and thus gain an escort. Like she couldn't take a piss alone.

"What are you doing?" Orv whispered when she slid out of her bedroll.

"Shh," she hissed, placing a finger on her lips just in case. "I need to pee."

"I will guard you." It shot out and hovered above.

Vona smothered a groan-giggle. She didn't need protection, but Orv was the worst at that, diving for cover when anyone approached. "Thanks," she muttered, tiptoeing past the bedrolls and into the bushes.

Squatting in the shadows, she kept one ear out for anyone stirring while she fixed her gaze on the stars above. A cool breeze swept over her, drawing a sigh. Bobbing her ass, she drip-dried, then yanked on her breeches, taking the time to button up. While notching her belt, she strolled along the riverbank before settling on a rock to dip a hand into the water. Blue tendrils swirled around her fingers and faded into her skin, sending a frisson of warmth through her.

A river held life and the purest form of magic. A bowl of water or a fountain was all she was afforded. If she had her way, she'd live in a cottage by a river, a cliff at the rear, and a garden filled with vegetables and exquisite flowers. Her family was wealthy, and such a life would be possible.

Except...obligations and bringing honor to their name was expected of her.

Father had discovered many treasures. Mother, the same, though her focus had centered around the *Whispers of the Lost Ones.* When Vona was younger and eager for tales of their adventures, Father had promised to take her with him one day. Thack had been there. Piers too, but he hadn't heard. He'd snored where he'd sprawled on the settee.

Whirring, Orv dove behind a bush, whipping Vona's head up.

"My apologies," Thomas whispered, cradling a sleeping River in the curve of his neck. His tunic gaped, and in the moonlight, his exposed throat was appealing. "I did not mean to alarm you."

She shrugged and faced him while keeping one hand in the water. "I could not sleep. You?"

"The same. I am usually anxious around strangers."

She smiled. "You need not be. Yrsa is ferocious, but she is not bloodthirsty."

He chuckled. "That is good to hear." Gesturing to the rock, he asked, "May I join you?"

She shifted to the side, granting him more of the ledge to sit. He sank beside her, tugged off his boots with his head tilted to keep River in place, then sank his feet into the water. With him came his alluring scent, a mixture of his magics and the muskiness of male.

"Moments like these should be enjoyed," he mumbled, raising his face to the moon.

"I prefer being in nature," she managed, blinking at him and trying to hide how much he fascinated her. Conversations with the popinjays were always over the latest Conclave gossip, what parties they'd attended, or their finest horseflesh.

"Water and earth requires you to be." He ran his fingers through the water. Instead of shaking them dry, he stroked her cheek. When her skin glowed blue, he smiled. "Those who do not know better exist on the impurest sources of magic. Nothing compares to an untamed river, to the sunlight baking a desert, to the maelstrom of a storm at sea."

She gasped, leaning toward him to meet his gaze. "You have experienced these?"

"Besides the river?" He grinned. "Aye, I have been far and wide. Our Sagua is beautiful." He lowered his voice. "They say, 'tis possible to travel from north to south and from west to east on horseback."

"So they say. I have yet to read of such adventures." She thrust her fingers into the water, rotating her arm as the blue tendrils burst into life. "I imagine sailing across the seas on a horse would be impossible."

"True, but then I suppose, they mean to ride around any great bodies of water."

She shuddered. Not be at the center of it all? With no land in sight? Perhaps what she longed for was to be alone amid the elements. "My father has seen so much. 'Tis my greatest desire." *To be free.*

He tilted his head to study her. "No family of your own? Children? A husband?"

"No one has asked me." She lowered her chin to her chest. "Yet I am expected to want these things. I must marry a man my mother will choose for me." Squaring her shoulders, she met his gaze. "I will flee, find a cabin at the edge of Sagua, and live there."

She pursed her lips, realizing she sounded like a spoiled child.

"We all long to be free, Ruvona." He patted her hand splayed across the rock between them.

She slumped with relief. He hadn't judged her. "True."

"Find the moments where freedom exists and revel in them."

"Like now?" she asked, sweeping her hand out of the water while trailing droplets frozen in time. They glistened silver, tiny reflections in their depths. She released them, allowing them to return to the river.

"There are many forms of freedom. Savoring the sun on your face halfway through a task. Or having the time to nap late morning. Choices also grant us such moments. Some eat the same meal day in and day out. Being able to choose between roast boar or fried fish is freedom."

"It's all a matter of perspective," she said, taking his words to heart. Here she sat, alongside a relative stranger, albeit a darkly handsome one, while her party slept. She may not have the choice as to their destination or length of stay, but there were other things open to her. "Thank you, Thomas." She gave him a tentative smile.

"My pleasure, Ruvona."

She hid a wince. He might as well have tagged on her title, so proper did he speak her name. "'Tis Vona to my friends."

"Oh?" He smiled, but something intense darkened his eyes. "Are you offering friendship?"

Warmth on her cheeks had her lifting her face to a passing breeze. "I could rescind it, kind sir."

"No," he chuckled. "I accept."

Pulling his feet out of the water granted her full view of them. A man's bare calves wasn't something she'd been blessed to see. With a sweep of her hand, she dried him, finding the black hairs dusting his skin intriguing.

"My thanks, Vona." He slipped on his boots and stood. "I bid you a good night." Bending to whisper in her ear, he said, "Your Yrsa is with us."

Ice curled around Vona's innards, not warmed by Thomas's breath on her skin. "I expected as much." For once, she'd hoped Yrsa would stay asleep. No, her conversation with Thomas had to be monitored. Vona pondered killing the woman, harsh in her desperation and nigh impossible, Mother would simply appoint another guardian.

Her only hope was Father. She had to find him before her future was cast in stone and without her say-so. 'Alone' again, she stared into the waters trickling past her, off on their adventures. The temptation to slip into their depths and let them carry her away was almost too much to resist. Besides, Yrsa would drag her out of the river and scold her, like usual.

A matter of perspective. From Yrsa's point of view, guarding Vona wasn't what she might have envisioned for her life when she'd been identified as an envoy. Perhaps she had had fantastical dreams to see Sagua as Vona did. She frowned. Not once had she asked Yrsa about this. Whether she was happy being a nursemaid. Come to think of it, Vona didn't know much about the woman other than the angry visage she saw every day.

"Yrsa, why do you do this?" she asked the shadows. "Did you not have hopes and dreams when you were younger? A life with a family and daughters of your own to torment?"

Yrsa strode from the bushes, the moonlight bathing her in silver. She sat on the rock beside Vona, crossing her legs beneath her. Silence fell while she fiddled with the beads in her braids. "When I was younger, my family gifted me to the Rikesia Temple. There, what makes me a woman, is stripped from me. In my training, I was taught discipline, sacrifice, and the use of all weapons, old and new. My ability to have children was removed on my thirteenth birth date."

She met Vona's wide gaze. Shock, sadness, horror warred within her. She sniffed. That she had never thought to ask, that Yrsa had suffered so.

"They say the procedure is painless, and for the most part, it was." Yrsa tapped her chest over her heart. "Here is where the scar resides and never fully heals." She captured Vona's hand in hers. "I chose to serve your mother, knowing the extent of my duties. In my eyes and heart, you are the daughter I can never have. I want only the best for you, Vona, in all things." A slow smile formed.

Despite the tears trickling over Vona's cheeks, she squeezed Yrsa's hand. She had never known this, how Yrsa felt, what she had endured, and that she had chosen her when she could have served the greatest sentinels in the Conclave.

"Do not believe I would let your mother marry you off to an unworthy man. You need love, honor, excitement, and passion. Without those, you will be hollow and bereft. So, I guard you for your husband, something I am certain he will be grateful for."

On impulse, Vona threw her arms around the woman, hugging her as if her life depended on it. "I am so sorry I was such a pain, resenting your training and teachings." She sucked her tears into her skin. "I shall endeavor to be better, to do more, to listen."

Yrsa chuckled. "You can try, little one, but a stubborn streak runs through you. You crave independence, and had I not made a vow to protect you, I would grant you this." She rose to her feet, lifting Vona with her. "Now, come, off to sleep. Tomorrow's journey may be a short one, but something has me anxious."

"About Father?" Vona asked, leading the way to the campsite. A glance back confirmed Orv trailing them. Thomas had warned her about Yrsa but hadn't mentioned her non-vigilant and shy gyro.

"Darkness lies ahead, Vona. A battle we will need to overcome to find the truth."

Cryptic words, but Vona trusted Yrsa's instincts. "Dream well," she whispered, while sliding into her bedroll.

Orv dove for the satchel. Resting her cheek on her clasped hands, Vona studied Thomas's profile. A grateful husband, Yrsa had said. Most men wanted docile wives, but Vona was far from that, she hoped. Did all ladies suffer through weapons training? History and geography tutelage? She rolled over to face a snoring Piers. Whatever man she did fall for, she prayed he didn't expect her to be anything but herself.

Six

DAWN BROKE AND SO did the camp. Groggy Piers mumbled about sleeping in, but Thack was energized, along with Yrsa and Thomas. Within minutes, they were mounted and heading north. Breakfast was a hunk of black bread and goat's cheese. Vona dutifully nibbled on her meager fare while Piers tormented their ears with a morning wail. She'd love a bowl of boar stew with sweet potatoes, onions, and garlic. Perhaps finished with blackberry pie and cream? The cheese tasted salty, and the bread stuck to her tongue. She grimaced, struggled to swallow, then coughed when it lodged in her throat.

A massive hand pounded her back, and through tears and aching ribs, she glared at Thack.

"What? You were dying," he chuckled. In his other hand, he fidgeted with a metallic object long and narrow, grooves along the sides. She'd learned a long time ago, unless she had all day, not to ask him what he was working on.

With nothing to look at other than the scenery, she had time. "What's that, Thack?"

He blinked at the object. "A whistle. Tiny holes need to go on the side, each a finger width apart."

As Baston plodded on, Thack focused on the gadget, fiddling with one end that held a tiny flap. Well, that was short. She'd hoped he'd drone on for at least an hour. A glance over her shoulder revealed Yrsa cleaning a pistol, while occasionally peering into the forests to ensure they weren't being followed. Piers had fallen silent, broken only by the braying of his donkey. In his hands was a silk cap he was painstakingly sewing. In crimson and yellow, it promised to be as gaudy as his purple one.

Behind him, staring at Vona, was Thomas. A slight smile curled one side of his mouth upward. He dipped his head in a curt nod, as if in greeting. Her heartbeat leaped. Had he been watching her? No, she was in front of him, so of course, in his line of sight. She tapped the side of her head with two fingers and faced ahead.

Besides the passing wagons and other travelers, by horse or foot, there was nothing to occupy her thoughts. Hours ticked past while she hummed a ditty. Under her breath, she sang,

"Her kisses are honey sweet.
Her arms heaven divine.
Into the night, we soar.
On wings of joy and wine."

A husky baritone filled the air, so deep and resonating, she twisted in her saddle to gape at Thomas. His gaze remained fixed on her as he sang,

"I miss thee, lass, my heart's afire.

Spend thy time kissing my—"

"We are almost there." Yrsa pointed ahead. "The road to Devenmere forks to the east. Netherbury to the west."

He laughed. "So 'tis, Yrsa. My thanks." Offering his arm, he clasped hers in a sentinel-to-sentinel greeting. She flushed, her eyes wide, but she recovered her usual stoicism. Cantering past Piers, he patted the man's shoulder then paused alongside Vona. "Fair lady, until we meet again."

"Until the Fates see fit to cross our paths, kind sir." She tapped her temple again and watched him shake Thack's hand before veering left, following the road to Netherbury. A wooden sign stated it was a mere three miles away.

As their party headed east, Vona willed herself not to look back, to seek out Thomas's broad shoulders. It was only as they rode toward the hill with a clear view of Devenmere that she realized he'd stolen her cat.

All thoughts of River vanished when Thack cursed. Vona drew her horse alongside his and froze. Her breath caught in her throat on a sob. Before her sat Devenmere Manor, its stone façade gleaming in the sunlight. Around it, the impeccable gardens were gone. Shacks and tents filled the fenced grounds, fires trailed smoke, and children played in the trees and the now-blackened fountain.

The manor's windows were gone, with tattered cloth billowing in the breeze. The once ornate wooden door was missing, probably burned for firewood. Of course Father wasn't here. He wouldn't have stood for this...destruction.

With a battle cry that chilled Vona to the core, Yrsa urged her horse into a gallop and descended toward the settlement at breakneck speed. Vona did the same, spurring Honey on while sucking in the tears at her ruined home. Thack and Piers brought up the rear. Before she could dismount, Piers roared, slid off Kit, and split his clothes as his bear formed. Those watching cried out and scattered. With a swipe of his claws, he shredded a tent, then stomped a fire into the soil. Children climbed trees to escape him while the men charged, thrusting pitchforks and spears at him.

Vaulting off Honey, Vona threw herself between them but faced Piers with her hands up. "'Tis all right. I am sure there is a perfect explanation for this. Draw in your bear, Piers. You are frightening the children." As if on cue, a baby wailed.

With a pop and crunch, Piers's familiar face reformed. He shrank from a massive bear into this tiny man, naked as the day he was born. Raising her gaze skyward, Vona tried not to notice. Thack draped a coat over him and steered him to Kit while Piers grumbled about his ruined jerkin. Such a mild-mannered man, it took pure fury to unleash his bear. She'd seen it happen only twice. When a man had beaten a donkey. Kit had become Piers's steadfast companion since then. The other time was in an argument with Thack and Father. She didn't know the details, but witnessing the transformation had been incredible. Her studies touched on morphers, but she'd dismissed it as myth until Piers had revealed this other side to him. Morphers were said to be rare without an outward indication of their abilities.

"Explain yourselves," Yrsa demanded, facing the people with her pistols drawn. "This is Devenmere grounds. You are trespassing." She hissed the last word, spittle dewing on her bottom lip. Anger had flushed her cheeks, and she trembled with it.

"We are here at Lord Devenmere's behest," a tall man said, lowering his axe.

"Where is my father?" Vona asked, scanning the house for any sign of him. The crowd whispered her name, reverence and gratitude flowed over them. A few gazed at her with happiness and bright smiles.

"He was taken." The man pointed at Thack. "You were here, good sir. Your...friend too."

"Aye, that was six days ago," Thack growled, "but I do not recall Walter inviting you to squat here nor granting you the right to destroy his lands."

"We had no choice," a woman called, cradling her swaddled baby.

"This is the safest place in Netherbury," another said. "Lord Emil—"

"Does not deserve that title," the tall man spat. "He has brought death and decay to us all. We do not know what magic he wields, but 'tis nothing I have seen."

"Explain." Yrsa lowered her pistols but didn't holster them.

"I was there," an old man waddled into their midst. "In the center of a farm, surrounded by sheep and crops, Lord Emil clasped the amulet around his throat and whispered to it." He squeezed his eyes shut, and for a second, Vona thought he might faint. "In a circle, barreling outward, everything decayed. The sheep died. Crops withered. Trees crumbled. My poor Bessie, a few feet between me and Lord Emil, turned black as if burned alive. She did not have a chance to scream. Death consumed her...killed everything." Tears clung to his lashes.

"An amulet did that?" Yrsa sounded skeptical.

"'Tis possible. There are a few artifacts powerful enough to do such a thing, but it would have to be of pure darkness." Thack pointed to the fence. "Walter ordered the posts to be made of iron, chains to be run between them, yet buried as deep."

"So, no death within the iron boundary but what of the manor." Vona faced the crowds. "Who destroyed it? Where are the windows, the doors?"

"Lord Emil sent his men. They stripped it of all its value," the tall man said. "We house our elderly in the rooms, hoping to spare them the chillier nights."

Hell's teeth, how was she supposed to chase them out. This was her home filed with cherished memories of the hallways, the library, and shooting stones across the nearby lake. "Where is Dunstan?" She met the tall man's gaze. "Where are my...servants?"

"I am here, Lady Ruvona," someone called from the back. The crowd parted to let him limp through. He'd aged, his dear face lined with worry and sadness.

She met him halfway, cradling his dirty hands. His once-impeccable garments were soot-stained and crumpled. She sucked in the tears, willing herself not to cry. He needed her strong, to take command.

"Start from the beginning," she said, straightening his collar before brushing a gray curl off his temple.

"I tried to stop his men, but they were...determined." Dunstan glanced at the house. "Thankfully, I had received warning and hid the most valuable items in the cellar. The beds remained, they were too heavy for us and his men. The books were ignored and, thank the Lord, not burned. I feared that."

"And this limp? You did not try to stop them, did you?" She dipped and ran her hand down his leg, uncaring that her delicate touch summoned a blush to his parchment cheeks.

Warmth left her when she reached his knee, sending a chill through her. Her magic, glowing green, disappeared through his pants.

He bounced his knee, a chuckle escaping. "My thanks, milady. No one among us is a healer."

"No one?" She straightened. "Who else needs care? Bring your wounded and sick."

"Vona," Yrsa whispered. "Do not overtax yourself."

Casting a smile at her nurse...no, her guardian, she said, "A few a day should be fine."

The sun tracked its path across the sky as she saw to the wounded first. Most had received the sharp end of a sword, the burns from fireballs, crushing blows from well-aimed fists. She healed where she could, drawing magic from the soil when needed.

When she swayed and staggered, the tall man from earlier gripped her elbow to steady her.

"That is enough for today, milady," he said, tears shimmering in his eyes. "My apologies for what we did to your home."

"Not of your doing, sir." Falling to her knees, she dug her fingers into the sand. "Let me replenish. Then I will attend to your sick."

"No, Sir Piers has done so, milady."

Relief slumped her shoulders, and the whimper barreling up her throat almost slipped past her lips. She smiled. "Good." Straightening her spine, she walked to Dunstan, holding a large pot and scooping soup into wooden and chipped bowls. "When you are done, I would like a tour...to see the extent of the damage."

She worried her bottom lip. The two bags of coins she'd brought with might not be enough to repair the windows and doors, never mind feed these people. Yrsa had a bag, but perhaps, if the lord's soldiers hadn't discovered Father's secret room, none of their coin would be needed.

"I will continue," Thack said, taking the ladle from Dunstan.

"My thanks, Sir Thack." With a bright smile, Dunstan led the way. "The door is in the cellar. Your father bought it on one of his many adventures. The windows were removed post-intrusion. I did not want them to return to steal them."

Vona sniffed, lifted her arms to hug the man, then thought better of it. When she was a child clinging to his leg and pleading for a sweetcake, that was fine. But she was the lady of the manor now and expected to behave with more...reticence. She caught his hand for a squeeze.

"You have my deep gratitude. And the servants?"

Dunstan hesitated. "Most begged leave to see to their family. With the devastation brought on by Lord Emil and his guards, I had to let them go."

"All of them?" She gasped. "You are alone?"

Dunstan smiled. "Not anymore, milady." He entered the foyer, the stone floor exposed without the thick Eryssian rug she'd played Horses and Dragons on. The room was stripped of its sconces, paintings, and statues. The cellar wasn't large enough to hide it all.

The farther he went, the more despair encircled her heart. Markings on the walls showed where paintings had once been. Each room, the parlor, dining room, sunroom, and conservatory were filled with make-shift beds. Upstairs, the beds held the sick, even in her bedroom. Yet her father's remained empty.

"I refused to let anyone sleep here." Dunstan held his chin high. "This is my lord's room and as such, should remain as is." As is meant no paintings and artifacts, the thick skin of a polar bear was gone, along with the smaller Eryssian rugs. What remained was the bed and the books, stacked tall along a wall far from the untouched windows.

She faced Dunstan. "This was why you were hurt?"

He lowered his chin. When he glanced up, he was grinning. "I fought like a demon, milady."

Not sure how to thank him for his loyalty, she patted his shoulder despite the weakness in her limbs. "To the library. I pray all is well there."

"They showed no interest in his many books. I did hide his most cherished trinkets."

She giggled. "Best not to let Father hear you call them such."

The library was almost untouched. Her father's desk in rare dark Thariq wood sat to the rear of the room. Books filled his floor-to-ceiling shelves lining every spare wall. His quill and ink jar were where he always left them. Scrolls of parchment were scattered across the desk. The painting of a ship adrift on the Somerta Sea was gone. The sconces were missing, with only the daylight to fill the room. She stroked the stone wall, along the grooves of a hidden door. Nothing had been disturbed.

Dunstan dusted a leatherbound book. "I did not remove the windows. Books are...sensitive to the weather or so milord has grumbled so many times."

Facing Dunstan, she said, "Summon one member of each family. Escort them here." She smiled at Yrsa who read the spines on the bookshelf closest to the door. "There is much to discuss."

SEVEN

WARRIC WILLED HIMSELF TO not glance back and seek out Vona's thick braid. He faced ahead, trying to force himself to focus on the task. He ran through scenarios of what to expect, not liking to be caught off-guard. He was lost, adrift, for as Serenity consumed the few miles to Netherbury, he couldn't grasp what had happened to the countryside. What he remembered the few times he'd passed through Netherbury was its lush fields, happy people, and abundance of livestock. Not the dark circles of blackened soil and vegetation. Abandoned homes with not a crow or chicken in sight. Ahead, the soot-stained castle. Smoke billowed up and enshrouded a once-bustling town with an ominous atmosphere.

He slowed Serenity to a walk, steering his mount along the muddied main road—the paved stones hidden beneath black soil and mucky water. No, this couldn't be Netherbury, but he hadn't turned onto another road. Dark structures towered on either side. Where flower boxes had added their color, now only blackened leaves and stems remained. White or brown stone was covered in soot. The smithy was abuzz—the familiar clang of hammer on metal was music to his ears. No stalls sold food other than pheasant or rabbit. He twisted to stare at a roasted rat.

The faces of the people, their horses as gaunt.

A large signboard swayed in the breeze. He drew Serenity to a halt and dismounted, tethering him to a ring mounted in the wall. With a sweep of his finger, he tested the dust. A bolt of heat shot up his arm, his veins glowing purple for a moment. Darkness? In dust? Yet, instead of empowering him, a bit of magic leeched from him.

"What brings you to The Clumsy Elf?" a woman asked, her belly bouncing as she moved.

"Not this day, madam." He gestured at the door to the building beside hers.

She grunted and left him. With a shrug, he strode into the Netherbury Guard. Behind a desk sat a man, his uniform black and crisp, a shock of blond hair falling over his temple.

He glanced up. "Aye?"

"What in hell has happened to Netherbury?" Warric demanded. Mud mewled so he removed the kitten and placed him on the scarred wooden floor.

"I do not answer to you, sirrah." The man circled the desk. Other men pushed off the walls, gathering around.

Warric clenched his jaw. There was nothing he hated more than a bully. Withdrawing the letter of appointment, he slapped it on the desk. "I want names, your duties, and the roster. Who is in the dungeons and why? For the love of all things wicked, I need an ale."

A man pointed his pistol. "Hang on—"

"Lower it, Nibbon." The blond unraveled the scroll, cast a glance at Warric, and snapped to attention. "Welcome, Sheriff. We knew you were due to arrive but weren't told which day to expect you." He gestured to a lad playing with Mud. "Get our sheriff's bags, Tims, and take his horse to the stables."

The boy bolted.

"Sheriff Thomas of Hasden at your service." Warric forced a smile. "So, what happened to Netherbury? I thought to procure a leg of lamb, but rat?" He shuddered for effect. "Not my first choice."

Another man offered Warric a tankard of ale. The scar on one side of his face wrinkled his eye and lip.

"My thanks," Warric said and took a long pull. He smacked his lips. "Ale's still good." *Barely.* Cradling the tankard to his chest, he stamped his feet as if his ass was numb. "It's been one hell of a journey. Weather's been a mean woman, that I can tell you." He swirled his ale. "Was there a plague? Folks do seem sickly."

"Lord Emil—"

"Will be delighted to hear you arrived." The blond glared Nibbon into silence.

Warric grunted, placed his tankard on the desk, then flicked a wrist at the blond. Into the air he hovered, his legs twitching as he struggled to breathe. He clawed at his throat in desperation.

"I do not appreciate having to ask three times, nor do I like being lied to. We are the last bastion of the law, and as such, must stand united." Warric released his magic and turned away while the man fell to the floor, coughing and sucking in deep breaths. "Now, explain." Warric pointed at Nibbon.

"Sir, Lord Emil has an amulet that requires immense power."

"We are forbidden to speak of it, *sir*," the blond rasped.

"Even to me when I will soon discover it? Do not be absurd, *fool*." Warric settled behind the desk and rested his boots on the open register, splattering dust across its surface. "I assume the usual applies: enforce the law, maintain order, arrest the riffraff?"

"The collection of taxes." The blond staggered to his feet. "The name's Guy. That's Nibbon, the twins Loaan and Iwen," hitching a thumb at the scarred man, "the lad's Tims, and the orc is Dul."

"Orc?" Warric sat up, curling his fingers around the dagger in his boot. He'd lost many a man to an orc. Resistant to all forms of magic, they fought like animals, lacked honor, and would sacrifice their lives for a kill. Such beasts couldn't be reasoned with. Yet now, he had one on his payroll. "Where is he?"

"His turn to collect taxes, sir," Guy said, pointing to the scrawlings on one wall.

Warric growled. "Since when do we do that? Where's the tax collector?"

"Pitchforked. The one before that, drawn and quartered." Nibbon ticked off on his pudgy fingers. "No one argues with an orc, sir."

Who were they taxing? "I did not see many people in the villages I passed through."

Nibbon smirked. "Those who fought us, Lord Emil dealt with. The others escaped to the surrounding forests. Trees are no obstacle for Dul."

Of that, Warric had no doubt. He scanned the scrawlings and snagged on Devenmere. Something cold, unwelcome, sliced down his back. Fear. He drew in a long inhale and released it slowly. Yrsa was there. He need not charge over to protect Vona. Tapping the word, he arched a brow.

Guy squared his shoulders and met Warric's gaze. "I sent Loaan to collect. Some of the townsfolk settled near the abandoned house."

Abandoned? Warric schooled his features to not react. "I pray he returns."

Guy frowned. "What—?"

"I met Lady Ruvona Devenmere and her party. She has an envoy with her." Choosing to share was wise. If they learned he'd known all along, distrust would result. He needed them on his side for the task ahead. Sparring with any of them was a hassle he didn't want.

"Here, in Netherbury?" Nibbon gripped his pistol, his gaze darting as if he searched for an escape.

"Weary of envoys, Nibbon?" Warric unsheathed his dagger to clean under a fingernail.

"Aye, sir. Them have powerful magics." Nibbon's Adam's Apple bobbed when he swallowed.

"Indeed they do. This one is air and fire." Testing the sharpness of his blade before sliding it into his boot, he faced Guy. "Where is my room?" he asked, when Tims scurried past him, Mud on a shoulder and Warric's satchels slung across the other.

Guy pointed up. "The room at the top of the tower, sir."

"The rest of her party, sir?" Iwen asked, his eyes narrowed. Darkness swirled in their depths, not the kind Warric used, the kind that fueled berserkers, tore limbs off animals, slaughtered innocents.

"An old tinkerer from Drezat, a bard who cannot sing for shit, and the lady herself."

"Is she as pretty as I remember?" Guy grinned. "Brown hair, big brown eyes, pale skin, and the sweetest smile?"

Warric clenched his jaw, not liking Guy's familiarity with Vona. "Aye, hence the envoy."

"That is new. It used to be Lord Walter, Thack, and Piers when she spent summers at the Devenmere Manor."

She'd implied other experiences, and a girl alone among three men would be privy to stories not meant for her ears. An image of her came to mind, two pigtails trailing her as she skipped along blossoming fields, chased chickens, and climbed trees. He smothered a smile, not wanting his men to realize he was a little besotted.

"I best check on Loaan then." Guy glanced at Iwen. "You, hie over to Dul. Make sure he has not set the forest on fire again."

"I will join you, Iwen." Warric's ass twitched in complaint.

Not that he'd been in the saddle long this morning, but over the past four days, aye. What he yearned to do was visit Devenmere Manor. He also didn't appreciate Guy taking charge, but then, the man must have been acting as the sheriff. Reclaiming that control would be a slow process, but Warric would manage it within a week. At some point, he needed to present himself to Lord Emil. The part he dreaded. Bowing to such a man went against his honor. Of course, not every man he'd deceived was worthy, but Warric despised Emil the most. Hiding in his brother's shadow while shooting arrows and sending bottles of poisoned wine to him? If a man was immoral, unjust, rotten to the core, then he needed to own that part of him. Warric respected such men despite their wickedness. Every person, no matter how much they claimed to be good, had darkness in their hearts. It took strength to acknowledge how tainted their souls were.

"Tims, go with Iwen to saddle three horses," Guy called.

"Tims, come here." Warric knelt on a knee and grasped the boy by his frail shoulders. "This is Mud." He transferred the kitten to Tims's twitching fingers. "If a hair on his head is harmed—"

"Aye, sir." The boy, with eyes a dark gray, tossed a smile at Warric. Poor Mud mewled from within the tight grip when the boy bolted out the door.

"Man the desk, Nibbon," Warric commanded before striding out of the guardhouse and onto the unsavory road. *My poor boots and breeches.*

Guy didn't speak. As soon as Tims hurried to them trailing two horses, Guy leaped onto one and galloped off. Warric tousled the boy's hair and stroked Mud under his chin. Iwen had mounted and waited, patience in his still fingers resting on his thigh. Warric vaulted into the saddle and gestured to Iwen to lead the way.

They crossed a blackened meadow south of Netherbury. Warric scanned the horizon and scowled at the surrounding forests in various stages of decay. Smoke billowed southwest of their location.

"What happened here?"

Iwen didn't respond, but the pursing of his lips spoke for him. There was evil here.

It took ten minutes to reach the edge of a forest, and indeed, flames licked the tops of the dead trees. Iwen cursed and charged, throwing himself out of the saddle when they drew close enough. He dived into the shadows, hollering Dul's name.

Warric followed, his booted feet sparking dark purple from the black soil. He paused alongside burning trees to snuff the air the fire fed on. One by one, he doused the flames, then dusting his hands, he ventured deeper into the grayed foliage. He cupped a leaf. It disintegrated on his palm, and a purple light sank into his skin. He shook his hand, trying to dispel the tingles. This was evil, darkness, some form of magic that was old. He'd experienced it when he'd touched an ancient tome in the Conclave's library. Covered in cracked leather with a silver medallion embossed on the cover, purple-black inked words were written in a language he didn't know, and yet, his soul recognized.

When he glanced up, Iwen had his finger in Dul's face, even though the orc was heads taller.

"They not give," Dul growled.

"What did we say about starting fires?" Iwen swept out a wide arm. "We hunt here, for hell's sake. Fire means no more boar for Dul."

Warric stared into the shadows. Was there still life here?

"Dul like boar." The big male rubbed his belly, scraping his dirty talons across his loose, black uniform.

Iwen narrowed his gaze on the sky as if he sought patience.

"Dul, return to the barracks," Warric commanded.

The orc straightened, sniffed the air, stared at Warric for a few minutes, then marched toward Netherbury, thundering his footsteps down the path his destruction had created.

Iwen eased his shoulders and faced the forest.

"I am the sheriff of Netherbury. Pay your taxes," Warric roared, using a blast of air magic to project his voice. The leaves on trees and bushes crumbled to the ground.

"An' what if we don' want to?" someone called.

With a flick of a wrist, Warric shot the man up and out from his hiding spot. Hanging in mid-air, he scrambled, as if his hands could grasp onto something, anything.

Warric peered at him. "If I insist?"

"Let 'im go," a boy screamed, no more than six years old. He brought the stick over his head and thumped Warric on the foot.

Pain shot up his leg, but he channeled it, not needing to react. Later, in the privacy of his room, he'd deal with the injury. Splaying his fingers wide spread the dangling man's limbs outward. He wailed, and the boy dropped the stick.

"Now, let me repeat this one more time. Pay your taxes." He, the personal assassin to Baron Gregory of Kenningthain, was arguing over taxes?

"We *have* paid," the man garbled. "We've nothin' more but our garments an' weapons."

Warric arched a brow at Iwen. "Is this true?"

The man scratched his scar and shrugged. "Lord Emil commands us to gather taxes, and we do so. He does not take kindly to excuses."

Clenching his teeth, Warric lowered the dangling man, who snatched the boy close to him the moment his feet touched the ground. "What did you do before...the forest?"

"I was a tanner, sir." The man shoved the boy behind him. "When we couldna give more, Lord Emil brought his darkness."

"As I see it, sirrah, you have two choices. Flee these lands, or find a way to earn coin."

The man spluttered, "My family has been in these—"

"Your family will die here if you do not choose a path," Warric snapped. If he had loved ones, he'd do everything within his power to protect them. "How many more are hiding in these woods?"

"Four score and something," the man muttered. "Most are farmers with no crops to harvest."

"This forest cannot sustain so many." Warric scowled. A boar for Dul would be a miracle. "What you are saying is that there is no food in Netherbury?"

"Lord Emil sends a wagon to the neighboring towns." Iwen leaned against a tree, crossing his legs at the ankles.

"With our coin," the man said, smacking his chest.

Warric grunted. This was worse than he thought. He needed to update the baron on the situation but hadn't found a place free of prying ears. "I should meet with Lord Emil this day."

"Best of luck with that, sir." Lifting the boy over his shoulder, the man faded into the foliage.

Warric flicked his fingers at Iwen, indicating they needed to return. The trip was made in silence, something Warric was grateful for. What did the baron expect him to achieve here? Thwart all Emil's plans? How? With so many lives at stake? He needed a plan, some way of restoring the balance. Stealing the amulet would be a start. Such power shouldn't rest in the wrong hands.

EIGHT

As soon as Dunstan left the library, Vona leaped across and tugged on the book labeled *The Fabled Antelope of Osiree*. The stone wall cracked and groaned when it swung open, exposing a small room lined with shelves and dust-laden artifacts. At the end, built into a windowed alcove was a desk. At the center of it was a bare pedestal.

She gulped. "Father's will is missing." Yanking open the drawers, she searched for the parchment. "Why would anyone take it, Yrsa?" She gestured to the bags of coins filling one shelf. "And not touch those?"

"Unless the document was in the library?" Yrsa blew dust off a silver figurine of a mythical faerie before setting it aside.

"Now is not the time to worry about this." Vona hefted a bag, tugged on the cord, and peered inside. Gold sovereigns clinked and shimmered in the minimal light. She palmed one, pulled the bag closed, and left the room, tipping the book to close the door as soon as Yrsa stepped through.

"What are you planning, Vona?" she asked.

"To help these people, Yrsa. I *must* do something."

Yrsa sighed, as if she dealt with a child. "Gold does not solve anything."

Vona frowned and set the bag on the desk. "We shall see."

One by one, Dunstan escorted men and women into the library until a sea of faces stared at Vona expectantly. They coughed, shuffled, shushed each other until silence settled.

She straightened and pushed off the desk to face them. "Should you want to stay in Netherbury, you must return to your homes." She held up a hand when they protested. "You will need to ring your property with iron as my father did Devenmere."

They mumbled among themselves, their eyes wide.

"Or you can flee and start over." She lifted the sovereign high. "I will grant each of you one gold coin. What you choose to do is up to you."

With color on their cheeks, their eyes alive with excitement, the group broke into a deafening chatter as they threw ideas around. While listening to them, she placed a coin in each palm. When but a few coins remained and all held theirs, she handed the bag to Yrsa and addressed the gathering.

"Dunstan needs hands if anyone among you is seeking honest work. I will head into Netherbury to get to the heart of this matter."

A fresh wave of murmurs filled the room, most pleading with her not to risk her life.

"Do not fear. I have an envoy with me." She nudged her head at Yrsa.

A bellow sliced through their concern. Vona bolted, hurrying outside to find a man on horseback, his pistols drawn.

"What is the meaning of this," she demanded, sliding to a halt beside a glowering Thack.

Piers was trembling, his cheeks turning red—still without a tunic on but at least wearing breeches. She dug into his pocket, pulled out a gumdrop and popped it into his mouth. He calmed on a hum but didn't remove his gaze from the mounted man.

"By order of Lord Emil of Kenningthain, I have come to collect taxes due."

"We have paid your taxes," an old woman called out.

"I will shoot you where you stand, woman. Do not test me," the man snapped.

"I accept your challenge," Yrsa roared, whipping the pistols out of his hands and splaying his limbs wide. His horse bolted from under his hovering body.

"How dare you attack a guard," the man spat. "I will have your head for this." He gurgled when Yrsa stretched his limbs. A pop sounded when his arm dislocated and tore a scream from him.

"Yrsa, lower him." Vona pointed to the ground at her feet.

Yrsa glanced at her, closed her eyes for a second, then dropped the man. Vona cupped his shoulder and reset it. He cried out then scrambled away from her and tried to draw his sword. That too went flying, landing firmly in Yrsa's grip. She swung it around her body in a demonstration of skill before tossing it aside. When he lunged for Vona, he bounced off an invisible wall.

Into this mix trotted another mounted guard. In the sunlight, his blond hair glowed golden. He vaulted out of saddle and drew the first man to the side. Whispering words to him drew grunts and glowers from Yrsa, so not good. Once calmed, the men faced the crowd.

"My apologies, fine folk." The blond man smiled. Vona peered at him. Something was intriguing about him—his gray eyes and charm, perhaps? "My men must do as tasked. Lord Emil expects much from us."

"Much? As in harassment and death?" Thack yelled. "Your man threatened this woman. Look at her, frail and in need of care. What coin does she have?"

"My man was overzealous. I *did* apologize." The blond scanned the crowd and settled on Vona, sending a frisson of anxiety through her. She stiffened. "Lady Ruvona, 'tis true you have arrived. What a delight."

She winced. So, her name was on everyone's tongue? How was that possible? Had Thomas mentioned her? Realizing all waited for her to respond, she gave them a tight smile. "Aye, to visit my father."

"You are most welcome," the blond man said. "I had hoped you would remember me, milady."

"You are indeed familiar, sir." She wasn't lying, though who he was, she didn't know.

"Sir Guy...of Tacourt."

"Guy." She smiled. "How fare's your sister?"

He beamed. "Well, Lady Vona. She will be most pleased to hear of your arrival."

"Guy, I see gold," the other man pointed.

Vona's breath caught. Hell's teeth, they wouldn't take what she had just given these people. Everything within her stilled, her senses heightened, and she watched Guy, waiting.

He didn't look away from her when he said, "Collect it then, Loaan."

"No." She threw up a wall of stone, startling his horse. Both men stumbled back. Loaan responded with orange swirls around his hands. They formed fireballs, spinning and gyrating an inch above his palms.

Guy's eyes went wide. "I must, Vona, as commanded by—"

"I do not give a damn what Lord Emil instructed, Guy. These people have given enough." Her limbs trembled, her core frozen. She had no more magic to draw on, not after all she'd spent this day.

Piers roared and beside her stood his bear. His shredded breeches clung to his hairy legs. Thack settled to her right, his pistols drawn, gyros whirring around him and blinking red. Yrsa joined the fray, her arms raised, white light circling her hands.

"Best not chance it today, boy," Thack called.

"I swore an oath to serve Netherbury and Lord Emil," Guy said, gesturing to Loaan to snuff his magic. "Please..."

"Take mine and leave," an old woman said, tossing her sovereign at his feet.

Loaan scrambled for it, his gaze shifty as if he expected to die. Guy mounted and offered his fellow guard a hand up.

He didn't ride off though. "You are newly returned to Netherbury, so take my warning to heart, Vona. Do not involve yourself in something you know nothing about." He met her gaze. "I do not wish to bring you harm, but if I must, I will." With that, he steered his skittish mount, galloping back to Netherbury.

As one, those gathered around her released a sigh. Vona staggered to the old woman and slipped another coin into her palm, the one she had originally pocketed from the bag. "Choose wisely, madam." She stared at the horizon and the shadow of Netherbury in the distance. "You can always return when things are...better."

"Come, rest," Yrsa said, slipping an arm around Vona's waist.

"No, I must visit with Nessa before her brother—"

"Milady, kind sirs, and Madam Yrsa, the cook has prepared a meal." Dunstan stood to the side, wringing his hands. "'Tis not much, but 'tis warm."

Forcing a smile, Vona dipped her head. "A meal would be wonderful, Dunstan."

She could spare the time, especially when he and what staff remained had gone to so much effort. Before she entered the house, she glanced over her shoulder at the poor folks. The campsite was abustle as they packed up their belongings. Had she handled this badly by chasing them off her land? She had in truth paid them to leave.

Hell's teeth, that wasn't what she meant. She spun, wanting to assure them they could return if they needed to, but Thack caught her wrist and shook his head. Piers hesitated, his gaze slicing between them. He clutched what remained of his breeches, barely covering his lower half.

Dunstan whispered something to him then led him away.

Smiling at Thack, Vona leaned in to say, "We should purchase a few extra breeches."

He chuckled. "Indeed. Something colorful, mind you."

A woman appeared, her apron stained, her cheeks bright red, with tendrils of gray hair plastered to her temple. She had the appearance of a cook but not the face of the woman Vona had known growing up.

"Please, this way." The woman gestured to the table in the kitchen laden with bowls, a pot of stew, freshly baked bread, and a tub of butter.

Vona paused, surveyed the scene, and clasped the woman's hands—excitement warring with hunger. The bread and cheese from earlier was but a bitter memory. "This is...wonderful. It smells," she inhaled deeply, releasing it on a hum, "delicious."

The cook dipped her chin. "'Tis nothing, milady."

"Not to me," Vona said. "Your name?"

"Ellia, milady." The woman bobbed, her knees crunching as she did so.

"Food first before you heal her too," Yrsa whispered, tugging Vona to a bench. Once seated, Yrsa left, returning shortly with a bucket of soil.

Vona cried out and shoved her fingers into it, sighing when heat and green tendrils seeped into her skin. While she relished the flow of magic, Ellia spooned wild boar stew into Vona's bowl. Lumps of potato and carrot peeked out of the thick sauce. Her mouth salivated as she stared at it. Before today, she hadn't realized how blessed she'd been. Choices meant freedom, Thomas had said, and he was right. If she could grant these people the right to choose, she might discover her purpose in this life.

While they enjoyed the meal, no one spoke, not after what the day had revealed. When her stomach ached, she pushed the almost-empty bowl aside.

She rubbed her belly. "Delicious, Ellia. My thanks. Tell me, do you know of a seamstress? I may need a few more gowns, and Sir Piers requires new breeches."

"Aye, milady, Alani is the best seamstress and services Lord Emil."

"Excellent." She beamed at the woman.

"We cannot stay long, Vona. Your mother was quite clear." Yrsa dipped her bread into the sauce to soak.

Vona stiffened her shoulders. Here was where she was needed. "I suggest you ride ahead and find Jacut."

Caught licking her fingers, Yrsa hastily wiped her hands on a cloth Ellia handed her. "Abandon you?"

Thack threw out his hands. "Perhaps *I* can head north."

"Not alone," Piers said, settling beside Thack on the bench. He drew a bowl closer to him which Ellia filled to the brim. Slices of bread followed. He flashed her a smile. "We will leave in the morning. If possible, I would like to spend a night in a bed."

"Agreed," Thack grumbled, rubbing his neck.

"I suppose that would be satisfactory." Yrsa slathered butter on a chunk of bread then bit into it.

"Thank you," Vona said, clasping Thack's hand.

"Do not endanger yourself, my girl." He met her gaze and held it. A tear shimmered on his eyelashes. "With Jacut here, we will have his authority to demand your father's return."

She bit her lip, hating that they believed she could do nothing without her brother. After today, she had learned she wasn't useless. "Ellia, please, step forward."

"What is it, milady?" the woman asked, inching closer.

Without saying a word, Vona cupped Ellia's knees through her thick skirts. Warmth drained from Vona, and a cold settled into her bones. Ellia whimpered, trembled, and crushed her apron in her hands. With a sniff, she stepped back to do a little jig. "Thank you, milady. I... Thank you." She bobbed again, this time without a sound, then hurried off to fetch a pewter jug and cups. "Apple cider from your orchard," she said, placing the jug on the table.

"Well, well," Piers chortled, pouring in a hefty amount then swigging it back.

Thack nudged him, grabbed the jug, and served her, Yrsa, and himself. "Selfish idiot," he muttered to Piers.

"A lady's maid?" Yrsa asked Dunstan. "I signed up to guard Lady Ruvona, not to help her dress."

"I shall assist until Dunstan finds someone," Ellia beamed.

"My thanks," Vona chuckled. "I have but one gown...for now." She pushed off the bench while downing the tart apple cider. "Dunstan, were your quarters ransacked as well?"

"No, milady. The door to the servants' quarters is hidden. I have asked a few men to help carry the furniture out of the cellar." He puffed out his chest. "I will have Devenmere Manor to rights before you return from your visit."

"I am sure you will." Vona squeezed his forearm. "I shall take my father's room for now."

"I thought as such. It needs tidying—"

"In time. For now, it will do." She ventured outside, amazed at how many folks had left, the trampled ground beneath their feet showing their passing. When she had fully replenished her earth magic, she would see what she could do to restore this area to its former glory. The fountain too.

Honey chomped on grass below a tree. Vona winced at having not thought to tether her horse, nor to see to her care. Were her father's stables empty? Where were the stablehands? Mac, the stablemaster was the grumpiest man she knew, but there was no one better with the horses. Father had often teased him, saying he had the ability to charm a snake.

She caught Honey's reins, and while crooning to her, she gazed at her family home. So much had changed. Familiar faces no longer there to greet her. The fragrance of the house altered with a deep sense of sorrow clinging to the hollow rooms and stripped walls. She *had* to fix this.

Urging Honey round to the stables, she walked the stone path, flowers and weeds not yet encroaching. Inside the massive stables able to house a dozen horses, one nag snorted a greeting. Tears slipped free. Vona gasped and jogged ahead with Honey trailing her.

"May, my sweet girl." She sniffed. Her father had taught her to ride on May. Many a day she'd spent exploring the fields, forests, and the lake with this gentle horse. Not once had May nipped at her or thrown her. Stroking her neck, Vona pressed her temple to hers, all while humming a lullaby.

May stomped her foot, pawing the freshly laid hay. Someone was caring for her. Spinning, she drew Honey closer and quietly introduce them. With a chuckle, she settled Honey into a stall, unsaddled her, then brushed her and May down. With a bag of feed over both their heads, she took the time to refill the water troughs.

If Dunstan was attending to this chore, no wonder he was exhausted. She'd removed what she could when she'd healed his leg. Still, she was here now. Jacut would expect her to do as much as she could and that included finding her father. Thomas might know. Perhaps if she stopped in Netherbury on her way to Tacourt Estate?

Removing the feedbags, she returned them to their hooks, and with satchels in hand, bolted for the house. She'd ask Piers to clean her. A swim in the lake would have been wonderful, but she didn't have the time. Not if she wanted to speak to Thomas. A frisson of excitement scattered her heartbeat for a moment. What she should do is inform him about his guards' behavior. She jerked her chin.

Piers was still in the kitchen, nursing a cup of cider. He wore beige breeches gathered at his ankles and a white tunic, no doubt Dunstan's finest. Without color to distract, he seemed thinner than usual.

"Piers." She swept her hand downward. "Please. I am filthy and smell of horse."

He flicked his wrist. "Yrsa will be traveling with you, Vona. Be careful."

She grinned. He'd cleaned her, but it didn't feel the same as a bath. As she carried her satchel to her father's room, she lifted her tunic for a sniff. She smelled clean, as in no body odor. Where was her jasmine soap? Beggars couldn't be choosy, though. That she did know.

As soon as she opened her satchel, out shot Orv.

"About time. Did you forget about me?" it whined, darting around the room.

"Aye, sorry." She dug in the satchel, searching for the blue velvet gown Mags had packed. Right at the bottom, rolled around matching slippers, was the garment. She withdrew and unraveled it, placing the shoes on the wooden floor. With care, she undid her tunic's ties, unbuckled the belt, then yanked off her boots, setting them to the side. She grimaced at their state. Piers had cleaned them, but they remained unpolished.

89

"Where are you going?" Orv didn't wait for answers while it explored the room.

"Oh, my dear gyro, so much has happened." She smirked. "You should come out of your shell and befriend someone other than me."

Orv whirred, "Why?"

"Because I cannot hide a gyro in a gown. So, if you want companionship, you will have to find a way."

Orv grumbled, dropped to the floor, and rolled under the bed to sulk.

She studied the redness on her fingertips. Her delicate hands hadn't known hardship. Forming fists, she vowed to learn how to polish her cursed boots. Flicking her hat onto the bed, she flipped the coat off her shoulders and tossed it over the back of a chair. Off went her tunic and breeches.

Standing there naked, she hurried to strap a holster to her thigh. Without a belt, she couldn't carry her pistols, but a dagger offered some sense of comfort. She held up the gown, groaning at the million buttons running down the back. How had she not noticed this? She set to undo them, groaning when her fingertips began to burn. What magic she could spare healed her as she went. By the time Ellia knocked on the door, Vona had shimmied into the garment. It was tighter than she remembered. Perhaps she'd eaten too many of Piers's sugary treats.

"Ah, milady, you look beautiful," Ellia spluttered when Vona called to her to enter.

"Not too small?" Vona admired the reflection in the polished silver Father had tilted against one wall. The dark blue paled her skin further, giving it a translucent glow. It had a narrow V in the front where she was supposed to shove a white kerchief, but she hadn't seen one in the satchel. The bodice cinched in just under her breasts to her waist, flaring outward. The skirts brushed her bare toes.

"A little." Ellia stopped behind her to tackle the buttons.

"The gowns we order, Ellia, please ask the seamstress to place the buttons and fastenings down the side." Vona tilted her head to smile at the woman. "Just in case no maid can be found."

"Wise, milady." She remained focused on the buttons. Only their breathing filled the silence. Ellia tugged on the gown's puffed sleeves then stepped back. "Done, milady."

"Thank you," Vona said while sliding her feet into the slippers.

"Your hair, Lady Ruvona," Ellia called when she ran out of the room.

"Not to worry, Ellia, Yrsa has air magic." She waved and hurried down the hallway, only to find her guardian waiting in the foyer. The Eryssian rug was back under a large wooden table with a jar of meadow flowers in the center. Paintings rested against the base of the walls in preparation for returning to their places. She twirled, giddiness making her giggle.

"Come," Yrsa said, flicking her wrists. She used her air-magic to unbraid Vona's hair. "Stand still."

"Can I not wear my boots?" Vona raised her foot, exposing her ankle and slipper. "I will have muddy feet on the way to the stables."

Yrsa exhaled. "Aye, boots might be better." She lowered her arms to fold them across her chest. Still in her tunic and breeches, she hadn't changed into something more formal. Her wide-brimmed hat rested on the table and dust coated her cheeks. "Well?" She arched a brow.

Vona ran to her father's room, sat on the bed, and swapped the slippers for her boots. While dancing down the hallway, she dodged Dunstan and the men carrying a tallboy.

Yrsa harumphed when Vona danced into the foyer. She spun on a heel and marched down to the stables. Vona struggled to keep up. Yrsa gathered the reins of her horse, Shasta. The dark-brown mare's coat glistened in the afternoon sunlight. Yrsa must have brushed her down before re-saddling her. Honey was also saddled and stomping her feet, eager for a ride.

Vona chuckled, gathered her reins, and led her out of her stall. As she pulled herself into the saddle, she groaned. In a dress, she couldn't straddle the horse, not without exposing her legs. Nor did she have a side-saddle. She scanned the stables, stripped bare of its tack and gear. Wincing, she curled her leg around the pommel and gathered her skirts, covering as much as she could.

Yrsa chuckled but didn't speak. She steered Shasta toward Netherbury. "Dunstan says the Tacourt Estates are west."

"Aye, but I wish to speak to Thomas first. He may help us find Father."

"Perhaps." On that note, Yrsa urged her horse into a canter, then an outright gallop when they hit the Conclave Way heading into town. Some folks waved as they passed, familiar faces filled with hope. Others trudged onward. One wagon, laden with goods and guarded by four men in solid black yelled at them, their fists ready.

The closer they came to Netherbury, the more her eyes widened. This...this wasn't what she remembered from the once lively town. Yrsa sliced glances at her over her shoulder. She too must think this alarming.

Vona grimaced and prayed she found Thomas easily. For as they rode on, many a man paused to ogle her, making her skin crawl. More so when they galloped through the town. Faces lined with soot, empty food stalls in the market, the stench of heat and metal from the smithy added to the despair in the air.

She drew Honey alongside Yrsa whose white-knuckled grip on the reins said it all.

Darkness had come to Netherbury.

Nine

Warric stared at the sovereign Iwen placed on the desk. That was the extent of the taxes his men had managed to gather? Guy bounced, his leg twitching, a smile slipping and forming at regular intervals. The man must have seen Vona.

Warric stiffened his shoulders then focused on the roster he'd been perusing when they'd disturbed him.

"Lord Emil will be most pleased," Guy said. "'Tis more than we brought in yesterday."

"He will want to know from where such wealth came," Warric muttered. "I assume Devenmere?"

Guy paled. "I... We..."

"'Twas an old woman," Iwen offered. "There was more, I swear it, sir."

"More gold?" Warric arched a brow. What was Vona doing, trying to get herself killed?

"Aye, when we tried to take it, she hit us with a wall of stone," Iwen continued, despite Guy glaring at him.

"She?" Warric faked a sigh of boredom.

"Lady Devenmere," Iwen ground out.

Smothering a chuckle, Warric turned a page. *So, she has claws, my cat thief.*

Iwen blurted, his words merging, "We were outnumbered. Her party rallied. One man morphed into a bear."

Warric hummed.

That had to be Thack, though he hadn't sensed a morpher among them. A few served the baron, not enough for Warric to be familiar with their tells. It was said it was impossible to discern a morpher in human form, but he didn't believe that. Life was about balance. Where there were strengths, there were weaknesses.

"I request we return, sir. Such bounty cannot be ignored."

He was tempted, not for the gold, but to see her. Glancing at Iwen, he said, "Would that be wise when you have them on the offensive? A morpher, you say?" He snapped the roster closed and faced his men. "I intend to request an audience with Lord Emil this evening. I shall discuss this matter with him."

"No need, Sheriff." A cultured voice sliced through the room.

As one, Warric's men hugged the walls, granting him a clear line of sight. Dominating the doorway stood Lord Emil, so similar to Baron Gregory, except for the narrow shoulders and scrawny arms. They shared the same height, but Emil's bulk was bolstered by his thick cloak lined with fur and in a resplendent gold and red. Jewelry dangled from his neck, thick chains of gold and rare stones. On his fingers, cumbersome gems glittered. Behind him hovered more guards, these marked with red sashes on their sleeves and not under Warric's command, he assumed.

He rose to his feet, circled the desk, and bowed with a flamboyant flick of his wrist—the kind Baron Gregory hated. "Lord Emil, welcome to the guardhouse."

"I was told of your arrival, Thomas. I am delighted you have already set these men to rights." Emil sashayed around Warric to slip the sovereign off the desk. "And with such bounty."

"Aye, milord," Warric grinned through his clenched jaw, silently cursing Iwen and Guy.

"Pray do tell, from whence came such treasure?" Emil pocketed the coin with a flick of two fingers.

"Devenmere Manor, milord," Warric said. Lying about it would only breed distrust. He squared his shoulders while scanning his men's scowls.

"Um, milord, Sheriff, I apologize for the intrusion," Loaan stuttered while bobbing his head. "A lady approaches."

"So?" Emil snarled.

Warric closed his eyes for a moment, begging the Lord for it not to be Vona, no matter how much he longed to see her.

Iwen peered over his brother's shoulder and cried out, "'Tis Lady Devenmere."

Warric swallowed a curse. His heartbeat thundered, but instead of rushing to see her, he met Lord Emil's gaze, awaiting his guidance as expected of a man not eager to see the lady.

"Oh?" Emil arched a brow.

"Aye, milord, and she is steering her mount toward the guardhouse."

Emil nudged his head, his instruction clear. *Deal with this.*

"Step aside," Warric growled and shoved past his men, taking up a position where he could grip the railing and peer at her.

His breath caught when he settled his gaze on her. Magnificent in dark blue with the sunlight picking gold strands in her hair, he couldn't recall a more beautiful woman. When she saw him, she smiled and scattered his thoughts. He scrambled for some composure, aware Emil watched from the doorway cast in shadow.

"Sheriff," she bowed her head.

"Lady Devenmere," he said, hoping he could convey with a stern tone that caution was needed.

When she stiffened, he allowed the tension in his shoulders to ease. Yrsa drew up beside her, dominating her mount with her muscled physique. Her sharp gaze missed nothing. She muttered, "He is not alone," to Vona whose brow furrowed.

"I wish to lay a formal complaint." She angled her stubborn little chin, drawing attention to the enticing dip in her gown. "Two men tried to assault a guest on my lands. They stole from her too."

"Tax collection is not an assault, milady." His tone dripped impatience.

She pursed her lips, a tiny smirk forming. "Is it now, when she is not a citizen of Netherbury?"

Warric clenched his jaw but kept a polite smile in place. "Indeed? Pray tell, can you confirm this?"

"You doubt my word, sir?" She lowered her chin, but he caught her mumbled, "If I had my pistols, I would shoot you where you stand."

Warric coughed to hide his bark of laughter.

"My apologies, Lady Devenmere." Emil sidled forward. "My men are often overzealous in their eagerness to please me. Join me this evening. I am holding a small dinner. Your presence would be a blessing and a delight."

"Oh, Lord Emil, what a pleasure." Her smile was bright but too wide.

Yrsa tilted her head and whispered with unmoving lips, "Be careful, Vona."

"Of course I accept your invitation. How kind of you to offer." She bowed her head. "Now with regards to my complaint?"

Warric relished this tenacious side of her. He held still, waiting for Emil's response.

"My men shall no longer disturb you, Lady Devenmere."

"Wonderful." She clapped her hands as if she was a simpleton. "'Tis Lady Ruvona, milord. Please, I insist." She batted her eyelashes which was a touch too much.

Emil chuckled. "Until this evening."

"You have one gown," Yrsa muttered.

"I cannot anger a lord, Yrsa. Even a Sundowner can be taken to task for such an offense," Vona hissed.

They bickered as they rode on. Warric faced Emil who stared after the two women, his thoughts in turmoil.

"An envoy in Netherbury is not a welcome sight," Emil said. "We need to be vigilant."

"I believe she guards Lady Devenmere," Warric said, hoping to imply where Vona went, so did Yrsa. Thankfully, a fur pelt hid Yrsa's Sundowner mark.

Emil flicked a glance at Warric. "Then she should be in atten-dance this evening." He turned on Warric's men. "Did anyone sense what magic she holds?"

"Air and fire." Warric folded his arms across his chest. "A level seven in air."

"Hell's teeth." Emil paced across the wooden balcony, his cloak brushing Warric's boots at each passing. "Music will be needed for more private discussions." He halted. "I expect you to be in attendance, Thomas. Any Devenmere plus an envoy at this stage is…"

"Unwelcome?" Warric suggested.

Emil's eyes narrowed. "Aye." He marched out of the guard-house and into his carriage. "I need your escort, and do not tarry." With a crack of a whip, the ponderous carriage shifted forward.

Escort to where? 'Twasn't Warric's place to ask. He grimaced.

At last, he could breathe. As first meetings went, he couldn't be disappointed. Although, it was too soon to tell if Emil had bought the act.

Now he had to play nursemaid *and* attend a dinner. Thankful-ly, he had one jerkin in black velvet and silver thread.

"How dare she complain," Iwen huffed. "No, Guy, I do not care. The more beautiful the woman, the more trouble she is."

"Well, at least we were not taken to task for the poor collec-tion," Nibbon mumbled.

"Indeed," Warric said.

"The lord defended us, Iwen," Loaan was saying.

"That he did, so cease nattering about a silly girl's complaint," Warric barked. "Where is Dul?"

"Why do you ask?" At the question, Warric glared at Guy. "I meant no disrespect, sir," Guy ground out.

"I tasked him to return to town. Has he arrived? Or do I need to send someone to find him?" Warric didn't trust orcs to do as commanded.

"He prefers the stables to the guardhouse." Guy hitched his thumb to the south.

"I would like him to stand guard at the dinner, even if 'tis in Lord Emil's stables." Yrsa couldn't take down something that big, could she? Warric couldn't so he had to hope she might struggle. As per this afternoon's forest incident, fire hadn't bothered Dul.

Not wasting anymore time, Warric stomped out of the guardhouse to the stables.

Dul *had* returned and busied himself brushing down Serenity. He jerked his head up, met Warric's gaze, then set the brush aside to saddle the horse.

Minutes later, Warric was mounted and riding along the path to the castle. The portcullis was raised. Men with red sashes on their sleeves patrolled. Most wore glowers, as if unhappy with the hand life had dealt them. He didn't greet them besides a nod.

Instinct told him they weren't in his command. If that was true, then to whom did they answer? Emil having men at his disposal meant anything beyond Warric's control could happen.

The carriage and its horses dominated the courtyard. Emil thrummed his fingers along the edge of the window. The ties on his sleeve were loose, exposing his forearm. Renowned for his foppish dress sense, seeing him so disheveled was odd.

Warric stayed mounted. He surveyed the lay of the castle, its outer and inner keep and the pale stone covered in black dust. Servants scurried, their gazes lowered, and shoulders hunched. No smiles or laughter filled the air. Emil's castle guards didn't budge, not even to swat a fly. Two guards sat mounted, waiting, their horses as still and silent.

The sour notes of terror saturated the air.

A weasel of a man, strands of gray-brown hair slipping out of a ponytail at the nape of his neck, scampered down the stone steps. His eyes were narrowed to pin pricks, his beaded brow knitted. When he climbed into the carriage, he twisted his pursed lips into a semblance of a smile.

Emil stopped drumming his fingers and huffed, "About time, Grokar."

"My apologies, Lord Emil." The unfamiliar older man, gifted in earth and darkness, must have trained at the Conclave years before Warric did.

The carriage rocked then lurched forward when the coachmen flicked the reins, spurring the magnificent gray horses on. Warric set Serenity into a canter alongside Emil's window. The two guards trailed. Silence reigned for the time it took to cross the bridge to the northern outskirts of Netherbury.

"Tell me, Sheriff, how do you find Netherbury?" Emil's tone was casual, but his unwavering gaze showed a keen interest in Warric's answer.

"The ale is as good as I remember, milord." Warric grinned, focused ahead, then said, "Yet, the once joyful townsfolk have lost their way." Forcing the lie past his revulsion, he growled, "Which I suspect is due to Baron Gregory's continued absence." He met Emil's gaze. "If you beg my pardon for saying so, milord, 'tis good you have taken over."

The man's lips twitched. His eyes, so like Gregory's, warmed. "Well said, Sheriff. See, Grokar, I told you he was the best man for the position."

"Aye, milord." Grokar may have agreed, but his expression said otherwise, steeped in distrust and ill intentions.

Emil broke into a cough, bending over as it racked his body. Warric frowned. Not once had reports indicated the man was in poor health. Flicking a glance at Grokar in passing caught the tell-tale trail of darkness soaking into his garments. So, the man poisoned Emil? Darkness could do that, could corrupt the body from within. It was a skill assassins were taught, and one he'd used. He should have recognized the symptoms. To be fair, he killed with mercy not poisoned as slowly as Grokar did.

The question was why? Why kill Emil? What did Grokar gain from this? Unless he meant to make the man dependent on him?

"Do you expect trouble?" Warric asked.

Emil shook his head while wiping a blue kerchief across his mouth. Blood dotted the fine silk. "This is something you should see and understand, Sheriff."

"Aye, many crave the power and may attempt to take it from us," Grokar hissed, spit dewing on his bottom lip.

Whatever *it* was. Warric ignored him, keeping his gaze on Emil. "My gifts and weapons are at your service." He thumped his chest for good measure.

Emil flicked his fingers, dismissing Warric. Grateful for the reprieve, he slowed Serenity so that he trailed between the guards and the carriage. Interacting with what the Conclave called 'superiors' was always tiresome, especially when they had no concept of how easily he could kill them. They behaved like children—naïve, arrogant, and oft times, foolish.

The carriage veered off the Conclave Way and cut across a meadow. Apple trees grew to one side. Bees flitted from flower to flower. The lush grass and blue sky whispered of joyful times spent frolicking in nature. A bunny watched them, it's nose twitching.

Into this, Emil and Grokar strolled, leaving the carriage, its coachmen, and the castle guards behind.

"Do keep up," Emil called, waving his kerchief.

Warric followed, his brow furrowing, and behind that, a throbbing ache formed. What were these two up to?

Grokar halted and cupped his temple, shielding his eyes, as he peered at the carriage in the distance. "I do believe this is far enough."

"It better be. I would not appreciate *walking* to Netherbury." Emil's lips curled in derision.

He faced the field while tugging something out of his jerkin. Grokar crowded him to the right. Warric inched closer on the left and set his focus on an amulet Emil clasped in both hands.

"Hold onto my elbow, Sheriff," he commanded, then closed his eyes and held up the amulet.

Warric did as instructed, finding it strange to hold Emil's bony elbow. Grokar had done so already. Before he could open his mouth to ask, ice, like a thousand needles, raged over him, whipping his hair off his shoulders and making his teeth ache.

The stench of decay and evil burned his nostrils, but none of that mattered, not when apples shriveled and tumbled off the trees just as they too withered into dust. The lush green meadow was gone. The flowers swaying in the gentle breeze a memory. Where the bunny had been, nothing but bone remained.

He tightened his grip and only released Emil when the man pocketed the amulet.

"What did it show you?" Grokar danced around Emil like a child begging for sweetcakes.

"Our time draws near." Emil beamed. "I saw him. Dead. In a casket of plain wood." Emil laughed and spun on the spot. The humor drained from his face when he settled his gaze on Warric. "See, Sheriff, 'tis this amulet that holds the power, and I possess it." Lifting his nose in the air, he strode to the carriage, the line of death ending but a few feet from the skittish horses.

Warric cast glances around him, unable to believe the death such an artifact could inflict. Send one man into a battlefield and the enemy would fall. It could end the battle with the wildemen. Yet, it was used so willy-nilly. Where was the Conclave? How could they let it remain with Emil? "So, it foresees the future?"

"Aye, and requires immense life to do so." Emil clambered into the carriage, Grokar on his heels.

It was a death dealer, mired in the purest darkness. Warric clenched his jaw. He mounted Serenity and cantered after the carriage. As soon as he reached the window, he asked, "Why did you insist I witness this, milord?"

"To choose sides, who to give your allegiance to."

"The Conclave will fall," Grokar muttered, rocking from side-to-side, his gaze wild.

"Aye." Emil smiled.

"My allegiance was to you the moment you hired me, milord," Warric said, though it pained him to do so. This night, he would need to inform Baron Gregory of the amulet and all it could do. A discussion he wasn't looking forward to. After they crossed the bridge into Netherbury, Warric bid Emil good day and returned to the stables.

He tossed the reins to Dul and strode to the guardhouse, the smell of death burned into his skin. "Tims," he roared, settling behind the front desk to yank off his boots. He needed them polished. A bruise had formed where the six-year-old had smacked him. Warric tossed the boots to Tims when the boy burst into the room. "I am to dine with the lord this evening."

"Truly?" Tims gathered the boots to his chest. "I shall polish these until my face shines in them, sir." Mud clambered along his shoulders and into a boot. The lad took the stairs two at a time.

Warric shook his head then scanned the few men watching him. "Off you go. Tasks to perform. Patrols to do."

They scattered.

"Nibbon, man the desk," Warric called before climbing the two levels to his room on threadbare socks. Anything thicker would have set him apart from the common man. The baron had been most generous over the years, and any extra coin Warric had earned, he'd deposited into the Bank of Lisbay, maintained, handled, and audited by the dwarves.

With two fingers, he pushed the door open, finding Tims in the middle of the room, legs akimbo as he polished Warric's boots. Mud had curled into a ball at the foot end of a narrow bed. Warric grimaced. His feet would hang over the edge. Tims had placed his satchels onto a nearby chair. The furniture was stark, but Warric hadn't expected more than this. A table nestled in the corner held a pewter bowl and jug. A piss pot peeked out from beneath the bed. A wide window overlooked the castle and town. This high up, the air was almost clean. Less dust marred the surfaces.

"Are you excited, sir?" Tims flashed a wide smile. "All those meats and the sweetcakes too."

The lad thought of food, as any should. Digging into his pocket, Warric dropped a coin into the boy's lap. "Go, find us something to eat. As much as you can buy."

"Truly?" Tims scrambled to his feet and fled.

Warric followed him, peered down the stairwell, then shut and sealed the door with air. No one would hear him or force their way in. He removed the disc from his coat pocket and held it to his lips.

"Baron, I am in place."

The baron's voice crackled across the connection. "Good. What are your initial thoughts?"

"Worse than anticipated, milord." How could he convey the devastation? "I am to attend a dinner this evening. Perhaps I can discern more when wine loosens tongues."

"Keep me informed." The call ended.

Warric released his held breath and sucked in his air magic, lest Tims returned early. Where the boy would find food, Warric had no idea. He removed his jerkin and flicked it out, summoning air to press the wrinkles out of the cloth. What he needed was a bath. Opening the door, he bellowed down to Nibbon, "Find me a water-gifted or send up a bucket of clean water."

"Aye, sir."

Tims footsteps scampered up the stairs, bringing with him the aroma of something roasted. He knocked then entered when bid to. With a flourish, he placed the cloth-wrapped meal on the table. He unraveled it to reveal roast chicken, chunks of buttered bread, and a date cake."

Warric hid a smile. "Take your pick, Tims."

"Truly?" the lad cried out, then snatched the cake, taking a massive bite of it.

Mud stirred and meowed, leaping from the bed to the windowsill to the table. Warric hastily tore off a piece of chicken and set it before the kitten. Without thought, he dumped a chicken leg and a slice of bread into Tims's hands. With his eyes bulging, the lad mumbled his thanks.

"Finish my boots when you are done eating." Warric sat on the bed and sank his teeth into the bread. He chewed while listening to the *thunk-thunk* of someone climbing the stairs. A knock preceded Nibbon and Guy carrying a wooden bathtub. They set it down in an empty corner. A woman entered. A smile curled her painted mouth.

"This be Kaethe," Guy said. "She serves the tavern's customers, but she is a water-gifted as requested, sir."

"Guy, stay. My thanks, Nibbon." Warric gestured with his chin for him to close the door on the way out.

He did so without a backward glance at Guy.

Warric didn't watch Nibbon leave or Guy fidget. His gaze was on the serving maid. Pale blonde hair escaped a messy bun. The harshness of life shadowed her beguiling green eyes. The gaping low-cut tunic and exposed leg to mid-thigh said she offered more than ale. "I would like the tub filled." He tossed a coin at her which she caught out of the air. "With clean water."

She bit the coin, pocketed it, then sauntered over to the window. With a flick and twirl of her hands and arms, water in the form of a snake slithered through the air to splash into the tub.

"Guy, warm it." Warric met the man's gaze. "Please."

Guy shoved his tunic's sleeves to his elbows and sank his arms into the water while she filled it. When steam rose off the surface, he withdrew his arms, taking a moment to shake off the droplets.

"My thanks to you both." Warric pushed off the bed, licked his fingers, then opened the door for them.

"He is a fine looking man," Kaethe whispered.

"'Tis best not to toy with him, sweetheart," Guy mumbled.

"You just want me all to yourself," she teased.

Guy chuckled. "Of course."

Warric closed the door on that little conversation, not needing to know where Guy spent his time. Tims was back to polishing Warric's boots. Mud licked his paws. Warric stripped off his coat, ensuring when he draped it over the chair, that the disc didn't fall out. Tonight, he would have to leave it behind. The jerkin was without large-enough pockets. He'd have to find a hiding place. Off went his tunic, his belt and breeches, then with a moan, he slid into the water. Tension eased out of him. He rested his head back and closed his eyes, wishing he was anywhere but in this shithole. *Keep him informed*, Baron Gregory had said, as if Warric had the choice not to.

What he'd said to Vona came to mind. He didn't have freedoms, not when he served Baron Gregory, not when he didn't have a choice in the tasks he had to perform.

"Pass me the soap, Tims." He held out his hand. The shuffle and scuffle marked the lad's journey from floor to satchel to tub. "I will hurry, that way you can climb in while 'tis warm."

"Me? Bath, sir?" Tims squeaked.

Warric popped an eye open to peer at him. "A man cannot be respected if he does not care for his person." He waited until Tims nodded, then soaping his hands, Warric set to washing himself. When thoughts of Vona's cleavage came to mind, he shoved it aside. Now wasn't the time. He would see her tonight wearing blue again.

He hoped so. The gown had been tight on her curves, accentuating her form. She was a distraction. He was stronger than this, trained to resist all manner of temptations.

When she had ridden up to him, he couldn't shake the sensation she had meant to speak of something else. Perhaps at dinner he would ask her? He would make sure to get her alone.

Without Yrsa eavesdropping.

Not difficult at all.

He snorted.

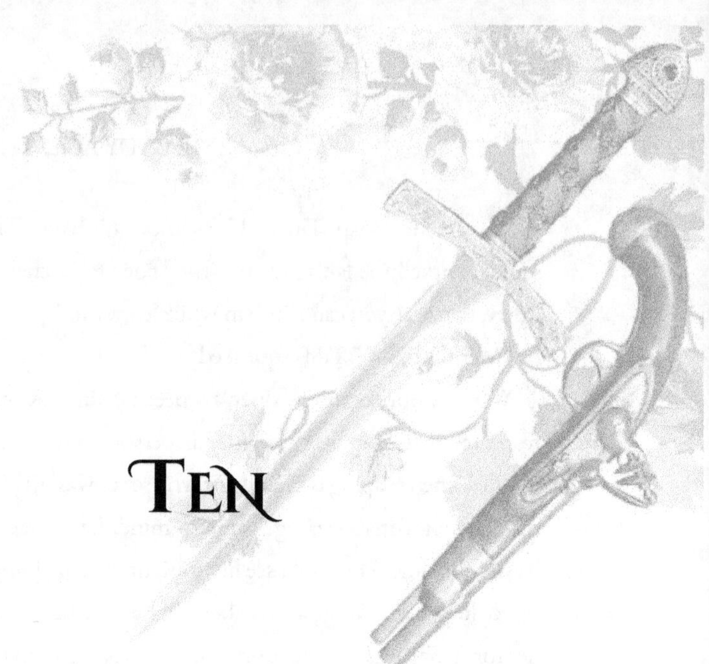

TEN

VONA RODE UP THE narrow road to Tacourt Estates. The house looked untouched and unspoiled. Rolling hills and pristine gardens spread out on either side of her. Roses in full bloom added a sweetness to the air. Stained-glass windows sparkled in the sunlight. Nothing had changed since she had last been there.

The door swung open to Barten, their butler. "Lady Devenmere, what a pleasant surprise."

"Barten." She smiled. "Is Lady Nessa home?"

The old man belied his age and hurried on nimble feet to help her dismount. "She will be delighted to see you." Yrsa vaulted off Shasta without assistance, gathered the reins and tossed it to him. He scowled but caught them then tethered the horses to a nearby ring mounted to a low-height wall. "This way, please." Into the house, he led them. Fresh flowers, rare mirrors from Marai in the east, and statues of semi-naked women filled the foyer. White stone and large windows flooded the entrance with light. A staircase ran up the right side, its balustrade curved and twisted iron.

"Vona?" A young woman with blonde hair glided down, her hand lifting her skirts an inch off the floor.

"Nessa?" Vona clasped her hands. Tears flowed for them both.

Giggling like young girls as if twelve years hadn't passed, they scampered into the parlor, choosing a double settee while chattering about everything and anything they could think to share. Occasional glances at Yrsa showed her snoozing, sprawled in a dainty chair in front of the cozy fire.

Vona lowered her voice to a whisper. "I need help, Ness. Lord Emil has invited me to a dinner tonight, and I have nothing to wear. I am sure to see you there, though. We can dance like we used to, pretending the circles of mushrooms were Fae."

"Oh," Nessa gasped. "I stopped attending those, but of course, there is bound to be something in my wardrobe to suit you." She leaned back to study Vona, tapping her fingers on her chin as she hummed. "I do believe I have a burgundy gown my aunt sent me. Most unsuitable for one of my pale coloring. I will have Tuala do the rest. She is amazing." With a yank, Vona found herself up and out the parlor, dragged to the upper floor, and into Nessa's room.

A maidservant tidying the pillows jerked back at their intrusion.

"Tuala, this is my dearest friend, Lady Ruvona Devenmere. She is desperate for our assistance. We will need a bath, and her hair, please, miracles are your forte."

Miracles? Vona winced while patting her braids.

Nessa waltzed off to fling a wall of doors open, exposing gown after gown. Choices, Thomas had said. "Where is that gown Aunt Gwella sent me?"

Tuala darted around her and pulled out a gown in burgundy silk. Nothing else adorned it—no beadwork, gems, or ribbons. With a square neckline, it was more than decent. Yards upon yards filled the skirt, sure to make riding difficult, but at least it would hide the state of Vona's boots.

"'Tis perfect." Vona gathered the fabric in hand, savoring its silken feel.

"A bath, please, Tuala," Nessa said, "and refreshments."

"Aye, milady." Tuala bobbed before leaving.

"You shall wear this." Nessa scooped something out of a wooden box resting on a side table. She faced Vona while holding a large ruby on a delicate gold chain.

"I...could not, Ness." Vona cupped the gem and hummed at its beauty.

"Of course you can," Nessa scoffed. "'Twas a gift from a suitor."

Vona blinked. Her suitors had brought her mother gifts. If one was thoughtful, Vona might receive a box of sweetcakes or a bouquet of wilted flowers. Nothing this precious.

"Milady, the bath is ready," Tuala said when she carried in a tray. On it was a glass jug, as rare as it was exquisite. In it, a deep blue liquid gave off an aroma of honeyed berries. On a silver platter was a variety of fruits, peeled and sliced. Still full from Ellia's wonderful stew, Vona accepted a goblet of juice but declined the fruit.

While she sipped savoring the tartness, Tuala stripped off the blue gown. She paused at the sight of the dagger.

"Oh, that." Vona handed the goblet to her and hastily unbuckled the blade and holster. She tossed them onto the bed as if they meant nothing.

Still holding the goblet, Tuala ushered Vona to the bathtub in an alcove overlooking more gardens. "Which soap would you like, milady? Honeysuckle, lavender, jasmine, or rose?"

Choices. Vona forced a smile. She *had* to stop thinking about Thomas. "Jasmine, please, Tuala."

The woman bobbed.

As soon as Vona sank into the hot water, she swallowed a moan when warmth seeped into her core, the bath glowing blue. Tuala handed her the goblet, then began to unravel Vona's hair. While she soaped a cloth and rubbed it along her limbs, Tuala washed her hair.

Nessa sat in a chair, nibbling on a tangerine. "How long will you be staying this time? Ten years has passed, Vona. How could you not visit?"

"Mother filled my days, Ness. Father went on his adventures." Vona scrubbed her face then splashed water until it dribbled off her chin. "How is your family? Has a man won your heart yet?"

Nessa shrugged. "Since Lord Emil's return, Father is always at the castle. Four years ago, my mother traveled to the healing pools, something about her frail nerves." Ness smiled. "I suspect she just wanted a break from Father. It was enroute that her carriage lost control and took her over a cliff. I could not bear to write you, Vona. Forgive me."

"I am sorry too." Vona squeezed Nessa's hand. "I did see your brother earlier today." She winced. How to explain that she'd almost buried him under a mountain of earth?

Nessa stilled. A frown furrowed her delicate brow. She brushed curls off her forehead with a dismissive flick of her hand. "He is...different somehow." Glancing at Vona, she offered a tentative smile that didn't quite reach her eyes. "Since he became a Netherbury guard, he has been...determined." She shrugged. "He is hoping to become the sheriff."

Vona pinched her lips. Thomas's bright blue eyes came to mind. That little smirk he wore when he glanced at her. This morning, when he'd glowered at her, his shoulders incredibly broad, and his hair brushing his shoulders in a stray breeze. Thankfully, she'd been admiring his features and hadn't missed his eyes bulging when he'd tried to warn her.

She opened her mouth to share that the sheriff had arrived, but Tuala poured fresh water over her head, rinsing her hair. With her face dripping, it took a few moments for Vona to absorb the droplets into her skin. Nessa had abandoned the chair for the table, fiddling with the items in the box.

It was for the best. Vona didn't want to mention Thomas and gush about him when she truly didn't know him *that* well. Tuala urged Vona from the bath to stand on a towel. Focusing on her magic, she dried herself, including her hair.

"Oh, not fair," Nessa pouted. "When I use my fire, I do dry, but it leaves me hot." She fanned her face for affect.

Tuala helped Vona into the gown. Too tight, it squeezed her waist and threatened to pop her breasts over the square neckline. The sleeves were diaphanous strips of transparent fabric, dangling past her elbows. Clasping her hand, Nessa ushered Vona to a stool placed in front of a wall-mounted mirror. She gasped and lowered her ass to sit. Never had her reflection been this crisp. Freckles splattered across her nose. Her eyes were a deep brown, something she'd never focused on when puddles and polished silver were all she'd used.

Father had to get one of these. She'd insist. Even better, she'd suggest she travel to purchase one. Taking Yrsa along, her mother couldn't say no. With flicks of her hands, Tuala sent slivers of air through Vona's locks, raveling, pinning, curling, and tucking. Using air and fire, she made quick work, floating clips and beads from the table and into the tiny braids maneuvered into a crown.

Nessa patted colored cream onto Vona's lips, smearing it with a gentle touch. Vona blinked at the reflection, not recognizing the woman, nor liking her red lips. She didn't have the heart to wipe it off now, but perhaps en route to the castle?

"Your dagger, milady?" Tuala brought over the holstered dagger then kneeled to strap it on Vona's right thigh.

"My thanks, Tuala. Mother says 'tis best to be armed than harmed." Vona grasped Nessa's hands. "Thank you for this. I shall have new gowns made on the morrow."

"This was a pleasure, dear Vona." Nessa tore her hands away to loop the ruby over Vona's head. She draped it, letting the ruby fall where it may, which happened to be between cleavage and belly button.

A knock broke the women apart. Tuala answered the door and returned with Vona's polished boots. It took moments to pull them on, and when she fluffed the skirts, only the tips of the boots peeked out.

"Now you are ready." Nessa clasped her hands against her chest. "Guy will be most upset he missed your visit."

Vona forced a smile. "I am bound to see him in Netherbury, Nessa. Once we have set Devenmere to rights, I shall invite you for tea."

Nessa clapped while bouncing on her toes. "I do hope your stay is a lengthy one, Vona. It will be wonderful to have someone to converse with."

Vona hugged and released her. "Tomorrow, you and I shall ride around Lake Uriell and dance around mushroom circles."

Nessa's eyes filled with tears. "Promise?"

Vona nodded, grabbed her blue gown, and followed Tuala out the room to the parlor where Yrsa paced.

"My apologies, Yrsa." Vona winced. An empty refreshment tray said her guardian had been cared for.

"None needed, milady." Yrsa caught Vona's hands and held them out wide. "You look beautiful." She smiled at Tuala. "Well done." Pulling Vona to the door, she muttered, "Now we must hurry. 'Tis almost sunset. I do not know what time dinner is, but 'tis best you arrive early rather than disrespect Lord Emil."

Barten handed over the reins when they stepped outside. Yrsa was correct, for the sun had begun to set. With Barten's assistance, Vona sat side saddle, her leg curled around the pommel, her skirts spread to rescue her modesty. With a wave, they cantered down the road toward Netherbury. Into a gallop, Vona urged Honey while praying Tuala's hard work remained in place. A pat behind the ear confirmed all was well.

Yrsa matched Honey's gait until they reached the stone bridge into Netherbury. There, Yrsa slowed to a walk, glowering at anyone who dared to cross their path. Instead of heading into town, she veered north and through the inner keep's raised portcullis. Red liveried grooms rushed to help them dismount then ushered their horses away, leaving Yrsa and Vona on the steps into the castle hall. The massive wooden doors were open wide, music and gaiety coming from inside. Many servants hurried hither and yon, some guards were in place, all looking resplendent in their uniforms.

Yrsa whipped out a kerchief, swept it across Vona's lips, then motioned for her to lead the way. Taking a deep breath, Vona gathered her skirts and climbed the steps, the plaintive melody of a flute luring her inside.

Eleven

Warric strode into the stables, his focus on an orc rubbing down a horse. That the animal wasn't wary of Dul said much. Just as Yrsa had trusted Warric due to Mud, he would do the same with Dul.

"I have a task for you," he said, halting in front of the orc.

Dul glanced his way, then continued to brush down the horse. "Aye."

"You like the stables?" Warric rested his arms on the stall wall.

"Aye, an' horses." A massive hand stroked the forelock of the gelding beside him.

"Good. Have you been to Lord Emil's stables?"

Dul's head whipped up. He smiled, showing an impressive collection of mismatched teeth. "This is task?"

"Aye. I want you to guard the horses, watching for men not supposed to be there." Warric's thinking was that stables weren't monitored—the perfect place for clandestine conversations. Not that he expected Dul to record every word spoken. Perhaps the orc could identify the men...or women involved.

Without a second thought, Dul balanced the brush on the wall, closed the stall, and waited. "I be ready, sir."

He trailed Warric when he strolled along the paved road into the inner keep. No one stopped him or Dul. None dared to. Abandoning his spy at the stables, Warric slipped into the hall. Few guests had arrived, more queued behind him while he waited to greet Lord Emil. Sconces were strategically lit, casting light and shadow as designed, granting opportunities for secrets to be shared. Silk and velvet banners bearing the Kenningthain emblem masked the walls, covered windows, and flittered in a faint breeze.

If Warric didn't know invisibility was impossible, he would think someone uninvited snaked through the guests. Or perhaps here at Emil's behest? Warric wouldn't put it past him.

"Sheriff Thomas, thank you for attending," Emil said the moment Warric stood before him.

"I live to serve, milord." Unfortunately, so much truth lay in that statement.

"Please, meet the citizens you protect." Emil gestured to those gathered around him. "Keep your ears open," he whispered, his gaze pointed.

Warric grabbed a goblet of wine from a passing servant, and strolled the hall until he found the perfect spot to observe. He didn't shuffle on his feet, no matter how much doing nothing pained him. Standing around sipping sweet wine wasn't an ideal way to waste an evening. Glances confirmed Emil meandering around the room. Each time he stopped to talk, sycophants surrounded him. No one dared touch him, though. In the four corners of the banquet hall stood his vigilant guards.

Warric dragged his gaze away from the gaped doors for the seventh time so far. Where was Vona? He refused to consider she wouldn't attend. Doing so would insult Emil.

Despite the clean jerkin, it itched and squeezed Warric's throat. With a flick of a finger, he unbuttoned the top two ties, drawing in a deep breath when the constriction eased.

A flute trilled, a qitary thrummed, and into this, a woman hollered in a husky voice. With his sensitive hearing set to listen to all whispered words, the singing was fast forming a headache behind his left eye.

Burgundy shimmered in the doorway. His gaze snapped there and snagged. Vona glided through, looking every inch a lady. She lifted her chin as she swept her gaze across the guests, her hands clasped at her waist, her shoulders straight. Behind her hovered her envoy shadow still in her Osiree garments. At least she'd taken the time to wash her face. Her cheeks glowed in the torch light.

Warric abandoned his goblet on a plinth and sliced through the crowd to reach Vona. "Lady Ruvona, good evening." He offered his hand.

Her eyes widened when she met his gaze. He was fascinated by the shape of her mouth. In a perpetual pout, when she smiled, he couldn't grasp how she did so and yet still maintained said pout.

"Sheriff, how handsome you look," she said, running an admiring perusal over his black embroidered jerkin.

"You, milady, are mesmerizing." His focus caught on her pale breasts threatening to escape the tight confines of the bodice, along with the ruby shimmering when she moved. With a nod at Yrsa, he guided Vona's hand to his forearm, then cupped it with his. A frisson of warmth passed from her bare skin to his palm, and in an instant, vanished the exhaustion and headache plaguing him. The healing power of earth, and she shared it without restraint or command.

"I do believe you stole my cat, sirrah," she huffed.

"Unfortunately, Mud is under the care of a page desperate for companionship. You are most welcome to take the kitten from the lad."

"A kitten does need constant supervision. I shall leave *River* with you for now."

"How gracious of you, milady." Leaning in, he whispered, "Be warned. Many are eager to make your acquaintance."

"Hell's teeth. Why?" she rasped and scanned the crowded hall.

He arched a brow. "A lovely lady in Netherbury?"

She smirked. "Desperate for gossip from the Conclave or Lisbay, or dare I say, companionship?" Drawing closer as if to share a secret, she brought with her the delicate fragrance of jasmine. "Perhaps you could rescue me?"

He hummed as if the idea had merit. "I would need a clear signal."

She chuckled. "I could rub my elbow, run my thumb along the bridge of my nose, press a finger to my chin?"

"All too obvious. Perhaps tap the rim of your goblet?" Snatching wine from a hovering servant, he offered it to her.

Her fingers brushed his when she took it from him. "Yes, a sound solution." The torch light softened her features. Her brown eyes darkened while she watched him over the goblet's rim. "How will I rescue you, Sir Sheriff?"

"Indeed," he croaked then cleared his throat. "I could grip my sword's hilt?"

"It might work." Her smile faded. She pulled away from him, her attention on those gathered. "I should greet Lord Emil. Until later, Thomas." She sashayed as she approached Emil whose lascivious gaze fixed on her...bountiful curves.

"Be vigilant, Yrsa," Warric muttered without glancing at her.

"Of course," came her response, just as faint.

He clenched his jaw and ducked behind the columns, his focus fixed on Vona. She was a dove among the wolves. So out of her depth, but he couldn't bring himself to whisk her away to safety. Nor did he think Emil would allow it. Yet, her presence made this evening bearable. As Warric dodged women's searching hands, drunk men eager to draw him into a debate or garner his alliance, he listened to conversations and dismissed them as quickly as they reached his ears.

"Good evening, Lord Emil. Thank you once again for the invitation." Vona dipped into a deep and graceful curtsey before rising.

Emil caught her hand for a kiss that didn't reach her knuckles. "My dear, you are a vision."

She blushed prettily but met his gaze without hesitation. "I owe this creation to Lady Nessa. As you must know, milord, I am newly arrived to Netherbury and have yet to acquire the services of a seamstress."

"I shall send mine on the morrow." He released her to circle his arm around her waist. "Now, do tell me what happened today at Devenmere. I am most eager for the details."

"A misunderstanding. I do not fault you at all, milord." She batted her eyelashes and gave him the sweetest smile. "Without supervision, men are like children. So trying."

Emil jerked back, his eyes wide. His lips twitched. He threw back his head and laughed. "That they are." Catching the chain around her neck with one finger, he lifted the ruby to the torch light. "What an exquisite bauble."

She slid it from his fingers, her touch innocent enough, but no less seduction. Warric shivered. "On loan from Lady Nessa. It does match the gown, does it not?"

"Aye," Emil said, his gaze on her heaving bosom. "I see you have found a champion in my sheriff."

Warric stilled. Torn, he wanted to hear what she truly thought of him but prayed she didn't acknowledge their friendship. Her announcing any sort of connection would jeopardize her reputation and his task.

"The sheriff?" She frowned, twirled on the spot as if searching for him while shifting away from Emil's cloying touch. *Good girl.* "Oh, aye, and I do appreciate him greeting me when I entered. I thank you for tasking him to do so, milord. I know no one here. Even his familiar face would do in a pinch."

Emil chuckled. "You cannot tell me you do not find him handsome, milady. Most ladies in attendance are falling over themselves to meet him."

"They are most welcome to him, milord, for my mother will determine the man to wed me." She blinked and smiled, appearing a simpleton and innocent at the same time.

Warric rolled his bottom lip over the top, trying to hide a smile.

"Your mother is a formidable woman, and you are a delight, milady." Emil raised his head, as if someone had drawn his attention. "I must greet my guests. Do enjoy the evening."

Vona dipped into another curtsey without spilling a drop of wine. "That was...stimulating," she whispered, glancing across the crowd at Yrsa.

"You did well, lass." Yrsa peeked over her shoulder, hiding that she had spoken. Not that Vona would hear her.

"Lord Walter's daughter, I do believe," a man said, snatching Vona's hand for a long kiss to her knuckles.

"Aye, milord." She bowed her head then blinked slowly as if stupid.

"Leave her be, Lord Panvaar." A blond man stole her hand for a gentle squeeze.

Warric stiffened, ready to rescue her, but her fingers remained firm around the goblet. When she beamed at the man, Warric realized she knew him. Odd when she'd claimed she knew no one.

"Vona, so delighted to see you. How fares your mother?"

She faced the man without glancing at the retreating Panvaar. "She enjoys good health. As you must know, Lord Juluan, I spent the afternoon with Ness. Your grounds are as beautiful as I remember, milord."

Ah, that explains it. The man is the father to a close confidant.

"Barten informed me of your visit." Juluan gestured to the gown. "This color suits you."

"Thank you. Nessa was most kind to lend it to me, along with Tuala's amazing skills." Vona patted her hair, unwittingly setting a thick curl free to dangle past her ear to her collarbone. She inched closer to Lord Juluan. "I will need to procure a mirror from Moriah, though. I never knew I had freckles."

Juluan chuckled. "As a homecoming gift, I will send one I have stored in the cellar."

"No, I could not accept." She caught the ruby in her hand and stroked a thumb across it.

"I insist." Juluan's expression turned serious. "I am sorry for the state of Devenmere. I arrived too late to stop it."

She stilled and offered a tight smile. "Nothing a little coin cannot fix, milord."

"True, but..." He glanced around before whispering, "I meant to save your father."

Warric paused. *Her father Lord Walter?*

She gripped Juluan's sleeve, crushing the blue velvet. "You know where he is?"

"I shall visit tomorrow. Expect me for tea." With a quick kiss to her knuckles, Juluan abandoned her.

So her father is missing? Mm. Warric intended to be at Devenmere eavesdropping when Juluan arrived for tea.

She gaped, color blooming on her cheeks. Her eyes sparkled and she fairly danced on the spot.

"I assume you need my assistance?" Warric glanced at Yrsa, who gave him a curt nod.

Leaving her goblet on a table laden with sweetcakes and roast pheasant, Vona weaved through the guests to reach Yrsa's side.

"I heard," Yrsa whispered. "Perhaps Lord Juluan is the key."

Vona grimaced when the music's volume increased. Yrsa stiffened and surveyed the hall. Warric did the same, suspecting foul play. The louder the music, the more secrets were being spilled. Emil laughed from amid two ladies, their gowns almost indecent, their lips a bold red.

"Guard her, Thomas," Yrsa ground out and faded into the shadows.

That the envoy trusted Vona's care to him puffed out his chest. He struggled to smother a sense of pride, wanting to castigate her instead. What could she know about him? He almost snorted. Nothing he hadn't wanted her to know. Cutting across the hall, he gathered Vona's hand in his a second before another man sought it.

"Guy?" Warric scowled. "Are you not on duty?"

"In a way. Filial obligation, Sheriff." Guy, in his pristine guard uniform and glowing blond hair, was the image of a young handsome man with excellent prospects.

Warric glanced at Vona, trying to discern what she thought of him.

Her lips formed a full pout. "Evening, Guy," she hissed. Lifting the ruby, she offered it to him without removing it from her neck. "Want to take this? I am certain 'tis worth more than a *sovereign*."

"Vona," Guy whined, pressing a palm over his heart. "I swore an oath—"

"To steal from the poor, even at the cost of their deaths," she spat. "No, I did not tell Nessa about your descent into evil."

A pulse ticked at the base of Guy's jaw. "My thanks, but serving the Lord of Kenningthain is not evil."

"The Guy I knew was noble with dreams of chivalry and valor." Vona arched a brow. "There is honor and self-respect, and you have neither." She faced Warric. "Please, escort me around the room, Sheriff."

Warric did as asked, sweeping her past a glowering Guy. "A bit harsh, Vona."

Her fingers tightened on Warric's arm. "I expected better of him."

"Our expectations of others can never be met." Why he was defending the man, Warric blamed on how forlorn she seemed. He couldn't bear the strange tightness in his chest. "Dance, milady?"

Gasping, she met his gaze. "Aye, please." She hesitated, casting a glance around the hall. "To do so will not be wise, Thomas. Unless you have partnered with others this evening?"

"No," he grimaced. "Then around the hall we go." He ushered her closest to the musical troupe. When she tried to walk past, he held his ground, forcing her to face him. "I must speak to you away from prying ears."

"Oh," she smiled politely while watching the guests and the few couples dancing—their hands above their heads, gazes locked in a parody of love.

"Where is your father?"

She didn't react other than to squeeze his forearm. Sucking in a deep breath that trembled the ruby, she whispered, "He is missing. About a week ago, he was taken from his bed."

"Is that why you are in Netherbury?"

"Partly." She glanced from right to left, then peeked at him through the veil of her eyelashes. "We do not know who took him. Perhaps he is in the dungeons?" She lowered her chin. "Nowhere else makes sense."

It was possible. Sir Walter *would* question the amulet's origins, stand against any darkness or injustices, or so Warric liked to believe. He'd never met the man, but he'd raised a fine son in Jacut. With Thack, Piers, and Vona's loyalty, Sir Walter had to have some merit. "You believe Emil—"

"If not him, then your guards." She turned toward him, clasping his arm and giggled, as if he'd said something funny. "I do believe we are being watched." She darted her eyes to the left.

He twirled her around, taking the opportunity to look where she'd directed. Behind a pillar stood Grokar. Frills gathered at the neckline of his white tunic. His dark blue breeches into polished black boots completed the outfit, but it was his intense gaze focused on Vona that Warric didn't like.

"I do not know who that is," he lied, guiding her hand above her head in unison with the other couples.

"Neither do I." She batted her eyelashes at him. "Best you find out, Sheriff."

"Oh, I serve you now?" he teased.

Her eyes darkened, and once again, her sinful mouth formed a smile-pout. "He has an...unsavory feel to him, if you get my meaning."

Warric stiffened. "Earth and darkness. A sentinel, though."

"Aye." She spun then dipped into a curtsey when the song ended. "I shall abandon you to your...admirers." With a nudge of her head at the gathering ladies, she waltzed off to stand beside Yrsa hovering nearby. "What did you find?"

"Later," Yrsa mumbled to Vona and gave Warric a curt nod.

"A dance, Sheriff Thomas?" A redhead held out her hand which he accepted by rote, brushed a kiss an inch across her knuckles, then drew her into his arms. As he smiled at her, he listened for conversations. Any between Vona and her envoy he would consider a boon.

On the edges of his vision, he tracked Grokar's movements. When the man settled behind Emil's throne-like chair, Warric smothered a grimace. Grokar's rise to that of an adviser was a loose thread, one

Warric needed to tug on. Perhaps Guy would have some answers. A quick search of the hall showed Guy hunched over a tankard. Beside him sat Lord Juluan. Their similarity indicated them as related. *Father and son?*

Warric bowed to the redhead, escorted her to the side, then strode over to Guy. He settled on the bench beside him.

With one glance, Guy drew his tankard closer. "Sheriff," he mumbled. "This is my father, Lord Juluan."

The older man had shown Vona kindness and, therefore, would receive Warric's respect. "The man in the shadows behind Lord Emil, who is he?"

"Grokar of Kerleau. He has been beside Lord Emil nigh on a year. When he arrived in Netherbury, Lord Emil became obsessed with finding a lost artifact." Lord Juluan held a goblet of wine to his mouth to muffle his words.

"He watches and whispers lies to Lord Emil," Guy said, his chin to his chest.

"Ah, so someone we need to be wary of?" Warric cast a glance at Yrsa.

She pursed her lips and ushered Vona closer to the musical troupe. A server paused beside them, offering slivers of fruit, marinated strips of meat, and sweetcakes. Both declined. Warric leaned back and surveyed the guests, searching for something out of the ordinary. Grokar was one, but there had to be more.

"There are many here not quite what they seem," Lord Juluan said, his tone low. "'Tis wise to keep one's head down and to remain in Lord Emil's good graces. Quite a few men have vanished, their wealth confiscated." He forced a smile. "A discussion for another time, Sheriff."

Warric frowned. "Why are you so…open with me? I am new to Netherbury and could be a spy for Lord Emil."

"If Vona is comfortable with you, then so shall I be." Juluan shoved a tankard across to Warric.

"My thanks." Warric clenched his jaw.

He needed to speak with her. They had to be more circumvent with their interactions. Perhaps put on a ruse of pure malice? He coughed to hide a chuckle, expecting her to play the role to perfection. On the morrow, he would discuss it with her.

As the evening dragged on, he made sure to dance at least once with every woman in attendance. Except for Yrsa, who glared at him when he asked. He kept his distance from Vona, not exchanging a glance or a word. Only to himself would he admit it was a struggle. She was by far the prettiest and most intriguing woman there.

Without a fare-thee-well to Warric, Yrsa escorted Vona out. They had, of course, bid Lord Emil good night. Warric was tempted to follow, but now was when his work began. Much could be learned from loose tongues. Without Vona as a distraction, he could focus on the guests.

"Who is closest to Lord Emil?" Warric asked Juluan.

"Besides Grokar?" The man stroked his beard, placing his hand in front of his mouth. "Lord Panvaar has been summoned in the wee hours of the morning."

"He has a mean streak," Guy muttered, then drained his tankard.

Warric shoved the platter of meats closer to him, giving him a pointed look. Guy's cheeks were ruddy from overconsumption, his eyes glazed. He dutifully nibbled on a strip of meat. Warric unfolded a napkin and placed sweetcakes onto it, then with flicks of his fingers, he covered them. "Return to the guardhouse, Guy, and give these to Tims."

"But..." Guy spluttered, slicing glances between his father and Warric. With a grumble, he snatched the bundle and left the hall.

"Please stop by Tacourt, Sheriff, for dinner tomorrow." Juluan offered a broad smile.

"My thanks, milord." Warric inclined his head.

At that, Juluan stood and approached Lord Emil. The man was greeted warmly. Not once did Emil narrow his gaze with distrust. Intriguing. Warric prayed he would learn more over a meal. As the guests left in pairs or alone, he waited, listening, but to no avail. No more secrets slipped past tired or drunk lips. He couldn't be done with this evening without permission, even if he was invited as a guest. When Grokar helped a swaying Emil to his feet, Warric bowed to them both.

"Milord, if you no longer have need of me?" It grated that he had to ask, but in doing so, he hoped to define his position and 'servitude' in Emil's mind.

"Why, of course, Sheriff, return to your post. Do present yourself in the morning."

"As you command, milord." He beat a hasty retreat, striding to the stables to collect Dul. The orc stood to one side, his arms crossed in front of him.

When he saw Warric, he lumbered over. "Sir."

"Dul, did you have a pleasant evening?" Warric asked while they strode through the opened gates, dodging horse shit and carriages.

"Aye. Many horses need care." Dul beamed.

Warric waited until they were in relative privacy. "Anything odd?"

"Aye. Man meet with other." Dul grimaced. "Not nice man too. Other man bleeding."

Ah, so a scuffle happened. "Anything said?" Warric was taking a chance here, but to not ask would be foolish.

"Aye. Not time yet. Must wait. Gold as promised. Conclave die."

Warric's eyes widened before he could control himself. "Well done, Dul." At the stables, he gripped the orc's shoulder. "On the morrow, I must meet with Lord Emil at the castle. Do you wish to visit the stables again."

The orc bounced, splattering mud over Warric's polished boots. "Aye, sir."

"I shall fetch you. Good night, Dul."

The orc grunted and disappeared into a room at the rear of the stables. *So, he lives here too?* Shrugging, Warric headed to the guardhouse and climbed the stairs to his room. The headache Vona's touch had kept at bay slammed into him. He clenched his jaw. Aye, he had earth magic, for each person was born with all five inside them. Still, having never used his weaker gifts, healing himself was beyond his ability.

Stripping off his garments, he sprawled onto the bed and stared at his feet dangling off the edge. Where the bruise had been, unmarred skin remained. She'd healed that too. He would speak to her about it, perhaps after he eavesdropped on her conversation with Juluan.

Sending out a wall of air, he settled on the bed and cupped the disc. "Milord," he whispered. It was late, and perhaps, for the first time in a long while, the baron had found his bed early.

"Speak."

Warric held the disc to his lips to say, "Emil used an amulet to foresee your death."

"Hell's teeth." Gregory muttered. "An amulet?"

Warric closed his eyes, recalling the devastation. "The cost was too much."

Silence settled.

"Draining life?" Gregory finally asked.

"Aye."

A slew of curses spilled from the baron. "Let me confirm the identity of this artifact. I would prefer not to make a...hasty judgment. My thanks for the warning. I will be on my guard." He paused. "Anything else?"

"No, milord." Warric tucked the disc between the bed and wall. Throwing his arm across his eyes, he willed the dead meadow's images to fade. He hoped he found sleep. There was much to do, and he needed his wits about him.

TWELVE

Vona waited in the center of her father's bedroom while Yrsa tackled the gown's buttons. Thankfully, Vona's magic had staved off the exhaustion, but no power existed that could kill boredom.

"I pray we need not attend another gathering for a while, Yrsa." She smothered a yawn.

"I agree. Too much happening at once. Too many people watching, whispering." Yrsa pinched the bridge of her nose.

Vona clasped her arm, sending green tendrils into her. Color returned to Yrsa's pale face.

She straightened and smiled. "Come, out of this gown lest you ruin it."

Vona shimmied until it pooled on the floor and moaned when a breeze cooled her skin. Stepping out of the garment, she scooped it up then draped it over a chair. The ruby lay between her cleavage, swinging wildly with her movements.

"The sheriff was most attentive," she said, setting the ruby on top of the tallboy. She unsheathed the dagger to slide it under a pillow before unstrapping its holster from her thigh.

"The sheriff is a mystery. Darkness-gifted should not be trusted, and yet..." Yrsa's brow furrowed.

"Aye, he seems a most capable man." A safe way to put it. Gushing about him would put Yrsa on high alert. "Do you think he will help find Father?"

Yrsa shrugged. "We can but ask."

Vona pulled on a nightgown Mags had packed then climbed into bed. In their absence, Dunstan had tidied the room and remade the bed with fresh linen. Pictures and artifacts had been returned to their rightful places. She wanted to discuss the state of their food stores, hiring help, and organizing repairs. Sinking into the bed, she vowed to do so tomorrow.

As to paying for it all, with earth magic, she could summon lost trinkets and gems from deep underground if her well was fully restored and her bare feet knee-deep in soil. Such an endeavor would drain her though, taking days for her to recover. Mother had sent for an earth-gifted sentinel to heal her the last time Vona had attempted a treasure hunt. Fishing for sunken gold was easier, although she could only breathe underwater for a limited time.

Yrsa bid Vona good night then left her alone. At last, as the night serenaded her, she relished her privacy. Unless she slipped out to Lake Uriell a mile or two north of Devenmere, Yrsa would leave her be.

Rolling onto her side, Vona tucked her hands beneath her cheek and stared out the window at the dark sky. Thomas had looked so magnificent in his black jerkin, matching breeches, and boots, with his hair disheveled. When he'd captured her hand, her magic had slipped from her, instinctively healing him. Something that should never happen when her magic was hers to give.

She frowned, reconsidering mentioning it to Yrsa. If anyone would know why, it would be a Sundowner. Still, the way he had touched and gazed at Vona, she wanted to savor the memory. Perhaps she was being a silly girl, liking his attention too much.

He'd reprimanded her for the way she'd treated Guy. Few had done so other than Yrsa and her mother, and only with him did his words smart. She *wanted* to please him. Flipping onto her back, she threw out an arm.

Nothing could come of any interactions with Thomas. He was to remain in Netherbury. Her mother would soon recall her to Bennedor, especially when Yrsa informed her that Thack and Piers would fetch Jacut.

The moonlight darkened, and she snapped her attention to the window, half expecting a passing cloud to have taken the light. Instead, a familiar face hovered outside.

She gasped and scrambled out of the bed to open the windows. "Thomas," she whispered. "What are you doing here?"

"I could not sleep. Too much to think about." He clambered into her room, forcing her back with his bulk. He loomed in a plain cream tunic and breeches, no coat. In the meager light, she'd never seen anyone more beautiful.

He gripped her elbow and drew her closer. Warmth drained from her, telling her he needed healing again. What did this man get up to? Tomorrow, she had to ask Yrsa about it.

"Why do you do that?" he rasped. "Heal me."

She shrugged. "You needed it."

"Your well should be guarded. To drain it is foolhardy." With his face in shadow, she couldn't read his expressions.

"Did you come here to reprimand me, Thomas?"

"No, I wanted to warn you. Emil was most intrigued by the sovereign. I suspect I will be tasked to collect taxes from you on the morrow."

She met his gaze with a glower. "Why? What I have will be needed for repairs."

"I must do as commanded, Vona. If you have a suggestion as to how to keep Emil happy and the overtaxed townsfolk alive, then I am all ears."

"I assume he wants his gold and will not take no for an answer?" She trailed a finger along the bedpost. "When do your men record the takings? As they receive it or when they report to Emil?"

"As we receive it, I assume."

She held up her hands, palms outward. "Hear me out. What if bandits were to rob you en route?" She wiggled her brows. "Those pesky outlaws."

He chuckled. "Are you implying that I, Sheriff of Netherbury, cannot stop a few bandits?"

"True, 'twould reflect poorly on you." She rested her hand on his forearm, leaning in to whisper, "What if you record it incorrectly? Not too much, but a little here and there will not be missed."

"How would that work? My men are always in attendance." He shuffled, directing her back to the wall, then crowded her, his warmth and magical scents making her shiver. "Somehow a bag of gold must fall out of the wagon without making a sound."

"Or without someone seen stealing it." She bounced, a muted laugh escaping her as she tried to defuse the tension thickening the air. "Modify the wagon with a hidden mechanism and compartment. Weight sensitive, perhaps?"

"Then I retrieve the gold later." He captured an escaped curl, rubbing it between his fingers. One by one, he withdrew the clips holding her hair up, floating them across the room to gather on the table.

"There." She cleared her throat, trying to ignore her hair spilling free. "Two minds are better than one."

"How would we distribute this wealth? If Emil hears of you handing out coins, he will demand a higher tax," he mumbled, his focus on running his fingers through her hair.

"We need someone unpredictable, unattainable. A legend." She smiled. "Perhaps someone disguised as a bandit? They would need a name we can whisper among the townsfolk."

He smirked. "A hero?"

She shifted from one foot to another, peering at him. "Or heroine, robbing from the rich to help the poor."

"In truth, 'tis robbing from the poor to *help* the poor."

She snorted. "When the gold was unrightfully taken, any of it returning to their callused hands is a Godsend."

"Yet, a sovereign was all my men brought in yesterday." He glided a hand along her shoulder to cup her neck, stroking his thumb across her jawline.

Her heartbeat scattered. She pinched her lips to smother her reaction, hoping to hide how much she liked his touch. "Emil had too much wealth on display this evening. It must come from somewhere."

"A vault?" Thomas's voice was huskier than earlier, his smile mesmerizing. "We might need that hero-heroine after all."

"Steal from Emil?" She frowned. That seemed far too dangerous.

"Aye, or find the source of his wealth." His attention dipped when he lowered his hand to hers, capturing her fingers in his. With their gazes locked, he raised her wrist to his lips and pressed a kiss to the pulse there.

She shivered again, heat of another sort barreling through her. *What is this?* It wasn't magic, nothing she could identify, yet the same frisson of warmth curled in her core.

"Thomas?"

He closed his eyes, his nostrils flaring. "I came to speak to you about our...familiarity. It did not go unnoticed, Vona. When we are not alone, please...snap and glare at me. I must be your enemy in the eyes of Sagua."

He was trying to protect her from gossip. Part of her wanted to rebel against yet another guardian, but her heart swelled at his thoughtfulness.

"I can do that," she managed past the lump in her throat. Now, if he could stop touching her, she might be able to calm her ragged breathing.

"Good." He straightened and released her hand.

Thinking he was done, she pushed off the wall and bumped into him. "Oh."

He caught her elbows and balanced her, his chest inches from hers. "Vona," he said, bending to peer into her eyes, his mouth hovering above hers.

What she ached to do was rise onto her toes and close the distance between them. That would be presumptuous of her. He came to warn her, and she took advantage of him? No, she wasn't like the women ogling him at the dinner. If he wanted to kiss her, the effort must come from him.

"Thomas?" she echoed his tone.

"Sheriff," he muttered.

"When we are not alone." She smiled.

He glared. "You let me in without hesitation."

"Should I distrust you?" She pointed at the window. "I knew it was you and not some stranger."

He grunted, pulling away, and at last, giving her the chance to suck in a deep breath. "You did so in a nightgown."

"Oh, aye, I lie awake, fully clothed and armed, anticipating visits from men." She chuckled. "Find something else to castigate me over, and," she shrugged, "wait your turn."

"Vona," he said again.

"Thomas," she replied.

He strode to the window, then glanced at her. Running a twinkling gaze over her, a smirk twisted his lips. "At least wear something not transparent."

She squeaked and bolted across the room to shove him. While laughing, he caught her hands and spun her. With his arms wrapped around her, he pinned her back to his chest. Nudging her hair aside with his chin, he whispered into her ear, his breath so warm, "You, my innocent, are too tempting by half."

Then he was gone, the windows closing behind him.

She peered outside but didn't see him. His words brought confusion, but her heart thumped in understanding. This she couldn't ask Yrsa about, not if she wanted to lose what privacy she had gained. As it was, she expected the envoy had listened in.

Even romantic conversations were not Vona's alone.

Romantic? She rubbed her arms and climbed into bed, pulling the blankets over her head. Aye, she did think Thomas handsome, so commanding, and strong—the kind of man she couldn't resist.

Yet, what could he offer her? Would her mother accept him? Mayhap if he helped find Father? Curses, she hadn't asked him about that. Stroking the wrist where he'd pressed a kiss, she relived the sensation. Such an intimate thing to do and so potent.

He hadn't kissed her, though, not on the mouth. She wouldn't have stopped him, and still, he hadn't with his lips so close to hers. What was his agenda? She grumbled, hating it when people played games. He should just tell her what he wanted, what he was after. Guessing his motives was a waste of energy.

She flipped onto her side, giving the window her back. Curse him, she had enough to do without this complication. Jacut would arrive soon. She couldn't leave Netherbury without helping the townsfolk. Father still had his garments from when he'd been a young adventurer. Could she wear them, cover the bottom half of her face, tuck her hair into a hat, and act the part of a man? She'd need to swagger. *Men did that, right?*

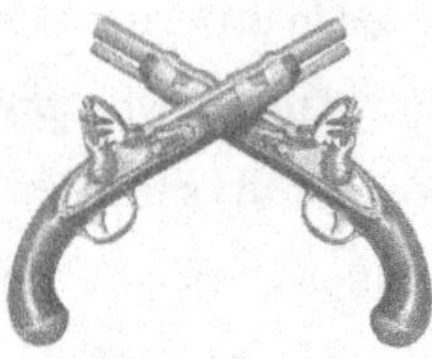

WARRIC WAS A FOOL. Morning had dawned, and he hadn't slept at all. *Vona*. He grunted and shoved aside a bowl of gruel Tims had found for him. What he shouldn't have done was visit her. He'd wanted to warn her, but in the end, kissing her was all he'd been able to focus on. She hadn't fought him, probably so innocent she hadn't sensed the tension between them and what it meant.

She fills my arms to perfection.

With a huff, he rose and strode out the door. Best to get this Emil-business over with. Only then could he present himself to Vona as Warric of Auriville and pray she didn't hate him for deceiving her. Every time she called him Thomas, it smarted. Especially in that breathless voice she'd used last night. He ached to hear her speak his true name.

Sharing his task with her was ill-advised. It would place her in a tenuous position, and she could let slip his identity. No, he couldn't involve her. He grimaced. Yrsa was another matter. When he'd left Vona, he'd found Yrsa waiting under an oak tree, her glower as ferocious as Vona had warned.

"This, I will not tolerate."

He landed on the ground and held up his hands in surrender. "I had to ask her to 'hate' me, Yrsa."

"What of the rest?"

"Unavoidable no matter how much I try to resist." He gestured to her to join him in the shadows, from where he threw out a dampening shield. "I am a spy for Baron Gregory of Kenningthain."

Her eyebrows shot up. "Go on."

"The baron has heard of Netherbury's plight. I am to thwart his brother until he can deal with this himself."

"You expect me to believe this?" She scowled, a formidable Sundowner in every inch of her taut body.

He withdrew the disc and spoke into it. "Milord, have you news on this amulet."

"Aye, Warric." For once, the baron answered promptly. "Myths of a trinket causing death and destruction exist in the Conclave's archives. Its lesser gift is that of foresight. Have you seen it?"

Warric met Yrsa's gaze while he said, "Aye, milord. Emil wore it around his neck."

"Curse my brother. The *fool*. It may reveal what may come, but what Emil does not realize is that the future is like an ever-changing river. My supposed death is but one strand on Fate's loom."

"He asked for my allegiance." Warric grimaced. "'Tis why he showed me the power of the amulet."

Gregory growled, "Making you complicit does not buy loyalty. Something my brother has never learned. Still, you are exactly where I need you to be."

"Tell me, milord, have you heard of Grokar of Kerleau?"

"Aye, an unassuming man, riddled with hatred and ambition." The baron paused. "If he is involved, Warric, this does not bode well."

"Until we can get to the bottom of this, I shall try and temper the hurt done to your people."

"Good. Do what you can. I might need to return unexpectedly. The Amulet of Amriel should not be in my brother's hands." Gregory sighed. "Keep me informed."

Yrsa waited while Warric pocketed the disc, then thinking better of it, he handed it to her. "Keep this safe for me. I have yet to find such a place in the guardhouse." He frowned, having balanced it on the roof outside his window while he was at the castle. Without her blood added to the baron's disc, Yrsa couldn't communicate with him. Although, she was an air-gifted envoy and a Sundowner. "If something happens to me, let the baron know."

"Your true name?" She gripped the disc in her palm then slid it into the back pocket of her breeches.

"Sentinel Warric of Auriville."

"That explains my instinctive trust of you." She closed the distance between them, peering into his eyes. "I sense a good man beneath the darkness, Warric, but if you harm a hair on Vona's head, or worse, break her heart, you *will* die." She scanned him, curling her lip in distaste. "Not in a nice way."

"Death is never nice, Yrsa, in any way." He squared his shoulders. "I do not wish to hurt Vona. I cannot explain the attraction, and I am struggling to fight it."

"Your honesty is appreciated." Yrsa folded her arms across her chest. "Still, the threat stands."

"Fair enough." He sucked in the silence dampener and launched himself into the air.

Returning to his room was easier than ridding himself of Vona's image, circulating conversations, the purpose of Grokar, and who Dul had seen bleed.

Shaking his head clear of last night's torments, he strolled into the inner keep. Dul lumbered off to the stables. He'd bared his teeth in a grotesque grin since Warric had fetched him. Emil's guards ushered Warric into a parlor where Emil sat too close to the fire. With fire magic, that made sense. Still, he was but a surpassor, less powerful than Gregory, a sentinel who'd been chosen to serve the Conclave as a baron.

A platter of chicken livers, thick slices of crispy bacon, poached eggs, and a crystal jug of orange juice sat on the table beside Emil. The wooden paneling lining the room, the imported Eryssian rug, Maraihan mirrors, statues, artifacts, and paintings all spoke of wealth. Except for the threadbare fabric on the brocaded chairs. The sconces added too much light and heat, but despite this, Emil shivered.

"Are you well, milord?" Warric asked. The man's death would end his task but not reveal what Grokar was up to and find the missing Sir Walter.

"I have tasks for you this morning, Thomas." Emil flicked a wrist at Grokar, who emerged from the corner to bow to Emil.

"Good morning, sir," Warric greeted Grokar.

"A wagon is due to arrive from Lisbay. Your men are to ensure 'tis not delayed." Grokar's gray eyes narrowed. "In three days, Lord Emil will hold an execution—a hanging. Escort the outlaw to the gallows after a thorough scrub. Let it not be said that we treated him poorly."

"What 'twas his crime?" Warric ventured.

"Conspirator," Emil barked, then broke into a nasty cough, bending over as he did so.

Grokar patted his shoulder and hummed something in an old language Warric didn't know.

Emil straightened and offered a small smile.

"The last would be to escort Alani, the seamstress, to Deven-mere Manor, and while she is there, ascertain what wealth can be taken for Baron Gregory's battles." Grokar held out a parchment, on which were listed Warric's tasks. As if he couldn't remember three instructions.

Dutifully, he accepted the scroll with a stiff bow. "Will that be all, milord?"

Grokar caught Warric's arm then released it. "Aye, report any-thing odd."

"As commanded." Warric itched to leave. Something about Grokar irritated him, but he couldn't react, not when the man followed him to the stables. After Warric collected Dul and marched to the guardhouse, Dul fairly danced around him.

At last, he glanced at the grinning orc. "What is it?"

"He is man."

Ah, so Grokar was in the stables. "Did he bleed?"

"He be stabbing."

Interesting. "My thanks, Dul. Start saddling horses, please." Warric strode into the guardhouse and addressed his men gathered around the roster. "We are to escort a wagon from Lisbay. Know anything about it?"

"Aye." Guy faced him, his face paler than usual. "Lord Emil had his guards bring a wagonful of goods from other towns, carrying delicacies, wines, cloth, and...gold."

Well, that explained his wealth, though he spent none of it on the upkeep of the castle. "Gold? From whom?"

Loaan shrugged. "Some say the Conclave. Grokar mentioned lords with coin to spare."

This went wider and deeper than Netherbury? Did Emil have a benefactor? Funded by higher powers? How wide did this plot go and how deep? What was Grokar truly up to?

Warric scowled. "Have you guarded the wagons before?"

"Aye," Guy said again, then struggled to swallow. His skin took on a greenish hue, no doubt from over imbibing last night. "They await us an hour outside Borfort. From there, we escort them to the castle."

Warric grimaced. Time wasted, and something he had to do today. He should have left early to attend to this. Facing his men, he assessed them. Could he send his men to deal with this in his stead? No, Emil had tasked him to go.

He pointed at Guy. "Man the desk, and for pity's sake, see a healer. The rest of you, mount up."

The twins, Nibbon, and Warric rode out, breaking into a gallop as soon as they crossed the bridge. It would take hours to reach Borfort. As the miles sped past, Warric couldn't shake the idea of somehow stealing a bag of gold. He blamed Vona. When his party veered south, past the road to Devenmere, he didn't dare glance in that direction.

Perhaps, during the long hours spent on the road, he might figure out what was between him and Vona and how best to thwart it.

Thirteen

Donning her father's garments from his younger days was a little more difficult than Vona had expected. His breeches were too tight, his tunic too loose, his jerkin more so. After tucking her braids into his wide-brimmed hat and pulling a scarf up to cover her mouth, she faced the polished silver mirror. The ill-fitting garments hid most of her curves, and her breeches would be more comfortable. She stamped an old pair of his boots, her feet had room to spare. Stuffing stockings in the front helped them stay on, but still, she thumped when she tested them out. Aye, the swagger was a no. She looked like an idiot. Instead, she minimized her movements, trying to mimic the confident and efficient way Thomas walked.

She did *look* like a boy. Twisting from one side to the other, she buckled on a belt, holstered Father's pistols, and grinned. This could work. All in beiges and browns was good. It meant she would blur into the surroundings and merge well with townsfolk. It took wealth to wear color.

She climbed out of the window, a bag of gold shoved inside her tunic. Sure, sneaking out was childish but truly, a trip to Netherbury didn't require an envoy's presence. When she hurried into the stables, she skidded to a stop on the straw-strewn ground. Yrsa leaned against a wooden post, her arms folded across her chest.

"Where do you think you are going?" She ran her sharp gaze down Vona then scowled. "Dressed like a boy?"

Vona spun on the spot. "Good?"

"For what?"

"I mean to deliver gold to the church. Doing so as Lady Ruvona will bring Lord Emil's guards down on Devenmere Manor."

"Aye." Yrsa pushed off the post with a curse. "Sending Dunstan or myself would do the same." She twirled on a heel and began to saddle her horse.

Vona slumped, straightened her shoulders, and started readying Honey, as well. "You cannot be seen with me, Yrsa."

"Aye. I shall wait outside the town's walls." She glanced at Vona. "'Tis wise to be near should you need me. I would, however, prefer you not go at all."

Vona rolled her lips, keeping silent. Tightening the last buckle, she gathered the reins and urged Honey out of the stall. Yrsa did the same before mounting, straddling the horse with ease. Together, they rode for Netherbury, choosing the northern most route and thus avoiding the Conclave Way.

Riding across the southern bridge meant reaching the church sooner while not passing the guardhouse. The fewer guards she saw, the better. Yrsa stood vigilant in the shade of a copse of trees—close enough to listen.

Vona dismounted outside the church—a rickety wooden building, weathered, tilting, and with a crumbling porch. A large cross was burned into the façade. A gaze up and down the main road confirmed no one paid her much attention. She slipped through the open door and into the dim interior.

"Father?" she whispered while venturing deeper. Even the carpet lining the aisle was threadbare.

"I am Friar Flynn." An old man, in a brown hessian robe, straightened and faced her, his hands clasped on top of his belly. "What is it, my child?"

"For those in need." She grasped his hand and dropped the coin in it. "More will be...given."

"This..." He stuttered, his eyes shimmering with unshed tears. "'Tis so much. The Lord bless you, my son." He beamed and clutched the bag to his chest. "Your name?"

She blinked. Hell's teeth. Not once had she thought to pick a name. What would one call someone robbing from the rich? A thief. She pursed her lips. "Um, Robbin?"

"My thanks, Robbin. I shall see to it that the destitute are cared for." The friar escorted her to the door. "Please, take care. We need you and more like you in these dire times."

"Good day, Friar." With two fingers, she tapped the brim of her hat. After mounting Honey, she steered south, riding past Yrsa in case she was being watched. Heat engulfed Vona's chest. To do good, to help people, flooded her with such warmth, that tears spilled free.

In the manor's stables, she waited for Yrsa, taking the time to attend to Honey.

By the time the woman rode in, Vona had brushed and fed Honey and Mags and mucked out one of the stalls. Dunstan had yet to appoint a stableboy. She frowned. Allowing Dunstan to do all the stable work wouldn't be good for his knees.

"See, nothing to worry about," she said, her breathing a little labored.

Yrsa snorted, dismounted, and said no more while she removed Shasta's saddle. When she was done, she took up a spade and mucked out another stall. With only three horses, there was still much to be done. By mid-morning, sweat glistened on Yrsa's skin. They'd worked in companionable silence.

"I shall ask Piers to clean me," Yrsa said. "I suggest you change lest anyone sees you." She gestured to Vona's bedroom window then stomped off.

Up Vona climbed, pulled herself in through the window then sprawled on the floor, her breathing still ragged.

Orv bobbed, its white lights flickering. "And this?"

"Part of my training." She pushed off the floor and removed each item with meticulous care. The disguise had worked on Friar Flynn, but the true test would be Thomas. Her silly heart fluttered.

"Truly?" Orv hummed. "Odd. Still, 'tis a lovely day for window climbing."

She bit her lip to smother a chuckle. "Aye, indeed."

Once more in her breeches and coat, her pistols on her hips and daggers hidden in her boots, she skipped to the dining room. Dunstan had things well in hand. Breakfast was a table laden with eggs, bacon, sausages, fresh-baked bread, and something her father liked...coffee.

The bitter beverage, though appreciated by Piers and Thack, wasn't something she was partial to. Dunstan assured her he had sufficient coin to send his son Kaval to the local villages to replenish their food stocks. He had hired a few hands to help around the manor—a stableboy to begin the next morning. Already the garden and fountain showed love and attention.

Trying not to cry, Vona bid Piers and Thack farewell. They would head north to find Jacut. Begging them not to go would mean she would have to, so she kept silent but hurried to the stables the moment their heads dipped below the horizon. Astride Honey, Vona rode to Tacourt to return the gown and ruby. As promised, perhaps she could spend a few hours dancing around mushrooms and swimming in the lake with Nessa. Yrsa once more trailed her.

"Are you planning on following me everywhere, no questions asked?" Vona twisted in the saddle to glance at her companion.

"Aye."

"No suggestions or advice either?" Met by silence, Vona faced ahead.

Guidance would be helpful. She was running around Netherbury trying to find her father without Yrsa saying a word. The Conclave Way was busy, but Vona didn't stop to chat to anyone, simply waved when they greeted her. Deliver the gown, visit with Nessa, then head to Netherbury, hoping Thomas had learned something.

If he asked her to be rude to him, she needed some other way to speak to him without being seen or overheard. Sending written messages would be dangerous with the possibility of them being waylaid.

"Yrsa," she said, holding Honey back to fall in beside Shasta. "What does it mean when someone draws my magic from me without my say-so?"

Yrsa snapped her gaze to Vona's before facing ahead. "By touch or syphoning it out of you?"

"Skin on skin. Without intending to, I heal in an instant."

"Huh." Yrsa's eyes narrowed in thought. "Leave it to me, Vona. I shall find out its meaning."

Vona stared at her. Something told her Yrsa knew and had no intention of sharing. She set Honey into a gallop, preferring to be far away from her tightlipped guardian. When she drew to a halt outside Tacourt, she vaulted off the saddle, threaded the reins through the hook, and marched past Barten, who held the door open.

"Good morning, Lady Ruvona."

She smiled and handed him the bundled gown with the ruby tucked inside. "Is Nessa in, Barten?"

"No, milady. She visits the church every morning."

Vona hid a wince. She might have run into Nessa. Then again, fooling Nessa would have convinced Yrsa the disguise worked.

"Please let her know I stopped by and how grateful I am for yesterday." Vona spun on her heel to leave.

"Vona, what a surprise," Lord Juluan called as he strode down the stairs. "Bring refreshments to the study, Barten." Juluan hesitated in front of Yrsa then held out his hand. "I did not have the pleasure last night. Lord Juluan of Tacourt."

"Yrsa of Osiree." A little peach color exploded across Yrsa's cheeks.

Vona smothered a smile. Yrsa had never reacted to any man. Juluan was good-looking with his blond hair, firm jaw, and kind eyes. An excellent choice.

"I hear the Mountains of Chalimar are exquisite." He closed his fingers around Yrsa's when she accepted his hand. With a gentle tug, he drew her closer. They peered into each other's eyes, leaving Vona to meander around the foyer, fluff her hair in a mirror, wipe the dirt off one cheek, then move from painting to statue. She extended a finger to stroke the top of a marble breast when Barten strode past, bearing a tray.

"Fetch a mirror from the cellar, Barten. Have it wrapped for transport." Juluan snapped out of his daze and gestured, with a sweep of his arm, for Yrsa to enter the sunroom.

Vona hurried to follow, delighted to witness their interaction. She chose a chair bathed in sunlight. Plants in a variety of pots spilled over their edges, some blooming, a few glistening, and they filled the room with such sweet fragrances. Drawing in a deep breath, she held it before releasing it on a whoosh.

"We shall take tea now, Vona, instead of this afternoon," Juluan said, breaking his admiration of Yrsa to spare Vona a glance. "Lord Emil has had your father imprisoned in his dungeons. There are whispers of an impending execution. If the prisoner to be hanged is your father, we do not have much time."

She gasped and shifted to the edge of her seat. "On what charge?"

"He unwisely compared Emil to Gregory." Juluan poured the tea, carrying the first cup to Yrsa. "He often contested Emil's new laws, and I suspect that played a part. Emil did not hesitate to have him taken from his bed. In the cover of night, none of Emil's court saw him do so."

"With your earth and my air, we can save him, Vona," Yrsa said, her shoulders straight.

"Indeed," Juluan rasped. "Of course, I cannot expect you to attempt this without assistance. I shall add my gifts to the mix." He settled onto a chair, then jerked back. With a look of chagrin, he stood to pour Vona a cup of tea. "I shall discover on which side of the dungeon he is located, and perhaps, we could blast our way in?" His brow furrowed.

"Or I create a tunnel?" Vona smirked. After she discussed this with Thomas, of course.

"I too have an ally I can call on." Yrsa sipped her tea even though she hated the hot beverage. Anything drunk hot was bad for the constitution or so she had spouted.

"Who?" Vona grinned. "Uldane?" Having the Lord Sundowner on their side would be helpful. "Stay and discuss the details with Lord Juluan, Yrsa. I shall return to Devenmere and not dally en route."

Yrsa hesitated, warring between duty and...temptation. She set the cup aside and rose. "I swore an oath. This I will not break. Thank you for the news, Lord Juluan," she scowled. "If we are to rescue Lord Walter, 'tis best you do not know any of it."

"Wait." Juluan cupped Yrsa's shoulder then quickly lowered his hand. "I need to mention the amulet."

"Of Amriel." Yrsa arched a brow. "I am aware."

Juluan gaped but recovered himself. "What of Grokar?"

"Who?" Cradling her cup, Vona settled in her chair.

"The adviser to Lord Emil." Yrsa folded her arms across her chest. "I trailed him into the castle stables last night. He met with Panvaar and had a revealing conversation about gold, allegiances, and power. Emil is but a pawn in a plot against the Conclave."

Vona blinked at her. Why hadn't Yrsa revealed any of this to her? Was she so untrustworthy? She dipped her gaze and drowned in the dark swirl of the tea, fighting to snuff her tears. They slipped free, spilling down her cheeks. She hastily sucked them in, the blue glow of her water magic blurring her vision. "You professed to wanting the best for me, yet you keep this to yourself?" She rose, set the cup on a side table, and slapped her hat on. At Juluan, she twitched a tight smile. "Good day, sir."

She stomped out, aware she acted like a child, but she was done with this, with everyone protecting her like she was a weakling. Barten held the reins for her and helped her mount. She offered him a tight smile, then urged Honey into a gallop.

"Vona," Yrsa called.

Without a backward glance, Vona ducked low, pressed her hat to her head, and spurred Honey onward. Gray clouds on the horizon matched her heart. Heading to Devenmere Manor shot pain through her. With a tug on the reins, she steered Honey across the fields to Lake Uriell. The vast body of water shining silver in the sunlight filled her heart with such longing. When she was younger, nothing had plagued her. She had remained a child, free to play, to dream.

Leading Honey to the north, she circled the lake to the secluded spot where she and Nessa had spent hours, whiling away their time talking about dreams and hopes. She leaped out of the saddle and tethered Honey to a nearby tree. Without wondering if she should, she yanked off her boots, tossing them aside, her daggers spilling out. Her pistols and hat landed beside them, her tunic and breeches on top until she stood there naked.

This far from Devenmere manor and other farmholds, she was alone.

When she waded into the lake, green and blue tendrils spiraled up her legs. The water was chillier than she'd expected, but she needed this. Diving in sucked the breath out of her. She stayed submerged, using her magic to summon air bubbles to form a pocket around her head until she could breathe. Dark gray fish glided past her, shimmering through the murky sunlight. She stroked one. Skittish, it dodged her fingers. With her feet sinking into the lake's bed and the water engulfing her, heat swelled and grew inside her, filling her with euphoria. She giggled, swirling her arms around her, creating eddies and stirring up plant life.

As the bubble shrank, she pushed off the floor and burst through the surface, wincing at the sunlight reflecting off the water. The air was sweeter though. Her smile dwindled. What joy this exercise had garnered, faded. Running off *had* been childish. She swam to the bank, planning on returning to Tacourt to fetch Yrsa, but with her well full, she couldn't dry herself.

Cursing, she stretched her arms to the lake, cupped her hands, then spun them left to right. Droplets of water hovered, rushing to form a giant ball floating a yard above the surface. She spread her palms wide, increasing the size of the swirling globe. With a flick of her arms, the ball exploded.

With her well emptier, she rolled her shoulders and sucked in the droplets dewing on her skin, drying her hair too. After scrambling into her garments, she shoved her hat onto her head while galloping west. A gust of wind swept off her hat, tossing it onto the lush green grass of the meadow. She guided Honey around and cantered back, sliding to the right side of her saddle to dip low and scoop up the hat.

When she smashed it onto her head again, she huffed at finding Yrsa before her. "Thanks," she gestured to the crushed hat.

"A pleasure." Yrsa hitched her thumb at the Conclave Way. A smile teased her lips, and seeing it eased the tension in Vona's jaw.

"My apologies." She patted Honey's neck and ran her fingers through her mane. "I should not have ridden off without you."

"Care to tell me why you did?"

Vona stared ahead, letting Honey fall into an easy canter. "You not sharing information."

Yrsa hummed. "I see."

"You know *everything* about me, witness and overhear *each* conversation, even those I have with the moon," Vona snapped, drew in a deep breath, and fought for calm. "What do I need to do to change yours and Mother's opinion of me. You have trained me well enough. I can defend my life, and yet, I am guarded as if I am a child." She faced Yrsa. "Were the last years for naught, or were you just there to keep me occupied?"

"A fair assessment," Yrsa said then fell silent. Only the passing wagons and horses intruded but made no impact on the tension in the air.

Vona waited, praying for something from her taciturn guardian.

"I shall remove myself when you are with the sheriff...in a more intimate setting."

Vona blinked at her, at the gift. It was a start. "Thank you."

Yrsa faced ahead.

"So, Lord Juluan?" Vona wiggled her eyebrows.

"Not up for discussion," Yrsa droned as if bored.

Chuckling, Vona tilted her face to the sunlight, letting it warm her lake-cooled cheeks.

"Out of the way. Lord's business," a gruff voice called.

She opened her eyes and frowned at the overladen wagon taking up all of the Conclave Way. Eight men in black uniform guarded it, red sashes on their upper arms stating their allegiance. The man to the rear was one she hadn't expected to see so soon.

Sheriff Thomas of Hasden, who now snuck a bag from out of the wagon and flung it off the side of the road. He met her gaze, trying to convey something. When he focused on Yrsa, Vona dipped her chin, struggling to summon rage. He'd asked her to be rude, and she needed a valid reason.

"I said, out of the way."

She lifted her gaze to the man in the lead—a bald head, beady eyes, with a thick beard falling to his chest. He showed no mercy, only impatience, slapping his reins across his thigh. Sweeping off her hat, she flicked her head to the side so that her unbound hair caught a stray breeze.

"Good day, sirs." She offered a sickly sweet smile. "I see I must lay yet another complaint at Lord Emil's feet," she bit out, then pointed her hat at the road. "This is the Conclave Way and not yours to selfishly occupy. Steer your wagon to the left and allow me to pass."

The man spluttered. "We serve Lord Emil and escort precious cargo at his behest."

"Fascinating." She arched a brow. "Now move to the side, or I shall inform Lord Emil of your rudeness."

"How dare you?" The man grasped his pistol only for pain to scrunch his face.

A glance at Yrsa showed her squeezing her fist. Vona had to assume she crushed the man's white-knuckled hand around the pistol's grip.

"This is Lady Ruvona of Devenmere, Kenet. I suggest you let the viper pass." Thomas's baritone cut through the tension.

"Viper?" she hissed, straightening in the saddle. "You, sirrah, are an uncouth imbecile. I pay my taxes to the Conclave, and as such, have right of way. What do you do but serve a lord?" She urged Honey past the wagon, her glower on Thomas.

His glare was fierce, yet it sent a frisson of delicious heat through her.

"I grow weary of these complaints, sirrah. Perhaps next, I shall challenge you to a duel for your impertinence."

He threw back his head and laughed. "You?"

She studied him for a moment, taking in his broad shoulders in that too-tight coat and his massive hands that could surely snap a man's neck. "No, my champion." She waved her hand at Yrsa.

His smile dwindled. "Very well. Kenet, veer the wagon to the left. Grant others the right to the Conclave Way."

Kenet gaped and twisted in his saddle to glance over his shoulder. "But—"

"Or do you wish to fight a Sundowner?" Thomas ground out.

Kenet paled and urged his men to obey, his gaze fixed on Yrsa when she cantered past him.

Vona bowed her head at Thomas. "Pray we do not meet again, sir."

With a flick of her head, she turned away from him, walking Honey east. She faced ahead, trying to sense where he'd thrown the bag. By his pointed look, she assumed she was to find and keep it secure.

Just like that, he'd stolen it from the wagon, amid seven guards and from under their noses.

Yrsa had her eyes closed, no doubt using her magic, as well. "Let them create more distance."

"If I had my shoes off," Vona muttered. "I could send my earth underground, find the bag, and drag it along the road until we turn to Devenmere."

"We will return for it," Yrsa said then grinned. "Because removing your boots after that display of ire would not seem...normal."

Vona chuckled. "Indeed."

"My thanks for volunteering my skills in a death match."

"Just adding some excitement to your otherwise dull life," Vona said with a shrug.

Yrsa's harumph was the only response.

Fourteen

A GLOWERING VONA WITH her eyes narrowed, her hair swaying in the wind, and her lips in a full pout, was the stuff of sensual dreams. She had risen to the challenge, as Warric had expected of her. *Uncouth imbecile?* Oh, he'd tease her about that...later.

At least she had served as a distraction, granting him the chance to steal a bag that had clinked since Borfort. What he could glimpse of the cargo were bolts of velvet and silk, crates of fruit, wines, brandy, cured meats, and of course, a chest of gold. For the last mile, he'd been slowly wiggling the clasp free, using the tiniest wisps of air. Now he painstakingly refastened it.

He dared not glance back, even though Kenet and a few of his guards did so.

"Viper or not, she *is* beautiful," a man mumbled to another.

"No longer friendly to you, Sheriff." Loaan smirked.

"Aye, 'tis her true colors we witnessed." Warric huffed. "I shall endeavor to stay away from her where possible."

"Did you not dance with her last eve?" Nibbon bounced in his saddle while glancing at Warric.

"I danced with all the ladies in attendance," Warric growled. "To not do so would be unwise."

"True. Many a man was brought low by a woman," Kenet threw into the mix. "My missus should be feared. Now *there* is a viper like no other." He chuckled, his voice carrying warmth, negating his words.

Well, well, the captain loves his wife. "Staying in Netherbury until tomorrow?" Warric ventured.

"No, 'tis back we go the moment Sir Grokar checks the cargo."

"I am intrigued. What is in the chest?" Warric grinned. "I pray 'tis new pistols or something exotic."

"That I cannot say, Sheriff."

"Fair enough." Warric faced ahead. The contents of the chest, he suspected, was in the document he'd stolen from Kenet during Yrsa's demonstration of her skills. The man had been writhing in agony, unaware when Warric whisked the scroll from his belt. Who would place it there for safekeeping? Had Warric been tasked to protect it, inside his jerkin against his heart was the safest place. Wiggling it off a belt was easy. Hell's teeth, it could tumble out, and Kenet wouldn't have noticed.

Aye, it was now inside Warric's jerkin.

Stumbling on Vona and Yrsa had been a godsend. Her 'tantrum' had served the perfect diversion. He would thank her when he escorted the seamstress to Devenmere Manor.

His stomach grumbled, reminding him he'd skipped the gruel that morning. Nor had he packed water or wine to tide him over. They were nearing Netherbury. Perhaps one of the stalls... He doubted it, but he could peruse. As he guided the wagon across the bridge and up the hill to the gatehouse, he surveyed those they rode past. Nothing was out of the ordinary.

When Kenet halted the wagon outside the keep, Grokar stood waiting. "I was told you were close, Captain."

"Aye, sir." Kenet dismounted and flipped the hessian back, exposing the cargo.

Grokar met Warric's gaze. "The seamstress?" He gestured to a woman seated in a wagon.

Warric hid his surprise. Had she been there since this morning? He dismounted Serenity and handed the reins to Nibbon. "I shall not be long."

When he approached the wagon, the woman bobbed her head in greeting. "My name's Alani, sir."

Climbing onto the seat, he smiled at her, gathered the reins, and urged the horse into a trot. Across the bridge he went. This day was turning out to be dull and long, his ass smarting from the saddle and now the hard seat.

Glancing over his shoulder, he scowled at the bolts of cloth lining the bed of the wagon. Alani clasped a bag to her chest, but she didn't speak, didn't fill the time with inane chatter. She was young though. Tucked under her cap was honey-blonde hair matching her eyebrows. Too-pale skin marked with spots made her appear sweet and innocent.

He wondered why Vona's freckles inspired something deep within him, yet Alani's didn't. They made quick time. He tried not to peer into the bushes where he had flung the bag of gold. If Vona had understood his look, she had retrieved it. Taking the turn a little fast, Alani let go of her bag long enough to grasp the seat.

"My apologies," he mumbled.

When he drew the wagon to a standstill, she rose and waited. He left the reins on the seat, then jumped out, hurrying around the horse to hold his hands up. She gripped his forearms and let him lower her to the ground.

Turning away, he gestured to the cloth. "These?"

"Gifts from Lord Emil." She said no more and marched to the massive front door.

Having not approached the manor from this angle, Warric took the time to assess the trodden earth around a scarred fountain. A path led up to a carved wooden door. The house had two floors. In white stone, pretty ivy grew up its side and stained-glass windows added color. A stone path curved around the side of the house, horse tracks stating its use.

"Good day, Mr. Dunstan." Alani bobbed.

"Sir, madam, this way please." The man ushered them through the door. "Please, wait in the parlor. I shall inform milady of your arrival."

Warric ushered Alani to a chair, then stood to the side, clasping his hands behind his back. This room was like Juluan's sunroom, filled with trinkets, intriguing statues, artwork, and well-cared-for furniture. Wealth was in every aspect. No wonder Emil wanted to strip the manor. A thick Eryssian rug was underfoot, and even on this sunny day, the sconces were lit.

Yrsa entered first. "Sheriff," she said in greeting.

"Madam," he replied. "I escorted Lord Emil's seamstress at his request. Bolts of cloth are in the wagon."

"A gift from my lord," Alani said, dipping into a curtsey.

Yrsa pinched her lips. "Let us begin with my garments. Come with me...?" She arched a brow.

"Alani, madam." Clutching her bag, she scurried after Yrsa.

Warric waited, assuming he had to spend the afternoon doing nothing while Alani took everyone's measurements. He explored the room, peering into the sunset on a painting then stroking the breast of a marble statue depicting an unknown goddess.

"Sheriff."

He snatched his hand away and faced Vona. "Viper." He grinned.

"Imbecile." She chuckled. "The bag is safe. Father has a secret room."

"Good. My thanks for the distraction."

"A pleasure." She circled the room opposite him, the space between them seeming insurmountable. "It was a great joy to snap and growl. I look forward to further interactions with you."

"Vona," he rasped, wanting to cross the space between them and draw her against him. Her hair was down and wind tussled, curling over a shoulder.

"Thomas." She smiled. "I can ask Dunstan to bring you refreshments while you wait?"

"Please." He cleared his throat. "I am famished."

"Oh," she gasped. "You will need something with more substance. Follow me. Ellia will have a meal for you." She marched out of the room and along a passage, down a few steps, and into the kitchen. He trailed her, content to admire the sway of her hair. The heat of the fire hit him first, then the rich aroma of baked bread.

"Lady Vona?" Ellia wrung her hands, slicing glances between Vona and Warric.

"This is the ravenous Sheriff of Netherbury, Ellia."

She beamed. "Greetings, sir. Do sit down." She pointed to the table. "I have cold meats, fresh bread, and cheese. Just this morning, Kaval arrived with dates from Drezat and wine." Bowls, tubs, and platters were shoved onto the table.

Vona sat across from Warric and picked a date, biting into it with a groan. "My favorite."

He blinked, lost in the way her lips wrapped around the dark fruit. "Coffee?"

Warric jerked out of his daze, praying his fascination went unnoticed. He nodded at Ellia, not sure how else to respond. He'd drunk coffee twice in his life, the smoky bitter flavor pleasant.

"The pot is not fresh, but it should still be good. A little honey to taste?" Ellia didn't wait for him to respond but placed a honeypot before him.

Vona scooped the honey dipper into the pot and dribbled the golden goodness onto a buttered slice of bread. She bit into it, then mumbled her thanks to Ellia who'd poured juice into a cup for her. "Now to find our legend. I know a few who are suitable."

"Where would he or she deliver...the news?" He sliced a glance at Ellia, not sure she was trustworthy.

"I would suggest *he* start at the church. The friar would know who needs the *news* the most." She licked honey off a fingertip.

He lowered his gaze, taking a moment to calm his breathing and hopefully his heartbeat too. When he peeked at her, heat uncoiled in his belly. She was so unaware, so innocent, without any understanding of what she did to him. Biting into the cured ham silenced any groan or remark that might have slipped from him. He followed that with a piece of cheese then a sip of coffee. With his mouth full, he couldn't confess his feelings, nor beg her to let him woo her.

Woo? He straightened, widening his eyes, then coughed when the food lodged in his throat.

"Are you all right, Thomas?" she asked, rising from the bench.

He waved her down, rather than have her touch him.

"I am well," he rasped, then sipped the coffee, swirling the bitterness around his mouth.

"Did I discuss my father with you?" She met his gaze while shredding a piece of roast chicken between her fingers. Discarding it, she wiped her hands on a cloth, then cupped the juice and rested her elbows on the table.

"That he is missing?"

She winced, tightening her grip on the cup. "Yes." Her mesmerizing mouth formed a full pout. "Lord Juluan revealed that Lord Emil had Father imprisoned for some slight." She sipped the juice then pinched her lips. "Please, could you find out if he is...in the dungeons? I do not want to launch a rescue if he is not there."

Warric stilled, a date halfway to his mouth. "What are you considering, Vona? Planning on risking your life and reputation?"

"I have Yrsa and Lord Juluan's assistance, Thomas." She huffed. "I am not without skills."

"Yrsa agreed?" Warric massaged his brow then clenched his jaw at smearing butter across his face.

Vona leaned across the table and dabbed at his temple with a cloth. "Aye."

Too furious, he ignored her magic easing his aching muscles and exhaustion. "You cannot break into the dungeons and just pluck him out, Vona," he whispered hoarsely. *Is she driven to madness?*

"He is my father, Thomas. I cannot let him die when I can do something."

"This is foolhardy." He slapped the table, rattling the platters and bowls. "There must be another path without placing you in harm's way."

Balancing precariously, her hand still holding his chin, the other wiping his temple, she shoved her face into his. "I am doing this, and if you try to stop me, I will—"

"Endanger yourself." Wanting to shake sense into her, he gripped her hands, drawing them together. "I can come and go with ease. I can suggest to Emil he pardon a few prisoners as a sign of good will." He cupped her cheeks, fixing her gaze on his. "Give me two days—"

"You have *one* day," she said, angling her chin.

His breath caught as he drowned in her warm and inviting brown eyes. "Must you be so stubborn?"

"If 'twas *your* loved one? Would you hesitate?"

He released her. "No, but I would also have a plan instead of going in there smelling of jasmine and wearing a silk gown."

She chuckled but didn't settle on the bench again. "You think I am unarmed?" She shook her head. "Believe me, Sheriff, I carry a full arsenal."

He tilted back to study the tunic she wore. The pistols he knew of, and the dagger's hilt glimmering from her boot. He grunted. "You are easily disarmed, milady."

She snatched his hand he'd stretched out to grab another slice of bread, then pressed said hand between her cleavage. "Feel that?"

His focus narrowed on where his fingers rested. His breathing hitched. His heartbeat became erratic. Warmth passed through her tunic to him, just heat from her body, not her earth magic. When she waited expectantly, he gathered his control and twitched his fingers, pushing past the soft flesh on either side. Something hard lay beneath his touch.

With a barely concealed tremble, he pulled away. "A dagger?"

"No." She smirked at him over the rim of her cup. "Do you believe my guardian would not share her skills?" She arched a delicate brow. "I often wished it was not so, hours spent thrusting a sword or leaping over obstacles she had a hand in creating."

He ran his gaze over parts of Vona he could see, remembering what molded feminine flesh lay beneath her garments. Closing his eyes, he took as long as needed to will the images of her moonlight bath from his mind.

"Here you are. Alani is ready for you." Yrsa stepped aside when Vona strode past her. Nodding at Warric, Yrsa sat and started buttering a slice of bread.

Into the silence, broken only by Ellia pouring a cup of juice for Yrsa, Warric asked, "Vona mentioned you trained her?"

"Aye." Yrsa said no more, simply stacked cheese and ham onto the bread, folded it, then bit into it. She chewed, her gaze fixed on him. "I best ask you. What are your intentions?"

He stilled. "Why do you report on Vona, and to whom?"

Yrsa harumphed.

He opted for a change in topic. "I visit the dungeons after this task. Perhaps I will find Lord Walter."

Yrsa stared at him for a while, quietly eating her meal. She leaned back, dusted her hands, and cradled her juice. "I pray he is not there, and yet, if he is, we can do something about it."

"I hope he is not the man I need to prepare for hanging." Warric popped a date into his mouth—its sweetness intense after the ham and coffee.

"Aye. I would prefer time to plan."

He gestured to the door. "You will allow her to participate in a rescue?"

"If Lord Walter is in the dungeon, I may be able to remove blocks of stone, but I cannot dig a tunnel wide enough to walk through. Like I said, days to plan and to dig would be helpful."

"Vona can do this?" Warric frowned. "She is but proficient in earth and water."

Yrsa stiffened. "Do not underestimate her abilities, Warric."

As much as he liked hearing his name, he wanted it to fall from Vona's lips, not Yrsa's. "Then why did you train her?"

"To learn control and discipline. Two qualities helpful in any situation life will throw at her." Yrsa rested her elbows on the table and clasped her hands together. "Also to realize that magic is not the only solution." She cast a smile at the door. "Do not tell her this, but I am proud to have spent these years with her. She is an incredible woman, flawed, spirited, quick to act, and yet, I would lay down my life for her."

"Indeed." So, Vona inspired that in others besides him? Relief slumped his shoulders. Here he had thought he had lost control of his sanity. "I dine with Lord Juluan this night. He has information on Lord Walter. I could return here with whatever I have learned."

Yrsa shook her head. "We will come to you. I believe you are being monitored, Sheriff."

Warric stiffened. "By whom?"

"Grokar is not as convinced as Emil that you are what Netherbury needs. He will either find or fabricate something about you to distort."

Warric grunted. "A slimier man I have never met." Frowning, he reached into his jerkin and removed the parchment. "I stole this from Kenet when you were crushing his hand." He smirked. "My thanks, by the way." He unraveled the scroll and skimmed over its contents.

G

With the gold, I have sent further information on our shared interests. I pray it may be of some assistance. I am eager to review your progress and await the promises made.

DT

So, not a detailed list of the chest's contents.

The best time to raid the chest was when it wasn't out in the open, perhaps in Emil's treasury somewhere deep within the castle. He would have to locate the room and play thief.

"Hell's teeth," he muttered. "I should have looked at this sooner."

"I see," Yrsa said after reading it over his shoulder. "Well, if we are to restore the wealth to the people, cleaning out Emil's coffers would be a start."

He tossed the parchment into the fire before returning to the bench. "You assume the chest is there?" As had he.

"Aye, for why have a chest if it does not carry precious gems, gold, or jewelry." She shrugged then assumed her seat.

"When he discovers the gold gone, he will up the taxes and send me out to find the thief."

Vona eyed him over the rim of her cup. "Hence why we are to use this 'legend' Vona mentioned. One cannot hunt a man who does not exist."

Warric tapped his chin. "She has someone in mind?"

"Aye." Yrsa said no more.

He glared at her. "You cannot spare a clue?"

"None." She pushed off the bench.

"You must have been with her when she met with the man. Or at least overheard their conversation."

"She resents my constant vigilance, but I am sworn to." Peering down the passage, Yrsa's brow furrowed with concern. "She has to be protected, Warric. This is paramount. If the Conclave—" Yrsa snapped her mouth shut.

He tried not to react, like Yrsa fearful of the Conclave wasn't alarming enough. What could an envoy and a Sundowner fear from sentinels less powerful than her? When he next had time alone with Vona, he would reassess her. Perhaps he had missed something, too dazzled by her smile and the memory of her toned body. Most women he had lain with had been soft, malleable, their curves filling his hands and mouth. He expected, if he should ever be blessed with the chance to sample, that iron ran beneath Vona's skin. So far, her elbows were all he had touched.

Visions rose to mind of her mouth, of testing the pliancy of her lips, of sharing a breath and reaching her soul. Under Yrsa's knowing gaze too. He shifted on the bench and refilled his cup with coffee, slowly using the dipper to add honey, all in an attempt to calm his body's amorous response.

Focus on the task at hand, Warric. "I have seen what the amulet can do, Yrsa. If I was Emil, I would store it in my most guarded room."

"Lord Walter first, then Emil's wealth." She gazed down the passage again. "I have trustworthy people I can call on in Lisbay. Let them investigate what history Grokar has with the Conclave. Knowing who 'DT' is would be helpful."

"My thanks," Warric muttered around his coffee. "What do I tell Emil about the state of Devenmere?"

"Undergoing repairs, furniture and food stocks being sent from Lisbay. Not a sovereign in sight." Yrsa sighed. "She is also impetuous, but her heart is too..."

"Generous?" Warric grinned.

"Aye, and stubborn." Yrsa marched off, leaving him to his thoughts.

"Anything else to eat, Sheriff?" Ellia asked while gathering the dirty platters and plates.

"No, thank you, Ellia. This was more than I could have asked for."

The woman smiled and left him. He hesitated. Returning to the parlor to await Alani was an option or he could stay here. Or he could stroll the house? Learning the layout might be of assistance at some point. "Ellia, is Dunstan around? I would like a tour of the manor."

"Aye, sir." She bobbed a curtsey. "I shall fetch him for you."

While he waited, he mused about the upcoming dinner with Juluan. Such an alliance with a man of good rapport may go a long way to completing this task. Or so he prayed.

After a tour of the manor, its many bedrooms, Lord Walter's messy study, and the cellar lined with bottles of wine, he sauntered back to the parlor. There Alani awaited him, sipping a cup of tea with a sweetcake balanced on a knee.

He let her finish, the poor girl too skinny, and the way Ellia baked, everyone deserved to savor her food. Once again en route to Netherbury, the time passed without conversation.

When he strolled into the guardhouse, Guy, all smiles, sat behind the desk.

"What?" Warric flipped off his coat and draped it over the chair, too tired for words.

"There is talk of gold among the townsfolk."

"Talk?" Warric arched a brow.

"Drunk Yail is spending what he has in the tavern." Guy rose to his feet and crowded Warric to whisper, "Sovereigns, Sheriff."

"Not all sovereigns belong to Lady Ruvona, but aye, 'tis the first place I would check." He clenched his jaw, cursing the woman. "From where do the coins come?"

"Yail did not mention this." Guy tapped his nose. "Some secret."

"Did you at least ask him if the giver was a woman?"

Guy winced and darted for the door. "Let me do that."

Warric sank onto the chair and flipped through the roster with unseeing eyes.

Minutes later, Guy bolted in, a little breathless. "A man."

Ah, so a 'legend' appears? He shouldn't have expected anything less from Vona. Still, could she not have given smaller denominations of coin?

"You best head over to Devenmere, Guy. I cannot stand that *viper*, and you do have history with her."

Guy paled then flushed. "Aye, Sheriff."

When he trudged out, Warric hid a chuckle. What he wouldn't give to be listening in on that conversation.

FIFTEEN

WARRIC DIDN'T HEAD FOR the dungeons. He stopped outside the stables to collect Dul, who sat in a stall, polishing a saddle. Warric had to admit, his initial bias toward the orc had been rash. So far, he trusted him more than he did Guy.

"Back to the castle we go, Dul. This time to the dungeons." Warric grimaced. Death was preferable to imprisonment. Perhaps a few more men would die this day, if he could help them leave this world.

"Dung'n stink," Dul growled when he clung to the back of the wagon, careful not to touch the bolts of cloth.

"Not with me there," Warric said as he steered them toward the castle's gatehouse, ignoring Alani's stiff posture.

The portcullis was up again, although he couldn't recall if he'd ever seen it down. A groom came out to unbuckle the horse. Warric lifted Alani off the seat and strode to the nearest guard with red sashes on his sleeve. Explaining his task and showing the parchment with Emil's seal, Warric was escorted along a dark hallway, down a spiraling staircase, then into a dank room. The stench alone told him what to expect. The sickly sweetness of rotten food, the foulness of piss and shit, and the rankness of unwashed bodies assaulted his nose. Waving his hands in front of him, he expelled the fetid air, filling it with something that hinted of salt and the sea.

"Sir, this way." The guard led him deeper into the bowels of the castle. Dul followed, ducking to fit, with one hand on the stone ceiling to protect his head.

Cells led off the passage. Glances revealed mangled limbs on cots, ragged blankets, and rats running across the stone floor, un-fazed by humans.

Warric paused. "Who is in there?"

The guard shrugged. "No one. Those are cleaned cow bones. Ah, here comes the jailer."

A man, as wide as he was tall, waddled toward Warric. His tunic was stained and torn. His breeches gaped revealing far too much of him than Warric had wanted to see and would never be able to unsee.

"Collas, this is the sheriff. He has come to prepare the prisoner for execution."

"Aye. 'Tis good." Collas giggled. "You asked about my the-atrics?" He rubbed his hands with glee. "'Tis but a show. The battle is in the mind. To have victory, I need to break those barriers. This way, Sheriff." He waved a hand then skipped along the passage, over water and sewerage into a vast room. "Here be my battlefield."

Warric halted and surveyed the massive room. Stone pillars ob-scured his line of sight. Rings of iron were mounted to every side of the pillars and along the walls. To every ring, a prisoner was chained. No women were present, no children either. Warric drew in a slow breath. That was a good start.

As he meandered through the room, he spoke to each man, assessing his responses, his reasons for being there, and the state of his health. When he paused in front of a better-dressed man to the rear of the room, he glanced at Collas.

"A recent addition and quite strong." Collas grinned when he pointed to between his eyebrows, his pupils following his finger.

Lest Warric stabbed Collas in the heart, he opted for distraction and glanced at the prisoner. "Good day, sir, and who might you be?"

"Lord Walter," the man said, lifting his gaze to Warric's. Vona's eyes stared at him. The man had her nose too.

"A pleasure, milord." Warric bowed his head. "On what reason were you imprisoned?"

Walter chuckled. "Many, none criminal."

"This one is to be readied." Collas pouted. "When I have yet to break his barriers."

Warric didn't react. He schooled his features to one of boredom. "What garments must he wear? For that thing is filthy." He gestured with his boot to all of Walter.

"Garments are set aside for such an affair." Collas shrugged. "'Tis the same all must wear."

Warric curled his lip in disgust. "Fetch me these garments. I shall be the judge."

Collas hesitated. Warric wrapped his air around the man's throat. Only when he garbled an agreement did Warric release him. As soon as the jailer skipped out of the room, Warric knelt to face Walter, enshrouding them in a small dampening cloud.

"'Tis good I found you, milord. Do expect a rescue and a reunion." Warric smiled.

The man's eyes widened then a scowl formed. "Pray you mean Thack and Piers."

"'Tis likely to be this night or the next." Warric expected Vona to charge ahead with her shaky plan. "Continue to act as if these are your final days." He straightened, sucked in the shield, and folded his arms, ready to glare at Collas.

Around the corner he trundled, bearing a small pile of garments. "Here, sir," he huffed, his breathing ragged.

"A lord to be seen in the garments of a commoner?" Warric shook his head. "I shall bring him something more suitable. Prepare a hot meal and bath this evening."

"Hot?" Collas grimaced, but when Warric settled a gaze on him, Collas nodded.

"Until then, milord." Warric continued around the room, learning of each man's crimes.

Most had stolen food, too hungry to consider the consequences. Others hadn't been able to pay whatever taxes Emil had demanded. One or two had earned the right to be shut up forever, darkness in their eyes, unrepentance in their attitude. When Vona tunneled into the dungeon, she would have to release them all. He would task his men to hunt the worst two first. To leave them chained would draw interest and tie him to the escape. If Yrsa was correct, he didn't need to garner any more attention from Grokar.

'Twas best if Vona, Yrsa, and himself came disguised. Juluan too if he involved himself further. Warric would find out at dinner.

He left the dungeons. A silent Dul trailed him.

Warric glanced at him, frowning at his angry visage. "What is it?"

"Iron on ankles to stop magic. 'Tis cruel."

"Aye, but most cannot be locked up without it." Warric said no more, for Dul was correct.

It was cruel to snuff one's magic. The well within each person formed part of their souls. At the Conclave, they were chained as such, to experience the void that engulfed their minds. Deep and endless darkness had consumed Warric, like the potency of grief. Few lasted being shackled for long. Those who did became assassins.

Dul veered off to the stables while Warric headed for the guardhouse. When he strode in, Guy sat at the desk. "Good day, sir. You missed a ruckus with Sir Grokar and Kenet. Seems the man lost a parchment en route from Borfort."

Warric cursed as expected of him. "Was one of my men tasked to find it?"

"No, sir." Guy grimaced. "Kenet received twenty lashes for his incompetence. He is next door at the Clumsy Elf paying for healing." A twitch at Guy's lips said it all.

Snorting, Warric leaned against the desk. "Anything else I need to know?" Before Guy could respond, a brown bundle of fur darted across the floor and climbed Warric. He chuckled and cuddled Mud. Running behind him came Tims.

"I am sorry, sir." Tims clasped his hands behind his back, his face paling.

"For what, lad? Mud looks well-cared for." Warric stroked the kitten's head. Taking to the knee to be at eye-level with the boy, Warric dug out a coin and placed it in Tims's hand. "I dine out again, so go get yourself and Mud some food."

The lad beamed and bolted out the door.

"'Tis odd, you having a pet," Guy said, gesturing to all of Warric.

"Aye. Wait until Mud becomes too cumbersome to carry."

"Let us hope he does not insist on becoming a guard." Guy laughed. "Although, Dul will take to him right away."

"A good orc." Warric scooped Mud off and placed him on the desk. The kitten started to bat at the quill's feather. "I dine with your father this evening, Guy. Will you be joining me?"

"No." His cheeks reddened. "I have plans."

"Very well." Warric chuckled. "I thank you for not sharing them. 'Tis best I not know."

"Perhaps you should if I do not return." Guy winced while shifting the quill from one side of the desk to the other, forcing Mud to crisscross to assuage his curiosity. "She could turn me to stone."

Warric forced a light note to his voice, but he knew to whom Guy was referring. "She?" Could *she* not stay out of his conversations for once?

"I mean to apologize to Lady Ruvona for my behavior. Father says our families have been friends for far too long and that I should be the one to ask for forgiveness."

"Well, you did collect taxes on her land. Still, she should not have disregarded your authority." He offered a polite smile mastered after years of use. "I wish you luck, Guy."

"My thanks, Sheriff." Scooping Mud into his arms, Guy gave him a cuddle, realized what he'd done, and shoved him back onto the desk. "Nibbon will be on duty."

Tims scurried in, carrying a basket that smelled heavenly. Mud mewled, leaped to the floor, and trailed the laughing lad into the barracks. Warric followed to watch their interaction. He stopped in the doorway, content to rest on the frame. Mud jumped onto Tims's cot and pawed the lad who had begun to unpack the basket. He broke strips off a drumstick and fed them to Mud, choice pieces too. Right then, Warric decided to give Mud to Tims especially when the lad, while biting into bread roll, scratched Mud's head. Better yet, perhaps Dunstan had use of the boy? Somewhere out of harm's way and with daily meals?

Turning on his heel, Warric headed upstairs to change his tunic and jerkin for the one he had worn last night. At this rate, he would need more garments, something he was loathe to do when traveling required he packed light. He washed his hands and face in the water provided, then peered out the window while drying himself. Asking for another bath would be time-consuming and frowned upon. Besides, poor Guy had to contend with Vona's wrath this evening. Warric chuckled. It was best to leave the man with most of his well.

Minutes later, Warric strode to the stables and waited for Dul to saddle Serenity. The sun had begun to set on a long day. By the time Warric reached Tacourt, dinner would be served. What could Juluan reveal that Warric hadn't already learned? Perhaps the details leading to Walter's arrest? Did those matter?

Still, it was a meal he didn't have to pay for. As he rode down the main road to the bridge, he couldn't help but notice the shadow watching him leave. Grokar's spy, no doubt. How had Yrsa discovered that before Warric had? She wasn't that more powerful than a sentinel. Perhaps when she had abandoned Vona at Emil's gathering? No wonder she was entrusted with Vona's care. The woman took her responsibilities seriously.

Warric rode up to Tacourt, its windows aglow with welcoming torch light. He vaulted off Serenity and tethered him.

A man waited in the open doorway. "This way, Sheriff."

The foyer was decadent by any standard, not that Warric was allowed to linger. He was escorted into a large dining room. At one end of a twelve-seater table sat a woman and Juluan, who stood and gestured to Warric to join them.

"My apologies, Sheriff. 'Tis customary to share polite conversations in the parlor prior to dining, but alas, I am famished." Juluan waved a hand at the woman who was as blonde as him. In the flickering torch light, she glowed with youth and innocence. "This is my daughter, Nessa. Please, be seated."

Warric bowed to Nessa then took the chair on Juluan's right. Servants streamed in to serve the meal. Judging by the bowl, he would guess soup.

Fresh bread was presented for him to choose a slice or two while his bowl was filled with thick brown liquid. Thankfully, his service to the baron had more than prepared Warric as to the expected etiquette. As the evening progressed from course to course, Juluan's shoulders relaxed, and his easy smile became genuine. Whenever Guy was mentioned, it brought to mind where he was and with whom.

At last, the dinner drew to an end. Juluan ushered Warric to the drawing room after they both bid Lady Nessa goodnight.

"Brandy?" Juluan waved a crystal decanter at Warric and poured a healthy amount into a glass without waiting for a reply.

"My thanks for a lovely evening, Lord Juluan."

"But get to the reasons behind the invitation?" Juluan chuckled. "I was there the night Walter lost his mind and took Emil to task for everything. Even though he was allowed to leave the castle and return to Devenmere Manor, I expected the worst. In his study, Walter ranted about the injustice of it all, the Conclave's apparent disbelief that the Amulet of Amriel had been found, and his pleas for their help had been ignored." Juluan stared at the burnished hue of the brandy. "One would think the Conclave would send someone to verify the amulet and its abilities, yet no one arrived to do so. How can they ignore this?"

"I stole a scroll today. It mentioned information hidden in the chest that arrived from Lisbay. I may have to discover what the sender meant." Warric took a sip of the brandy and savored the fullness of its woody flavor before swallowing, then relished the burn and heat it resonated. "I found Lord Walter this afternoon, shackled to a ring like a criminal. 'Tis he Grokar and Emil wish to hang two days hence. I will need garments if you have any to spare."

"'Tis good that he is still alive." Juluan met Warric's gaze. "Have you told Vona?"

"Not yet. I plan to do so after dinner." Then hie back to the dungeons to deliver the garments. Exhaustion drained him, bowing his shoulders.

Juluan placed his unfinished brandy on a table and leaned out the drawing room's door. "Barten, I need breeches, a tunic, jerkin, and boots, but not my finest. Let us not raise questions. And saddle my horse." Juluan waved Warric over. "Come, let us tackle this united."

"All right," Warric said, though frowned at the suddenness of their departure. He downed his brandy and trailed Juluan outside. Once a horse was brought around and a bundle tied to the back of Serenity, they galloped toward Devenmere. They bypassed the Conclave Way to cut across farmland and meadows, circled a lake, and approached from the north.

It was late, but torch light glowed from Vona's window.

Juluan launched himself off his mount, looped the reins to the ring provided, then pounded on the door. Dunstan opened it and gestured to both men to enter.

Yrsa stood there, arms folded across her chest, her expression pursed as if she sucked on a lemon. "And this?"

Juluan tugged her hands into his and nudged his head at Warric. "He found Walter."

She smiled and peered around Juluan to meet Warric's gaze. When he nodded, she glanced at Dunstan. "Fetch Lady Vona." Still holding hands, Juluan and Yrsa strode into the parlor.

With an arched brow at their intimacy, Warric followed. They paused by the dying fire, whispering to each other—cheeks pinkened, nervous smiles flashed, and trembling fingers in clasped hands. What was this? It did explain Juluan's eagerness to visit Devenmere Manor when Warric could have delivered the message alone.

Vona burst into the room, straightening her tunic and stamping her boots on. Her hair cascaded down her back in wild disarray. "I thought Guy had returned." She glanced at Warric. "What news?"

"Your father is well," he said.

"You found him?" She squealed, threw herself into his arms, and hugged him. Warmth soaked into him, easing his exhaustion in an instant. When she buried her nose in the curve of his neck, he crushed her to him. Her body against his was perfection. "Thank you, Thomas."

He winced. "We have to rescue him, Vona. He is in the dungeons as you so rightly guessed."

She pulled away, her damp cheeks glowing blue for a moment. "We need him close to an outer wall."

"The dungeons are beneath the gatehouse. If you plan to tunnel in, the cover of darkness is a given, but more than this, you need the correct entry point." He cupped her face, wishing they were alone. "Southwest is best. We will need disguises. Any retrieved prisoner must not be able to identify us."

"Us?" She beamed, the warmth of her eyes calling to him.

"Aye." He stroked his thumb across her chin then released her. "Not this night for I visited there today. Tomorrow night would suit. The hanging is two-days hence." Aye, he had thieving to do this night.

She gulped. "One more day." Closing her eyes, she drew slow breaths in and out. "This is such wonderful news, Thomas. That you found him." She grabbed his hands, giving them a firm squeeze.

"Tomorrow, I shall mark the outer wall. Tunnel there, and you should come across his exact position. I would suggest we release all the prisoners to act as a diversion."

She smiled and scattered his thoughts. Strong affection filled her gaze. "You have thought this through?"

"Someone had to," he smirked. "I cannot have you charging ahead and endangering yourself again." He cast a glance at Yrsa and Juluan whispering still. Closing the distance between himself and Vona, Warric hovered his lips an inch from her ear. "After all, did you not bathe in the moonlight, give away sovereigns, and throw stone walls at my men?"

"Wait... Bathe in the moon—" She gasped, covering her mouth. "How did you know?"

"I camped on the other side of the river." He dragged her hand away to kiss the inside of her wrist, savoring the sweet silkiness of her skin. "Mud is mine. I found him in Borfort, but when he tumbled into the river, I could not save him and thus reveal my presence."

Heat poured off her. "You saw—"

"Every glorious inch of you." Meeting her gaze, he tried to convey how magnificent the sight of her bathing had been.

"Hell's teeth." Her sinful mouth parted on a groan. "Is that why you joined our party?"

He chuckled. "You stole my kitten."

Her eyes widened. She threw back her head on a husky laugh. "My apologies. How thoughtless of me."

"My thanks for saving him," Warric rasped, wishing he could kiss her.

"An hour before midnight." She dug her fingers into his waist. "That is when I will tunnel."

"Aye. Then perhaps keep your father in that hidden room you mentioned. My men and I will, no doubt, search your home."

With a furrowed brow, she met his gaze. "Perhaps you should be seen at the guardhouse and, therefore, waylay any suspicion."

He stilled, emotion swelled, fell, rose, and broke over him—hot, aching, and yearning. All at the realization that she cared for him. She had the right of it, though. He had to be seen. "Aye, 'twould be wise. It goes against all that I am to leave you to do this without me."

"What in hell's teeth is going on?" a familiar man demanded from the doorway. He slapped his hat on his thigh then handed it, along with his gloves and coat to Dunstan.

Why is General Jacut here? Had the baron sent him to aid Warric?

"We did good." Thack beamed, shoved the general aside and strode into the parlor, heading for the brandy crystal decanter.

"Aye, I shall take a healthy dollop of that," Piers called, straightening his wrinkled bright-red jerkin.

"Jacut, welcome home." Vona pulled away from Warric to kiss her brother on each cheek. "Hungry?"

"I asked a question, sister." He glowered at her with hazel eyes so not like Vona's.

Warric cast glances between the siblings. Jacut's dirty blond hair was trimmed neat—the mark of a soldier and unchanged since Warric last saw him. *Hell's teeth, they don't even share noses.*

"Baron Gregory sent me to attend to Father's disappearance, and I arrive to this?" Jacut flicked a hand at her and Yrsa then accepted the brandy Thack shoved at him.

"This is a celebration, brother," Vona gritted out, settling beside Warric. "The sheriff discovered Father's location today."

Jacut faced Warric. Not an ounce of recognition crossed his features. Warric couldn't help but be impressed. "Sheriff, what news?"

Warric bowed curtly. "Lord Walter is in the castle dungeons and is to be hanged in two days." With Jacut here, perhaps Vona's recklessness could be curbed. Warric doubted it though. If Yrsa, an envoy, had no sway... "Tell your brother your plan," he whispered to Vona.

Her eyes widened, and she shook her head.

"Vona," Warric grumbled.

"Thomas." She offered him a sweet smile.

"We will be breaking into the dungeons tomorrow night," Yrsa said to the room.

"Vona?" Jacut glared at her. "Were you ever going to tell me?"

She crossed the room to grasp his hands, sending green tendrils into him. "There? Better? Now can you please be less grumpy? Dunstan, prepare nourishment, please. Nothing requiring too much effort."

Dunstan bowed and left.

She straightened Jacut's coat as if they discussed the weather. "I will do the tunneling. Yrsa will conceal any noises from the falling rock."

Juluan splayed a hand across his chest. "I shall be there to assist in any capacity."

"I will be attempting to be otherwise occupied." Warric held up his hands in surrender.

Vona patted Jacut's chest above his heart. "We will be masked, and Thomas suggested we release all the prisoners."

"Thomas?" Jacut frowned.

"The sheriff," Piers mumbled. "I could do with some action. Sitting for days does not agree with my bowels."

Thack grumbled, "'Tis all those sweets you devour."

"Piers, as much as I would love your assistance, your bear is far too recognizable." Vona kissed him on the temple.

Warric gulped down a gasp. He'd thought Thack the morpher.

"Perhaps rest, sleep in a bed, eat your fill, and restore your strength." She tilted her head at Thack. "You too."

He waved her away. "Nonsense. I can sit a horse a little longer. Never let it be said that these bones are too frail."

She wagged a finger in Piers's face. "Fine, but my oath, if you do not control your bear, I will bury you beneath a mountain of sand."

Tugging on his collar, Piers grimaced. "Not something I wish to endure again, I assure you."

"What about me?" Jacut scowled. "You cannot expect me to *let* you do this."

"You have no choice. Father is about to be hanged. Do you have another plan?" She tapped her foot, her brow arched.

He winced. "No, not at this short notice."

"Then 'tis settled." She grinned. "You, my dear brother, need to present yourself to Lord Emil."

"If I must," he huffed. "Fine, but if you die, I will wake you so you can explain yourself to Mother. For now, I bid you all a good night." He glanced at Warric then stomped from the room.

"This complicates things," Vona muttered.

"'Tis best to follow his example and get some rest." Yrsa pulled out of Juluan's arms and ushered Vona through the door.

Despite wanting to hold her a little longer, Warric needed to meet with Jacut as the look had conveyed. Sighing, Warric faced Juluan. "Return to Tacourt until tomorrow eve. I shall circle Devenmere to ensure all is well then head to the dungeons."

"Aye. Until tomorrow." Juluan strode out the door.

Warric waited.

It wasn't long before Jacut snuck into the parlor. "On a task for the baron?" he whispered.

"Aye," Warric said.

The general squared his shoulders and clasped the pistol's grip at his hip. "Intentions with my sister?"

Warric stilled. His heart hammered in his ears. "Honorable," he rasped.

"Fair enough." Jacut pursed his lips. "Might be best to have yours and the envoy's guidance when it comes to Vona."

"You mentioned she was special. In what way?"

Jacut tapped his chin and narrowed his eyes. "I cannot divulge this. The Conclave spies are everywhere. Mother will share when you commit to a life with Vona." He gave a curt nod and left.

With his back straight, Warric marched out of Devenmere Manor, mounted Serenity, and set off for the dungeons. Hopefully, by midnight, he would see his bed for a brief hour or two.

Sixteen

"Choosing your father's garments was wise." Yrsa pushed out of the chair and circled Vona. "Looks good. Your eyes are too pretty so keep them downcast."

"Aye." Vona laughed. "You do realize that is the first time you have ever complimented me."

Yrsa snorted. "Those you do not need."

Smirking, Vona watched her in the mirror's reflection when she said, "Still lovely to hear. I bet Lord Juluan—"

"Not up for discussion," Yrsa snapped, but a peach-colored blush spread across her cheeks. "I suggest you move to your old room. Let Dunstan prepare this one for your father's return."

Vona faced Yrsa. "I assume you tasked him already?"

"Aye."

Vona pursed her lips. "Now, to test this." She marched to the door, but Yrsa blocked her. "I do not want to find out when the need is great that this disguise fools no one. If Thomas, who knows me best in Netherbury, cannot see me behind the scarf, then it will work." She smiled. "Besides, we need to share the gold he stole."

"I can whisper anything you need to convey. He is an air-gifted sentinel, after all."

Vona tapped her foot, her hands on her hips. "How do you know no one else is?"

When Yrsa had nothing more to say, Vona ventured a quick trip via Father's hidden room to fetch the bag Thomas had stolen.

Yrsa trailed Vona to the stables, her scowl saying it all. Without further protestations, they rode toward Netherbury. As they neared, Vona slowed Honey to a canter. "We approach from the road. You vault me onto the roof, and I shall enter through the uppermost window."

"Adding architecture and the most common designs to your studies, in hindsight, was unwise," Yrsa muttered. "In this case, the sheriff's bedroom closest to the tower will help us in this silliness."

Vona grinned, threw her head back and laughed. "I do love you, Yrsa-my-guardian."

"Right now, lass, I do not feel any affection for you." Yrsa glared ahead.

Vona chuckled but said no more, circling Netherbury along the shadows to pause outside the church. She slipped through the door while Yrsa waited, silencing both horses.

"Friar?" Vona whispered.

"Ah, Robbin, a sight for sore eyes." The old man scurried toward her, nimble on his bent legs.

"I have come to bless our Lord's people." She slipped the coin across to him.

"You are truly a miracle, Robbin."

"I merely do what I can, Friar." She ducked through the door, closed it quietly, and mounted Honey. "That went well," she whispered to Yrsa. Her vigilant guardian muttered something about 'luck not being the same as skill.'

Minutes later, they drew up to the outer wall of the guardhouse. Once in position, Vona dismounted and handed Honey's reins to Yrsa.

"I still think this is foolhardy," Yrsa grumbled, peering up the wooden walls of the guardhouse, to the roof two levels higher.

Vona snapped, then softened her tone, not wanting to sound like her mother. "We went over this. Unless you can guarantee no one will hear your whispers, this is the only way."

"What message is so important that it requires this much effort?" Yrsa swirled her arms in great round movements, then without another word, floated Vona to the roof.

She instinctively scrambled for something to cling to, realized it was futile, then calmed the blinding panic blurring her vision, and in time to step onto the roof. Glancing at Yrsa's upturned face, she flashed a smile as if to say how easy that was. Yrsa's frown darkened before she scanned the surroundings. An envoy behind the guardhouse would rouse curiosity. "Do hurry," she said, then headed to a copse of trees to wait.

Vona's heart thumped in her ears, and a fine sweat coated her temple. A cool breeze calmed her as she tiptoed across a narrow rafter. Such obstacles had formed part of her training, this one no less daunting so high up. Although, not once had Yrsa floated her anywhere.

When Vona was younger, prior to the Conclave testing her gifts, she'd dreamed of flying on clouds of air. Alas, useless earth and water were hers to use. She doubted she could summon a puff of anything. Rounding the corner, she caught the ledge and swung into Thomas's room, landing on her feet just as he pressed a dagger to her throat.

She gasped, froze, and swallowed, her skin prickling when the cold blade scraped her. "I bring a message from Lady Ruvona," she gruffed her voice, praying he'd believe her ruse. With his arm heavy across her chest, she acknowledged how silly this plan was. He wasn't an idiot, no matter how much she'd enjoyed calling him an imbecile.

The dagger disappeared, and his face appeared, bathed in the moonlight spilling through the window. The silvery light didn't stop there. It illuminated parts of him: those mesmerizing eyes, the defined arch of his nose, the right side of his mouth and chin, and pooled over his bare chest. Muscles rippled as he moved. Lord help her if her gaze didn't trail the dark hair to his breeches. Hell's teeth, he was breathtaking. She raised her hand to discover if his chest hair was as fine as those dusting his arm. Thankfully, she realized her intentions before touching him, then to compensate, checked that her scarf was in place.

"What, pray tell, does milady have to share at this hour?" He stepped into shadow, granting Vona a little breathing room.

She fell into a 'relaxed' stance—one she had practiced in the mirror. That meant thrusting her hip to the side and hitching her thumbs in the low-hung belt.

"This is a test. The lady needs a way to communicate with you without anyone seeing or hearing," she said hoarsely, her throat beginning to sting then burn when her magic rushed to heal her. "She was most adamant I venture here this eve."

He growled. "Why must she interfere?" His eyes narrowed as he ran his gaze over her.

She tried not to twitch or freeze, tried to keep her shoulders relaxed and humor in her eyes. The slightest change could shatter her disguise.

"Never mind, I will discuss this with your mistress." He caught her shoulder when she turned to leave. "Who will be dispensing? You?"

"Name's Robbin, and I have taken care of it."

He grinned. "Did Vona come up with that?" Without waiting for a response, he gave her his broad back to swirl his hands at the door. "I need assistance breaking into Emil's most guarded room. Think you can handle it?"

She blinked at him, then nodded, not trusting her voice. Excitement swept through her, squeezing her throat and trapping the joy inside her.

When he waited, she mumbled, "When?"

"The room is in the northern tower. I would prefer we do so soonest, as in this night."

She stilled at the urgency. "What do you seek?"

"A letter in a chest with information from Lisbay. It might reveal a wider plot than we had anticipated."

Yrsa was not going to like this change in plans. Still, if doing this convinced Thomas Robbin was an ally... "You know for certain it will be there?"

He shrugged those broad shoulders of his. "If not, there is still Emil's gold he keeps in that same room."

She frowned. "You speak to me freely, sir. How do you know I am trustworthy?"

"If Lady Ruvona trusts you, lad, then so do I. Besides, Yrsa would have killed you before your first deception."

Vona winced. *So, Yrsa's approval matters more than mine?* "Aye." She gestured to the window. "I shall meet you outside the tower's outer wall."

"We go together. As in now."

Shit. Not that she needed to tell Yrsa what was happening when she listened. Her concern was Thomas spotting Yrsa and realizing who Robbin was, never mind Honey he might recognize as Vona's horse.

"I have no mount, sir." She dipped her chin to her chest as if she was ashamed of such a thing.

"We need a wagon, lad." His voice muffled when he pulled on a tunic then a jerkin. Pistols slid into the holsters on his belt, powered by his magic. His hair swept up, tying itself at the nape of his neck. He sat on his bed to yank his boots on. The sight of his toes brought to mind the time he'd sat beside her on the riverbank, linking her longing for freedom to choices.

As she looked back on the past few days, any decision she had made had led to this moment. Yrsa no longer strangled Vona's freedom. Thack and Piers had agreed to fetch Jacut on her behalf. Jacut himself hadn't waylaid her plan. Now all she had to deal with was her...mother.

Without warning, Vona floated out of the room, landing, with a squelch, boots first in the mud. Thomas dropped beside her and skirted the shadows to the tavern where someone had abandoned their wagon. He merged with the darkness, so much so, she struggled to see him to follow.

She hesitated alongside the wagon, used to having someone assist her. When Thomas clambered in, she did the same, trying to find unfamiliar footholds. She settled on the seat, out of breath for an able 'lad.' At a flick of the reins, the wagon lurched forward. He held the strips of leather firmly in his hands. She shivered and forced herself to face ahead.

Her breath hitched.

Two Netherbury castle guards paused on their stroll into town. One palmed his pistol. Another held out a hand, fire flickering to life.

Beside her, Thomas stiffened. Hell's teeth, would blood stain her hands at the end of this evening? *Think.* Drowning them in sand or pelting them with rocks would work for a few minutes but not solve this dilemma. Her heart fluttered in her chest while her ears rang with deafening silence.

"Who goes there?" the guard demanded.

She flung her arm around Thomas's shoulder as best she could and burst into slurred song.

"The bonny lass was naught but sass,
With curls of fire and eyes of green,
Her coffers were full, her tongue crass,
For a coin, her sweet treasure to be seen."

Thomas flicked a glance at her, and for a second, she waited, watched, not sure what he would do. He hiccupped, then in that husky voice of his, he sang,

"'Twas but a moonless night,
When she stole my heart.

And aft I took flight,

The wench'd taken me gold."

The guard chuckled and snuffed his flames. "Leave 'em be, Maz. They but be drunkards on their way home."

"An unlikely pair," his friend muttered but holstered his pistol.

As they rode past, unhindered, she clung to Thomas, not daring to peek.

He shrugged her arm off. "You can release me now, Robbin."

She did and the breath she'd been holding. "That was close. Me, they would'na recognize, but you, sirrah, are memorable."

He jerked to the side then scoffed. "I blend in, dear boy."

She almost laughed at that but managed to swallow it. The man was tall, dark, and handsome. Sure, he blended in. "Without your gift of darkness, you stand out like a sore thumb."

After that, any guard or drunk on the road let them pass without a by-your-leave, and as they traversed on any sort of soil, she smoothed their tracks with a little earth magic. When they crossed the bridge, she glanced both ways, hoping to appear as if she checked for travelers. Instead, she searched for Yrsa. There was no sign of her or the two horses. Vona allowed her shoulders to slump in relief. Thomas not seeing through her disguise was a good start, but that didn't guarantee there wouldn't be hell to pay later.

Hell's teeth. This might end badly for her. Yrsa might use this as an example of why neither of them should leave Devenmere...ever again.

"This way," he whispered. The horse's hooves and the wheels on stone or mud made no sound. He pulled on the reins and urged the wagon to a slow halt. Three or four levels of a stone tower loomed over them.

Vona swallowed. The guardhouse had been high enough. Here, there was no window. Just a dangerously steep roof, then nothing below.

"I will lift you to the edge of the roof. Grab onto it and shimmy around to the window."

"Shimmy?" she squeaked then cleared her throat.

"Do not be afraid, Robbin. I will not let harm befall you." His gaze was sincere, setting her heart aflutter.

"I am not *scared*, sir." She puffed out her chest.

He smirked, then with a swirl of his hands, hoisted her skyward. This time, she managed to not scramble for air holds...much. When he plonked her onto the roof, she slid off. Nothing halted her descent. Screaming was out, so she bit her tongue and prayed he was a man of his word. When she didn't fall to her death, she peeked with one eye, then flicked both open. He held her there, her face in line with the roof's edge. She gripped it, digging her fingers into the shingles. Not sure when he'd remove his magic, she inched along the edges as fast as she could. Every few feet, she twisted to glance down, hoping to find some sort of opening.

In the silence of the night, when a shadow fell across her, the air in her chest seized. Thomas hovered beside her, scaring the hell out of her. Her heartbeat thudded in her ears. Worse, as if he generated a gust, it whipped past her, threatening to steal her hat and reveal her identity. She yelped, smashed the hat in place, while hanging by one hand.

"Just a little farther," he said.

She glared at him, waited for the breeze to calm, then released the hat to shimmy along. The window was above the wall walk where a guard patrolled. With a flick of her hips, she swung her body. Her toes hooked on the ledge. For a second, she hung there like an idiot.

Thomas tutted and opened the window with his air-magic. She pulled herself through, tumbled and landed on bags of coins. She scrambled to her feet, righting her hat and scarf just as Thomas floated into the room.

"You could have done all this without me," she grumbled, dusting off her breeches. "Or I could have waited in the wagon." She folded her arms across her chest. "Or were you planning on tossing the bags willy-nilly and us spending the evening searching for them?"

He paused, then flicked bags through the window, zinging them away. "You in the wagon would accomplish what?" He hitched a thumb at the wall walk. "I need a lookout. Just in case."

"Of what?"

"In case I do not hear them approach." He grinned. "It can happen, even if 'tis most unlikely." Once he'd cleared a path to the door, he flung open a chest set in front of it. More bags flew out the window as he emptied the chest. In each hand, he grasped parchments. "This one is for your mistress." He handed a scroll to her.

Her breathing froze, and she, inch by inch, unrolled it.

SEVENTEEN

ROBBIN TOSSED WARRIC THE last bag of coins which he sent to the 'x' he'd placed on the bed of the wagon. He chuckled, liking the lad's sense of humor. Spend the evening searching for the bags? He was correct that he hadn't been needed, but a true test of trust was to place the person in a trying situation. Where had Vona found this lad?

Darkness and air aided their stealing, something Warric had done before, but for a cause. He frowned, praying this wouldn't jeopardize the baron's task, but he could justify it as thwarting Emil's madness. After all, he was distributing the wealth to the people of Netherbury and finding out what was in that chest.

Well, not him. Robbin.

Warric patted his jerkin, the parchment secure. The information was gold promised, allies lined up, and the supposed locations of Baron Gregory for the next week.

Robbin had snatched Lord Walter's will, upon which was scrawled, "Where is the Devenmere deed?" The lad had snorted. "The idiot does not realize Devenmere belongs to Lady Ailith and not Lord Walter. Killing him would have granted Emil nothing but 'worthless' artifacts."

Odd that the lad knew this about a new acquaintance. Unless, he'd known Vona for longer? Warric pursed his lips, his instincts prickling.

Staring at the Amulet of Amriel at the bottom of the chest, he hesitated to take it. From the moment Emil had demonstrated its power, Warric had confiscated it. Now, he hesitated. Gold? Emil could tax or ask his allies for more. The letter was damming but not enough to start a manhunt for the thieves. The loss of the amulet would, though. He was tired despite Vona healing his earlier exhaustion. Certainly not up to hying all over the countryside for something in his possession.

Still, having it would thwart Emil and please the baron.

Before closing the lid, he ran his hand along the sides and the bottom, searching for hidden compartments. His fingertips snagged on a fine crack. He flicked out a dagger and wiggled the blade in the crack until a small door popped open. Inside sat another parchment, folded to the size of his palm. He opened it and stared with wide eyes at the message.

AD is being difficult. While I deal with that, my men have infiltrated GK's closest ranks. 'Tis a matter of time until he dies. I have also discussed with the Conclave the ongoing war and its drain on our coffers. I pray, soon, we will know peace and freedom. I trust that you are handling our combined problems?

DT.

Sliding the note into his pocket, Warric took the time to run his finger along the seam to hide his presence. With a last glance at the amulet, he strode deeper into the locked and guarded room, all while silencing their movements.

Whispering outside the door had him sidling closer to the young man whose face remained hidden behind the scarf. He had pretty eyes though, sure to charm the girls of his acquaintance.

"Ready to be lowered?" he asked.

"Aye," Robbin chuckled, darting to the window ledge to climb onto it. "Once on the ground, I shall take the wagon to the church." He peered out, studying the sky, the ground below, then faced Warric. "That is, if you do not mind the walk?"

"Be vigilant," Warric said as something scraped along the door.

Robbin touched his temple with two fingers in a familiar salute. "Until the Fates see fit to cross our paths."

Warric jerked back. His eyes widened before he could hide his shock. The lad could be spending much time around Vona to learn her mannerisms, but he doubted it. Running his gaze over the scuffed boots, breeches, narrow hips, and loose tunic, he settled on the hat and scarf hiding the lad's identity. No hair curled against his collar, and aye, his eyes and eyebrows were too feminine. The scent of Jasmine did linger in the air.

Come to think of it, when she'd touched him during their bawdy singing, his perpetual exhaustion had eased.

"Hell's teeth," he growled, leaning out the window to lower *Vona* to the ground.

How had he been so easily duped? He an assassin, a master of deception, manipulation, and intrigue? He'd seen exactly what she'd wanted him to—Robbin, the lad she had chosen to deliver the coin to the people. Pacing across the room now empty of gold, he tried to calm his breathing. It *was* possible he was wrong. Short of stripping the hat and scarf off and possibly exposing an innocent in this? No, he would go to the source, to Vona herself.

Just as a key slid into the door's lock, he swirled air and darkness around him. He launched himself skyward then took the time to conceal their presence where he could while "guards, guards," sounded. During the wagon ride to the castle, not once had he sensed her using her magic to sweep away the wagon wheel's tracks. How had a proficient hidden that from him?

If Robbin was Vona, it would take time to deliver the bags to the church. He had planned to await her in her bedroom. Instead, he veered south, aiming for the church steeple, in case something happened en route. Had it been Robbin the lad, then Warric would have trusted him to handle whatever obstacles arose, but leaving Vona unguarded didn't sit well with him.

It was a good decision to make, for not minutes later, aggravated male voices snagged his gaze.

"I tell you, 'tis the same wagon," Maz, the castle guard, said. "Oy, you, state your business."

Warric clenched his jaw. He couldn't descend to assist her, not when they would recognize him. He could hide his face, but she was correct as to the rest of him. Nor could he choke the two men for they would surely report such an event. He'd used the same skill on Guy. It wouldn't be hard for the young man to leap to the conclusion of Warric's involvement.

Nor did they deserve to die for being vigilant.

No, he had to let Vona handle this on her own, for the most part. Casting darkness across their vision and smothering their voices might help. No sooner did he do so, a rock struck Maz on the temple. He collapsed, sprawling at the feet of his friend. Before Warric could engulf the other man in shadow, he gaped, glancing between Vona and his unconscious companion.

When she vaulted off the wagon, pistols drawn, Warric swallowed a curse.

The guard swiped his eyes, trying to clear his vision and missed seeing the barrage of rocks flying toward him. He stumbled back when a few hit him. Drawing his sword, he swung it wild, where he must have remembered she stood.

She gasped, leaping to the side with astonishing agility, but not soon enough. The blade sliced across her temple. She cupped the wound, then pulled her hand back to look at the blood smeared across her palm. With a deep breath, she threw out her arms, green swirling around her. Massive rocks hovered off the ground, spun around the guard, then stacked tightly together, entombing all of him except his face. While cursing her, he jerked his head side-to-side but couldn't budge the wall she'd formed around him. She stomped toward him, shoved her face an inch from his, and rasped, "the name's Robbin, sirrah, and you have made an enemy of me."

Turning away from him, she didn't watch as one of her rocks knocked him out. Without another word, she climbed into the wagon and continued through the town as if nothing had happened.

Tension burned between Warric's shoulders and didn't ease until he stepped onto the roof to wait as she gave the wooden door of the church a faint knock.

The friar crept out, sweeping a gaze south then north. "Robbin?" he whispered.

"Another...gift, Friar Flynn," she said in a roughened voice. "Best to dispense it all immediately. I have word that Lord Emil will be most upset."

Warric clenched his jaw, planning on giving her such a tongue lashing *if* what he suspected was true.

He felt...used, kept in the dark, not trusted. It grated.

"You have been injured. Come..." The friar gestured inside the church. "...Inside. Let me tend to it."

"Not to worry, Friar." She patted his arm then hitched a thumb at the wagon behind her. "Do you need assistance?"

The friar opened the door wider, and a few men and women spilled out of the church into the night. Warric summoned his magic, ready to kill if need be. No one bothered her. Within minutes, the wagon was emptied.

"Bless your heart, Robbin," the friar whispered.

With two fingers to her temple, she steered the wagon to the tavern, a slight shimmer of green on the wheels. No wonder Warric hadn't seen her cast her magic. She did it so well that there was no way he could've known, unless he was looking for it. After returning the wagon, she jumped off and faded into the shadows.

He trailed her across the bridge and meadow to a shadowed copse of trees where two horses were tethered. Out of the shadows emerged Yrsa. Heat burned in Warric's core when both riders turned east, avoiding the Conclave Way, but heading in Devenmere's direction.

He curled his hands into fists with the urge to wring Vona's neck and lambaste Yrsa for her lack of control. Both knew his stance on Vona's safety, and this recklessness, this involving him in endangering her? Anger barreled up his chest, his throat throbbing with unsaid words he ached to roar at them both.

He was patient while they settled their horses in the stables, even more so when Vona swept off the scarf and hat then creeped into Devenmere Manor. Braids tumbled free, and a backward glance gave him a glimpse of a familiar stubborn chin.

"At last," Yrsa growled while gripping Vona's chin to assess the healed wound. Only a smear of blood remained. With a huff, she released her and faced ahead. "This...was not what I agreed to, Vona. I could not guard you. Anything could have happened. What would I say to your mother?" Yrsa sucked in a deep breath. "It went well?"

"Aye." Vona grinned. "Thomas and I emptied Emil's coffers, now in Friar Flynn's hands."

Yrsa said, her tone that of amazement, "I cannot believe the sheriff did not doubt your disguise."

Vona's response was slow to come. "He must have accepted what he saw?"

"Perhaps," Yrsa said. "I bid you good night." Fading footsteps implied she had turned in.

On the morrow, he would have a talk with her too about allowing her charge to be this foolhardy, about not including him in this ruse.

Right then, with the pain crushing his chest, he realized why he was so furious. Why deceive him? Aye, he would've protested Vona being in harm's way, but he hoped he would've at least listened to the plan before rejecting it. Circling the manor, he hovered outside her window, but when the door didn't open, he frowned. Tilting his head, he listened, followed her steps while hovering from one window to another. She had moved bedrooms, one where the moonlight didn't venture deep.

He allowed his magic to reveal her movements with full visibility. After tossing the hat and scarf onto a tallboy, she stripped off her boyish garments, draping them over the chair. Each item removed sank a nail into the coffin of her duplicity. Despite that she stood there naked, every inch of her beauty on display, he couldn't assuage the hurt her actions had inflicted.

Leaning over a bowl of water, she washed and dried her face, peered at her reflection in the mirror, then pulled on the same transparent nightgown from the other night. Without a care in Sagua, she slid between the sheets.

He shifted forward to grip the edges of the window, staring at her while fighting for calm. Words burned the tip of his tongue. What would he say first? Resting his forehead on the cool glass, he tried to see this from her perspective. She may have had a reason to hide this from him. Not one he could think of but possible.

Opening the window on silenced hinges, he floated in, stepping with care when he landed. He crossed to the chair and fingered the tunic, still warm from her body. As he rounded the bed, his gaze fixed on her face, the way her hair spilled across the pillow, the rise and fall of her chest with each breath. Emotions swelled within him like a crescendo—musical instruments discordant at the start then merging into the sweetest harmony. Longing inflamed his heart. He brushed a curl off her temple.

In an instant, she sat up, a dagger at his throat.

"Hell's teeth," she muttered, flicked the blade away then slipped it under the pillow.

He balanced on the edge of the bed to cup her cheeks, burying his fingers in her hair, and forcing her to meet his gaze. "Explain, *Robbin*."

Beneath his palms, her skin warmed.

"We decided on a 'legend,' Thomas. I did not have the heart to endanger anyone. Besides, what I did was not *that* dangerous." She placed her hands over his. "Stealing all of Emil's wealth has made this disguise redundant for now."

Did she think this was a children's game? A chance to risk her life *and* his for a bit of fun? He wasn't sure he believed her, that Robbin would be no more. Her pulse was erratic under his pinky. Her breathing ragged. The heat from her cheeks on his palms also gave her away.

He clenched his jaw. Could she be lying to him even now? His feelings for her jumbled his intuition, muted his instincts, and cast his control to the winds.

"Thomas," she said, her voice a caress.

He shivered, hating that name but didn't move or release her. "I do not know whether to believe you, Vona."

She twitched, her eyes widening. How had she deceived him so easily when she never masked her tells?

"Your erratic heartbeat implies you lie." To show her, he tapped her neck to the rhythm of her heart.

"Um," she glanced to the side then met his gaze, "you are on my bed *touching* me."

He jerked back, withdrew his hands and took hers with. Before she could pull away, he rested a thumb on each palm, stroking her soft skin.

Her breath hitched, proving she reacted to him. Her eyelids fluttered shut, and she tilted her head back on a sigh. Her mouth, his weakness, parted. Rising, he leaned over her, descending slowly, savoring each moment, until he brushed his lips across hers.

She blinked at him then dipped her gaze to his mouth. When she brought up her hands, he assumed she'd push him away. Instead, she slid her fingers up his chest to cup his neck, then she tugged him down to press her lips to his. He groaned, gripped her hips, and sank into the kiss. She buried her fingers in his hair, stroking his ears in passing. His thoughts spiraled and narrowed on her in his arms, on her jasmine fragrance, on the honeyed sweetness of her lips. Gathering her against him, he delved in, conquering her mouth as he'd longed to do since her moonlit swim.

Heat swept through him, tingling across his skin. He growled then crushed her to him, needing more, aching for her touch. This moment, now, here, would forever remain a cherished memory, but he couldn't rob her of her innocence, not when she would gasp, 'Thomas.' *When* she experienced her first orgasm, he wanted his true name to tumble from her.

Pulling away, he lingered, sipping at her lips while squeezing and releasing her hips. To touch another part of her would be hazardous. "No more Robbin?"

She nodded. "I promise."

With everything he could muster, he sauntered across her room to the window and slipped out. It may have looked like he vanished after closing the window and glancing one last time at her, but he didn't. Instead, he summoned his shadows and rested his forehead on the stone wall of the manor, relishing the cool rough texture while he wrangled his breathing into something normal. Parts of him throbbed, demanding he return, to ease the ache. For this, her magic couldn't heal him.

Eighteen

Galloping horses woke Warric, the sky touching dawn. Two hours sleep was all he'd had. Scrubbing his face with his hands, he resisted the urge to lie down again and let them 'awaken' him. That left him vulnerable and unprepared. Neither position he liked to find himself in. This task had become as tedious as he'd anticipated, but denying Gregory was something Warric couldn't do. He pulled on a tunic and sat there in his braies. What he would like, in that instance, was time away, with no care in the world except what to eat for dinner. Clenching his teeth, he donned his breeches then boots, followed by his jerkin, all while he tasked his magic to buckle on a belt and tie up his hair. He met the heavy tread on the stairwell, peering down at Emil's guards.

"What is it?" he demanded, despite knowing full well why they had come.

The first guard hesitated then stuttered, "Lord Emil requires your immediate attendance."

"Very well." Warric gestured to them to leave then took his time down the stairs and into the main room of the guardhouse. His sleepy eyed men gathered, their weapons in hand. Nibbon gaped. Loaan and Iwen tightened their hands on their pistol grips. All watched Warric, waiting for a signal, as if pitting the town guards against those from the castle was commonplace.

"At ease, men. Lord Emil has summoned me. 'Tis nothing to be concerned about, so head to your beds and continue with your tasks should I not return for breakfast."

They nodded but didn't lower their weapons. When Warric stepped onto the muddy, cobbled road, Dul towered over the four horses he petted. Emil's guards halted, half reaching for their pistols or swords.

"Be this about wagon?" Dul asked, stomping toward Warric in his usual gait.

Warric's heart leaped. They had been spotted, that he knew, but not identified. Could Dul have seen it all? "What wagon, Dul?"

"I wake to wooden wheels. Clackity clack." Dul cupped his ears.

Mm, perhaps when Vona had returned the wagon? *Good.* So, he hadn't seen Warric or Vona. "At what time?"

"Past moon." Dul pointed to the sky.

"My thanks." Warric smiled at him while thumping him on his upper arm, the highest he could reach.

Dul beamed then chose a castle guard's horse, offering Warric the reins. He mounted and trotted to the castle, expecting Emil to be waiting for him in the hall. Not the red-faced, unkempt man standing in the courtyard, yelling like a tavernkeeper's wife.

"At last." Emil faced him, his shadow Grokar behind him. "Where were you, *Sheriff?*"

As disinterested as Warric was, he didn't need this nonsense. While he dismounted, he studied the guards lingering around the courtyard. At Emil's feet sat a chest, similar to the one Warric had emptied last night.

"In the guardhouse, milord," Warric said.

Emil glanced at his men he'd sent to escort Warric.

"It was as he says, milord," a man stated then dipped his head in a show of respect.

As if he didn't believe the man, Emil huffed before facing Warric. "Some*one* snuck past my *useless* guards and entered *my* treasury. All but this," he touched the amulet hanging around his neck, "was taken."

"Baron Gregory's funding is gone, Sheriff," Grokar added.

Warric scowled. "Why leave jewelry behind?"

"Jewelry?" Grokar jerked back as if Warric had slapped him. "This... This is the Amulet of Amriel. You have seen what it can do."

Warric blinked at him. "To a thief, 'tis a worthless trinket." He ignored Grokar's gape. "No one *saw* anything?"

When the guards shuffled on their feet, Warric snapped his fingers at one who chanced to meet his gaze. "Search around the castle wall for tracks." He doubted the guard would find any trace, but it looked good if Warric took charge. Selecting two more guards, he hitched a thumb at Netherbury. "Head to the tavern. Question folks. Someone must have *seen* something." Meeting Grokar's gaze, he said, "Please, show me the treasury."

Dutifully, he followed Emil and Grokar. Step-by-step they climbed the tower stairs, slower due to Emil's bad health and an unfit Grokar, both wheezing the higher they traveled. When they moved aside to grant Warric access, he kept a frown in place as if he investigated a serious matter. First, he analyzed the solid metal door, stroking the untampered lock a few times before striding to the window. There on the stone was a clump of mud he'd missed.

"They entered through here. Big men too." He studied the stone floor lined with circular dust marks where the mountain of bags had sat. "Odd that your men did not see them leave with the coin." He peered out the window at the wall walk where a guard patrolled, not once glancing up.

Emil joined Warric. "Could they have gone over the roof?"

Warric leaned out and twisted to look up. "'Tis steep. Not sure where they could hold onto."

"Perhaps it was one of our guards assisting the thieves?" Grokar asked while wringing his hands.

His concern was too much for just gold. Warric narrowed his eyes on the weasel. "What of worth was stolen? Gold? Gems?"

"Gold and a note." Emil glared at Warric. "That is sufficient for concern."

While Emil shouted to the guard on the wall walk to pay attention, Grokar sidled closer to Warric to whisper, "Lord Emil was awaiting a special...letter from someone of great importance. He did not have the opportunity to remove it when the chest arrived." His smile showed blackened teeth from too much black root. "Not your problem, of course."

So, Grokar is hiding the secret letter? Perhaps Kenet's scroll wasn't intended for Emil? Warric didn't peek at Emil but kept his focus on Grokar, on his tells and finger twitches. "Parchment is harder to find. The thief could burn or soak it. 'Tis not as traceable as coin spent at a tavern." Perhaps Emil knew not what his adviser was up to.

"All this started when that...that Sundowner came to Netherbury." Spittle formed on Emil's bottom lip while he swung his arm in Devenmere's direction.

"Without evidence, I cannot storm Lady Ruvona's manor." Warric curled his lip for affect. "That viper will stone me for the audacity."

Grokar cackled. "She is but proficient—"

"You will do as I command, Sheriff. Search the tavern, the inn, every stall, all estates on the outskirts of Netherbury...and....and the guardhouse too."

Warric fake-blustered. "My men would never—"

"My watchtower, as well." Emil's red face twisted into a monstrous glower as he roared, "find my gold."

Warric bowed and stormed to the watchtower. He gathered what men loitered, giving them a look if they hesitated.

"Captain Ollar will not like this," a man grumbled. A jagged scar curved around his chin, dimpling the skin.

Warric halted and faced him. "Where is this captain?" Not once had he met the man, nor had anyone mentioned him.

The scarred man paled. "He's... He—"

"Spends his days in the tavern, sir." A young man stepped forward, his hand gripping the pistol holstered to his hip. "Name's Mita, that's Petran." He gestured to the scarred man. "I assume we search for the thieves."

"Aye. To merge you with my men means none can blame the other. Whoever stole the gold knew what they were doing."

"Sir," a sweat-drenched blond man jogged toward him. He paused, bent over, and gagged. "No...tracks," he gasped.

Warric pursed his lips as if this was dire news. "Who hates Emil enough to bring the law down upon their heads?" He studied each man's eyes, searching for tells. "Why did none of you hear anything? Patrols are in place."

"Perhaps the baron?" Petran whispered, bowing his shoulders.

"Mm," Warric hummed. "Do they hate each other, the two Kenningthain brothers?"

"No," an older man rasped, his voice like coarse stone. "Name's Nolan, sir. I was here when the baron took over from his father—God rest his soul. Baron Gregory, as the elder, was a studious lad but skilled with pistol and blade. 'Twas his younger brother who hated him, his success, and popularity. My lord would not steal from anyone, let alone kin."

"Indeed," Warric said. "The baron would have taken the amulet, not left it behind." He gazed at the castle, glad he'd listened to instinct or his exhaustion. The missing amulet would have cast suspicion on Gregory.

"'Tis a shame, if you do not mind me saying so, sir." Nolan cleared his throat. "That thing is pure evil."

"Aye, but as men who serve, as long as we keep ourselves honorable, our consciences are clear." Warric gestured to them to follow him to the guardhouse. There, he split the men into teams of two, tasking them to search the town and neighboring villages. Only Nolan remained. "You are with me." Warric strode to the door. "Have a problem with orcs?" He paused and glanced over his shoulder at the man nursing his left leg.

Nolan faltered, then squared his shoulders. "Aye, in my youth, but Dul is a decent male."

"Regardless, we need him." Warric headed for the stables. As he stepped inside, he met Nolan's gaze, offering a lip curl laced with disdain. "I pray a Sundowner cannot lift him, and Lady Devenmere will not bury him alive."

"Ah, that sweet lass?" Nolan chuckled. "Her heart's too pure to hurt Dul."

"You know the viper?" Warric scowled for good measure.

"In my youth." Nolan shrugged then peered at the castle. "Her father too."

"Let us pray she is in a good mood," Warric muttered, then gestured to Dul to saddle three horses. Within minutes, they crossed the bridge, heading east to Devenmere. Vona better be ready for this.

Orv woke Vona at the crack of dawn, humming a tavern song she shouldn't know. While wearing a silly smile, she caught its hovering mass and hugged it. Thomas had kissed her. Sure, he had seen through Robbin's disguise, and she should have expected that from him, the Sheriff of Netherbury.

"Is that necessary?" Orv harumphed.

"Where have you been?" She released it.

It shot away and bounced around her. "You said I needed to face my shyness. Dunstan has been a wonderful guide."

"Truly? I am so proud of you." She swiped at it, trying to catch it for another hug. It swerved while squealing, dodging her in mild panic. She chuckled and climbed out of bed. Strolling across the wooden floor to the window, she gazed at the lake. A bath would be lovely.

Not that her mother would let such a man as Thomas woo Vona, never mind wed her.

She huffed. Marriage? After one kiss?

"Oh, good, you are up." Yrsa burst through the door. Orv dove for the bed, hiding under the covers. So much for facing its fears. Not that Yrsa tolerated it much. "Come, Vona, your mother has arrived."

"What?" Vona squeaked, her heart sinking. She pressed her temple to the cool window. "Did you ask her to come?"

"No, Jacut spoke to her, and of course, with your father still missing, she was too concerned not to make the journey."

"She will not like the plan to free Father." Vona grimaced. Her brother, the traitor. "So like Jacut."

"As long as I am with you, I do not foresee an issue."

Flicking a disbelieving glance at her guardian, Vona hurried to don breeches and a tunic. Stamping on the boots, she rushed out the door while Yrsa air-braided Vona's hair. When she entered the parlor, her mother sat on the edge of a chair, her back ramrod. Not an expression crossed her face.

"I do not tolerate disobedience, Ruvona." She clasped her hands on her lap. "Sending Piers and Thack to do a task I assigned to *you*? I am…disappointed." Her gaze settled on Yrsa and didn't budge. "Step outside, Ruvona. I need to speak to Yrsa alone."

Vona opened her mouth to complain, but Yrsa shook her head. Slumping, she left the parlor but plastered her ear to the door.

"Do I need to request a replacement?" Fury dripped from Mother's tongue. "I thought we had an understanding."

"When she was a child, strangling her freedom made sense." Yrsa sounded unfazed by the reprimand. "We have trained and educated her. Do you expect her to never use those skills?"

"May I remind you, Yrsa, we do not yet know what triggers the…madness."

"What madness?" Vona whispered.

"I did not spend all these years hunting a cure for her to lose her life to a wayward pistol shot." Mother clipped her words, but all Vona could focus on was 'cure.' Was she dying or did she have a sickness healers couldn't eradicate? "Now, let us discuss Walter. What do you know?"

"He is in the castle's dungeons. We will rescue him this evening."

"We?" Mother barked.

"Aye. Ailith, he is to be hanged in the morning."

Never had Vona heard Yrsa use Mother's name. In the silence that followed, she understood the sense of urgency doing so brought to the conversation.

"Truly?" A swish of skirts implied her mother paced the room. "Have you appealed to Lord Emil—?"

"No, Lord Juluan is adamant there is no mercy in Emil's heart."

"I see." Mother exhaled. "A rescue it must be. What is the plan?"

"Vona will burrow a tunnel. I will silence where needed, and together, we will remove the stone wall a block at a time. Lord Juluan has involved himself. Thack and Piers too."

"Good." Warmth filled Mother's voice. "And Jacut?"

"He will present himself to Emil. I suggest you join him."

Mother gasped. "Why? I could better assist—"

"You will take charge, and in this instance, Vona must succeed on her own."

"Yrsa," Mother hissed. "I—"

"'Tis done, decided. Your part is to draw attention and suspicion away from the rescue. Understood?"

Mother grumbled, "I do not like your tone."

"You cannot protect her anymore, milady. Vona will wed and move away. What then?"

"Hence why I hoped she would fall for one of the men I chose for her." Mother's swishing skirts resumed. "All are weaklings, but they are malleable. Also, they were willing to live...at Bennedor."

Vona scowled. Remain in her mother's house forever? She would rather die.

"'Tis time to trust what we have taught her, milady."

Mother's groan was most unladylike. "Walter warned me this day would come. I hoped...that I would be ready." She sniffed. "I am not."

"She will need to be told. Her suitor too."

"Truly?" The swishing skirts halted. "None of the signs have manifested, Yrsa. We could have been wrong all these years."

Yrsa's response was slow to come. "No, the discernment was correct. I have...sensed it."

"What suitor?" Mother's voice was high-pitched with alarm.

"Would you require breakfast, milady?" Dunstan standing beside Vona snapped her back straight. She tried not to blush at being caught eavesdropping.

"That would be lovely." Dragging her feet, she trailed him to the dining room.

A side table groaned under a mountain of food. Despite the early hour, Thack and Piers were elbows deep into their eggs and sausages. In one corner of the navy wallpapered room stood her brother, talking to a disc. A mechanical clock clicked the seconds, adding a comforting hum to the ambiance. Not this morning. The whir, grind, and tick sent a shiver down her spine.

"Good morning, Vona." Thack patted the chair beside him with one hand, while the other held a leg of roasted pork.

Obedient for now, she settled beside him. With a polite smile pasted on, she nodded or shook her head when Dunstan offered her juice or coffee.

"What has you so quiet?" Piers peered across the twelve-seater table, his fingers shining with oily residue.

"Do not fret about this night. No harm will befall you." Thack glanced at her while biting into the pork.

She dipped her chin to her chest. Thomas had said the same thing. Why did everyone feel the need to protect her? Did someone want her dead?

"No, of course not," Thack said around a mouthful, wiping his hand on a cloth to squeeze her shoulder.

She stilled, having not realized she'd asked aloud. "I heard Mother mention a cure, signs, and other such nonsense. It has me..." She chewed on the inside of her cheek. "What do you think she and Yrsa are hiding from me?"

Neither of the men would meet her gaze. *So, they know.* Sadness settled over her heart like a wet and cold blanket.

Pushing out of her chair, she rose, then hesitated. Splaying her hands on the dark wood table, she dipped to snag Piers's gaze. "Who will tell me?"

"'Tis not our secret to share, sweetheart," Thack said.

"How long have they hidden something from me?" She smacked the table. "You can tell me that, at least."

Piers swallowed, glanced at Jacut, then shook his head.

Jacut knows too?

Tears burned at the back of her eyes. *How dare they.* She stormed out of the dining room and the manor. Anywhere was better than here.

Standing hip deep, fully clothed in the lake, she spent an hour forming and shattering globes of water. Mother strolled to the shore and watched her. Yrsa would have been preferable.

"Come, Vona, sit with me." Mother gestured to a fallen tree, tried to dust it off, then sat anyway.

Vona didn't want to talk to her mother, but if it got her answers, perhaps even *the* secret, then she would play along. She waded out of the lake, dried her clothing, then settled next to her mother.

"I...may not have been the mother you wanted." Tears glimmered in her eyes. "I am the mother you needed."

Vona gritted her teeth. "Yrsa is more of a mother than you are."

Her mother winced. "Aye. When 'tis time, you will understand—"

"Now, now is the time." Vona slapped her thigh.

Her mother shook her head. "I need Walter with me. 'Tis for us...to divulge."

Vona scowled. A reunion with Father was a day away. "But—"

"Milady, there are guards demanding access to Devenmere. They mean to search it." Dunstan stood on the path, wringing his hands.

"For what purpose?" Mother demanded, then leaped to her feet. She hesitated, cast a glance at Vona, and said, "we shall resume this discussion tomorrow."

Slumping, Vona trailed her, expecting the guards to be led by Thomas. He'd warned her of such, that Emil's men would be searching for the gold. She prayed the friar had emptied the bags last night. Touching her hair, she frowned. The same braids she had worn since she was a girl fell down her back. The urge to chop off the mass called to her, but now wasn't the time. She released a breath with a whoosh, squared her shoulders, and summoned a sharp tongue.

She stomped around the corner of the house, hardening her expression. With her mother here, the anger, frustration, and resignation simmered on the surface of her emotions.

"What is the meaning of this, Sheriff Imbecile?" she demanded, striding toward him.

Mother squeaked, faced Vona, and gritted out, "a lady—"

"I do not venture here by choice, Lady Viper." Thomas rested an elbow on his pommel, and in the morning light, he was the glorious image of virile male—the broad shoulders and brow, the angular jaw, those lips she knew to be soft, and that piercing blue gaze.

She smothered a fission of heat and pushed past her gaping mother. Yrsa strode through the front door, Thack, Piers, and Jacut behind her. Dunstan followed, a broom in hand as if he'd been caught sweeping. As a child, she'd seen what he could do with a 'stick.'

"State your business, Sheriff," Yrsa said, spreading her legs in a battle-ready stance.

"Shit," Piers cursed and started unbuttoning his jerkin while toeing off his boots. "I just made this," he muttered. "Here, hold my cap." He shoved the purple monstrosity at Dunstan, who stared at the thing now in his palm.

"Morphing is not necessary." Thomas held up his palm. "Lord Emil has commanded me and his men to search all holdings, villages, shops, and towers. Gold was stolen from his treasury last night."

"You believe it to be here?" Vona rested her hands on her hips.

"I must search, milady." He vaulted off his mount, striding toward her as if to throttle her. His glower almost had her taking a step back.

Yrsa bristled.

Mother rested a hand on Yrsa's shoulder before standing between Vona and Thomas. "By all means, Sheriff, search. You will find none of Lord Emil's gold here."

"Thank you, milady." Thomas gestured to the older man still mounted. "Nolan, search the east of the manor. Dul, check the stables. I shall search what remains." He faced Mother and bowed his head. "Lady Ailith, welcome to Netherbury." He held up a finger, waiting until Nolan disappeared into the manor then he threw out his hands. A wind whipped Vona's braids back. Still wearing a tense expression, he said, "Emil's in a panic. 'Tis a good thing we did not take the amulet, Vona."

Mother twisted to glare at Vona. "What did you do?"

"Cripple Emil, milady. Without gold, he cannot pay his guards or fund this insane quest to ruin the Conclave." Thomas frowned. "Please forgive my angry visage. I have dampened sound but cannot pretend to be jovial when one glance from Nolan will raise suspicion."

Mother stomped her foot and spun on Yrsa. "Much you did not reveal to me."

Yrsa shrugged. "Consider that my final mistake, Ailith. Once Lord Walter is secure, I shall return to my beloved mountains." She gazed east, her eyes glistening.

Vona froze then stepped closer to Yrsa. "I might travel with you."

"You will not," Mother snapped.

Vona crowded her mother, peering down her nose at her. "Your hold over me vanishes when Yrsa leaves." Giving her mother the cold shoulder, Vona grabbed Thomas's hand and healed the shadows beneath his eyes.

He squeezed her fingers. The subtle gesture snatched her breath. Without a word, she returned to the manor and the breakfast she'd so readily abandoned.

NINETEEN

"WALK WITH ME, SHERIFF." Lady Ailith gestured to the manor. "'Tis best you do your search and leave."

Warric hesitated, dragging his gaze from the door Vona had left through. "Thank you, milady."

In silence, she escorted him from room to room. He flipped through a book, lifted a trinket, peeked behind a mirror, all token searches. When they stepped into Lord Walter's library, Yrsa waited, a few sovereigns in her palm.

"Take these. Returning with nothing from a rich holding will reflect poorly on you. I have had no news from the baron."

"The baron?" Lady Ailith scowled.

"My true lord." Warric accepted the coins from Yrsa and slid them into his jerkin. "Are you prepared for this night?"

"Aye." Yrsa glanced down the passage. "Much is dependent on our success."

"Jacut and I will be dining with that...fool," Lady Ailith muttered. "Against my better judgment."

"I understand your frustration, milady. I too will be visible and thus blameless." He tugged his jerkin down, his fingers twitching for action.

What if he did help this evening? What if his name was linked to freeing the prisoners? Warmth flooded his belly. Aye, he could do so much. Be there for...Vona. He stiffened. No, he swore to give his all in service to the baron. One pair of lovely eyes...and breasts, could not change his vow.

He opened his mouth to blurt out his intentions, then snapped it shut. After the way Vona had reacted to her mother, revealing his affections would not be wise. Besides, Lord Walter was the focus. Warric prayed Vona didn't lose her father in the coming days.

He stroked his chest where his grandmother's ring hung from a chain. It had been decades since he'd thought of her. When she gave him to the Conclave, he didn't have fond memories of that day the Sundowners stormed their tiny hut. Years later, before he'd begun his service to the baron, he'd found what remained of their home. As frail as she was, she hadn't lived past his tenth birthday. No one had let him know she'd died.

Her gnarled fingers had trembled when she'd slipped a simple gold band into his palm. It was all she had left from his grandfather and something she had not once considered selling to buy wood or food.

"This way, Sheriff." Lady Ailith gestured to the door. From bedroom to bedroom, they moved, until they marched into the dining room. His nose had twitched. His stomach had growled on cue.

"Breakfast?" Vona hitched a thumb behind her at the overladen side table. Thack had a mountain of food on his plate. Piers was adding teaspoons of honey to his tea. Jacut waved at the chair beside him.

Warric hesitated. "I should not intrude."

"By all means, Sheriff," Dunstan said, entering the room while carrying a fresh platter of bacon pies. "Ellia is feeding Dul and Nolan in the kitchen."

Warric accepted the plate Thack handed him. With eagerness, he approached the side table, leaning toward the bacon pies because of how well Ellia baked.

"Coffee?" Dunstan asked, a pot in hand.

Warric nodded, settled into his chair, and placed his filled plate on the table. When he glanced up, he paused. Opposite him sat Vona, her elbows on the table, a cup cradled in her hands. She said nothing, but it was enough for him to gaze upon her. This woman, with her naked beauty and strong will had swept aside the walls surrounding his heart.

Jacut cleared his throat, dragging Warric from his thoughts. "I have spoken to the baron and informed him of the situation with my father. He is not pleased."

"I pray something can be done before tomorrow morning," Warric managed around a mouthful of fluffy scrambled eggs. He resisted the urge to glance at Vona. "My thanks for the welcome." He gestured to the room. "I anticipated the worst."

Vona jerked back. "Why? You warned me this would come."

"True, still, our ruse has to be maintained."

"Aye." She lowered the cup. "Where to after Devenmere?"

"Tacourt, of course. The other holdings are without company. I shall ride past them to be sure." He winced, halved a strip of bacon and popped a piece into his mouth. Chaos, that's what this had become. Who knew what his and Emil's men would find? After all, the friar must have handed out the gold last night. Most would have spent it already. The unwise few would have held onto their coin.

Today would try his honor, for no man, woman, or child should die over this lunacy. He could not allow it. With the way Emil had behaved this morning, madness lay on the horizon. His stomach twisted and throbbed. He pushed aside his half-eaten meal and nursed his coffee after adding an extra dollop of cream.

"An hour before midnight?" he asked, slicing a glance at Vona and straying no further.

"As agreed."

He dipped his head. "I shall ensure the wall is marked."

"'Tis not necessary, Sheriff," Thack said between licking his fingers. "I know the layout of the castle and its dungeons."

Warric offered a smile. "Good. Then I shall see you all tomorrow morning at the hanging?"

Lady Ailith squeaked, "Why?"

"If we arrive to witness Lord Walter's hanging, you sobbing and pleading with Lord Emil, Jacut bargaining, then he will not think we played a role in his escape." Yrsa tore into a sausage, her eyes twinkling.

Lady Ailith's lips twitched. "Sobbing and pleading, you say?"

Vona grinned. "Aye, it should be your best performance."

Thack slapped his greasy palm on his thigh. "I look forward to Emil's expression when no Walter is led to the gallows."

"Indeed," Warric chuckled. "This morning, his face had turned crimson. Grokar is a concern, though. I stole Captain Kenet's letter, along with the hidden one in the chest. It seems Grokar is up to something and Emil his pawn."

"What did the letter say?" Piers bit into a sweetcake.

Warric rattled off the gist of it, and ended with, "If only I knew who 'DT' was. I might need to travel to Lisbay to investigate."

"Mm, a 'DT' in the Conclave?" Lady Ailith tapped her chin then splayed her fingers on the table. "No one comes to mind, and I am familiar with most with sufficient power."

"The why is my concern." Yrsa held a half-eaten sausage in each hand. "What does this 'DT' stand to gain? I spoke to Lord Sundowner Uldane and he too had no thoughts on this man's identity."

"I shall call him later. Perhaps our two heads together might jar our memories." Lady Ailith pushed off the table, forcing every man to rise. She gestured to them to sit. "I will not say it was a pleasure to meet you, Sheriff. Intriguing, though." With that said, she sashayed out of the dining hall.

Warric stayed standing. "Thank you for the meal. I should finish Emil's task. May the fates bless your mission this night." He smiled at Vona and left before he said something stupid about not doing something foolish that would endanger her life. She was about to break into a dungeon. How much more in danger could she be?

After a trip to the kitchen, a chatting Dul and Nolan trailed him to their horses. Serenity whinnied a greeting. Taken a moment to breathe, Warric stroked Serenity's forelock while gazing at the manor's façade. Something pressed on him, like his instincts were warning him to duck, to fight, to run. His skin prickled as his senses swept over him.

He mounted, gathered the reins, then steered his horse north-west to Tacourt. Juluan would participate tonight, along with Thack, Piers, and Yrsa. Vona would be fine.

"Sheriff," she called, striding around the fountain. "I shall come to you should I hear any rumors." She glanced at Nolan and Dul, then at the clear sky. "It might be at an unsavory hour."

Warric nodded as if she brought him valuable information when she meant she planned to visit him after the prisoners were freed. "Whatever time, Lady Ruvona, I am grateful for the assistance."

"See, not a viper at all," Nolan muttered as they cantered away.

A trip to Tacourt was fruitless. Warric hadn't expected otherwise. When Lady Nessa heard Lady Ailith had arrived, from Warric's mouth, no less, she pestered Lord Juluan to escort her to Devenmere. A day spent in the sunlight, enjoying a picnic alongside the lake, was what Warric dreamed of doing. Perhaps one day soon. First, he had to win over Lady Ailith. She hadn't taken to him as well as he'd hoped.

Passed holdings they rode. The shutters in the windows, undisturbed dirt at the doors, and empty stables said no one used the manors as hide-outs. Why would anyone return to Netherbury? He had no doubt that news of its deterioration had reached Lisbay and the Conclave. He scowled and steered his party to town. The coins Yrsa had given him should convince Emil the Devenmeres had nothing to do with the theft.

When they crossed the bridge, the wailing and sheer chaos stiffened his spine. Before him, in the center of the town, men, women, and children were gathered. Worse, his men and Emil's corralled them like chattel.

Warric leaped out of the saddle before Serenity had drawn to a halt. "What is the meaning of this?" He caught his horse's reins and patted his neck, calming him.

"Each had a coin on their person," Petran said, waving his pistol across the crowd.

Warric cursed under his breath. As he had feared... If the friar had only hidden the gold for a few days, these people would not be in this position. "Did they say who gave it to them?"

"Robbin," a few cried out.

"We did not steal our lord's gold. I swear." From amid the smudged faces, the friar emerged.

"A man of the cloth? Petran, are you insane?" Warric strode through the crowd to stand in front of Friar Flynn. "Do my men speak the truth, Friar?"

"I do not know this Robbin. I do know these are honest folk."

"Lady Devenmere gave us sovereigns, Sheriff," a tall man said. "That is what your men found on us."

Warric scanned the crowd. "That was days ago. You did not spend it?"

Chins dipped, revealing their deception.

"Take them to the dungeons." He could do nothing else. They need only endure a few hours until Vona released them that night.

They begged for mercy. A few attempted to break free and run. When his men took the tall man down, Warric hurried to intercept.

"Do not harm a hair on their heads. 'Tis not for our consciences to bear." Warric met each man's gaze. "Inform Collas of that too. I will not tolerate undue torture. These people are to be tried in accordance with our laws. I will see justice done."

Iwen straightened, and with a gentler hand, lifted the tall man to his feet.

Warric marched alongside the procession, not looking forward to speaking with Emil or Grokar. Word of this must have reached their ears, for both waited in the outer keep.

"Well done, Sheriff." Emil pointed to the ground. "How much?"

One by one, his men came forward, dumping a bag or two.

Emil's eyes bulged. "That is all?" he roared.

"Aye, for most have left Netherbury, milord," Guy said. "The butcher and tanner have abandoned the town. A few food stalls, as well."

Emil shook his fists at the sky, as if he cursed the Fates. "Taken my gold and fled? Did they say who gave it to them?" He glared at Guy. "You cannot have me believe peasants thwarted my well-trained guards."

"No, milord." Guy shifted from foot to foot. "There is talk of a lad named Robbin."

"A lad?" Emil squeaked. "Is that not worse than a peasant?"

"What does this lad look like?" Grokar asked the gathering.

"Aye, anyone who reveals this is spared the dungeons and a hanging." Emil offered a kind smile and spread his arms wide in a welcoming gesture. "After all, you did not betray my trust, venture into my home, and steal from me. Someone else did. How could you have known the coin was stolen?"

"'Twas dark, milord." An elderly man hobbled forward, bowing as best he could. "He was well-armed, though: two pistols holstered to his hips, daggers at his thighs. He wore a mask covering the bottom half of his face. Dark brows I did see."

Emil's face mottled red. "So, nothing?" With a backhand, he slapped the older man, sending him to the ground. The poor man's blood was striking against his pale cheek.

The crowd quietened.

"Ask the friar," someone called out and was swiftly hushed.

"Ah, Friar Flynn." Emil flicked his fingers at him.

The friar waddled across to the elderly man, helped him to stand, then ushered him to the crowd. "Aye, milord, I did see this Robbin." The friar faced Emil and Grokar. "'Tis as Old Gamis said. A wide-brimmed hat hid the lad's features."

"You took gold from a stranger?"

The friar's eyes widened, then his great belly bounced as he guffawed. "My lord, when the need is there, people will take gold from the devil himself."

Warric held his breath. Gamis had been slapped for telling the truth. What would Emil do to the friar for laughing?

Emil pursed his lips. "Aye, true, and for your mirth in the face of my sorrow, you shall be hanged second." He pointed at Warric. "Take them to the dungeons, Sheriff. I want them all hanged tomorrow. Spare no one."

"But...the children, milord." Warric hesitated. "We cannot tax them, sire, if they are not earning gold."

"Tax?" Emil spat. "They have stolen from me. What do I care for taxes?"

Warric clenched his jaw then nudged his head at his men to escort the prisoners to the dungeon. Instead of trailing them, planning on warning Collas himself, he paused. "Milord, none of the holdings bore fruit. Lady Ailith and Sir Jacut wish to present themselves to you at your earliest convenience. I did gather this from Devenmere." He was loathe to hand over more ill-gotten gains, but to be found with sovereigns in his pocket would not go well for him. "These were from Lady Ailith herself." Warric handed the coin to Emil.

"Lady Ailith?" He smiled. "A beautiful woman—petite, demure, and the perfect lady."

"Her daughter must take after Lord Walter," Grokar cackled.

Emil chuckled. "Still, no less beautiful. Aye, she and her son may dine with me this evening. Send word, Grokar."

"Thank you, milord." Warric bowed his head and ventured to the dungeons, praying he wasn't summoned back. He wanted to ensure none were abused and that Lord Walter was where he'd left him.

TWENTY

Vona prayed the message she tried to convey to Thomas was understood by him alone. She hoped to share with him how well the rescue had gone. With Yrsa beside her, it was destined to be a success.

When Vona returned to the manor, her mother awaited her. "The sheriff?" She arched a judgmental brow.

"What about him?" Vona refused to rise to the bait. Whatever her mother wanted to say, she could get on with it.

"The man is not of high standing."

"So? Do I need a man a heavy wind could blow over? One obsessed with his cravat, flopping hair, or fine horseflesh? Aye, I see the appeal of a *malleable* man." Vona swiveled on a heel and strode into the parlor to pour a decent splash of Brederburg brandy.

"Ladies do not drink at this hour, Ruvona," her mother snapped.

Vona met her gaze and downed the burnished liquid. "When said lady has you for a mother, then aye, I shall drink whenever I have need to."

Mother jerked back. "What has gotten into you?"

"As in? This is the most you have spoken to me in over a year. I do not know you. I care not to." Vona faced her with a refilled glass, acting complacent when she was far from it. Her heart fluttered in her chest, threatening to break free from her ribcage. "A few days ago, you showed your opinion of me. Untrustworthy, weak, a...burden is all I am to you. Shall I continue?" She sipped the brandy, savoring the delicious warmth from her throat to her belly. It fueled her ire and loosened her tongue.

Her mother frowned. "I... That is not... You are still a child."

"Am I?" Vona cupped a breast through her tunic. "Aye."

Mother recoiled. "And vulgar."

"Mm, not that I would imply Yrsa behaved in an unladylike manner, but as my guardian, she has been the only influence as decreed by you. How I turn out rests on your shoulders alone."

Mother gasped and sank onto the closest chair. "It does not."

"Aye. I do not share your morals, sense of honor, or humor, for that matter. I care for none of your passions or dreams. Hell, Mother, I do not know your favorite color. I doubt you know mine."

Into the silence, Mother whispered, "When you were young, it was the blue-green of the ocean. You saw a painting of the Somerta Sea and fell in love with the color."

Vona's breath caught. Tears pressed at the back of her eyes. "Aye, 'tis still my favorite."

"You like brandy over wine and tea instead of coffee. You prefer chess to cards. Love jasmine above all other scents. You used to steal Jacut's sweetcakes when he was not looking, even though you do not have a sweet tooth." Mother smiled. "You would do so just to tweak him." She sniffed and glanced at her clasped hands. "I am not ready for you to be your own woman. At home, I could keep you safe." She stood, leveled her gaze on Vona, then slumped her shoulders. "When Walter is home and well, you may leave with Yrsa. Travel the world as we have." She wagged a finger. "You call often."

Vona froze, disbelieving her ears. "You...mean it?"

"Lady Ruvona, Lady Nessa has arrived." Dunstan bowed at the door. "Lord Juluan has accompanied her. I have notified Yrsa."

"Yrsa?" Mother glanced between Dunstan and Vona.

"Aye." Vona grinned. She squeezed her mother's hands and skipped from the parlor. "Nessa," she called. "Come, to the lake we go."

Nessa laughed and crushed the fabric of her skirts with her hands. "I am too old to—"

"Nonsense. Let us enjoy this beautiful day as we once did." Vona looped an arm through Nessa's, and with a nod to Juluan, escorted her oldest friend along the path to the stables. A glance over her shoulder confirmed they were alone. "You will not believe this, Ness. Mother just gave me permission to travel without her."

"With Yrsa?"

Vona beamed. So many times she had ranted at the restrictions Yrsa's presence placed on her. Nessa had a right to mention it, but her dear friend knew not Vona's change of heart. "Aye, that I do not mind. Not anymore."

"What of the sheriff?"

Vona's steps faltered. "I have hopes. If nothing comes of it, then I shall see the world."

"I envy you, Vona." Nessa lowered her gaze to her slippered feet, somehow remaining unsoiled. "I have no suitor or plans for my future."

"Then come with me," Vona said, dancing around her while twirling her on the spot.

Ness squealed and dismissed Vona's suggestion with a flick of her wrist. "My father would not—"

"If Yrsa is with me, then perhaps your father will be, as well."

Nessa's eyes widened. "Aye."

Vona tilted her head. "We could swim in all the waters of Sagua. Write a book on our adventures. Which fish bite. What lakes are too cold, seas too warm. What brilliant sunrises and sunsets await those blessed to view them." She released Nessa to spin with her arms outstretched, the forest, lake, and meadows blurring past her.

"We could visit all the markets, return with fine silks and sackcloth." Ness giggled. "How different the breads will taste from Osiree to Thariq."

"Father once ate the smelliest fruit. It stank so bad he thought it spoiled." Vona formed a ball with her hands. "A deep purple skin, thick and rubbery, but beneath it, the nectar of the heavens." She faced the lake, admiring the beauty of the mirrored surface. Her father was locked in a dungeon, eating gruel. She shivered. They would have shackled him in iron, the bastards. Curling her fingers, she vowed she would do everything within her power to free him. She gritted her teeth. Just let Emil and his amulet try and stop her.

"Vona?" Nessa paused beside her. "Are you well? You do not seem yourself."

"I worry, Ness. What if tonight—"

"Father says you cannot fail." Ness threw an arm across Vona's shoulders for a side-hug. "As does everyone else. Why would Thack, Piers, and Yrsa come with you if they did not believe you could do this?"

Vona snorted and cast her a glance. "To protect me from myself?"

Ness chuckled. "Perhaps. I am a weak novitiate, but if Father would have allowed it, Vona, I would be there for you."

Tears prickled. Vona gasped and hugged Ness. "Thank you, but he is right. 'Tis not safe for you. I have my daggers, pistols, and magic."

"Aye, so I shall keep a vigil by torch light." Ness swept out an arm. "Are we going to swim or not?" She flicked a button at her throat, gaping the delicate silk of her fitted tunic.

Vona laughed and tugged off her boots, tossing them over her shoulder, one by one. "What a brilliant idea, Lady Nessa."

"'TIS ONE THING TO drown falling sand with silence and easy enough to do with Yrsa with us, but anyone could peer over the parapet and spot our horses." Vona rested her hands on her hips as the time drew near.

The dining room table was laden with an assortment of weapons, some handcrafted if she eyed Thack's selection. She had no doubt they were lethal, or worse, if she handled them, she might lose a finger. Not that she had the time to ask him about them either.

"What we need is a thunder-only storm," Piers croaked before biting into a sugar cookie. "The kind in legends."

Vona grinned. "Aye, but alas, no empyrean is among us." She glanced at her pistols, polished and glimmering in the torch light. When no one spoke, she met the gazes around the table. "No ideas? We make do with what talents we have. I shall mask our tracks."

"I could lead the horses to the nearest outcrop of trees, then join you by foot." Juluan captured Yrsa's hand and cradled it to his chest.

"Or we head first to the forest, tether the horses to the trees, and as one, approach the wall," Vona said. "Once I have crafted the tunnel, we will rush in and free as many as we can." Excitement swamped her chest with warm tingles. She drew in a calming breath.

Thack wiggled an antique lock pick. "Without magic, 'twill take some time."

"While you work on the shackles, I shall guard the inside entrance leading from the outer keep." Piers slapped his stained thigh. Old breeches and a tunic were his garments, along with a pair of ragged boots. "I shall not morph unless I have to, Vona." He winked, though she wasn't sure it was meant to put her at ease.

"I shall send out a dampening shield. Still, urge the prisoners to whisper." Yrsa frowned. "I may be an envoy, but no one's well is bottomless. Let us conserve mine as much as possible."

"Aye," Thack growled. "We might need your magic to escape."

"Cover your faces and wear hats. Roughen your voices so no one can recognize you. I will not lose one of you this night." Mother met everyone's gazes. "Vona, take care. If your father cannot be saved, come home. I...have petitioned the Conclave." She wrung her hands. "Had hoped to hear from them by now. Uldane said he would do everything in his power."

Thack huffed. "When the man was your ex-beau? When Walter dying would free you to wed again?"

Mother's cheeks flushed. "'Twas many years ago, Thackeray, and you know it. Uldane has been a steadfast friend to the Devenmeres and not once given us...*me* reason to doubt his loyalty."

Old suitor, was he? Vona arched a brow. Mother was right, though. Not once had Vona seen him behave in a more affectionate manner. Since Father welcomed the man into their home at Bennedor, that put paid to any lingering animosity between them.

"Mother and I will behave above reproach." Jacut tapped his dagger on his thigh. "Except for when Mother pleads for mercy."

She smiled, a darkness in her hazel eyes. "Emil's days as Lord of Netherbury are numbered."

"Aye, aye," Thack called, lifting his goblet of brandy.

Piers waved a cookie, scattering crumbs everywhere.

"Dunstan has saddled the horses." Vona holstered her pistols, sheathed the daggers, and grabbed the hat her mother offered her.

Under her mother's critical perusal, Vona patted her chest where a small pistol nestled in her cleavage. The memory of Thomas's hand there, his fingers pressing into her breasts, summoned a blush she would have a hard time explaining. Before she could dip her chin or spin on a heel to leave, Jacut yanked her into a bear hug, crushing the air out of her lungs.

"Take care, sister," he gruffed, then shoved her back as if touching her was offensive.

Mother laughed, tears shimmering in her eyes, then with a sniff, she glared at Yrsa.

"Aye," the envoy muttered.

One by one, they marched out of the dining room to the fountain. Dunstan and the new stable boy Tims, with Mud balanced on his shoulder, held the reins. Kit would be staying behind, a donkey as a mount was too noticeable. Piers grumbled then squeaked when Thack tossed him onto Baston. The poor man scrambled to hold onto any part of the saddle he could reach.

Without a backward glance, Vona followed Thack northeast, around the lake, the northern side of Tacourt and Netherbury to approach the castle wall from the west. The clouds thickened, blocking out the moon and its revealing light. *Please rain.* Along the route, she watched the skies, the bolts of lilac-blue lightning, the murmur promising thunder. Her heart fluttered. She smiled and angled her face to the cooling breeze sweeping across the land. It carried the sweetness of rain and the muskiness of soil. She inhaled deeply, held her breath, then released it on a hum.

Thunder rumbled closer. Lightning illuminated patches of stone, sky, and ground. A few drops splattered off the leaves and bark. One landed on her nose and dribbled off, trailing a path of blue and warmth. God had blessed their endeavor. She beamed.

About ten feet into the dead trees, they dismounted in silence as they'd traveled. Thack led the way, running along the edge of the forest until he broke away and bolted across the field. Despite being nimble for one of his age and girth, he still clanked as he ran.

A cursing Yrsa thrust out an arm. Their footsteps quietened, as did Thack's discordant tools and creations, along with his heavy breathing. He pressed himself to the stone wall, rapping his knuckles on random spots while shuffling from side-to-side. Short of gaping at him, Vona plastered herself to the now damp wall a good distance from Thack's crab-like antics. Piers settled beside her. Juluan and Yrsa took position on the opposite of a scowling Thack.

"'Twas here. I swear it, lass." As he spoke, a stone wobbled. He spun, shoved his ass out, and wiggled the block free. Inside was a cloth-covered object which he pocketed. He beamed at Vona. "Behind this is the dungeon."

She tugged off her boots, took five long steps away from the wall, then faced the castle. Damp dirt clung to her bare toes. Magic was there, but faint. She frowned. Whipping out a dagger, she plunged it into the soil to form a patch of exposed ground. She splayed her fingers into the hole and hummed when green light curled around her hand. As soon as she sank her feet into the sand, she drew on her well, closed her eyes, and envisioned a tunnel forming.

Details mattered—the darkness of the clumped soil, earth worms and beetles crawling free, networked branches and roots merging like lace and tapestries, and iridescent mushrooms adding light. With her fingers, she mimicked dragging the sand and rock behind her. Wind and magic, smelling of earth, life, and decay, toyed with her braids and hat. A comforting roar filled her ears, like she was submerged in the lake. Time was meaningless. Only the vision mattered. Scorching heat traveled up her legs, blooming in her core until her cheeks and eyes stung. Darkness had merged with earth magic. Weaker in darkness, she accepted its power filling her well. What else could she do? Desperate for relief, she summoned water, moaning when it pooled around her.

"Shit," Piers muttered.

Without peeking, she smirked and flung her hands out, sending the rivulets into the tunnel's walls to create damp, dark mud. With a muted hum, she sang encouragement to the roots to bolster their growth. Opening her eyes, she chuckled while admiring her handywork. The tunnel dipped steeply to the sand-caked stone wall at least ten feet down. The latticed branches curved around her, and as she waited, mushrooms shoved their caps through and bloomed, glowing a pretty green.

When she lowered her arms, the makeshift walls shuddered.

"No," she sobbed, throwing out her hands and magic. *This is not part of the plan.*

She was to slip inside and save Father. Not stand outside to support the wall. Tears spilled free, but she bit her lip and rolled her shoulders, fighting the agony building in her spine. Now wasn't the time to fall apart. Father needed her. With her fingers splayed, she ventured closer to the castle wall. Everyone trailed her. Lifting her trembling arm high, she supported the tunnel's weight while flicking a forefinger at the mortar between each stone, sending it floating through the air to pile on one side.

Yrsa settled beside her and whisked the blocks out, placing them with care to keep their stacking order. Piers kneeled and tossed out a ball of fire. Yrsa sent it deeper into the exposed room cast in shadow.

"What?" Thack peered through the hole in the wall. He glanced over his shoulder, his mouth parted. "A hidden treasure trove Emil knows nothing of? For had he known, the room would be empty."

Vona peeped, half-focused on holding up the wall. Her arm throbbed and tingled, growing heavier as strength drained from her. She pulled more from her well, risking drawing too much. Heat barreled up her legs, her knees spasming. As fast as the magic was replenished, she used it. Using her body like a conduit could only last so long.

A glimpse of the hidden vault revealed gold sovereigns spilling from gaping chests. Suits of armor, vases, mirrors, jewelry, golden plates, and weapons filled every inch of space.

Without another word, Yrsa returned the blocks to hide the untold abundance and loosened the stones above.

The stench of unwashed bodies hit Vona first. She winced and tucked her nose down, preferring to inhale her familiar sweat. Yrsa squeezed through the hole first, then silence fell—no coughing, moaning, gasps, or cries of delight reached Vona. Thack, Piers, and Juluan followed Yrsa, leaving Vona alone. Her tears flowed at having been denied the chance to see her father's surprised and delighted expression or hug him. She rubbed a cheek across a shoulder, her arms thrumming with agony, fire, and exhaustion. Lowering them wasn't an option when it would trap everyone inside the dungeon.

Time ticked on until one by one prisoners streamed past her. They cast her glances, brushed reverent fingers over her shoulders, touched her hat, but none removed the handkerchief covering her face. She focused her gaze on the tunnel's roof, fighting for strength while draining what little magic remained in the soil. Only trickles soaked into her, no longer the flood of power she'd initially endured.

"Yrsa," she croaked. Every muscle in her body was taut, straining, and burning. With her well depleted, she couldn't heal herself and didn't know how much longer she could hold the tunnel up. When Thack stepped through the hole, relief flooded Vona. She peered around him, Piers, Juluan, then Yrsa, searching for her father. When

Yrsa began rebuilding the wall, the bottom of Vona's stomach fell out. A darkness consumed her.

"Lass, he is not there." Thack rested a hand on her shoulder.

"What?" she squeaked. "No, no, Thomas said—" *He would not lie to me, would he?* She shook her head, not wanting to believe that.

"They must have moved Walter, Vona," Piers said, his chin slack.

Yrsa gestured to the entrance of the tunnel with a nod. Piers, Thack, and Juluan waited on the grass in the pouring rain. Yrsa trailed them, walking backward, her steps slow.

Vona hesitated, her gaze on the stone wall, half expecting her father to burst through.

Yrsa said, "Come, we must leave."

Not moving, Vona sobbed, "I have failed him."

"I shall search the castle. They must have secured him somewhere else. You two," Yrsa gave Thack and Piers a pointed look then bolted out of the opening and into the night.

Vona staggered and lowered her arms to collapse the tunnel, hurrying to grab her boots before the soil swallowed them. As much as she wished she could, returning the land to how it was before wasn't possible. Sure, the grass could grow over, but she'd drained her well. She yanked on her boots while gazing at the mess she'd created. The rain drenched her, doing little to replenish the emptiness inside her. Still, she welcomed the warmth seeping into her clammy skin.

Piers stood beside her and threw an arm across her shoulders. A flash of heat seeped into her, chasing away a chill, and in an instant, she was clean and dry. He extended an arm. Green tendrils streamed from his fingers, and with the fragrance of dirt and growth, the grass regrew on top of the settled soil.

Prisoners swarmed her and Thack, thanking them while begging for a name. Still reeling with sorrow circling her heart, she rasped, "Robbin of Netherbury."

With Yrsa not with them, the night filled with screeching insects, owl hoots, the gurgling stream nearby, and Pier's heavy breathing.

She grabbed his tunic. "Did you look everywhere?"

"Aye, Vona, but I could not question the dungeon master, not after the prisoners killed him." Piers grimaced. "'Twas good you did not see that."

"Come, we must hurry," Juluan whispered, gesturing to the forest with a sweep of his arm and spraying rain droplets in a beautiful arc.

Vona paused and scanned the parapet. Flames flickered in the wall-mounted sconces, adding a welcoming glow. "Yrsa—"

"We will await her return in the shadows." Juluan grabbed Vona by the hand and tugged her into motion.

As one, they sprinted across the meadow and into the darkness. She didn't approach Honey, choosing instead to hover on the edges of the forest, one hand splayed across a tree. The bark dug into her palm. She dipped to collect a clump of soil, needing to heal her exhaustion. She sucked in the water from her hair and garments, but it was futile. Not even the downpour restored her as much as she hoped. Perhaps with more magic she could try again...or make another plan.

"Father is not dead," she muttered.

"Aye, they have him in the watchtower." Yrsa appeared from the shadows, her mouth drawn into a thin line.

Vona slumped on a sigh of relief. "Excellent. Then let us—"

"Surrounded by six guards and Grokar." Yrsa folded her arms across her chest. "There is no way we can rescue him without awakening the castle."

"No," Vona moaned. "We have to try, Yrsa."

"There is still tomorrow morning when he is out in the open." Thack looped an arm around Vona.

She shrugged off his comfort and glared at them all. "Alert the guards now or tomorrow, what difference does it make?" She swung her hand out. "'Tis night. We can hide better and flee into the shadows."

"Aye, but we cannot get inside the tower." Yrsa's stance remained unyielding.

"I came prepared to spill blood," Vona snapped. "I see you did not."

Thack jerked back. "Now, lass—"

"Fine." She pinched her brow to hold back the tears. Perhaps Yrsa was right. How could Vona sneak into the tower unseen? Thomas might know. She would ask him...now. "We will do this your way. Tomorrow at dawn, I will stand on that wall walk, bow and pistol ready. You three merge with the crowd and be prepared to kill or bleed for my father, the man who has been your friend for decades." Glaring at Thack and Piers without revealing her upset took all her control.

She stomped off, then tossed over her shoulder to Yrsa, "Do not follow me. I will be with Thomas until dawn."

The walk to Netherbury gave her the chance to smother her tears. The rain lessened, forming a fine mist that painted a romantic air across the fields. Arriving in Thomas's room in a mess wouldn't convince him to help her. She had to be strong. A damp breeze cooled her cheeks. Her strides became more confident, especially when she took the time to grab soil. By the time she reached the outside wall of the guardhouse, she could draw rocks out of the ground and stack them in a step formation. Three rows was all she needed.

Exploding into a run, she leaped off the steps, scrambled up the wall, and perched on the top. With her arms outstretched for balance, she inched along until she could touch the side wall of the guardhouse. Now what? She leaned back to assess the trusses, then vaulted to reach one. Her fingers brushed along the coarse wood, but she couldn't get a grip. A squeal lodged in her throat when she plummeted.

She threw out her arms to shield herself, instead, she flipped in mid-air and flew up. After being dumped on the roof, she crawled to the edge and peered off it. Below, Yrsa waited. Mounted on Shasta with Honey's reins in hand and Juluan behind her, she tapped two fingers to her temple and headed home.

Vona pressed her forehead to the roof's tiles, bemoaning her inability to do anything well. Mother had been right to question her inexperienced daughter's decision to 'save' her father. Someone else should have done it. Father would have been home and asleep in his bed.

She sniffed, scrambled to her feet, and hurried along the roof to Thomas's window. She absorbed any lingering dampness, straightened her handkerchief and hat then jumped off the roof, catching the edge of the tiles with her fingers. When she swung into Thomas's room, he stood before her with his pistol drawn. Seeing his solid shoulders, that arched brow in query, she tore off the handkerchief and hat to hug him. Tears spilled free despite her best intentions. One moment, she squeezed his torso, her face buried in his tunic, the next, he crushed her to him, collapsing all her barriers. She melted into his embrace.

"What happened, Vona?" he asked while rubbing a hand up and down her back.

"He was not there, Thomas." She met his gaze, uncaring that her face was a mess. "They barricaded him in the watchtower."

Thomas jerked back, then scooped her into his arms. "I am sorry, Vona. Had I heard of—"

"I know," she managed past the lump in her throat. "Is there a way to sneak in without Grokar and the guards seeing us?" Unable to resist, she cupped Thomas's jaw and ran a thumb across the dimple in his chin.

"No."

She slumped, letting her head fall onto his shoulder. "Thought as much, but I hoped you as darkness-gifted might know of a way."

He sat on his bed, cradling her on his lap. With the gentlest of touches, he smudged aside her tears even as they warmed her cheeks. "Where is your guardian?"

"I demanded to be left alone." She lowered her gaze. "I planned on sneaking in with your help." Her nose twitched as fresh tears pressed against the back of her eyes. "I know now that 'tis impossible. Would... Would you mind if I stayed here with you? Just for the night?" Her breath caught. If he said no, she had nowhere else to go. Returning to Devenmere to be judged by her mother? She shuddered. No, she would rather sleep under the stars than face that.

"Aye," he rasped, then flipped onto his back, flicking her so that she sprawled across him.

His kindness, the strength of him beneath her, a comforting hand he rested on her hip all solidified in one terrifying realization. She loved him. Eyes wide, she lay still with a cheek pressed to his chest. The steady rhythm of his heart calmed her. Hers thumped, deafening in her ears. She sucked in gulps of air, her lungs squeezing shut.

"Vona, follow my breathing. In...and out." He placed a kiss to her temple, sparking a fiery path of tingles to her chest.

When her breathing settled, mimicking his, she snuggled into the curve of his arm wrapped around her.

"Good, now sleep. Dawn promises to be an event we dare not miss."

She pinched her lips. *Should I confess? What if he does not return my affection?* Her cheeks warmed. Mayhap Yrsa might best advise. Thomas's caressing hand on Vona's hip drew her deeper into slumber, until all she could focus on was his hypnotic heartbeat. His breathing deepened, but she didn't sleep. Instead, she cherished every minute in his arms while playing scenarios in her head: how to rescue her father and reveal to Thomas that she loved him.

Twenty-One

Dawn came too soon, even though Vona had watched its soft light crawl across the scarred wooden floor. When she tried to move, Thomas tightened his hold and spun her, trapping her beneath him. She gasped, grabbed his upper arms, and whipped her gaze to his.

"Morning," he drawled.

Her heart skipped a beat at the twinkle in his eyes and the sweetness of his greeting.

"Morning," she whispered.

He brushed hair off her face. "Please do not get yourself hurt or killed." He closed his eyes for a moment, his cheeks trembling, then with a released breath, he met her gaze. "Please, for me."

She nodded, though promising that when the future was uncertain was foolhardy. Although, she could vow not to willfully endanger herself.

"Good. I cannot assist without—" He clamped his mouth shut then rested his temple on her chin. A swath of his hair brushed across her face. "I will help you save your father. 'Tis the right thing to do."

She froze, fresh tears prickling behind her puffy eyes. "Thomas, you would lose your position."

"Aye." He jerked back then rolled off her.

Smothering a shiver at the loss of his body heat, she sat up then grimaced at her mud-caked boots. The least she could have done last night was remove her boots. She pushed herself off his bed and uncoiled her mussed braid from where Yrsa had pinned it. Her hat lay on the floor next to the discarded handkerchief.

While wrestling with the braid and hat, she studied him standing in a pool of sunlight. "I do need a way to get onto the wall walk unseen." She flicked the handkerchief out, preparing to tie it in place. "Want to fly me up?"

He frowned. "Why?"

"Vantage point. I plan to challenge Emil from a distance." She met his gaze. "As Robbin. If all else fails, I will fight to free my father. Mother, Jacut, Yrsa, Thack, Piers, and Juluan will be in the crowds, begging for Father's release."

"As Robbin?" A pulse ticked at his jaw. "You vowed—"

"I did, Thomas, but how else can I save my father without bringing Emil's wrath down on my family?"

He stared at her, his expression hard. "Robbin's name was on everyone's lips last night, Vona. You are a target, in danger, and I—" He tilted his head, lunged for the window, and groaned. "We are out of time." He pointed at the handkerchief. "I will do what I can. Just do not...die."

She harrumphed at his silly expectation that she could thwart death.

He looped an arm around her waist and kissed her. Heat swirled, her throat closed, and in his arms, she melted, settling into the kiss. The way his warm lips touched hers, the way his tongue took liberties she found addictive, all addled her thoughts and played havoc with her heartbeat. He thrust her away, his breathing labored.

She hastily tied the handkerchief before he noticed her flushed face. "Do not do anything foolhardy either."

Without warning, he whisked her onto the roof. She landed like a cow pie thrown at a wall. A glance below revealed guards dismounting and marching into the guardhouse. Aye, they were out of time. The raised voices implied the discovery of the missing prisoners and dead dungeon master.

It had all been for naught.

She scrambled to her feet and scurried along the roof to the rear of the building. From there, she dangled off the edge, praying she didn't miss the wall and fall. Worse, break something. Worst, die. She landed, teetered, caught her balance, then sprinted along the top of the wall.

"Shit, Thomas did not say he would help me sneak in," she muttered when she dove into a shadowed alcove where the morning sunlight had yet to reach. "Where is your bow, Vona?" she snapped. "On Honey, fool."

She spun on her heel and snuck behind wagons, snickering horses, and a gathering of women on their way to the markets, to slip into the church. Pressing herself to the door, she listened for stamping feet or cries of alarm.

"Robbin?" rippled through the church.

She faced those gathered in prayer and grimaced at the many faces staring at her, some familiar. Facing the friar, she gruffed, "I need a bow."

Friar Flynn waddled toward her. "This is a house of God, we do not have weapons." He grinned. "Except for those I have confiscated." He flipped open a wooden chest that had seen better days. It sat to one side, as weathered as the wall it leaned against. "Take what you need."

Daggers, rusted swords, two bows, three arrows, and a cracked crossbow lay before her. She tested a bow of elm wood, trusted that it would fire true, then grabbed the arrows. Three wouldn't be enough, but perhaps she could find more inside the castle. If all else failed, she could use the pistols. They were loud, announcing their intention, which was why she was hesitant. An arrow could fly through on silent feathers.

"Why do you need these, my son?" Friar Flynn rested his hands on his ponderous belly.

"An innocent man is to be hanged this morning, Friar." She glanced at those watching. "I mean to stop Lord Emil, to stand against his tyranny."

Tapping two fingers to her temple, she slipped through the door and out into the morning light. No, she wouldn't ask these people to join the fight. They had suffered too much. This was her battle alone. She studied the bow in hand. With what she planned, she needed both hands. If she tucked her tunic into her pants, she could gape it and slide the bow and arrows in, nestling them down her back. Jumping up and down, she tested the make-shift holster. It wasn't ideal, but it was all she had. She sucked in a deep breath, squared her shoulders, and headed for the nearest bridge. A jog around the outside of Netherbury's walls to the castle would mean encountering fewer guards. Which was true on normal days, not after a recent intrusion into their 'impenetrable' dungeons.

Guards came and went, patrolling the perimeter though paying their surroundings no-never-mind. Almost as if they believed their task pointless.

As soon as she could, she weaved through the forest, her focus on the guards scouring where she'd created the tunnel. Despite Pier's assistance, the uneven surface gave their presence away, along with the bright green of fresh grass on the blackened soil. Hiding their tracks hadn't been a concern. It wasn't now, not when the guards couldn't possibly discover who'd been involved.

She circled to where she and Thomas had stolen from the vault. A sprint across the exposed lifeless fields wouldn't go unnoticed. The sun marked the passing of time. She was running out of it. Tunneling under again would be heard and would take too long. Not to mention, she'd hit stone floors, walls, and other rooms before she reached the outer keep.

She muttered a curse.

Fresh tears scratched her throat and twitched her nose.

She rocked on her heels, prepared to risk it, then froze. Thomas rode toward the men, his black hair unbound, his shoulders broad, his mouth pulled into a grim line. He bellowed orders. The guards scattered, some returning to town, others trailing him. A few minutes later, the fields were clear.

She sobbed, chuckled, then laughed while running pell-mell toward the castle. All humor dwindled when the wall loomed. She flicked her magic, trying to peel away clumps of mortar. Some tumbled free, granting her fingerholds and footholds. As she climbed, she removed mortar, her arms trembling with each yard she progressed. This hadn't been included in her training, not to the extent she needed today.

Wind whipped her hat but didn't remove it, thank the Lord. She didn't have a spare hand to hold it in place. Inside her boots, her feet cramped with every toehold. From below, talking reached her. Two guards scuffed the dirt, searching for tracks, she had to assume. Why hadn't they left as Thomas had commanded? The fools.

She held her breath, expecting them to glance up. Her body began to shake—keeping her in one spot wasn't easy. Nor could she continue up without alerting them to her presence. Time dragged. Chatter from the outer keep implied the crowds were gathering. She pressed her chin to the wall and stared at the last few feet. One or two more clumps should prove to be enough.

Peering over her shoulder, she released a breath at finding the guards farther along the wall. With two flicks, she removed the mortar, watching as the clumps tumbled to the ground.

"What was that?" a guard asked, swinging his gaze wide.

"I heard nothin'," his partner barked. "Quit wasting time. Lord Emil wants the entire wall searched. 'Twill take us all day."

She scrambled up the last bit but didn't throw herself over the parapet wall. A peek was in order. Getting herself killed now would be stupid. A guard patrolled, his focus on the courtyard, the gallows, and the milling crowds.

She shimmied to the left, then climbed higher, aiming for the top of the tower. 'Twas too high for her needs, but it was the safest spot. With a last glance at the guard, she threw herself over the parapet and crouched low. Her gulps for air overwhelmed her ears while she listened, waiting for the alarm to sound. When none came, she smirked. Her good humor dwindled. That had been *too* easy. Her instincts darted like skittish fish, from success to failure and that it would cost her family a daughter.

The chatter intensified into a din as more people gathered to watch. When the sun bathed everything in gold and shadow, she sat on her backside, stretching her legs to ease the cramping even as her magic healed her. It was almost time. The distance from the tower to the gallows wasn't too much for the bow. She removed it and the arrows and laid them on the stone floor. On the parapet wall, Emil's guards could easily overpower her. Still, to remain on the top of the tower was to trap herself.

She peeked over the wall to study the layout between the gallows, the crowds, the exits, and the dais upon which Emil and Grokar would sit. Within the drab folks, hooded figures in black stood out like knights among pawns. She frowned. Thomas's or Emil's guards in disguise? That didn't make sense.

Not when Thomas and his men pressed their backs against a wall, close to the raised portcullis. While gripping his sword, he surveyed the crowd, his brow furrowed. She smiled. He'd said he would help, and he had, allowing her to cross the field. Part of her prayed he helped again, the other wished he didn't, not when doing so would cost him so much. If his assistance saved her father's life, then she would ensure Thomas was compensated somehow.

Ropes crisscrossed the outer keep, with colorful banners flapping in the wind. She grimaced, like today was a fair? Bile rose to choke her. Emil was pure evil to treat her father's hanging as entertainment.

Regardless, the ropes might serve as her escape route. The clanking of armor reached her. More guards lined the parapet, no doubt expecting trouble.

She settled on her backside and leaned on the wall, her gaze on the trapdoor at the center of the tower.

The crowds quietened then burst into cacophonous cries of 'mercy' or 'hang him.'

She swiveled onto her knees and gaped when her father was ushered onto the gallows. The sun picked up the gold in his hair and the gray. She sniffed. He looked thinner, tired, but other than that, well-dressed and clean. His hands weren't shackled behind his back, but she suspected that was a courtesy due to his status.

Emil stood and held up a hand, silencing the crowd. "Thank you for joining me on this momentous day where justice will be served for treason."

"Treason?" someone in the crowd squeaked.

"'Tis foolishness," another called.

"My husband is no more a traitor than you are a lord," Mother snapped, glowering at Emil in all her furious glory.

The crowd gasped and stepped away from her. She stood isolated for but a moment until Thack, Piers, Juluan, and Jacut flanked her.

"Did my husband impugn the Conclave?" She arched an imperious brow. "I think not."

"I said that if a lord does not improve his lands and people, then he should not rule." At her father's gruff voice, Vona smiled.

"Treason." Grokar jumped to his feet, his mouth contorted.

"Is it?" Thack bellowed. "No name was mentioned, Lord Emil. Or does your guilty conscience place yourself as the 'bad' lord?"

"Guards, arrest that man," Grokar demanded, pointing a finger at Thack.

"Executioner, are we not here for a hanging?" Emil sat on his throne, resting an elbow on the arm.

"No," Mother cried out. Her gaze flew to gallows as the executioner slipped a noose around Father's neck.

Vona crouched, pulled her pistols free and splayed them on the top of the wall. Alongside those, she placed a bag of musket balls. With care, she withdrew a few cloth-wrapped balls, ensuring they didn't touch each other by accident. Doing so could trigger a spark and an explosion. She didn't know how the fire-gifted made these using fire and iron when iron was the antithesis of magic. Thack tried to explain once.

When she pulled the trigger, the pistol's hammer struck the firing pin, sending the ball along the barrel and out of the muzzle. Bows were logical. Strength was required to pull the string back, to notch an arrow, and release it. Striking one's target came with practice. So did aiming a pistol.

With a steady hand, she loaded the pistols. One shot each for now.

She notched an arrow, focused on the rope, exhaled slowly, and fired. The arrow embedded in the wooden upright behind Father, narrowly missing the executioner. The name 'Robbin' swept across the crowd. Folks pointed and cheered. With a flourish, she waved a hand and bowed. She readied another arrow and aimed at Emil. Killing him wasn't her intention, not with children present. Scaring him was. The arrow flew across the outer keep. She chuckled when it pinned tufts of his hair to the padded throne's backrest.

His squeal pierced the silence. The crowd laughed. Grokar rushed to his aid, but Emil swatted him away.

Chaos ensued. A few castle guards barreled along the wall walk toward her position, their weapons drawn. Without thought, she withdrew a dagger and slid it into the trapdoor's handles, slowing their approach.

She returned to the wall and smirked at Emil. Arrows flew toward her, but at the boom of a pistol, she ducked, praying the shooter was a poor shot. A spray of stone showered upon her. She slumped. That was too close.

A roar then cries of alarm forced her to peek. Piers was in bear form and charging the row of guards in front of Emil. Yrsa flung men aside, hard enough to slam them against each other, walls, or the platform of the gallows. She hoisted Father into the air, pulling him toward her. The crowd dispersed to the perimeter of the outer keep, probably not wanting to miss the entertainment. Mothers gathered their children and ushered them through the gate.

A thump-thump at the trapdoor caught Vona's breath. The dagger rattled but didn't dislodge. She dragged the pistols off the wall and aimed at the door. If anyone broke through, she'd shoot. If only she could escape the tower, but alas, water and earth couldn't aid her. Yrsa was too busy to notice.

"Vona, lass, open the door."

She laughed and pulled the dagger free, sliding it into her boot in a smooth motion.

Thack pushed through and grinned at her. "I always knew the beaus would be beating down your door."

She snorted but scrambled toward him, abandoning the bow and the last arrow. With a backward glance, she snagged the bag of musket balls and slipped them into a pocket. "Shall we?"

"Aye," he sang and shimmied down the ladder.

When she joined him on the floor below, unconscious guards littered the circular room.

"Your eager beaus needed to rest." With a wink, Thack slid down the ladder to the lowest floor. There he waited for her. "Ready?"

"Aye," she smirked, holstering one pistol to grab her sword.

With a battle cry, they burst through the door and into chaos. She tried not to kill, but a little blood spilled wouldn't be too terrible to heal. Spinning while back-to-back, she and Thack worked their way to Yrsa, Juluan, Jacut, Father, Mother, and Piers, roaring and growling, at the center of the courtyard.

Amid the guards surrounding them stood the cloaked figures. They didn't assist, nor did they join the fray. No emblem marked their identity or fealty.

Juluan had Yrsa's back. Father and Mother held hands while swinging swords or wielding magic. With a cut on his cheek, his white tunic torn, Jacut hefted his swords, looking every inch a warrior of old. Vona's chest swelled. This was friendship, loyalty, and love at its purest. She fell in beside Thack, facing outward. Trapped behind the crowds, Thomas struggled to push through, but his focus was fixed on her. She spared him but a glance. Soon she would allow herself to gaze in peace at his handsome visage.

When Grokar flung balls of fire, Piers threw himself in their path. He chuffed in a sort of bear-giggle when they fizzled on his hide.

Grokar's face mottled. Standing center on the dais, he pointed a finger, his mouth gaping.

Yrsa extended her arm toward him.

When he bounced off the stone wall to land at Emil's feet, the pale-faced lord wailed, "Sheriff, do...something." With his hair still pinned to the throne, Emil hadn't budged. Tears streaked his cheeks.

Vona swiveled in Thomas's direction. She lunged forward, crossing the distance between him and her family. His familiar scowl yet warm gaze swept her doubts aside. She smiled and flicked up her sword, holding the blade an inch under his chin.

"Robbin," he clipped. "At last, we meet." His focus shifted to the sword. His head tilted, and a sinfully gorgeous smile formed. He held out his free hand, his fingers curled slightly.

Something tickled her throat. Her eyes widened as her breath lodged. Heat exploded in her core, forced air out of her lungs, and soothed the tickle.

He jerked back, the warmth in his gaze fading. When he stretched out his hand again, shards of glass squeezed her throat. Pain radiated outward. Her vision circled with black. The blade she held at his neck trembled. Her cheeks flushed when her magic met his. This was him helping her? She couldn't clasp her throat, fight for breath, and lower her guard.

"Sheriff?" she rasped, then with a slow blink, summoned her healing again. It rose into a crescendo and engulfed her, tingling the tips of her ears to her toes. She coughed when the burning in her throat eased.

A pulse ticked at the base of his jaw while he studied her. He holstered his pistol and threw out his arm. Her feet left the ground.

Fear slithered down her spine, cold and dark. She glanced at her mother, Father, and Yrsa, who had one arm up, keeping Vona in place. Squaring her shoulders, Vona flung out her hands and yanked stones from walls, throwing them at Thomas. They bounced off an invisible shield.

She huffed, tired of this nonsense. To defeat him, she had to attack him from within. She slapped her palms together, targeting what water or moisture resided in his body, then flicked her arms wide. Droplets of water lined his shield.

He staggered back and fell to a knee, releasing her. She hit the ground, caught herself, and faced him, angling the blade once more to his chin.

While clutching his torso, his gaze swept the courtyard. The castle guards sprawled across the stone floor. His men had their hands full dealing with the excited crowd. Thomas lifted a hand, palm outward.

Into the silence, a man called, "Bravo." He flicked back his hood to reveal a grin and a familiar face. Vona slumped and lowered the sword. It was done. They were saved. She cast a glance at Thomas then offered him a hand. He accepted it, draining her magic to heal. Later, when they were alone, she'd discuss this display of power with him and the point behind it.

"About time you showed up," Yrsa gritted out.

"Uldane, you came," Ailith rushed across, throwing her arms around him in welcome.

"Too many rumors with Netherbury at the center, my dear." He slipped off his coat and revealed his uniform that of the Lord Sundowner.

Emil uncurled from the fetal possession to point at Vona. "Arrest that man."

"Man?" Uldane frowned while handing his coat to a nearby cloaked Sundowner.

Vona froze. She settled her gaze on Emil and Grokar. Who Robbin truly was didn't matter to her anymore. Still, she didn't want to drag the Devenmere name into disrepute.

"Robbin is innocent." Yrsa bulged her eyes at Uldane. "*He* is simply preventing a murder."

Vona rolled her bottom lip under the upper and prayed Uldane didn't reveal her deception.

A smirk formed on his lips while he studied Vona. "Indeed. Seems I arrived just in time." Swiveling on a heel, he strode toward Emil, and with a flick of his sword, unpinned the man from his chair. His hair stuck out like the back end of a turkey. "I believe this is a misunderstanding, milord. Do you not agree?"

Emil clambered to lean against the balustrade.

Uldane wrapped a hand around Emil's fist cupping the amulet. "What have we here?" He squeezed until with a cry, Emil released the amulet.

Yanking on the chain to bring it closer, Uldane forced Emil to grip the wooden balustrade or tumble off the dais.

"It is...my amulet," Emil whispered.

"Interesting." Uldane's brow furrowed. "I apologize, Lord Emil, that I must foist myself on your mercy and request refreshment. The journey was most taxing."

Emil hesitated, cast a glance at Father, then lingered on Vona. "Matters are not settled to my satisfaction, Lord Sundowner." He flattened his lips into a grim line.

"Life is filled with disappointment, Lord Emil. If you insist on pursuing this, I will have to set aside my patience and investigate this...situation. On behalf of the Conclave, of course." He curled his lip in disdain. "And perhaps confiscate that...amulet. A year spent in our catacombs should derive its origin."

Emil paled, flushed red, then stepped back, pulling the amulet with him. "I extend a most hearty welcome to you and your...Sundowners, milord. The gates to Netherbury are open to you." With a last glare at Vona, he gestured to Thomas with a flick of his finger. "Escort these...*citizens* from my castle and Robbin to the dungeon."

The crowd booed. Thack yanked Vona behind him and drew his pistols.

"Enough." Uldane's voice sliced through the growing uproar.

"That man emptied my vault." Emil pointed at Vona while clutching his amulet.

Uldane met Vona's gaze over Thack's shoulder. "Did he now? You have proof?"

Emil sputtered. "I am a lord, my word is—"

"When a man's life is at stake, I need more than your word." Uldane faced Emil. "Do you have witnesses?"

"Aye," Grokar spat. "They were freed last night." He glared at Vona. "No doubt *his* doing as well."

Uldane chuckled, then threw back his head on a guffaw. "A lad thwarted your skilled guards to steal your gold and free your prisoners? Come now, milord, surely you do not expect me to believe this?"

Emil hesitated, straightened, and scanned the crowd. "I will richly reward any who speak the truth."

"Bribery?" Uldane pinched his brow as if a headache was forming. "Witnesses must speak of their own free will."

"Aye." An old man ambled forward. "'Twas Lord Emil who killed the land."

"Who taxed people to death or drove them to leave Netherbury," a woman called out, hidden behind many.

"Who imprisoned for any slight." A tall man gestured to himself.

Emil grimaced. "Let us adjourn to my hall for refreshments, Lord Sundowner."

Grokar snapped his gaze to Emil and scowled.

Uldane bowed his head. "My thanks for the offer."

Vona held her breath until the door closed on Grokar's ass.

Mother cried out and hugged Father amid the cheers from their dearests and the crowd. Vona stayed still, despite the smile hidden behind her handkerchief. Something could go wrong. It paid to have friends in high places. She just wished Uldane had deigned to let them know of his intentions. All this effort... She nodded at Thomas, praying he didn't see the shimmer in her eyes. Had Uldane seen fit to inform Mother of his arrival, Vona would not have spent the night in Thomas's arms.

The good Lord had blessed them this morning. Without losing his position, Thomas had managed not to involve himself. Perhaps he'd 'attacked' her to avoid Emil's questioning? The crowds dwindled in excited chatter along the road into Netherbury. With the town guards crowding Vona and her family, they sauntered out of the castle. Not that she got a chance to talk to Thomas, not with Piers on one side and Thack on the other.

One last glance was all she was afforded before they mounted their horses tethered outside the church.

Friar Flynn greeted her from the porch, many of his congregation around him. "You did well, Robbin. I never doubted it, although, I did send up a few prayers, just in case." He swept his gaze heavenward then settled a beaming smile on Vona. "May the Lord shine his face upon you and bring you peace."

"My thanks, Friar." Vona gathered Honey's reins and veered the horse around.

Only once they crossed the bridge and cantered toward Devenmere did the tension in her shoulders ease.

TWENTY-TWO

As expected of an escort, Warric stared at Vona's back. All the while, he hoped for a glimpse of her exquisite eyes. He thanked the Lord for her good health. She lived, had no injuries, and had walked away with her family restored. All thanks to Lord Sundowner Uldane Tellalouise of Harvet. A decade older than Warric, yet he knew the man, how he had tormented those beneath him, and vaunted his deep well and connections to the echelon of the Conclave. In Warric's world, how hard one worked decided the reward. If cunning, conniving, blackmail, and coercion meant hard work, he'd been doing it wrong all these years. He snorted. Serving the baron meant more to him than rewards. Something he doubted Uldane 'Dane' Tellalouise knew anything about.

Yet, the man had saved the Devenmeres.

Warric scowled and veered south, marching to the guardhouse. Despite wanting to gather Vona into his arms, he and his men had prisoners to find. Not that he liked wasting his time. He wanted done with this task. Though, had the baron not sent him to Netherbury, Warric wouldn't have met Vona.

When she had swung into his room and arms, her sobs had nigh broken his heart. He shouldn't care this much, but he did. She shouldn't have such a control over his emotions, but she did. He frowned. Perhaps it was time to resign from the baron's service if Warric's focus was this compromised.

With all watching, he couldn't succumb without a fight. When he'd used his darkness to 'throttle' her, the level of power she'd slammed into him had hit his senses, trembled his well, and rattled him. He rubbed his torso, nausea still churning his gut. In an instant, she'd made him ill. Sweat had beaded his skin, and pain rippled along his bones. How she had managed that, he couldn't say.

"What news?" he snapped at Nibbon.

He gaped, his face paling. "Of?" he squeaked.

"The prisoners." Warric pinched the bridge of his nose. He couldn't expect Nibbon to have abandoned his post to gather information, but knowing his men, the tavern was a frequent haunt.

"Aye, two are at a table next to the tavern's fire, causing poor Kaethe all manner of trouble. They have yet to pay her. She has asked for assistance, of course." Nibbon gestured to the guardhouse, implying the woman had complained.

With a smothered sigh, Warric spun on a heel and trudged to the tavern, snagging Guy and Loaan to follow.

At the door, he hovered and listened, enhancing his hearing to capture whispered conversations. Discussions swung between Robbin's bravery, Lord Sundowner's arrival, and Emil squealing like a girl. Kaethe weaved through the room, placed hefty tankards on tables, and dodged wayward hands, all while smiling. Warric cut through the rowdy crowd to reach her.

She faced him, her cheeks flushed, and strands of her pale hair escaped her chignon. In her cinched-in waist, low-cut tunic, and heaving bosom, she was a striking woman. She narrowed her eyes, a smirk playing on her lips. "Sheriff?" She rested a hand on her hip.

"Kaethe, Nibbon said you needed...assistance?" Warric met her gaze over the seated patrons.

"Aye, Sheriff." She hitched a thumb at a table in the corner, then sauntered off.

Recognizing the purple 'x' he'd placed on their foreheads, he veered toward the men in shadow. A glimpse of gold had him clenching his teeth. His and Robbin's theft was being put to good use. The stack of empty tankards said it all.

"Good day, sirrahs, what brings you to *sunny* Netherbury?" Bile pooled on Warric's tongue at his happy tone.

"Who's asking?" A man sniffed, sucked on his top teeth, then sipped his ale.

Warric glanced at his own black tunic and breeches, at the Netherbury coat of arms on his cloak, then at his men dressed like him. "You know full well who I am. Anders and..." He clicked his fingers. "Truan."

The other man straightened, squared his shoulders, and splayed his hands on the scarred table. He was a big bastard, one an orc would struggle to subdue.

"Fetch Dul," Warric said to Loaan.

"There ain't no need to be calling an orc," Anders spat.

"I will not be carrying you, dead or alive." Warric grinned. "So, aye, Dul is needed."

Truan leaped to his full height, meeting Warric at eye-level. "Now, listen here, Sheriff—"

"Ah, so you *do* know who I am."

Anders's cheeks flushed as he too stood.

A thump-thump on the wooden walkway sliced through the hum. A shadow fell on the doorway, grew bigger and darkened until Dul appeared.

Anders reached for a dagger that had seen better days. It didn't glimmer in the light, or was that blood not rust on the blade? Warric summoned his air, keeping the magic ready.

When Truan lunged at Dul, Warric didn't hesitate. He targeted Anders, who dropped his weapon to clutch his throat. Dul gripped Truan by the jaw, hoisting him off the ground. The man swung fists and kicks without much success.

With a final gurgle, Anders collapsed to the floor in a dead faint. Truan cast a glance at his unconscious friend and slumped.

"Take them to Lord Emil's dungeon."

"No." Truan clasped Dul's wrist. "Anything but that."

"Death?" Warric arched a brow.

Truan paled and lowered his gaze at Anders. "If we must."

"Tell me, what did you do to be jailed?" Warric had not thought to ask the first time he met these men. The darkness rolling off them had convicted them in his eyes.

Truan drew in a deep breath then muttered, "My...son was murdered when *Lord* Emil used that cursed amulet." Truan scanned the crowd avidly listening. "Many have suffered such a loss: Anders's parents, Ol' George's daughter, Kaethe's father... I chose to do something about it." He lowered his chin to his chest. "And failed." A tear slipped free and trailed a path down his dirty face to hide in his scraggly beard. "I truly am sorry." He swept his gaze across the room. "Most of you stayed honorable. We...did not."

Regret Warric could work with. "Lord Emil will receive his due." He crooked a finger at Guy. "Escort these men to Baron Gregory of Kenningthain care of me, the Sheriff of Netherbury. He will put them to good use." Warric squeezed Guy's shoulder. "Do not share their past...misdeeds."

Guy nodded. "Dul, please saddle three horses."

"The best we have for the long journey." Warric smiled at Kaethe, who offered him a foam-topped tankard.

"Lord Emil will not take kindly to this, Sheriff," Guy whispered. "Take care."

Warric raised the tankard in salute. "Let him think us incompetent, but I refuse to imprison Anders and Truan when they have shown remorse."

Loaan cheered, drained his ale, then wiped his wrist across his mouth. "Aye, Sheriff, wisely said."

Warric ignored him and focused on Truan. "You have a fresh start. Do not waste it." He slapped Loaan on the shoulder. "Come, let us proceed with this *hunt*." Both handed their empty tankards to Kaethe and strode out. Warric paused, studied the bright sky, then loped off the walkway. "Fetch your brother."

"Aye, Sheriff." Loaan veered toward the guardhouse.

In the stables, Dul glanced at Warric over a saddled horse. "More?"

"Aye, Dul, three. One for yourself if you want to join us?"

"Sir asking?" Dul met Warric's gaze. "'Tis good, but Dul stay here."

"Very well," Warric said, leaned against a wooden beam, and waited. What he wanted was this day done. This evening, he planned to sneak out, to seek Vona, and explain his behavior. Her eyes had widened, fear darkening in their beautiful depths. What warmth for him had vanished. He hoped not for good.

He rubbed his chest. A sense of fullness swelled his heart. It was time he called the baron and resigned. He straightened. "I will return shortly."

Across the muddy road, up the stairs of the guardhouse, and to his room he hurried. There, he threw out his shield and cursed. Yrsa had his disc. Whatever he wanted to share with the baron would have to wait until this night. He bit into the chunk of black cheese someone had left for him. While he chewed, he reviewed what he would say to the baron. With the seed bread in hand, he barreled down the stairs, across the common room with Nibbon at the desk, and to the stables.

Loaan and Iwen were saddled and waiting. Dul held the reins while Serenity nudged the orc with playfulness. His coat shimmered under Dul's diligent care.

"Thank you, Dul." Warric mounted and accepted the offered reins. "We head north then east, south, and finally west. Let us search out these escaped prisoners to the best of our abilities." He grinned at Loaan. "Perhaps Lady Fate will be on our side." He didn't believe so, wished she would be otherwise occupied, but to say that aloud when he'd already revealed his opinion wouldn't be wise.

"Aye, Sheriff." Loaan chuckled.

Iwen sliced a glance between them while they trotted along the Netherbury road to the bridge.

Warric left it up to Loaan to explain, but he hoped his men chose another life after he resigned. He smothered a laugh, sheer joy engulfing him at a future with Vona. Convincing Lady Ailith was his next hurdle, but having charmed many termagants, he didn't consider her a problem. Leaving the baron's service lay heavy on his heart. Staying on as sheriff with a wife didn't sit right either.

He had yet to inform Vona of his true identity.

Tightening his grip on the reins, he spurred Serenity into a gallop. Perhaps this night would be the perfect opportunity to come clean.

He grimaced.

VONA PACED THE LENGTH of the dining room. The Eryssian rug silenced her footsteps until she crossed onto the wooden floor. Whipping around on a heel, she stomped to the door. Thack and Piers were on their third tankard of ale. Jacut nursed a glass of Brederburg brandy. Yrsa had just left to see Juluan out.

Mother was with Father in his...their bedroom.

Piers had been banished to the dining room after he'd healed Father. When an impatient Vona had approached the bedroom door, Mother's giggling had chased her away. She blushed at what her parents were up to.

"How long—?" She faced the room.

"Now, lass, 'tis not something I wish to discuss," Thack grumbled, his cheeks warming. "Let them be. Walter will appear when he is ready."

She huffed and glanced at her brother.

He waved a hand. "No, Vona, I shall not share also. A lady—"

She growled and threw her arms in the air.

"I think 'tis sweet." Piers hiccupped. "Their love is the stuff of legends." He peeked over his shoulder then slumped, no doubt searching for his qitary. The spot was empty where he usually rested it.

She sighed, grateful for small mercies. "Now what? Father has been rescued. Do we return to Bennedor?"

Thack shrugged his massive shoulders. "'Tis not cast in stone." He pulled out a gadget and fiddled with it. He didn't meet her gaze which meant bad news was coming.

Well, if anyone bothered to ask her, she wanted to stay at Devenmere, or failing that, she would travel with Yrsa as Mother had promised. Vona's breath hitched. Her plans depended on Thomas. What would a life with him look like? Did he even want her as a...wife? How would she spend her days if he remained the sheriff? She accepted the glass of brandy Piers handed her, downed it, then coughed. Her eyes watered.

He whacked her on the back hard enough to crack ribs.

"Swallowed it too fast," she rasped while stepping out of reach.

Jacut caught her and swung her into a quadrille. "I return to the wall."

As she followed his lead, she blinked at him. "You cannot stay one more night?"

"Aye, but on the morrow, I must fare thee well."

She hugged him, splaying her fingers across his back. "I shall miss you, dear brother."

"Lies," he chuckled. "Yrsa says you will be traveling with her. Take care, sister." He leaned back to pinch her chin. "You have done well these past few days, Vona. I am proud to know you."

Tears of another sort stung her eyes. She sniffed. "You would swear one of us is to die soon."

He scowled. "'Twill be a while before we see each other."

"How so?" Uldane asked from the doorway, a welcoming grin on his handsome face.

"Your timing was perfect," Vona said, pulling away from her maudlin brother. "Thank you."

Uldane bowed and sank into a chair beside Thack. "And this?" He gestured to her still in Father's garments sans handkerchief.

She tugged on the tunic's hem, smoothing the wrinkled fabric. "A necessary evil. You will not believe what has been happening."

"I have learned much this day." Uldane pinched his lips. "The Conclave will not be pleased."

"At least you saved Walter from the noose, dear man." Thack slid the brandy decanter to Uldane.

He rested his elbows on the table then poured an unhealthy amount into a glass. "Aye. Had I been delayed by an hour, 'twould have been too late." With a ferocious frown, he threw back the brandy.

The air thickened with dark intent. Vona stilled. What was this? Was Uldane disappointed? Angry? At what? Possibly being too late to save father? Or did he mean he arrived too early to 'let' Father die? No, that made no sense. Uldane had no reason to want Father dead.

"Where *is* Walter? Ailith?" He glanced from Jacut to Piers.

"They have yet to leave the bedroom." Vona chuckled but kept her focus on Uldane. Any reaction from him could ease her concerns...or heighten them.

The man grunted, but his stiffening shoulders revealed much. She glanced at Jacut, wondering if he'd noticed, as well. With his brows furrowed, her brother stared at the golden disc in his palm.

"Ah, here you all are," Father said, striding into the dining room. Mother trailed him with her hand gripped in his. "My thanks to my dearest friends and family." He rested his gaze on Vona, scanned her garments, then settled on the room at large. "Much was risked by all. It is thanks to you that I stand here."

"And to Thomas," Vona added, peering around Jacut, who'd taken the chair next to her.

Father's brow knitted. "Who?"

"The Sheriff of Netherbury shared with us your circumstances then aided in your rescue." She cupped the empty glass and held it out to Uldane. He poured a dollop, but she waited until he filled the glass half-way. As Father ventured farther into the room, she sent out her magic, checking that Piers had healed him well.

"May I serve the midday meal?" Dunstan asked from the doorway.

"Please. I am famished," Father said, but he clutched Dunstan by the elbow, halting his departure. "Thank you, my friend."

The older man blushed then with a mumbled, "I live to serve, milord," hurried out.

"Brandy?" Thack waved the bottle.

"Please." Father pulled out a chair for Mother before sitting next to her. "Now, tell me everything." He sipped his brandy and listened to the story unravel with Piers taking center stage.

Despite Piers's entertaining embellishments, Vona's attention stayed on Uldane. Something about him scratched at her happiness. She whipped her gaze to the door, wondering where Yrsa had gotten to. Her guardian's thoughts on Uldane's strange behavior would add light to this since she knew him best. Was Vona imagining things? After all, Uldane was a close family friend.

Dunstan placed platters of food on the side table. Ellia carried plates, while little Tims, with Mud on his shoulder, laid out the cutlery.

The aromas of roast chicken, freshly baked bread, sweet oranges, and steaming venison pie twitched Vona's nose. She clasped her fingers on her lap, waiting for Mother, who stared into Father's eyes like a lovesick fool. Vona hadn't seen them act this way in a long time.

Yrsa sank into a chair on Vona's left. "I have an errand to run," she whispered.

"Oh?" Vona glanced at her.

Yrsa's pursed lips said she wouldn't reveal anything further. "When Dunstan returns from the kitchen, ask him to set food aside for me."

"Sheriff of Netherbury," Ellia announced and stepped to the left.

Vona's gaze whipped up. Her breath caught. She absorbed everything about Thomas, from his dusty boots, tight black breeches, and gaping tunic granting a glimpse of the chest upon which she'd laid her head last night. His hair brushed his shoulders as he strode into the room. He met her gaze. A smile widened his lips.

"Sheriff, 'tis good to see you. Do join us." Mother gestured to the chair beside Yrsa.

"Thank you, milady. I trust Lord Walter is well?" He bowed his head toward Father.

"You are a man true to your word." Father stood to shake Thomas's hand. "My daughter assures me we have much to thank you for."

"I did what I could," Thomas said and settled beside Yrsa.

"Do not worry about Dunstan," Yrsa mumbled.

Vona jerked back and studied her guardian. Thomas's arrival had canceled Yrsa's errand?

Ellia set a plate before Thomas, who cuddled the kitten while Tims bounced beside him, whispering a few words. As much as Vona loved looking at Thomas, she didn't like this secrecy between him and Yrsa. She kept her gaze ahead, watching the play of sunlight across Pier's purple-covered shoulders.

"How goes the search for the prisoners?" Thack asked, then coughed to cover a snigger.

"Well." Thomas grinned, revealing a dimple. "As in none found so far. They seemed to have left Netherbury and the surrounding holdings. Wise under the circumstances."

"Thomas?" Uldane glared. "Sheriff?" He scanned the table, his face contorting between disbelief and mockery.

Thomas squared his shoulders and met Uldane's gaze. "Aye, Lord Sundowner. Thomas of Hasden, Sheriff of Netherbury, as appointed by Lord Emil himself."

"Is that so?" Uldane twisted his lips into a smirk. "I knew an assassin with just your visage. A sentinel in darkness and air. Met such a man?"

"I have known many such men, milord." Thomas swirled the brandy Yrsa had kindly poured for him. "Will the Conclave be removing the amulet in Lord Emil's possession?"

A pulse ticked at Uldane's jaw. "'Tis not for you to know."

"Fair enough, Lord Sundowner." Thomas leaned to the side to accept the fresh loaf of bread Ellia offered. "Thank you," he whispered to her.

She bobbed and moved to Yrsa.

Uneasy silence settled on the table as the food was served. Uldane glowered at Thomas or Father, but when his gaze rested on Mother, his expression softened.

Jacut tapped the table. "I will be leaving in the morning. I have...duties requiring my attention."

"So soon?" Mother pouted.

"Send the baron my gratitude for sparing you, my son," Father said.

Jacut glanced at the disc he'd set on the table beside him. "I find it odd that the baron is not responding to my calls."

"What?" Thomas's fork clattered onto his plate. He paused, drew in a deep breath, and smiled at Mother. "My apologies, Lady Ailith and Lord Walter. Please excuse me. I have lost track of the time." He pushed away from his barely eaten meal and leaped to his feet.

Yrsa did the same. "I shall see you out, Sheriff."

"But..." Vona winced when they had left the room without further explanation.

Jacut hurried out with a mumbled excuse about asking Dunstan to pack for him.

"Well, who else needs to leave?" Piers asked around a mouthful of pie.

Vona had wanted to follow, to eavesdrop if need be. Now she couldn't. She clasped her plate and stared at the food, having lost her appetite. Here she'd thought rescuing Father would restore peace and order.

Something was amiss from Mother and Father acting like lovebirds to Uldane's odd reactions to Jacut, Yrsa, and Thomas fleeing like the gates of hell had targeted them. Like usual, Vona was kept in the dark.

She gritted her teeth.

Enough is enough.

Piers gasped, then choked on his chicken. In the center of the table, the vase of wild-flowers withered and crumbled into dust. Ice cooled Vona's cheeks at what she'd done.

Yrsa returned a moment later, assuming her seat beside Vona. "What happened to the flowers?"

Uldane laughed between downing glasses of brandy.

"Dane?" Mother rose, concern furrowing her brow.

"You are so naïve, Ailith. All of you are." He swept out a hand, encompassing everyone gathered at the table. "That man," he pointed at the door, "is not a sheriff nor is his name Thomas."

Vona frowned. *What now?*

"Who he is does not matter," Mother snapped, but her gaze rested on Vona. Had fear not darkened her eyes, Vona wouldn't have given her mother a second thought. She knew something, that Uldane spoke the truth.

Yrsa pushed to her feet. "I vouch for him, Lord Sundowner."

Uldane blinked at Yrsa, his humor fading. "I expected better from you, envoy. Tasked to guard… "He stared at Vona. "You let her fall for such a man. He is a sentinel and no match for our Vona."

"You love him?" Father's calm voice sliced through Uldane's tirade.

Silence settled.

Vona raised her chin but didn't glance away from her father. "Aye."

"Fool," Uldane spat, drawing a glare from her mother. "His name is Warric of Auriville, and he's a Conclave-trained assassin."

Ice entombed Vona's heart. She shook her head, not willing to believe Uldane, despite sensing the truth. She studied the anger twisting his face. She had no reason to distrust him. Why would he lie? Then again, why would Thomas? Regardless, it wasn't his name she had fallen for but the man behind his actions. He'd behaved with honor, compassion, and resolve. There had to be a reason for the fake name.

"He serves the Baron of Kenningthain." Yrsa tore off a chunk of bread and popped it into her mouth.

Vona gaped. Of course, Yrsa knew who he was. Anger barreled up Vona's throat, squeezing tight. She flicked a gaze at her mother, at the resignation in her sigh. Thomas deceiving them all, that Vona could bare. This...this was another thing withheld from her alone. She studied Thack and Piers. Her shoulders slumped as air whooshed out of her lungs. They hadn't known either.

Still, to not tell her? Knowing his true name wouldn't have changed how she felt about him. So hiding this from her was for what purpose? Their silly insistence on protecting her?

"'Twas not my secret to share," Yrsa whispered, her breath apple-scented from the tartlet she had bitten into.

Vona stiffened, saving her ire for Thomas-Warric. What were his reasons? Surely not to protect her too? All that time alone and he couldn't reveal this one thing? Unsummoned tears scratched her throat.

"I support Vona's choice," Mother said to Uldane.

Warmth engulfed Vona, slipping a tear free. She dipped her head to hide her reaction. Mother hadn't approved of Thomas, thought him beneath her. What had changed her mind?

"For the love of the gods." Uldane threw his glass at the fireplace, shattering it. He stormed out, cursed Dunstan in the passage, then slammed the front door.

"Thank you, Mother," Vona said into the stunned silence.

"Forgive Dane, Vona, he wanted a betrothal with you when you were but a child." Mother glanced at Father and rested her hand on his shoulder.

"We thought his interest stemmed from your status, a chance to connect his name to ours." Father captured Mother's hand for a kiss.

"Aye. Thack advised against it, my pet." Piers sniffed while dabbing his eyes with a bright yellow silk kerchief. "I do like your sheriff."

Hers? She huffed. "He is not mine...yet."

Juluan appeared in the doorway. He panted for breath. His face was mottled red. Yrsa hurried to his side.

"I...bring bad tidings." He paused. "Baron Gregory is dead. The funeral procession approaches Tacourt from the north. Come, let us hie to Netherbury."

"Aye, to be certain 'tis the baron and to..." Father grimaced, "swear fealty to Emil."

A clamber followed as everyone bolted for the door. It took minutes for the horses to be saddled with the men helping Dunstan and Tims. In that time, no one spoke, no doubt cowered by the thought of Emil in power.

If so, Vona and Robbin would have to stay at Devenmere to ensure the people of Netherbury survived. She wasn't sure about Thomas, though. If he wasn't a sheriff but an assassin, then what future lay ahead for him? For them?

Twenty-Three

Warric palmed the disc Yrsa had returned to him, his gaze fixed on Jacut. They had spent the past few minutes in the stables, trying to reach the baron.

"Truly, no response, Warric." Jacut tapped his disc then pocketed it. With a sigh, he hoisted the saddle off the wall and settled it on his horse. "It has me concerned enough to leave once Dunstan has packed my bags."

"I am here, milord," Dunstan called, hurrying down the path with a leather satchel in each hand. "Ellia wrapped food for the journey." He offered all to Jacut, sliced a glance between him and Warric, then left.

"Aye. I cannot return to aid the baron and must rely on you, Jacut." Warric grimaced. "He set me on this task. I will not abandon it no matter how much I wish to."

"Ah, hence your question to Uldane. If he confiscates the amulet, you are free."

"No, but it minimizes the destruction under Emil's rule." Warric grabbed the pommel of his saddle and mounted Serenity. "I had hoped to have a moment with Vona to reveal my deception." He glanced at the manor, searching the windows for a shadow while listening for her footsteps. "Perhaps tomorrow."

"Aye, before she travels with Yrsa to the east."

Warric slumped. Would she stay at Devenmere for him? Would she wait for him to finish this task? "Keep your mother informed on what you find. She knows who I am."

"Aye, Warric," Jacut called while tightening the girth.

Warric veered west, urging his horse into a gallop. The baron's silence didn't bode well. He was tempted to stop under a copse of trees and test the disc again. He cursed. It would be futile. What he should have done was called more often.

Crossing the bridge into Netherbury, he didn't spare a glance for the castle. Not when he was expected to inform Emil of his 'failure' to find the prisoners and the treasure. Peeking over his shoulder, Warric caught a glimpse of a shadow slithering between stalls. He halted, vaulted off Serenity, and strode toward it.

"Who are you?" he demanded.

No one spoke. No movement reached his ears, as well.

He clenched his jaw and veered around the stalls. Sending out his magic, he probed the darkness and found...nothing. With a huff, he stomped to Serenity, gathered the reins, and walked his horse the last bit to the stables. There, Dul waited with brush in hand.

Weariness dragged Warric's steps when he strode into the guard-house. They'd combed the forests, meadows, searched the closest barns, houses, and manors for any of the escaped prisoners. He hadn't lied about that. Every holding had been checked so he could tell Emil he'd done all he could with conviction. When he'd arrived at Devenmere, his intention had been to speak to Vona. He hadn't accomplished it, hadn't even finished a delicious meal.

"The night is yours, men." He forced a grin at the men he'd come to trust. "You have earned it. I shall man the desk." He ushered them out, grateful for a little quiet.

Dropping into the only chair in the room, he raised his booted feet onto the table and leaned back.

The night sounds settled into an ebb and flow, a rhythm only altered by the wind. A crisp breeze cooled the room. Warric closed his eyes and relaxed, sinking into the chair. He snoozed as only an assassin could, fully aware of his surroundings.

The steady thump of horse hooves hitting the ground snapped him to attention. He titled his head, listening. The clamber of boots on the wooden walkway preceded the man filling the guardhouse's doorway.

When the baron's messenger in full dark blue and gold regalia emerged in the flickering torch light, Warric tried not to react. The scroll gripped in the man's hand could be for him, Warric-the-spy, for the sheriff, or for...Emil.

"What is it?" he asked.

"Kiran of Endoval, messenger to the Baron of Kenningthain." The man shoved the parchment at Warric, who snatched it out of his hand to unravel. "News, Sheriff. The baron was adamant, in case of his death, that you be notified first."

Disbelief warred with the dark sorrow engulfing Warric's heart and sending chills across his body. No wonder the baron wasn't answering his calls. Had Emil finally succeeded in killing his brother? Warric's mind whirled, shooting from one thought to another. His future was adrift. Not once had he thought past a life serving Baron Gregory. Sure, he had amassed wealth, but what could he do with his skills to while away his time? An option was to seek vengeance for a life taken. Indeed, this was dire, and something he needed to bring to Emil's attention. One last task for the man who'd been like a father to Warric.

Nibbon entered the common room, bearing a bowl of venison stew. He veered around Kiran to set it on the desk. "Need assistance, Sheriff?"

Warric met his gaze, but his voice lodged in his throat.

"The funeral wagon is less than an hour away," Kiran continued, his shoulders slumping. There was no doubt the man had pushed his horse to its limits.

Warric cleared his throat. "Nibbon, see to Kiran's mount. Task Dul to give it special care. Then escort our guest to the Clumsy Elf." He tossed Nibbon a coin. "This man needs an ale."

Tucking the scroll into his jerkin, Warric marched to the stables, wishing he had a drop of Vona's healing. He sucked in deep calming breaths while poking at the darkness coating his soul. No, the baron couldn't be dead. The man was so capable, strong, and formidable. What had killed him? He spun on his heel to ask Kiran then sighed, for he was closer to the stables than the tavern. Still, the more information he had, the better.

He found the man cradling a tankard, his gaze far away. "How did he die?"

"A recruit and his incompetence," the messenger muttered, then downed the ale. "Fired his pistol into the air. A cry rose from the baron's tent, a hole in the cloth, and the baron on the rug. The odds of such a thing happening…"

So, the Fates had decided. "My thanks." Warric abandoned the man.

It was best he delivered the news to Emil. Did this mean his mission was complete? No, not until Netherbury was restored, and Emil thwarted. Perhaps now he could just kill Emil, Grokar too? Perhaps travel to Lisbay and deal with this 'DT' he still didn't know the identity of. He marched through the gatehouse and entered the hall, striding to where Emil held court like a king. Grokar hovered in the shadows as per usual. Uldane's dislike of Warric was illogical. Despite attending the same lessons, they were years apart and hadn't spoken once during their training. Warric hesitated at the sight of Uldane seated to the right of Emil.

Their casual discourse interspersed with chuckles confused Warric. This morning, neither man had appeared to know each other. Warric stormed past the ladies and lords in attendance and shoved the scroll at Emil. "My condolences, milord," he gritted out.

Emil snatched the scroll and read the message. Giggling like a girl, he waved his hand. His guards hurried the muttering gentry out of the hall. "My dear sheriff, when you first arrived, I was skeptical."

Warric glanced at Uldane, expecting the man to denounce him again. When Uldane did nothing but arch a brow while swinging his goblet between extended fingers, Warric faced Emil.

"Grokar more so," Emil continued. "You have proven your worth over and over. This is excellent news. At last, my oh-so-magnificent brother has died." He broke into a jig, his lank hair trailing him. "Netherbury and all it entails is mine."

Uldane took the scroll to read for himself. "I am torn between elation and disbelief."

Elation? Warric hid a lip curl of disgust to say, "The funeral wagon is en route, milords."

Emil applauded.

Aching with the need to see justice done, Warric hurried to snuff the man's wicked delight. "I suspect the Conclave will arrive once news reaches them. When do you head north to the battlegrounds, milord?" The Conclave's Sundowners and emissaries would insist Emil continue in Gregory's stead.

Emil gasped then coughed. His cheeks trembled. "I am *too* ill for such a life. What do you think, Dane?"

Warric stilled. A thought shot through his mind like a streaking star across a moonless night. Uldane 'Dane' Tellalouise? Could Lord Sundowner be the mysterious DT?

"Indeed, you are not well, Emil, but the Conclave has excellent healers." Uldane's gaze flicked to Grokar. "'Tis strange that you are not improved."

"A side effect of the amulet and impervious to our weak magical healing, so Grokar informs me. I am willing to suffer for its power." Emil tapped his chin then spun on a heel, flicking out his cloak. "Task another baron to guard against the north."

Fury barreled up Warric's chest. A great man had died, given his life so that filth like Emil could sleep at night. "I cannot stand against the Conclave, milord. Should they insist, you will have to obey."

"The Conclave this, the Conclave that," Grokar spat. "They are not as powerful as you believe, Sheriff."

"Whatever I believe, sir, I must face them. They will decimate my men, destroy Netherbury, and siege the castle. We do not have enough soldiers to build an army, only what farmers and merchants remain."

Emil squeezed Grokar's shoulder, calming the blustering fool. "The time has not yet come, and Thomas, we will tackle each obstacle as it arises. Perhaps we are too concerned over what might happen."

"Wise, milord." Warric managed to bow, hoping to hide his hatred for the men before him. How far had Uldane fallen? Which part of Emil's plan did he know of? That Emil still clasped the amulet revealed much. That Grokar still breathed damned Uldane in Warric's eyes.

"Lord Emil, Lord Juluan, Lord Walter, Lady Ailith, Lady Ruvona, and Sundowner Yrsa are demanding entry," a guard asked from the doorway.

A flutter formed in Warric's chest. He was to gaze upon Vona again and perhaps for the last time if she traveled east tomorrow.

"They escorted a funeral wagon bearing...Baron Gregory?" Sorrow crossed the guard's face for a moment.

So, not all of the castle's men are loyal to Emil?

"Bring my brother to the dining hall, and let our guests in." Rubbing his hands together, Emil faced Grokar and Uldane.

"Milord, I came at once." Lord Juluan hurried in first, trailing him was Lord Walter, Lady Ailith then Yrsa and Vona.

Vona was a sight for sore eyes as always. The urge to go to her gripped Warric. He twitched but managed to set his feet and hold his ground.

"Is it true, milord?" She curtseyed, her eyes wide with tears shimmering in their depths.

In breeches and a tunic, she wasn't dressed as a lady but as Robbin. Pistols hung from her hips too. Except for her unbound hair, would Emil recognize her?

Still, she was beautiful, humming with untapped energy. Warric drank in the sight of her when admiring her was all he'd allow. For if he was stuck as Sheriff Thomas indefinitely, he couldn't court her. He could never have her, never taste her lips as he longed to do, never gather her close, wipe away her tears, or share in her laughter. Like a thick horsehair blanket drenched in ice water, the loss of Vona settled over Warric, adding to the well of sadness Gregory's death had formed within him.

"Aye," Emil sniffed. "My dearest brother has...died." His shoulders shook as if he tried to smother his sobs.

Grokar, all concern, patted him on the back.

Juluan offered a silk kerchief.

Emil 'gratefully' accepted. "My thanks, Lord Juluan."

Men trundled in bearing Gregory through the hall to the dining hall. Warric caught the tell-tale hooked nose of the baron—a feature shared with Emil. The guards slid Gregory onto the wooden table then left. Emil staggered to his feet and weaved into the room, pausing for effect to lean on pillars and doorframes. Warric and Grokar followed. It was Uldane who closed the door on Juluan's face, granting Emil privacy.

Emil peered into the coffin at the baron's corpse then threw back his head and laughed. "At last," he roared. "All this effort, and for what, when you could have died so many times. When I pushed you off the wall and told Mother you tripped. Eating 'tainted' meat from the food stocks. Surviving my assassins, even the women I bribed to poison you." Emil glanced at Warric. "What killed him? My wine?"

Warric didn't meet Emil's gaze. He studied Gregory, searching for a bloodstain marring his impeccable blue jerkin. "No, milord, a stray musket ball." Despite his experience, it hit home, that something so small could do this.

"Oh, ho. The Fates aided me. What a blessing, indeed." Emil chuckled at Grokar when they shared a knowing look. "This amulet revealed the path I had to take." Emil patted the silver and diamond disc hanging around his neck, then grimaced. "It cost a fortune to find it. I sold everything, promised whatever. Aye, I found it but had to tax the people and align with filth to repay my debts. If you had just died..." He ran his fingers along the cuff of Gregory's velvet jerkin. "Well, you did, and now, Netherbury is mine."

"Nothing stops our plans from here on." Grokar cackled.

"Indeed," Uldane said but stared at Warric. "After we have dealt with loose ends."

"True. How are things on your side?" Emil traced a finger along the edge of the coffin.

"Proceeding. Once we give the signal, all will fall into place." Uldane unsheathed a dagger and gestured to Warric. "And him?"

"The sheriff is on my side," Emil said without glancing at Warric.

"Is he now?" Uldane pursed his lips. "How did an assassin become your sheriff? Do tell."

"An assassin?" Grokar scowled.

"A skill we will need." Emil waved a dismissive hand then stared at his palm. "All the blood on my hands is *your* fault, Greggy." He draped over the baron's chest and rubbed his cheek across the velvet. "What would Mother say?"

"She would say, 'I did not want to believe this of you, Emmy.'" Gregory sat up.

He climbed out of the open casket, forcing Emil to stumble back.

Joy exploded like a thousand cannons fired. Warric took a step forward then halted. He averted his gaze to wrestle with his grin. How he admired this man.

"No," Emil cried out, then fell to his knees. "Why can you not die?" he wailed.

Grokar charged with his dagger drawn and raised. Warric flung out his air, caught the man, and threw him back until he bounced off the stone wall. The blade tumbled from his hand and skittered across the floor, whacking Emil's slippered foot. Wanting done with the vile snake, Warric flicked his wrist and snapped Grokar's neck.

The door opened. Yrsa filled the frame with Vona peering over her shoulder. The envoy assessed the room and ventured in farther. With one glance, she conveyed she was ready if Warric or Uldane needed her. Warric prayed Uldane didn't ask for her aid.

"I do believe good triumphs over evil, baby brother." Gregory bent over Emil. "Mother would be most disappointed." He sighed. "I suspect she knew, though, forcing that deathbed promise from me." He gripped Emil's shoulders. "I should have done Sagua a favor and killed you years ago." He grimaced. "Still, I am a man of my word." He released Emil and nodded at Uldane. "Lord Sundowner. I see we have much to discuss. My men will have arrived along with emissaries from the Conclave. I could not understand how my brother had deteriorated so fast, nor where he found the funding for his mad expeditions. A little digging—"

Into the room slid a thin man dressed in gray. He slithered, falling in and out of shadow, as he circled them. Warric gripped his hilt and extended a hand in warning. White swirled on his palm.

"Xensi, you have served me well." Baron Gregory gestured to the door. "Escort the emissaries in."

"All has worked as planned, Baron." The dark-haired, dark-skinned man bowed. His gaze lingered on Vona. He paused beside her, placed his hand on his chest, and bowed. With "An honor, milady," he left.

The shadow stalking Warric was from the baron? He frowned. Was his ability to serve Baron Gregory in question? Had the man doubted Warric would succeed?

"Lord Sundowner?" Yrsa tilted her head.

By instinct, Warric did the same, picking up the educated tones of the Conclave's emissaries whispering about Uldane's duplicitousness.

Sorrow darkened her eyes, and she gasped. "No, this cannot be true. Lord Emil's rantings I dismissed as that of a madman, but this? What lies are these? You would not betray all we stand for." She settled a pleading gaze on Uldane. "Why?"

He smiled, charm in every pore. "Those in power rule without earning it, Yrsa. Do you not bemoan the loss of a life with children? What of those too magic-weak to choose their destiny but must bow in servitude? Are you not more powerful than anyone in the Conclave?"

"Aye, but 'tis ruling with too much power that corrupts." She flicked her hands open, white tendrils wrapping around her fingers. "I swore a vow, and should you resist arrest, we shall see who is the most powerful of the Sundowners."

"Now, Yrsa…" He showed his palms as if in surrender.

"Milord." Lady Ailith pushed past Vona to curtsey to the baron. "'Tis good the rumors of your death are false." Clasping her hands to her chest, she faced Uldane. "Dane?"

He paled and threw out an arm in pleading. "Do not believe this nonsense, sweet Ailith. I would not dare—"

"The evidence is damning, old friend," Lord Walter called from the hall. "We shall get to the bottom of this. It cannot be true." Parchment shuffled. Walter's whispers became cries of alarm, denial, then resignation—all within minutes.

He strode into the room and waved scrolls in Uldane's face. "What is this? Why? We welcomed you like family." With a pulse ticking at the base of his jaw, Walter stared at Vona then glanced at Ailith. "My dear, 'tis true."

"No," Ailith whimpered. Her tears streamed free. Lord Walter gathered her in his arms and ushered her from the dining room.

Vona, with her hands hovering above her pistols, fell into place beside Yrsa.

"You." Uldane pointed at Vona. "Had you left things alone, your silly father would be dead, Ailith would be alone and weakened, and what power lies in your veins mine to control." He lunged at Emil and yanked on the amulet, trying to rip it from him. "Give me this. I shall win this still."

With a cry, he flew across the room, crashing through the chairs and almost smashing the stained-glass windows set in an alcove. Warric stared at his hand, having never thrown someone so hard. He glanced at Yrsa with her arms extended and grinned. No, it hadn't been him this time either.

"Where...?" Spitting blood onto the Eryssian rug, Uldane rocked onto his hands and knees. "Where is your loyalty? You swore an oath to the Sundowners, to *me*, not to the Conclave and its antiquated ideals."

"I vowed to protect Vona. That supersedes anything prior."

He coughed then chuckled. "How fair weathered of you, Yrsa."

She stepped aside, letting the emissaries pass her.

In black with white piping, their hooded robes brushing the floor, five men and women circled Uldane. The fragrances of rain on dark soil, rich grass and foliage, the sweetness of mountain streams, and the flower-scented warmth of the sun filled the room.

"Uldane Tellalouise of Harvet, your vile actions have been revealed," a woman said, her voice crisp and cold. "Your nefarious plans have been documented."

"You have been tried," another stated, tucking his hands into his sleeves. "You have been judged."

"As one, we command your soul to eternal darkness," they sang, leaned over him, and clasped hands.

"No." Uldane tried to scramble to his feet, but something held him down. He raised his arms to shield himself, but the hum grew until deafening. A kaleidoscope of colors burned Warric's eyes. With a *'pop,'* Uldane was no more but a pile of ashes. The emissaries turned and strode from the dining room.

"Warric." Smiling, the baron veered around Emil on the floor to grip Warric's forearm. "You have done well, better than I had hoped. Your service to Sagua has been exemplary. I have petitioned the Conclave for baron status as reward. In addition, I made you my heir. Not that my brother was aware of this." The baron spared his brother a glance. "You inherit Netherbury regardless of the Conclave's approval."

Warric blinked, torn between gratitude and surprise. He gazed at Vona, who smiled at him. The warmth in her eyes renewed his hope.

He opened his mouth to spew some form of thanks, but the tension in the room shifted. Emil grabbed Grokar's dagger and lunged at Gregory. With the baron in the way, Warric couldn't use air without harming him, so he shoved Gregory aside and drew his pistol.

A boom echoed through the hall. Darkness swirled around them, and as Emil plunged the dagger into the black cloud above Warric's chest, the blade disintegrated. That didn't matter when red bloomed across Emil's stomach, spreading and staining his gold-embroidered tunic. Warric had fired true. Emil gurgled, gaping when he crumpled to his knees, his eyes wide in his dying moments.

Gregory returned to Warric, his pistol drawn. "My thanks, Warric. For you did what I could not." He paused beside his brother. "I bequeathed Netherbury to Warric years ago, dear Emmy. My death would have gotten you nothing but my title, and even that, the Conclave would have stripped from you."

Blood dewed on Emil's lip before his lifeless body slumped to the floor.

"I—" Warric frowned and clutched his chest, pulling his hand back to blink at the blood smeared across his palm. He fell against the wall, glanced at Vona, then sank, landing on his ass. Pain radiated outward, ice at its edges. He shivered.

"No!" Vona tossed her smoking pistols to kneel at his side. She hovered her hands over his body. Green faded through his garments and chased away the chill.

He smiled. "The name's Warric of Auriville," he rasped, then winced when she splayed her hands on his wound. "I love you."

Her gaze flicked to his. Tears flowed and glowed her cheeks blue. "Love you too, imbecile. Getting yourself wounded like this, what kind of a sheriff are you?" Her teasing was meant to hide her concern, but her face was pale. Her eyes were round and dark, and she nibbled on her bottom lip.

"Assassin," he coughed.

"Yrsa, I need soil." Vona met the envoy's gaze. "Please."

Yrsa hesitated, glanced at the door, the stained-glass windows, then at the amulet. She looped it off Emil and slipped it over Vona's head.

"What are you do—?" A scream tore through Vona, arching her back. Blue and green tendrils spiraled outward, pulsing, shining, then sucked into her. Hunched over, she whimpered, while studying her hands. "Out of the room. Skin to skin works faster."

After the baron cleared the room, Yrsa closed the door on him, glowering at him when he hesitated. By then, Vona was cutting the jerkin off Warric's chest.

"If you wanted to see me naked, sweetheart," he chuckled then coughed. The familiar salty tang of his blood pooled in his mouth. That wasn't good.

"You owe me a moonlit bath, Warric."

He closed his eyes at his name on her tongue. Sheer bliss swept through him. He could die now. When warm skin layered his, he opened his eyes to find her lying on top of him. Her soft breasts crushed against his chest registered through the pain.

"Survive this...for me." She rested her temple on his chin and engulfed him in a blinding green light.

Pain of another kind shuddered his body, and he moaned, wanting to shove her off, but his arms wouldn't budge. The heat from a thousand fires coursed along his veins, and with a thunderous thump, a force shot outward. Yrsa raised an air shield to protect herself but stumbled back.

Warric watched this play out as if he hovered above his body. Where the dagger had plunged into him now burned. He wanted to push through, ached to stay with Vona, but even for an assassin such as he, the pain was too much.

"I love you, Warric," she whispered just as his eyes shut.

Sweet darkness consumed him.

Twenty-Four

Vona cried out, forcing more of herself into Warric while begging him to live. Pulse after pulse pulled from her, snatching her breath. As she expected, touching him triggered the healing. She couldn't control the amount he drew, couldn't slow it either. So she sank into it, letting it guide her. Through his body she traveled. The exhaustion was easy to dismiss. His wound and where it had sliced through the skin and muscle didn't deter her. She painstakingly knitted the fibers. His pierced lung proved the biggest hurdle. Blood pooled and bubbled with each breath he took. She wasted precious minutes trying to find the hole, to seal it, then longer to drain the blood into a vein.

By now, her well should have dried up, but the amulet granted her more power, a deeper source she didn't hesitate to use. Questions could follow *when* he lived.

While she checked his body one last time, her thoughts and heart recalled his confession. Emotions blossomed and swelled. He loved her... Warric of Auriville. His deception didn't matter, not when she was close to losing him.

Warric... Aye, this name suited him better.

She pulled herself off him, amazed at how good she felt, as if she hadn't risked her soul to save him. There on his chest where the wound had been, was an imprint of the amulet seared into his skin. Hell's teeth, had she done that? She held her hand over it, but the symbol didn't heal nor fade. In fact, it glowed a mixture of green and purple.

"Here," Yrsa said, returning Vona's tunic to her. "I assume he is well?"

Vona studied Warric's handsome face. Relief set fire to her core. "He sleeps."

When Vona was covered, Yrsa opened the door and granted the baron access. The man strode toward Vona, concern furrowing his brow. Juluan took Yrsa into his arms, gathering her close. Mother watched from within Father's embrace.

"How fares he?" the baron asked, snagging Vona's gaze.

"Well." She leaped to her feet then palmed the amulet. "Thank you for this, milord." Looping it over her head, she handed it to him. "Odd," she said. The boost to her magic should've vanished with the removal of the amulet, but it hadn't.

The baron blinked at her. "I am honored to have met you, Empyrean. What is your name?"

"Empyrean?" She chuckled. "No, milord. I am but a proficient. Lady Ruvona of Devenmere, at your service." She dipped into a quick curtsey.

He frowned, opened his mouth to speak, then raised his chin, instead. "Guards, carry Warric to a bedroom, and take care. This man is dear to me." He took Vona's hands in his, forcing her stay. She'd wanted to follow Warric, to see him settled. "Tell me, how are you involved?"

"I shall explain. Vona, go to Warric." Yrsa pulled away from Juluan to cross the dining hall. "Sundowner and Envoy Yrsa of Osiree." She bowed.

The baron released Vona and gestured to the chairs placed in front of a fire.

Vona didn't hesitate and bolted past Juluan, kissed her mother and father on their cheeks, then sprinted past them. She hoped to find someone who could show her the way. When she accosted the first servant she came across, a heartbeat not hers thumped within her chest. She paused, took a few steps, and waited. The sound was muted. She swiveled on a heel and marched the other direction, listening for the heartbeat, testing its strength. Up a spiral stone staircase she hurried, only to stop on the landing. Two passages split off. Within minutes, she found herself outside a wooden door. Pushing it open with two fingers revealed a chamber worthy of a king. Thick Eryssian rugs, paintings, Maraihan mirrors, and an orchid from Thariq sat on a table before large arched windows.

The massive four-poster bed in dark wood dominated the room. In the center sprawled Warric. He watched her, his crystal blue eyes unblinking. Humor curled his upper lip. His chest was bare above the blankets. The amulet-shaped burn mark flickered green and purple.

"How do you feel?" she asked, closing the distance between them a step at a time.

"I should be dead," he rasped.

She slumped, savoring the sweetness of his voice. "Aye."

He patted the bed beside him.

After yanking off her boots, she dutifully climbed onto the bed and faced him, folding her legs beneath her.

"What happened, Vona?"

She shrugged. "When I asked Yrsa for soil, she gave me the amulet, instead." Gesturing with her hands, she pretended to hold a ball. "My well went to this, Warric." She flung her arms wide then lowered them to grip her knees. "For some strange reason, when we touch, you trigger my magic. It pulls out of me as you need it." She gestured to his chest. "Skin on skin made sense. I am sorry about the mark. That just...happened." Wincing as she waited for him to reprimand her, she glanced away.

"So much *just* happens with you." With a groan, he sat up and cupped her cheek, forcing her to meet his gaze. He brushed his fingers over the shell of her ear. "Where is the amulet now?"

"I returned it to Baron Gregory." While layering her hand over Warric's, she frowned. "Odd that I feel as if I am still wearing it. Like my well has grown."

"That is impossible," Warric scoffed.

"Aye, I am aware," she mumbled.

He closed his eyes and drew in a deep breath. Doing so granted her the opportunity to admire his face in this unguarded moment. Hell's teeth, she *adored* him and ached to kiss every inch of him. Across his raven-winged eyebrows, to the tip of nose, then to feather her mouth along his jaw. To kiss *him*. He gaped. His eyes opened and widened.

A grin formed, splitting his cheeks. "How... How is this possible?"

"What?" Unable to resist, she ran a hand up the column of his throat to his jaw then stroked it to the center of his chin.

"Empyrean," he whispered, awe in his voice.

She broke away from his touch. "The baron said the same thing." She shook her head. "I am proficient. Just like Jacut."

"What you are…is mine, Vona." Warric grabbed her by the shoulders and dragged her across to meet his descending lips. His breath warmed her chin then mouth before he kissed her.

She moaned, sagging against him.

"Tell me you love me," he commanded.

Awkwardness splashed warmth across her cheeks, but she refused to lower her gaze. "I love you, Warric."

Groaning, he twisted, trapping her beneath him. "Vona. Sweet, troublesome, Vona." He chuckled.

She smiled. "As long as you kiss me, you can call me whatever you want."

"Mine. Love. Wife." He placed a kiss on her lips with each word.

Wife? She wanted to squeal, but when he slanted his mouth across hers, she pressed her body against his.

Splaying her fingers over his chest, she tested the texture of his skin. With a swipe of his tongue, he plundered her mouth. She melted, unable to resist him, his kiss, his musky fragrance, his hair tickling her cheek, and the exploding warmth of her love for him.

He slid his fingers under her tunic to cup her breast. She squirmed, darts of bright joy ricocheting inside her to liquify in her core.

He broke the kiss to stare into her eyes. "When I lay with a woman, she is not wearing pistols, Vona, nor this many garments."

She jerked back and scowled at him. "I am not one of those women, Warric."

"Aye, you are more, my hope and my future. Marry me, sweet Vona." He flicked a thumb across her nipple and stole a gasp from her with his lips. "I shall petition the Conclave for your hand if your mother rejects my suit."

"Oh?" Vona arched a brow.

"For an empyrean should take an envoy as husband, Vona."

She huffed. "Empyrean? I told you—"

"Test your well, my love." He dipped his chin to meet her gaze. "'Twould be wise to wed before the Conclave discovers your existence."

"'Tis nonsense," she whispered, but when he didn't relent, she did as he suggested. Prodding the ball at her core, she squeaked when it unfolded like a flower in full bloom. Its petals reached to the very edges of her body and beyond. She sucked in a sharp breath and raised her face to his. "What...what is this?"

"We shall find that out later," he whispered. He patted his chest then stiffened. "My ring."

She gulped and dug in her back pants pocket for the chain she'd removed before healing him.

"'Twas my grandmother's." He stared at it, unlatched the chain, then offered her the gold band. "'Tis not much—"

"'Tis beautiful, simple, and perfect," she said, holding out a hand for him to slide it on.

"I am the blessed one. Let me love you, dear, sweet, Vona. I have longed to hold you thus, to kiss your beautiful mouth, to know every inch of you."

He feathered kisses along her jaw, over her cheekbones, then down the column of her neck, sending out sparks of white pleasure so exquisite, she forgot to breathe. Air cooled her skin as her tunic unbuttoned.

"That is cheating," she chuckled when he used air-magic to undress her. Pistols flew out of their holsters to the table by the window. Her belt unbuckled, her pants unbuttoned, then with sharp tugs, slid off her legs to fold and stack on a nearby chair.

"Is it?" He grinned, and with a flick of his fingers, she floated off the bed while he removed her tunic.

"Aye, for I am naked but you are not." She twitched to cover herself but hesitated when he ran an admiring gaze over her. Tingles followed in the wake of his perusal.

"As beautiful as in the river, Vona," he rasped. The blankets flipped aside revealing his long muscled legs dusted with fine black hair.

Her eyes widened as she took in all of him, as naked as she was. His arousal bobbed.

"Keep looking at me like that and..."

She scoffed. "And what?"

"I ache for you, Vona." His expression turned serious. "Please have mercy on me."

Her heart beat skittered. "Flip me over."

He did and lowered her into his arms. Warmth swept over her, amid a blast of excitement when he crushed her against him. A groan slipped past his pinched lips. "'Tis good to hold you." A pale green glow formed where their skin touched, and a little of her magic drained from her.

"You are not well yet, Warric," she said between kisses to his chin.

"I am well enough." He rolled her over, pinning her beneath him.

"You almost died," she whispered, willing the tears to not fall.

He cupped her cheeks, forcing her to meet his gaze. "Aye, but I did not, my love." After snatching a quick kiss, he brushed his mouth down her throat and across her collarbones. She shivered when he stroked his fingers along her arm to her fingertips, curled her hand into his and kissed her knuckles.

"Warric?" she squeaked. "I...do not know what to—"

"I have you, Vona-love, trust me."

She willed herself to relax, letting him dust kisses where he pleased. When he sucked her nipple into his mouth, the jolt of fire twanging through her drew a cry.

"Oh," she gasped. "Do that again."

He chuckled and obliged, tweaking one nipple as he laved the other with short licks.

Something gripped her thoughts, scattered them, yet narrowed her focus on the dark crown of his head. She sank her fingers into his hair and clung to him, arching into his mouth. Whimpers escaped her under his constant barrage. With a nipple receiving his attention, he slid a hand down her waist to grip her hip.

He released her with a 'pop' and rose to kiss her, his tongue dueling hers drew a moan. "Vona, I... Please."

"What is it, Warric?" she rasped, struggling to catch her breath.

He glanced at where he held her hip. "Spread your thighs for me."

Though frowning at his strange request, she did as asked. When he slid a finger between the folds of her womanhood, her lungs seized, and her heartbeat pounded in her ears. The sensations shooting outward from his exploratory touch drove her wild. She cried out, unable to understand what he was doing to her, what these joy-filled bolts of pleasure meant.

"Do not stop," she begged, clinging to his shoulders.

He pressed wet kisses to her neck and lower, pausing to nip her skin where her shoulder started. The unexpected burn merged with the flick of his finger. She screamed, tumbling off an unknown abyss into a sea of exquisite delight. She trembled, her hips gyrated, her nipples shriveled into tight points, with every muscle tensed for more.

"So damn beautiful," he gritted out and positioned himself between her legs.

Something hard pressed at her still-sensitive sex. She writhed, sparking residual ecstasy when she brushed against him.

He leaned over her, resting his weight on his hands he splayed beside her shoulders. "Vona," he whispered, "lie still."

She did, gazing at him. A smile slipped free at the warmth in his eyes.

"This will hurt, but only this once."

The biology of mating wasn't unknown to her, but never would she have guessed how good it felt. A little pain wouldn't deter her from experiencing everything he offered her.

He sank into her, an inch at a time, stretching her until he froze. A shudder twitched his shoulders. Concern darkened his face. He withdrew and thrust into her, claiming her mouth when she screamed. Her vision spun black, fiery darts of agony shot outward from within her. The familiar heat of her earth-magic radiated like a steady heartbeat until all she could sense was him...in her.

She ran her fingers up his arms and around his neck. A pulse began where he joined her—a slow thump like a distant tribal beat or the warning of thunder. It built until she throbbed. Twinges merged with the beat. By the time he pulled back and plunged in again, she was amid a world of pleasure.

The culmination of ecstasy she had just moments ago enjoyed, grew, intensified, until she pleaded with him. For what, she could not say. More, faster, harder? Would any of those make sense to him?

He kissed her, long and slow, teasing her tongue from its safe caverns within her mouth. Nibbling on her top lip, then sucking the bottom lip between his, she succumbed to his sensual prowess. She chanted his name amid gasps for air when he allowed her to breathe.

In this time, tension built inside her, tightened her muscles until she gripped him as if her life depended on him. Withdrawal, thrust, repeat, his shoulders stiffening, his hips frantic. A cry tore from her, when joy too much, too soon, convulsed her body. All thanks to him. Everything exploded—colors behind her eyes, the ebb and flow of magic, and a thousand delights across her skin.

His roar echoed in her ears before he slumped, crushing her beneath him. She didn't mind, needing the contact: his heat, touch, and presence. He held her to him while feathering kisses to her temple.

"Lord, I love you, Ruvona."

She smiled and pressed a kiss to his collarbone, the only spot she could reach.

Epilogue

Vona laced her fingers through Warric's and tugged him down the stairs. The castle's silence was calming. Along the stone passage, the setting sun cast golden squares through tall arched windows. The sky was a vivid display of streaked pinks, oranges, and lilacs. Never had she seen anything so beautiful.

When she stepped onto the landing, she hesitated.

"To the dining room," Warric said, tugging on a too-tight white tunic a servant had found for him. He wore his original breeches and boots.

Her cheeks heated at what everyone must think of their prolonged absence. She had to face them at some point. Now or after the wedding night mattered not.

Before she opened the door, Warric swung her, spinning her into his arms. Cradling her against him, he smiled then dipped to brush a kiss across her lips. "Remember, I love you. Nothing they say will change that."

She pursed her lips, teasing him, but it did worry her. If this was true, her life would change. "Even if I am empyrean?"

"Nothing, Vona-love."

The door swung open to a beaming Yrsa. "At last."

Behind her were Vona's family and dearest friends. Even Jacut sat beside the baron, their faces shining with laughter.

Yrsa stepped aside then closed the door once they passed her. "A wedding is in order?"

Vona held up her hand to show the ring. Mother squealed and leaped out of her chair, dancing across the room to hug Vona and Warric. The scent of vanilla floated around her. She gathered Vona's hand to admire the gold band on her finger.

"Oh, this is old...and filled with such sorrow." She stroked the metal. "But so much joy too." She met Vona's gaze. "I...no, *we* are happy for you."

"Step aside, Ailith," Father wrapped an arm around Mother, then pumped Warric's hand and kissed Vona on the cheek. "Delighted, my girl."

A gruff Thack and a weeping Piers congratulated them on their joyful tidings.

Nessa crushed Vona in a hug. "Does that mean you are staying in Netherbury?" she asked while flicking away her tears.

Vona glanced at Warric. "I do not know. We have not discussed what follows."

Jacut thumped Warric on the shoulder then clasping Vona's hands, beamed at her. "You are in good hands."

"Indeed," the baron said as he bowed to Vona and hugged Warric. "A fine choice, my son." He swept a hand out to the room. "Perhaps now we can discuss how you all managed to hide an empyrean?"

Vona stiffened. She hadn't wanted to think about this, to consider how much had been hidden from her. With the implications came sorrow, disbelief, and a sense of betrayal. So she'd kept her focus on the man beside her.

Warric curled his arm around her and surrounded her with the heat of his body. "Listen before you react, Vona-Love," he whispered in her ear.

Yrsa pulled out a chair and gestured to Vona to sit. She did so. Warric settled beside her.

"We bribed Lord Sundowner Mintlock to keep silent. 'Twas easy to do when the fool had gambled away his heirlooms and was about to be hanged for his mountain of debt." Father snorted.

"'Tis why I was so distant with you, Vona." Mother studied her clasped hands. "'Twas not my intention, but I had to spend every waking moment searching for a way to prevent the inevitable madness."

"I do not follow." Vona frowned.

"You are an empyrean." Yrsa's beamed with pride. "Your powers and depth of well is beyond anything the Sundowners have seen. Believe me, they search for one such as you."

Vona slumped. "How can this be true? Sure, my well has expanded since...yesterday." She squeezed Warric's hand resting on his thigh. "What you are implying is a deception that goes beyond this room and is easily unraveled. How could you have hidden me from Uldane? What about the emissaries who visited often?" If she hadn't done as Warric had suggested and tested her well, this conversation would be laughable. "Now, setting this nonsense aside, how has my well grown bigger?"

"Come," Yrsa said, rising to her feet.

After glancing at Warric, Vona joined her.

"See what you managed while wearing the amulet." Yrsa pointed out the window.

Vona blinked, gripped the sill, and leaned out. All around the castle were verdant green forests, lush fields strewn with wildflowers, and to the south, the roofs of the town gleamed in the sunlight. The soot was gone, as if a strong wind had swept it away.

"When did this—?" She froze and gazed at Warric. When she had saved him, she had healed the land too?

"Emil's wickedness guided the amulet's power, casting the town in darkness and dust. So too had it drained the forests and lands, stripping it of all its magic. It took a healer wielding the amulet to cleanse his corruption."

"Empyreans are legends, Yrsa." Vona met her gaze, allowing a smile to form. "You can hide a level or two from someone, everyone, but not that much power."

Yrsa gestured to all of Vona. "Yet, here you stand."

"Did you not question why we had thunder but no storm when you wanted one?" Thack huffed. "Nor how you could move a mountain of soil and stone while keeping the river and underground water at bay?"

"I was desperate. Besides, even if what you say is true, how did you hide it from everyone?" Vona shook her head. "Hiding one's power is impossible."

"Not true." Mother smiled. "An old text showed us that the gifted could be made to believe themselves a lower level."

"We had no other option. So we told all and you that you were a proficient. No one questioned it. After all, Lord Sundowner Mintlock had confirmed it."

"What?" Vona squeaked. "Because I believed, I became the lie?"

Mother nodded. "We never tested you with spells beyond this ability."

"Except that one time you tried to summon buried treasure." Jacut studied the bottom of his glass. "Your findings that day bolstered the Devenmere coffers for generations to come."

Vona laughed. "I found a gold coin."

He pulled a coin from around his neck. "That day, when you almost died, I realized you were not a level five. I too had believed you proficient. By now, you must know how much I...we love you, my dear sister, and would do anything to protect you."

"It took many healers. Even unconscious, you controlled how much of your well they could refill. We were frightened that one would discover the truth. In the end, Walter placed you in a freshly dug grave." Mother clasped Father's hand. "'Twas nature that restored you."

Vona crossed to Warric and grasped his shoulders, needing his strength. "Do you believe this, my love?" She met his upturned gaze and silently pleaded with him to save her from this...lunacy.

He swept her into his arms. "It does not matter what I or they believe. You have tested your well and found this to be true."

She closed her eyes and focused on the rise and fall of undulating warmth. He squeezed her fingers, power flowing into her... His magic.

Sending out an exploratory wave, she 'saw' by their magical auras where everyone was in the room. With a slight tug, she drew a little energy from Jacut. Her well changed, enlarged, like a bag could bulge if overstuffed. Hers accommodated the influx of power with ease. She shoved green tendrils out, aiming for her father.

"Enough," he rasped. "I am well."

When she glanced at him, his cheeks were pink and his hair had lengthened to his shoulders.

"My well grows and shrinks as needed," she whispered.

"Indeed. In saving Warric, you broke the limitation you had placed on it decades ago." Yrsa grinned. "'Tis why your magic slipped from you without you control. You love him." She sniffed, wiped an eye, and straightened her shoulders. "Juluan, Nessa, and I leave for Chalimar in the morning."

"Piers and I have agreed to serve the baron on the wall." Thack thumped the table. "These old bones still have fight in them. We shall join Jacut in his endeavors."

Her family was disbanding. Sorrow scratched at Vona's throat. None mentioned her changed status, as if an empyrean wasn't something newsworthy. For that, she was both frustrated and grateful. It would take some time to come to terms with it.

"A text I search for bears instructions on how empyreans should be trained and channeled." Mother giggled and pressed her temple to Father's arm. "I am close to discovering its location. Perhaps one last adventure, Walter?"

"It would be my pleasure, Ailith." Father kissed her knuckles.

"The Conclave will investigate the depth of Uldane and Emil's duplicitousness." The baron steepled his fingers then tapped his chin.

"I would prefer not to split my time between the northern battles and restoring normalcy to Netherbury. Since this will become yours, Warric," he twirled a finger, "I suggest you handle the latter." With a nod, a servant placed a wooden box before Vona. "Take the amulet and use it as you see fit, Lady Ruvona."

She flicked the box open and stared at the diamond-studded amulet nestled on green velvet. "Um, milord, perhaps I should mention a hidden vault beneath the dungeon. 'Tis rightly yours and should be used as needed."

"Indeed," the baron mused. "You could have omitted it and kept the wealth for yourself." He glanced at Mother and Father, then at Warric. "'Tis likely treasure left from my forefathers. Take it as my wedding gift to you. Perhaps it could make recompense for my brother's actions." The baron gestured to his empty glass which a servant filled. "Once the baronship is granted, I assume more property and responsibility will be added to you."

"My thanks, milord." Warric bowed his head. "I shall not disappoint."

"You never have, my son."

Warric rose and drew Vona to his side. "I need a moment." He ushered her to the alcove, but instead of disclosing his reasons for privacy, he gazed out of the window. She waited, content to admire his profile. At last, he glanced at her. "All this, Vona-love, could be ours. I shall decline the offer if you wish to travel as you longed to." He gathered her into his arms and tucked her face in the curve of his neck.

Her breathing faltered. She blinked away the tears, looped her arms around his waist, and pressed a kiss to his throat. "Restoring Netherbury and saving these people is in our hearts."

He jerked back and blessed her with a heart-stopping smile. "True, Robbin."

"Who's Robbin?" She pulled away to rest her hands on her hips while smirking at him.

"Just a lad I once knew." He stole a kiss then threw his head back to laugh. "Fetch Friar Flynn," he commanded a nearby servant. "I do believe there is to be a wedding this eve."

ABOUT THE AUTHOR

Sevannah Storm is a fiction writer who immerses herself in fantastical worlds both magical and science fiction. She has a flare for the creative, having studied art and interior architecture, and spends her time drawing, oil painting, and writing. An avid reader from an early age, Sevannah finds her inspiration from various sources: games, novels, music, and the land of make-believe. The unique versus the practical has brought on numerous debates.

IN HER SPARE TIME, she does CrossFit and Krav Maga and rereads novels that snatch her breath away. Having embraced the social media world, you can find her on most platforms.

Her home is a land south of Wakanda, where animals roam free. Born in Zimbabwe, she grew up in South Africa. The crisp blue skies with cotton-candy sunsets expand her heart and soul, encapsulating a sense of freedom.

Words she lives by: "Know your pothole and dodge it. Don't work in a pencil factory if you're a vampire."

Sevannah loves to hear from her readers. You can find and connect with her at the links below.

Website/Newsletter:

https://www.sevannahstorm.com/

Facebook:

https://www.facebook.com/sevannah.storm

Instagram:

https://www.instagram.com/sevannah.storm/

Twitter:

https://twitter.com/sevannah_storm

Thank you for taking the time to read *The Lady and the Assassin*. If you enjoyed the story, please tell your friends and leave a review. Reviews support authors and ensure they continue to bring readers books to love and enjoy.

Stay tuned for sample chapters.

https://sevannahstorm.com

Xiaxan Fox

An orphaned princess battles across realms to reclaim her kingdom.

Born under a calamity star, Princess Jenaso 'Joi' of Letoura survived the massacre of her family and the burning of Tennaba. Taken in by the neighboring King of Meideon, he raises her as his daughter alongside his two sons.

Years later, at a pre-coronation event, revealing her identity has old enemies once more after her, not to mention all the suitors for her hand. To secure her safety, she escapes with a Xiaxan fellow trainee and secret admirer, Prince Sohar of Greyad.

Across five realms, she battles her family's enemies, old and new, with magic and sword but must decide whether to pledge her life to her kingdom or follow her heart.

Read it here:

https://books2read.com/u/3LY6X7

IRE OF SILVER

As the bastard daughter of an orc chief, Thugari is nothing more than a slave. After her last beating, disguising herself as a stable-boy, she escapes, stealing as she runs. Unfortunately, her victim is the orc Rukk Knaraugh, a lawbringer from the Council.

When Rukk finds her, she tries to run, fearing for her life, but he's skilled in tracking her. Claiming she is in his debt, he takes her with him, heading north as he hunts wild witches stealing babies. He agrees to release her from the debt in the dwarven city of Dussoum, where, for her, magicless people are welcome. Yet, he fascinates her, awakening something addictive within her along with the claim that she's not without magical powers.

In the sinister Chaosthane Mountains circling Dussoum, it is not shelter she finds. Despite discovering the reason behind the stolen babies, a magic blossoms within her as does her love for a lawbringer. Across five realms, she battles her family's enemies, old and new, with magic and sword but must decide whether to pledge her life to her kingdom or follow her heart.

Read it here:

https://books2read.com/u/bwQYgO